# PROPHETS
# OF THE
# GHOST ANTS

# PROPHETS OF THE GHOST ANTS

*The Antasy Series*
Book One

## CLARK THOMAS CARLTON

HARPER

VOYAGER
IMPULSE

*An Imprint of HarperCollins Publishers*

This is a work of fiction. Names, characters, places, and incidents are products of the author's imagination or are used fictitiously and are not to be construed as real. Any resemblance to actual events, locales, organizations, or persons, living or dead, is entirely coincidental.

Digital Edition DECEMBER 2016 ISBN: 978-0-06-242973-5

Print Edition ISBN: 978-0-06-242975-9

Harper Voyager, the Harper Voyager logo, and Harper Voyager Impulse are trademarks of HarperCollins Publishers.

HarperCollins is a registered trademark of HarperCollins Publishers in the United States of America and other countries.

FIRST EDITION

10 9 8 7 6 5 4 3 2 1

*For Jim M.*
*What you said was so inspiring!*

# ACKNOWLEDGMENTS

The author wishes to thank Michael Colleary and Mike Werb for their expert analysis and suggestions. For their enthusiasm and support, he thanks Lawrence Bender, Caren Bohrman, Mike Dobson, and Janet Jeffries. Thanks also to Ann Howard Creel, Robb McCaffree, and Robert Rodi for their careful reading of the manuscript. Special thanks to Dr. Edward O. Wilson, the Second Darwin, for his magnificent contributions to science.

"Humans arose as a fortuitous and contingent outcome of thousands of linked events, any one of which could have occurred differently and sent history on an alternative pathway . . ."

—STEPHEN JAY GOULD,
EVOLUTIONARY BIOLOGIST

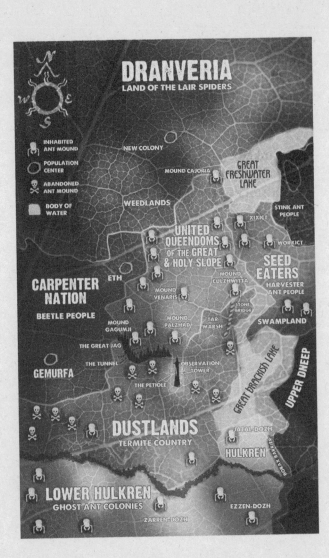

# PROLOGUE

*Locust, the Sky God, was enraged with His Creation. Humans had come to dominate Mother Sand and, in their arrogance, built towers of Her grains that poked through Locust's clouds. In His anger, he hurled a Great Boulder, sending up a dust storm that plunged the world into a freezing darkness that spared few beings. Surviving humans went underground, grew smaller, and waited for the Age of Dust to subside. When they reemerged, the humans starved, for all other creatures of red blood were extinct and plants and trees would be dormant for ages. Over a thousand eons, the humans who endured grew smaller and smaller still, shrinking to a ten-thousandth of their original size. They competed for food with the Sand's other survivors, the six-and eight-legged creatures whose blood runs green, which had returned to their true, greater size.*

*Too tiny to ever threaten the gods again, the humans'*

dominion over the Sand was regained when they realized their survival was not in warring with insects but in living among them. Different gods granted different tribes the knowledge that enabled them to deceive, infiltrate, and exploit the ants, but no race of men was more loved by the gods than the Slopeites, a semi-divine tribe, descended from Goddess Ant Queen and Her mortal consort, Rahtsu, the Warrior King. Ant Queen gave the Slopeites the holy leaf-cutter ants: the growers of mushrooms and the fiercest, most beautiful and useful of all insects.

—FROM THE ORAL TRADITIONS OF
THE SLOPEISH PRIESTHOOD

## PART 1

# THE ROACH BOY OF MOUND CAJORIA, A HUMAN-INHABITED ANT COLONY OF THE GREAT AND HOLY SLOPE

# CHAPTER 1

## THE LOWLIEST SUBJECT
## OF THE SORCERESS QUEEN

"**S**hit," muttered Anand, the word that summed up his existence. He had been knocked to the sand by a blowfly as big as himself. It crawled over his prostrate body and mopped his face with its pulpy mouthparts. Anand kicked out from under the fly, then stood and used his batting pole to beat it back into flight. He wiped his face, and sighed before resuming his harness.

The morning was typical for him, stinking and noisy with hovering insects as he lugged a vat of human waste away from Mound Cajoria. The most merciless of gods, Sun, was shining with all His cruelty and Anand sweated and strained as he trudged through a stretch of scorching sand. He beat his feet over the flattest part of each sand grain and avoided those with edges that could slice through his sandals.

At last he reached his destination, a density of weeds on Cajoria's northwest border. He looked up at a stalk of mint leaves and took a moment to rest in its fragrant shade. Once he caught his breath, he pulled back a leaf-tarp and dumped his loathsome cargo. The flies that had shadowed him dropped from the air to converge on the waste. The fattest of them buzzed her wings, scattering the others as she crowded them off the muck.

As one end of her ate, the other sank its abdomen into the moisture to lay an egg. In her compound eyes, Anand saw a thousand reflections of himself, indistinct and tiny, one of the countless masses. When the fly turned its iridescent body, he saw himself in a large and single reflection: a brown-skinned boy with defiant eyes, strong limbs, and hair as black and glossy as tar. He smiled to see his mustache had thickened. It prompted him to finger the fifteen chits he wore around his neck, one for each of his years. *I am almost a man,* he thought, but then he frowned.

*What kind of life is this for a man?*

Blowflies interrupted Anand's thoughts when they flew back to fight over the waste. Their buzzing made his skull vibrate with a terrible ache. He wanted to kill the flies with the sharp end of his batting pole, but that privilege belonged to the sons of the hunting caste. And as for those hunters . . .

Where were they? They should have been there to slay these pests and then port their corpses to the merchants. From the faint sound of it, Anand figured the hunters were deeper in the weeds and locked in some delightful combat. He wandered into the thicket to see what made them whoop and holler.

He followed their voices to a dandelion flower that had just turned to a great and towering seed clock. Under its leaves were several boys of Anand's age surrounding a black, glistening centipede. The creature was huge and hairy and looked to be two-headed as it rose up on both ends and waved its hundred claws. Scattered over its loamy home were droppings full of bones and a skull from a human it had eaten.

"That's the head, to the left," shouted Skylo, a young man of sixteen with yellowish skin and leaf-green eyes. He pointed to the true head with pincers below its mouth, the points of which were beaded with poison. The boys ran under the centipede's safer end where they thrust spears between its belly scales. Each puncture sent the creature into violent convulsions . . . but didn't kill it. As it snapped and thrashed, it whipped the boys with its legs and knocked them to the ground. It rose up, turned on them, and then lunged with its pincers. The boys ran under leaf cover, laughing when it missed them.

Weak and leaking blood, the centipede wobbled as it poised to strike again but when its head dropped, the rest of its body collapsed on the sand. The hunters ran in with their swords. Skylo skewered its brain as the rest chopped off its legs. Nearby was a hollowed acorn that one boy played like a barrel drum. Another joined him and started a chant. The rest picked up the centipede's legs and danced with them around the corpse.

As he spied on them, Anand was filled with an envy that choked him from inside. He wondered if he had ever known such joy in his life. His envy grew as he watched the hunters climb the stalk of the seed clock. Skylo was the first to reach the seeds and plucked a few by their stems. At their ends were the fluffy domes of threads that caught the wind. He widened his arms, waited for a breeze, then jumped.

Anand watched as the boy bobbed and floated before he alighted on a distant barley comb. After Skylo released the seeds, he bounced down the spiral of the barley stalk's leaves. When he reached the ground, he ran back, eager to do it again. He paused when he noticed Anand peering from behind the pebble.

"Step out from behind that pebble!" Skylo commanded and Anand complied. He saw the hunter recoil at the sight of his dark skin and his rags.

"Why aren't you at work?" Skylo asked.

"Why aren't *you*?" Anand whispered, and turned away.

"*What*? What did you say?"

Anand was quiet.

"Don't dare speak to me, shit-scraper, especially like that," said the hunter, pinching his nose as if

Anand stank. "Hang your head and apologize or we can find a centipede to throw you to."

"I'm sorry," Anand said, as he turned toward Skylo and knelt. After a moment of silent shaming, the hunter ran back to the others.

Anand was dragging his pole back to the vat when he heard a thump and a muffled scream. He turned in the sound's direction and froze to see a bloodsucker flea with Skylo bleeding in its barbed fore-claws. The bristled, disc-like monster was five times as tall as a man, crouching on powerful hind legs. Anand felt his heart jump into his head, beating like the acorn drum in his ears.

The flea clamped its head around Skylo's torso. A dagger-like stipe emerged from its mouth and plunged between his ribs. Dual suckers from deeper in the mouth slithered over the boy's chest, then sank into the incision. With a sickening slurp, Skylo was turned to a bloodless husk. The flea's body was translucent and Anand watched as its abdomen reddened and bloated with blood.

"Fleas!" Anand shouted to the others climbing to the seeds, but they were too distant and lost in their chatter to hear him. The bloodsucker dropped the shriveled corpse as tiny antennae popped from its head and waved their hairy sensors. The flea caught Anand's scent, pivoted towards him, then crouched to spring. Anand knew it was useless to run. He dropped to his knees and held up the sharp end of his pole.

Anand jerked upright when the flea jumped. As the insect dropped on him, he thrust the pole upwards and pierced its middle. The flea toppled, pressing Anand to the sand, with its wound smearing him with human and insect blood. He was excited he had killed it, but he knew fleas traveled in hordes, so he reached for his dagger as he wriggled out. "Fleas!" he shouted, running towards the seed clock. *"Fleas!"*

Once the boys heard him, Anand raced to the open sand under cover of the lowest weeds. The hunters leapt to the sand to run and hide.

Dozens of fleas were plummeting into the weeds as Anand ran. He heard the hunters' screaming and then their sudden silence as the fleas drained their blood. Zigzagging through a rain of fleas, Anand ran over the sand and reached the closest of the warning towers built among the weeds. He scrambled up a ladder to a platform under a wooden bell with a scent-bladder tied to a post at his right.

Anand slashed the bladder with his knife, releasing a powder of pungent *alarm-scent,* then grabbed the rope that trailed from the bell. As he swung up and into the air, a flea sprang at him. Anand raised his feet, kicking into the flea's head and sending it into a spiraling fall. As the bell sounded a warning to the humans, the flea landed on its side, righted itself, and attacked again.

The flea was in mid-leap when an arrow pierced it, sending it into a spin. Anand jumped from the rope to the platform to see a leaf-cutter sentry ant rushing over the sand, its antennae a blur as they waved. Riding on the back of the sentry was its master, a human soldier from the border patrol nocking his bowstring.

Anand watched the ant's antennae twitch in the direction of the fleas as she raised her gaster and sprayed *recruit-scent* on the breeze. Within moments, dozens of sentry ants and their human riders rushed into the weeds, flushing out the fleas. As the blood-suckers jumped up, the humans pierced them with spears and arrows. The ants rushed to the fallen fleas and used their pincers to slice through their bellies and shear their legs.

Atop the platform, Anand caught his breath as he watched the fleas retreating north, vaulting over the weeds. Smaller ants without riders converged on the flea corpses, slicing them into pieces to haul away in a column. Surviving hunter-boys emerged from the cracks of rocks or pebbles they had burrowed under. Anand almost grinned to see one boy had lodged himself in the ribs of a fallen but poisonous mushroom and his skin was swollen with itchy bumps. A moment later, Anand was shaking, waiting under the bell as a group of officers abandoned their ants to climb the tower he occupied. Their honey-colored armor creaked as they took the rungs. Anand feared these soldiers more than he feared the fleas. He kept his head down as they mounted the platform and dared not look them in the face.

"Look up," said their captain. Anand revealed his

dark face and the clipped earlobe that identified his status.

"Good gods. He's from the midden," said a soldier, pinching his nose.

"And he's got skin as brown as a roach-eater," said another.

"This entire tower is polluted," said the captain. "It will have to be chopped down and rebuilt."

He addressed Anand but did not look in his eyes. "We must cut off your arm, middenite, for polluting royal property. Stick it out . . . left or right as you wish."

From the corner of his eye, Anand could see the captain's skin was so fair that he had blue blood pulsing in the veins of his temple.

"Good soldier, allow me to speak," said Anand, staring down.

"What's this?" the captain asked, surprised at the outburst. "You dare speak to me?"

"I sounded the alarm because others were under attack—it was not to save myself," said Anand surprising himself. "Several hunter-boys died, but I see that some live—thanks to the keen aim of you and your men."

"That's true, Captain," said a soldier in the back. "The survivors all pissed themselves . . . unlike this one."

The captain sighed and stared at his sword with its cunning engraving of Mantis, the war goddess. "I'm not going to ruin my blade with the blood of some filthy middenite," he said. "Come on, men. We must collect the husks of the dead and return them to their families. And you," he said to Anand, "should praise Lord Grasshopper for His mercy."

Anand knew not to thank the soldiers as they filed down, for even his gratitude was polluted. Besides, he had new worries. He would be late in returning to the midden. Despite it being the most reviled place in all Cajoria, he hurried home, wondering what punishment his foreman had in mind.

## CHAPTER 2

## THE PLACE OF THE LOWEST CASTE

It was only midday, but Anand's father, Yormu, was numb with fatigue and his brown skin was slippery with sweat as he toiled in the midden, the place where both ants and humans brought their waste and enemy corpses. Yormu had spent the morning dissecting a dead tarantula, a messy and tedious process that always made him itch. Just as he was finishing, soldier ants—the largest leaf-cutters of all—filed in from the east with human and insect corpses held aloft in their jaws. They had come in triumph from a border skirmish with the men and ants of the Seed Eater Nation.

Yormu moaned as he watched the corpses pile up. The dead humans and their harvester ants were dumped together and would have to be sorted. The human dead had to be hauled to the swamp, but their ants, with their giant, seed-milling heads, would be salvaged for parts, food, and fluids. For Yormu, that meant opening the harvesters' gullets to extract their puddings of crushed seeds.

He was frowning at the enormity of his task when sentry ants poured in from the Western weeds from the flea attack—even more corpses. These had to be salvaged right away since fleas were a favorite food of the military caste. Yormu suddenly remembered his son had been sent to the weeds. Had Anand fallen to a bloodsucker?

He would have shouted Anand's name, but Yormu the Mute had no front teeth and only a stub of a tongue, the rest of which had been cut off by a sheriff. Yormu clutched his blade in panic and raced to the water station. He sliced a drop into a mushroom cone and snuck off to look for his boy.

Close to home, Anand was slowed when his route was overwhelmed with the caste of ants that gave the leaf-cutters their name. The foraging ants had stripped leaves from a distant tree and were returning to the mound with their pieces. The ants paraded past him with their leaf shards up high, at least providing Anand with some flickering shade.

As Anand was jostled in the foragers' traffic, a few dropped their cargo to rub their antennae and sniff the pair he wore in a headband fashioned from straw.

Anand's antennae, like his skin and clothing, were coated in the ant's kin-scent. "Yes, I'm one of you," he said as they identified him as one of their millions of sisters before moving on. He saw his father in the distance, a look of panic on his face as he took in Anand's bloodstained clothing.

"Don't worry, Dad," Anand shouted. "I'm not bleeding."

Yormu wiped at his eyes and ran to his son to hand him the cone. Anand's mouth was fuzzy with thirst and he sucked down the drop in an instant. He was eating the cone when Keel, the foreman, tromped over with his whip. "Yormu!" he shouted. "Who said you could bring water to your bastard?"

Keel was the largest of the middenites and had a lipless slash of a mouth. Like all in his caste, his right ear lobe was cut off to identify his polluted status, but his left lobe was newly clipped to distinguish him as foreman. Good with the whip, he lashed Yormu, who fell to his knees from the force. Blood surfaced from gashes in his back as Keel raised the whip again—but this time he didn't strike.

Anand had thrown himself between the men.

"Whip me if you have to whip someone!" the boy shouted. No hint of fear was in his voice as his eyes pierced Keel's. The foreman lowered his arm.

"I won't whip you, Roach Boy," said Keel. "Your blood might blind my eyes. Why are you so late?"

"I was caught in the flea attack. I had to sound the alarm."

Keel addressed Yormu as he struggled to stand. "Your bastard's a liar, Yormu, like all roach people. Now get back to it, both of you, or I'll dock your mushrooms for a month."

Anand watched with concern as his father limped back to the corpse piles. Anand returned to his usual work, the cleaning of chamber pots. He reached for one with a lid that had a quartz inlay of the emblem of Cajoria's Sorceress Queen. Inside it were contents that were rather less elegant.

As he scraped, then washed it, Anand was coming to understand that royal night soil was as malodorous as any commoner's. Lost in his thoughts, he had not realized a pack had gathered behind him. When they pitched sand grains at his back, he turned to see who provoked him.

It was his usual enemies, led by Tal, the eldest son of Keel. Since his father had become foreman, Tal had grown fat from stuffing himself with insect salvage. He had great and drooping cheeks, giving the impression that his chin and buttocks had switched places. He looked over his shoulder to see that his father and the men were distracted in the distance.

"Those are royal pots, Roach Boy," said Tal, "and they're for decent Cajorites to clean, not some roach-eater's son."

Anand's anger felt like maggots feasting inside him. Not a day passed in which his mother was not insulted. He was aware that all the boys had dropped their tasks. Like manure flies, they were buzzing around the two, ready to revel in the Roach Boy's weekly humiliation. Anand knew what was coming next, but after a morning of fleas that wanted to drain his blood and sheriffs who wanted to sever his arm, he wasn't going to take it.

"You want to clean these shit pots? Be my guest," Anand said, taking a pot and swinging its contents into Tal's face.

Tal was doubly startled; he was not used to defiance and now he was blinded and choking on excrement. As he scraped at his face, the others rushed Anand and grabbed his arms, stretching them back.

"It's time you were dead, you black bastard," said Tal. "Time to wash your kin-scent off you and give you to the ants!" And with that, he kicked Anand with a powerful thrust to the stomach.

All he could manage was a whoosh of air as the breath was forced from his lungs—not that any of the others heard it over their own howling laughter. The world around him grew dark and quiet. He felt the boys lift and toss him in the vat where he sank to its bottom. *So it ends like this*, was his final thought. His panic gave way to a strange and gorgeous relief as a sudden path to the Next World glowed before him with the soft light of stars.

# CHAPTER 3

## THE SORCERESS QUEEN
## OF MOUND CAJORIA

The foraging ants, pincers full, continued their climb up the mound with the essential task of delivering their leaves. After skirting the midden, they passed through 127 levels where different castes worked at specific labors. The first rings were the colorless slums of the laboring humans, an expanse of one-room shelters made of sand grains glued together by ant dung and perched atop stilts. Nearer to the mound, the leaf-cutters crawled through the rings of craftsmen and traders. These castes were privileged to live in two-room hovels of sand bound by sulfurous tar.

At a higher elevation were the treasure-stuffed homes of the merchants, constructed from white sand fused with fragrant resins. At the next level were the black sand barracks of the soldiers and above these were their generals' austere mansions. On top of these, and in marked contrast, were the priests' ornate rectories. These were fashioned from grains of pinkish sand and embedded with images of the Slopeish gods.

Finally the foragers reached the crystal palaces of the royal family. As the ants marched over these magnificent structures, their leaves were reflected in a golden lacquer. The palaces encircled the mound's opening, which was guarded by four ants with giant heads that locked and unlocked as a living gate.

Once inside the mound, the foragers descended to deliver their leaves to the dark, deep chambers of the chewing ants. This caste would make a rough carpet by shearing the leaves into tiny pieces. Smaller ants, the fungus growers, would chew these pieces into a fine paste, fertilize it with liquid manure, and then infuse it with threads of fungus. The threads would stalk and fruit into the sacred mushrooms, the staple food of both the ants and the human parasites that lived among them.

Once they made their delivery, the foragers exited for a second trip and more leaves. They spiraled past a stately train of silk-draped riding ants with noisy bangles clasped above their claws. Atop the lead ant was Queen Polexima, the most important human in all Cajoria. She and her entourage were just returning from the essential ritual she practiced as the mound's sorceress.

In the ninth month of her ninth pregnancy, riding had become difficult for the queen. Two things were on her mind as she entered the tunnel that led to her palace: lunch and a comfortable seat. Once in her chambers, she sat down to savor a sun-baked swamp fly as her servant informed her of the flea attack.

"Good gods," she said. "Did anyone die?"

"Eight hunters . . . all of them boys," said Mulga, a woman from the servant caste with freckles as numerous as stars.

"Children? How horrible." Polexima pushed her food away, having lost her appetite. She tried to hide her moistening eyes.

"Majesty," said Mulga, somewhat shyly. "Your hair could use a bit of brushing."

"Oh, thank you. Bring me my toiletries, please."

In a hand mirror fashioned from the wing of a water beetle, Polexima saw her yellow-white hair was now streaked with silver. Her pale skin with its golden undertones had grown more wrinkled about her eyes and mouth. After thirty-nine summers, she saw she was somewhere between being a fabled beauty and a faded one. "What did you expect?" she muttered to herself. "That it wouldn't happen to *you*?" Suddenly, the queen dropped the mirror and clutched her belly.

"Mulga . . ." she gasped.

The queen's tone frightened the servant as well as

the twenty others in the chamber. They were as still as stone as they stared at their queen.

"Yes, Majesty?"

"It's time."

The servant continued to stare.

"Mulga, will you run and summon the priests, please?"

"Yes, Majesty. Apologies."

As her cushion soaked with fluid, Polexima's mind flooded with painful concerns. After eight deliveries, it never really got any easier. Panic was throbbing inside her but she knew giving into it would accomplish nothing. She drew deep breaths as she rubbed the belly of the Grasshopper idol in her bedside altar and chanted all his names in prayer.

**M**ulga scurried through the vast chamber and its furnishings of carved amber. To reach the outside pathways, she had to crawl through a short tunnel, then push through a portal whose flaps kept the ants out.

Standing under the shade of the mound's rain shield, the servant tied on her band of antennae before entering the dense traffic of ants and humans. She was trembling when she stopped before a gathering of others from her caste. They were picking up the day's drinking water at the royal dew station where a man wearing a bucket-shaped hat stood on a sand-sled and used a broad knife to slice water from a barrel.

"What's wrong with you?" asked Mulga's sister, who served the crown princess.

"The queen—her water's broken."

Everyone gasped. The dew collector dropped his knife. Some fell to their knees and others fainted. All of them turned to their gods in prayer.

Mulga knew they should have been praying for the queen's health and blessings for the new heir. Instead, like her, they were muttering prayers that she give birth to a male.

Or at least a female whose life would be brief.

# CHAPTER 4

## SURVIVING THE STING

"He's drowning!" said a shaky voice some distance from the vat of excrement. It belonged to Terraclon, a twig of a boy, who squeezed through the circle of Anand's abusers. Terraclon was held in almost as much contempt as Anand, and his presence repulsed the others.

Terraclon thrust his arms, as thin as threads, into the vat. Using all his strength, he managed to pull Anand out, but he also sent the vat tumbling, something sure to set off the foreman (even more than the attempted murder of the Roach Boy). Anand coughed and flopped in the spreading filth. The other boys scurried back to work just as their fathers noticed the commotion.

**Y**ormu felt stabbed to see what had happened to his son. How many times had they thrown him in a vat this month? Yormu was running towards his boy when Keel grabbed his arm.

"Don't run to him, Yormu. He makes his messes. Let him clean it up."

Yormu clenched his fists with rage. If only he could speak his mind! He wished for a tongue so long and sharp it could lop off Keel's head. He saw Keel glance at his fists.

"Are those fists for me, Yormu? Take a swing and I'll knock out what few teeth you have left. Get back to work."

Yormu panted as he strained to keep himself from leaping onto his foreman to climb his chest and rip his ears off. He shook his head, defiant.

"I said get back to work!" Keel bellowed.

Yormu shook his head again, waiting for the moment Anand could rise and walk. Keel was coming towards him, fist cocked.

"Stop!" shouted Terraclon, yanking Anand to his feet. "He's up. Look." Terraclon held Anand's wobbling body up as he coughed.

"Go back to work, Dad," Anand choked out. "I'm fine."

Keel glared at them all before pushing Yormu back to his tasks.

After Anand and Terraclon refilled the vat, they removed their muck with several baths in nutshell tubs. As Anand sank under the last dome of water, he imagined the time he could leave Cajoria and return in the trappings of the richest trader. He would go to the Cajorites' priests to purchase Keel, Tal, and his other tormentors. Afterwards, he would sell them to an enemy nation where, for the rest of their lives, gawkers would pelt them with trash in pits at public showings.

*Dreams beyond dreams*, he thought as he continued to wash.

As they bathed, the caste's idols keeper stood nearby repeating the names of the Slopeish gods as he rubbed his generous belly stained from the dye of his yellow sash. When the boys were dried, he handed them oily cloths soaked with leaf-cutter *kin-scent* and muttered a prayer to Goddess Ant Queen. The boys were coating themselves when they heard a hubbub among the middenites. All had left their work to gather and stare at the top of the mound. Banners were hanging from the rain shield's edges.

"Look, Anand," said Terraclon. "Yellow banners! The queen is giving birth again. You know what it means if it's a girl who lives."

"Fission," said Anand. "A new princess may mean a new colony."

Terraclon shuddered. "Don't say it out loud, Anand!"

"Why not? Fission would be a good thing."

"Fission is never good. It tears families apart." Looking at Anand, he added, "And friends. Tears them apart, too."

"The people of this mound are starving. It's better they divide than die."

A northern breeze sent dead leaves and dust whirling over the boys. Anand sniffed the air and savored the strange scents of some distant land. He had no fear of being forced to a new colony for a few more months. As the most miserable boy in the most miserable caste, any change was welcome.

Queen Polexima was used to giving birth to triplets and quadruplets. It was more difficult with this single infant, whose enormous head was crowning.

"Push, Your Majesty," said the midwife as the mound's high priest, His Most Pious Dolgeeno, arrived with his entourage. Through all her pain, the queen almost smiled in contempt. She could see it had taken the priests a good part of the day to dress for the royal delivery. Their pollen-powdered faces of yellow contrasted with cassocks of deepest purple and as hats, it appeared they had agreed on fuzz cones over the usual skullcaps. Each wore twenty-eight head-to-floor necklaces of moonstones that rattled across the tiles as they teetered in on the cube-shaped shoes that gave them height.

A man of fifty-three summers, Dolgeeno had small eyes lost in a heavy face. He had three, sometimes four chins. He looked to the heavens, then led the other priests in a slow and cumbersome chant circle around Polexima's bed that drowned out her screams as the baby broke through. The midwife gasped.

"Show it to me," said Polexima.

The midwife hesitated before picking up the infant and turning her to the sight of the others.

"Good gods," said Polexima, "a girl!"

The queen could not hold back tears. Flooded with emotion, she had not realized her legs were apart when Dolgeeno glanced between them. She knew he had done so only for the pleasure of humiliating her. Her hatred for him flared as he approached with his knife, crafted from the tip of an ancient ant queen's mandible. He severed the umbilical cord, held the infant upside down, and slapped her buttocks to make her cry.

Polexima saw that the infant was large and strong and perhaps could survive the poison. *Please, Grasshopper, let her live,* she prayed to the god of riches and mercy. The infant was freed of her placenta as the jaw of a patrolling sentry ant broke through the greased flap of the chamber's window. Alerted by the newborn's odor, its antenna slid through the window in search of an intruder it would have to kill.

"Hurry, please!" the queen said.

"That sentry is too large to break through," said Dolgeeno.

"But she's spraying *alarm-recruit* scent," Polexima shouted back. "Smaller ones will get through."

"My good queen, I have never lost a baby to sentry ants," said His Most Pious, even as he was immersing the infant in a basin. Once the baby was doused in kin-scent, he raised her and the ant moved on. Dolgeeno nodded towards something buzzing in the corner.

Strapped into a twig frame, a living mud dauber wasp was lifted onto the shoulders of the priests and brought to Dolgeeno. He held up the baby and pressed her buttocks to the wasp's stinger, already glistening with poison.

Polexima had previously witnessed this ritual eighteen times. Seventeen times she had seen daughters die. The newborn would expire in a moment or live to wail in agony. The wasp fluttered its clipped wings as its stinger pumped its toxins. Dolgeeno pulled the infant away. She made tiny fists and squirmed.

Polexima's heart sank as she watched the infant shiver, then grow still.

"No, she's . . ."

Suddenly, blood rushed to the girl's face and turned it a deep pink. Her little body spasmed and she shrieked.

This daughter would live.

"Thank you, Lord Grasshopper!" said the queen, collapsing into her sheets.

"The gods have found this baby worthy. She shall be called Pareesha," said Dolgeeno, naming her after the south wind goddess.

One of Dolgeeno's men handed him a bladder of aphid milk. He smeared a bit of the sticky syrup onto the newborn's lips.

"May the days of Princess Pareesha be sweet and may her descendants be numerous," sang the priest. When the infant stopped crying, she was set in an amber rocking crib.

Polexima drifted into a shallow slumber as she waited for her family's visit. She knew one of them would be most unhappy, a thought that somehow made her smile as she closed her eyes.

**M**aking their way through the palace's tunnels were the new baby's sister, the Crown Princess Trellana, and her father, the Warrior King Sahdrin. They sat together on a couch set over the thorax of a carrying ant. Behind them, on their own ants, were twenty of Trellana's twenty-one brothers, most of whom were twins or triplets. They laughed and sang as they sucked from bladders of honey liquor. Trellana found them loud and irritating and it deepened her usual pout. She had been summoned prematurely from a day with a hairdresser who had fresh gossip from the neighboring mounds. What unsettled her most was pondering that this new sibling was her first surviving sister, a teensy thing that would be adored and spoiled by all.

Accompanying the procession were hundreds of tiny grooming ants that clustered about the princess as Trellana mixed her perfume with *queen-scent*, the potion that sparked grooming behavior. The little groomers crawled on her trains and her towering but unfinished coiffure with their mouths opened to offer their regurgitation. Trellana brushed one away from her eye with more violence than usual to see the king staring sideways with his good eye.

"Are you well today, my pretty?" Sahdrin asked.

"Certainly I am, Father."

"You do not seem excited at the prospect of having a sister."

"Well, yes, of course I am excited," she said with all the enthusiasm of a corpse. "But I am not excited at the idea that I might have to leave you within a year."

When they reached the portal to the queen's chambers, Sahdrin's servants helped him down from the ant and plucked off his false legs. Trellana began her entry, slowed by her ten-layered costume. Once inside, servants straightened her trains as she fanned herself with the clipping of an eye moth's wing. She waited for the commoners to draw away before floating to the crib. Peeking over her fan, she stared silently at the infant's face as the king, refitted with his legs, swung towards his wife on crutches carved from cricket femurs. He set his hand on her arm.

"Was it a painful birth, Polly?"

"The most painful since Trellana," said the queen. "But I have the comfort of knowing it shall be my last."

The king swung himself toward the crib to join Trellana and look at the second female heir. "Congratulations, Mother," Trellana finally said without making eye contact. "You have done very well."

"Thank you, Trelly. Her arrival will make us a little less sad when you leave," said Polexima, but rather flatly.

"She shall be very pretty," Trellana said, pursing her small lips, glossy with green paint.

"If she becomes even half the beauty you are, she will be very lucky indeed," said Sahdrin.

"Indeed," said Polexima through a sigh, betraying her disagreement with her husband about her oldest daughter's appearance. "That's . . . that's a rather ambitious coiffure," said the queen as she looked up at her daughter's jewel-embedded tower of hair.

"It's what they are wearing at the Kulfi and Goojinet Mounds," Trellana said, continuing to stare at the baby.

"I always have a learned orator in my chambers when I get my hair done," ventured Polexima. "Perhaps you should be learning more about our history now, of the kinds of difficulties you and your pioneers might encounter."

"Oh, how tedious, Mother. We have plenty of people to address any complications."

"It's not tedious. As you get older, you'll realize there are advantages to cultivating yourself. You should be learning our poetry and sagas, our—"

"But I'm not old, Mother," Trellana snapped. "You are. I should like to enjoy my youth before cramming my head with the words of your 'learned' blatherers."

Polexima sighed again as Trellana frowned and fixated on a crack in her fingernail. The princes entered the room, drunk and noisy, and their sloppy entrance allowed the unwanted grooming ants in. Some of these ants surrounded the crib and frightened Pareesha with their offers of vomit. A servant swatted the groomers away, then brought the baby to the shushing queen, who saw the newborn was rooting for milk. As Polexima nursed, she broke into a folk tune from her native mound of Palzhad.

> *Little one, life is short,*
> *But very long on sorrow.*
> *Make the most of every day*
> *And don't live for tomorrow.*

The servants smiled at the song, especially as it used words from their caste dialect. Trellana, her brothers, and the king did not understand the lyrics, though, and looked annoyed by the queen's singing. The priests did little to hide their distaste before Pious Dolgeeno interrupted.

"If Her Highness will excuse me," he said, before turning to his men. "Priests, the Princess Pareesha has survived the sting. We must descend to the cathedral and consult with the gods to tell us when Princess Trellana's Fission trek should depart."

"Before you do," said Polexima. "I should like to speak with the scouting party about the new site."

"Why?" asked Dolgeeno. "The site was determined and approved nearly a year ago."

"Who approved it? Not me. I will not send my

daughter and thousands of our people into the wilderness without some assurance of their safety. I should like to speak with the scouting party before you leave for the cathedral."

"As you wish, Majesty," said Dolgeeno, sending his quickest novitiate as a messenger.

Trellana trembled. She wanted to be a queen but had never wanted to leave Cajoria and found a new colony. She had always been told this was her destiny, but the arrival of this infant was turning those words into a reality. She suddenly felt constricted by her clothing and unable to breathe. She fainted, and fell softly into the thickness of her own costume, her mouth open. Before they were chased away, grooming ants responded to the signal that she was hungry and she came to and realized the ants had regurgitated into her opened mouth.

**A** short time later, the men who had found and approved the site of the new colony arrived at Polexima's chambers and stood before her and the king and Trellana. Their expedition had begun nine months earlier when the priests' oracles indicated the likely birth of a healthy princess.

"The site of the new mound, a meadow surrounded by woods, is north and slightly east of here, a journey of eleven days by caravan, or two days on fleet ants, in the uninhabited territory known as Dranveria in the old tongue," said Pious Estaine, the priest of the tree god Bortshu-mox. He wore a twin-winged seedpod as his miter and drew a map with his finger in a dust-box.

"Eleven days by caravan? Two days by fleet ant? No Slopeish mound is supposed to be more than one day's ride from another by fleet ant," said Sahdrin, his voice loud but trembling.

"How can I be so far from you, Father?" asked Trellana through whimpers.

Estaine bowed to the king before responding. "Majesty, it is some distance, but the oracles were correct. The new site is a meadow surrounded by glorious stands of untouched bortshu trees . . . an ample supply of leaves for twenty generations."

Commander General Batra, the officer whose soldiers had accompanied Estaine, jutted out his box-like chin before speaking. Around his chest was a necklace of dried human ears from tree cannibals he had personally killed on the journey. "Pious Estaine is correct, Your Majesties. The new site is distant, but treaties with the Seed Eaters prevent us from going east and we risk war with the Carpenter tribe if we venture west."

"What is the terrain like?" Polexima asked.

"It is still an extension of the Slope, so not prone to flooding, but with reddish sand," Estaine answered.

Polexima flinched when she heard "reddish sand," unsure of why it disturbed her.

"And it is not occupied?" she asked.

"Not by ant peoples. The tree canopies are full

of cannibal tribes, but they are primitives who pose little threat."

"Why have we not colonized it before?"

"Our journey was not without incident," said Commander Batra. "In the old tongue, the name Dranveria means 'domain of lair spiders,' of which there are many. Some in our party succumbed to them. Others were carried off by . . . night wasps."

At the mention of night wasps, a long silence chilled the room. Sahdrin sighed through his nostrils. "Very well," he said.

"I don't know that it is very well at all," said Polexima, searching her memories.

"Fission has happened hundreds of times in the history of the Slopeish peoples and in conditions just like these," said Dolgeeno. "Nearly always it is peaceful and successful. Princess Trellana will be protected by Commander General Batra's army, as well as by me, my priests, and all our magic."

Polexima's eyes shifted as a rush of images filled her head. "One remembers old stories about a previous attempt to colonize the land of red sand," she said, "and of the mysterious and brutal . . . Dranverites."

"Stories? What stories?" Trellana asked. She shot her mother a piercing look, then turned to Dolgeeno.

"In one legend," said the queen, "the dried bones and bloody clothing of Kulfish pioneers were returned to their original mound in neat, cube-shaped piles."

With slit eyes, Dolgeeno turned to Estaine and Batra.

"Pious Estaine, did you see even one little *Dranverite* on your expedition?" he asked, as if he were speaking to a child. "How about you, General?" he sang with a smug smile. "Anyone mounted on a . . . *red* hunter ant?"

"Of course not," said General Batra. "I give my word as a soldier."

"By all the gods, no!" swore Estaine in agreement with the general. Polexima watched as both men blinked at each other, then looked away in haste.

"People tell lots of silly stories for the fun of being scared," said His Most Pious, turning to Trellana. "Fear not, Princess. The omens for your new mound are exceptionally good. There are no such beings as Dranverites and certainly no one to challenge Slopeish supremacy."

Trellana and Sahdrin sighed with relief, but Polexima was still not sure. She searched the faces of the men for signs that they had lied. She did not sense an out-and-out deception, but she was sure of an unease between them.

"I overheard a conversation," Polexima said, "whispered between my servants, in their own tongue." The queen began to whisper herself. "They said the laborers that accompanied your expedition were not killed by insect and spider predators, but by our own Cajorite soldiers."

"Ridiculous," said Dolgeeno with a roll of his eyes. "Soldiers have no right to kill your subjects without cause—they would risk their own execution."

"Perhaps these laborers saw something," said the

Queen, "something you did not wish them to report to the mound."

"Like what, dear Queen?" Dolgeeno asked impatiently, his words worked into a melody.

"The border walls of another nation which they were ordered to clear . . . as their last act before dying."

"Polexima, really," said the high priest as he shook his head and sent ripples through his wattles. "What calamitous shape we would be in if we believed the stories of the simple folk." He turned to Batra and Estaine. "Again, under oath to Mantis, did either of you see red ants or anyone riding on one?"

"Certainly not," said Estaine.

"By Mantis, no," said Batra.

"Then you are dismissed," said the high priest, cutting short the meeting. "If Your Majesties will excuse me, we must prepare for our divine audience."

Polexima watched Dolgeeno's weighty buttocks jiggle under his robes as he exited the room.

*How I loathe that man.*

**A**fter changing into their evening robes, Dolgeeno led the priest of each of the Slopeites' gods on an ant train down the spiral path to the cathedral deep inside the mound. Since he had left the queen's chamber, he had been preoccupied with Polexima, once again irked by her endless and unwomanly curiosity. *Perhaps this new daughter will turn her away from affairs of state and back to motherhood,* he thought.

"Stop thinking about her," said his seat mate, Pious Estaine, who was sure of why the high priest silently frowned in the soft light of their torch topped with a lightning-fly egg. "You can't change her and you can't kill her."

"Are you so sure about that?" Dolgeeno asked, smiling ever so slightly.

Estaine feigned a gasp and slapped his chest. "Why, Pious, unless you include me in this plot I could have you stripped of scent for treason."

"Perhaps then you might finally succeed me as our mound's high priest."

The two chuckled as they patted each other's thighs.

"Here's something that will help you forget Polexima the Palzhanite," said Estaine. He handed Dolgeeno his consecrated wafer of the Holy Mildew, the precious fungus the priests scraped from the ceilings of the mushroom chambers. The two chewed their black, bitter wafers and the effects were almost instantaneous once it was washed down with a slug of honeysuckle liquor. Once inside the sanctuary, gorgeously lit by a thousand torches, the priests paced in a chant circle before a gaudy altar with their hundred idols. Their feet disappeared and they floated in a joyous trance. Soon, the walls would melt and the idols would transform into the real gods—gods who would make pronouncements and answer the questions of mortals.

# CHAPTER 5

## THE TRIP TO THE SWAMP

Anand and Terraclon had no rags to change into, but nudity was a serious crime on the Slope. They cut shoots of new grass, pierced the middles with holes and made capes of them. They fashioned antennae from grass fibers, wiped them with kin-scent, and tied them to their heads. No sooner were they dressed than Keel put them to the gruesome work of porting corpses to the swamp at the edge of the Freshwater Lake. The lake was considered polluted since it was shared with the enemy Seed Eaters, so there was no worry they were ruining Cajoria's drinking water. Not that this made dragging dead bodies any more pleasant.

The boys reported to a man from the steering

caste, who, like most of the mound's workers, was starving and had sunken cheeks. Using his shriveled limbs, he handed the boys turbans scented with *leaf-finding-scent*. The boys strapped themselves into reins attached to trucking ants hitched to vats stuffed with stinking dead men. Once the boys put on the turbans, the trucking ants could not help but follow and lug the vats behind them.

The two friends dreaded the tedious hike to the Punk Weed Wilds, but they picked up batting poles from a pile. "The end will be in sight," said Anand, "once we take the first step." Terraclon, who was usually chatty, was as silent as stone as they trudged along.

"You're quiet today," said Anand.

Terraclon exhaled, looking away from Anand.

"My parents have stopped speaking your name, Anand. They just call you 'that half-breed boy.'"

"So?"

"So they think you will make me unmarriageable and tempt me into eating roach flesh. They say I am too old to spend time with you."

Anand rolled his eyes at this. "Again, Ter. I've never eaten roach flesh. Neither has my mother. Her people eat roach *eggs*, but only when there is no other food to be had."

"You know what my dad says about her . . . that she worships a roach demon. And she steals Slopeish babies and stains them with roach dye to make them dark. Some are raised as Britasytes and some are fattened and eaten."

"Ter, you know my mother. She's never been a cannibal and neither are her people. And they would never raise a Slopeite as one of their own."

"Why not?"

"They think the Slopeites, and the Cajorites in particular, are as stupid as they are ugly."

"They think *we're* ugly?"

"Hideous. And you are, you know. All of you Slopeish people. And you stink."

"*We* stink?"

"The Britasytes think the smell of ants is nauseating. They can't understand why anyone would link their lives to creatures as vile as leaf-cutters."

Terraclon laughed, revealing his oversized teeth. Using their poles, they swatted at the flies buzzing about the carts. When one refused to fly off, Anand looked around to see if they were alone, then used his pole to stun the fly with a hard knock to its head. When the fly fell, Anand used the sharp end to stab thorough its brain.

"Impressive!" said Terraclon as he slapped Anand's back. "Who taught you this?"

"All roach people are hunters, including my mother."

Anand tore open the fly's abdomen with his knife, scooped out some of the lymph, and ate it.

"What are you doing?" asked Terraclon, suddenly wary and looking both ways.

"I'm eating. Come on. Let's get some fat on your frame."

"That fly belongs to the royals!"

"The fly belongs to us if we eat it," said Anand.

"When you're hungry, it's hard not to see the point in that," said Terraclon as he quickly scooped out some green flesh. When they finished eating and resumed their trek, carrion beetles crawled up from their holes to munch on the fly's remains, effectively removing the evidence.

Terraclon was singing in a high, clear voice as they walked around a defoliated bortshu tree. It took the boys thousands of steps to traverse the trunk. Ter stopped singing when they heard war song in the distance.

Heading their way were the last of the Slopeish soldiers returning from the conflict with the neighboring Seed Eaters. As usual, they were singing the Hymn of Glories that boasted of Slopeish invincibility. Some of the men were carrying upright pikes with the severed heads of Seed Eater soldiers on their points.

The boys pulled their vats off the path as the soldiers approached. Ter bowed his head and glued his eyes to the sand as the procession made its way. Anand bent his head to the ground, but his eyes peered up. The soldiers rode on the tallest of ants with mandibles that were large and lethal and exoskeletons that were a deep and glossy yellow. Around the men's necks were the breathing filters they wore when fighting the Seed Eaters, whose harvester ants sprayed noxious battle fumes.

Slopeish soldiers may have spent all their days

in preparation to kill and be killed, but to Anand it seemed they were always smiling, something he resented. When he stole an upwards glimpse, his head was smacked by the flat of a sword. He looked up to see a chiding soldier, nearly as young as himself.

"Eyes to the sand, boy," said the soldier and Anand's ears went hot. He gazed at the ground until the procession passed.

The boys reached the edge of the marsh with towering punk grass that waved its brown cylinders in the wind. They dumped the contents of their carts, then backed away as water bugs swam up from the swamp and converged on the corpses.

"I hate them and what they do to us," Anand said. "But sometimes I wish I was with them."

"With who?"

"The soldiers," Anand said as he kicked up a sand grain.

"You will be with them—some time when they go to war. Even soldiers have to wipe their bottoms."

"I'm not talking about carting off their shit. I'm talking about fighting."

"Fighting? You? Let them fight and die! Look at our legless, one-eyed king at the next assembly and then tell me you want to be a soldier."

"But at least he's lived!"

"At least we're intact."

Anand rolled his eyes. "Come on, Ter. Haven't you ever wanted to do something besides clean chamber pots?"

"No point in thinking about it. We are born to our tasks, just as the ants are hatched to theirs."

"But you have thought about it."

Terraclon obviously had. He looked over at a tuft of razor grass where he kept something hidden.

"Can you keep a secret?" he asked.

Anand nodded and Terraclon disappeared behind the grass. He huffed and puffed as he pushed aside a pebble, then unfolded something wrapped in rags. "Turn your back," he said, as he snapped a flower from a spray of dwarf lilies. Anand kept his back turned and heard the sounds of dressing.

"All right," Terraclon said. "Turn and bow before me."

Anand turned, then burst into laughter. Terraclon was arrayed in a parody of royal dress with jackets and trains. It was a patchwork of rags that had been salvaged from the royal trash. He wore the lily as a miter and its yellow pollen was smeared on his face. He strutted about, wielding his pole as if it were a scepter.

"I have a secret, too," Anand said when he could stop laughing. "Time to turn your back!"

Terraclon obeyed. Anand cut a shard from a saddle-leaf plant and draped it over the spiny thorax of the trucking ant. He took off his turban and wrapped it at the end of his pole. Terraclon heard Anand climbing and then the ant taking steps.

"Turn around," Anand said.

Terraclon screeched. Anand was riding on the ant, guiding it with his turban.

"Anand! What are you doing?"

"I'm riding."

"Get off that ant *now*! It's forbidden!"

Anand laughed as he rode the ant in a circle. Terraclon trembled, then climbed the ant's leg spikes and yanked Anand to the ground where they fell in a tangle.

"If the sheriffs see you on an ant, they'll cut your legs off!" Terraclon shouted as the two rose to their feet.

"Why, then I'll look like our king. And with that outfit, you can be queen. Your turn—get up there," Anand said, pushing him.

"No! If you ever ride on an ant again, I won't be your friend."

"All right, all right," Anand responded. "Trucking ants are boring as rides anyway. Help me hitch her to the cart."

On their return, the boys detoured into a dense growth of bucket orchids whose roots clung to the shady side of an old tree. After docking the ants, they climbed an orchid to steal a nap in the tubular beard of its flower. It was sweet and waxy inside, with lavender light that bled through the flower's freckles.

When Anand drifted into sleep, he dreamt of himself in a soldier's armor riding atop a saddled ant. He saw himself leading an army of thousands against an even greater enemy. He woke from the dream, startled and sweating. *Why have I seen someone else's future?* he asked himself. *Roach people are traders, never soldiers.*

*And right now, I'm neither.*

# CHAPTER 6

## THE FISSION LOTTERY

His Most Pious Dolgeeno was fatigued after a sleepless night of sanctifying the lots prior to the assembly. To stay awake, he paced in the tunnel outside his chambers as he waited for Dorfen, the foreman of the blinders' caste, whose grim and messy work was deep in the brood compounds. The foreman's garment was filthy with the dried blood of ants whose eyes were gouged out as soon as they emerged, and from the slaughtering of winged hatchlings who might be potential rivals to the ant queen. After Dorfen was bathed and given a clean robe, he was escorted to the rectory. He crawled to Dolgeeno and used his antennae to nuzzle the hems of the holy robes.

"Blessings of all gods upon thee," said His Most Pious Dolgeeno. "You may look upon me."

Dorfen raised his head and peered behind Dolgeeno's legs to gawk at the high priest's spacious chambers and his table covered with platters of foods. When Dolgeeno noticed the blinder was distracted, he shifted to cover the portal.

"Good Worker Dorfen, until I say so, you are not to blind or slaughter any winged nymphs that hatch. They are to be taken to a separate chamber by the hauling caste."

"Yes, Holiness. If I may ask a question . . ."

Dolgeeno nodded.

"How soon is the Fission?"

"Sometime after the next rain. The winged ones you protect will be the new colony's progenitors."

"One other question, Holiness."

The priest cocked an eye. "Yes?"

"May I wear this garment to the assembly?"

"Certainly not."

Dorfen fell to his knees and crawled away backwards. Once he had reached the priest's servants, the robe was quickly removed and his crusty rags were thrown at him.

As Dorfen returned to his caste, Polexima prepared to fulfill her duty as the mound's Sorceress Queen. As usual, she dressed in a simple garment, then mounted an ant at the head of a team that took her to the ant queen's chambers. Once there, she would lay down the divine essence that safeguarded the mound's existence. Joining her that morning was a newly ordained priest, Pious Frinbo, who was Dolgeeno's current favorite. He had long, thick eyelashes that weighted his blinking and the kind of square jaw and broad cheekbones that Dolgeeno rewarded with quick promotions.

"Your Majesty," he said, and bowed before helping her mount her ant. "I will accompany you this morning. Pious Dolgeeno is exhausted from a night of blessing the lots."

"The lots!" said Polexima with surprise. "Why was I not informed of this?"

"You were already in bed. We did not wish to disturb your sleep."

Polexima hid her alarm but her head throbbed with worries. Sooner than expected, her daughter and a third of her subjects would be making a perilous march.

She was jostled from these thoughts by the chaotic traffic of ants that thickened on their way to the ant queen. Some of the smaller ants, with food for their mother, crawled over Polexima's back and her mount. It seemed longer than usual before she reached the egg-layer, a massive ant of thirteen summers. She was nearly three hundred times the size of her smallest daughters—the grooming minims—a few of which paced inside her emptied eye sockets. At her massive gaster were ants from the hatching caste that took her chains of eggs to the brood chambers.

A dozen priests near the ant queen circled around Poleixma as she dismounted, then helped her spread out her skirts before discharging her urine.

"*Holy is the essence of Polexima,*" sang Frinbo in the priests' holy tongue, "*that holds back the Yellow Mold whose demon tendrils weaken walls and tunnels, and whose poisons kill ants and mushrooms. Gods bless and protect our Urine Sorceress, Queen Polexima.*"

Once Polexima had finished, the priests returned to the ant queen where they rubbed rags over different parts of her to absorb her different essences. Some of them dashed into her mouth to dab at the glistening lumps inside it. As they did so, streams of feeding ants ran in and deposited their liquid food. When the ant queen's mouth started to close, both ants and priests rushed out.

After Frinbo returned Polexima to her apartments, he rejoined the priests, who were back in the secret chambers of the rectories, immersing their essence-soaked rags in barrels of water, oil, or spirits. Around them were other priests extracting essences from leaves, seeds, twigs, or insect parts to bottle or dry and powder. As they did so, they made lists and practiced their greatest secret of all: the inscribing of symbols on sheets of paper that only they could decipher.

When their morning's work was finished, Frinbo opened a barrel of honey fermentation and made an announcement. "The Fission Robes have arrived from Venaris! Let's dress up and . . . more important, let's drink up!" Even as he shouted, he was dipping in a paddle to slurp up a golden drop. As the priests drank, acolytes entered setting down chests that the priests ran to and flung open. They gawked and gasped at the ancient robes that were heavily embroidered, spangled with jewels and trimmed with fresh bee fuzz. The priests laughed and swooned as they pulled them on, then shoved each other aside to gaze in a full-length mirror, boasting about who looked more menacing and godly.

Anand's mother, Corra, sat in the shade under their shelter using her muscular arms to grate a barley seed. Like all from her Britasyte tribe, she had nut-brown skin and black eyes. She had broad cheekbones and blue-black hair that fell down her back and coiled on the sand. Corra watched as her neighbors gathered for the march to the stadium, all of them pacing with fear. She sniggered as she handed Anand some wrapped meals to take.

"Why do you laugh, Mother?" he asked.

"These Cajorites are so afraid," she said. "If they only knew the pleasures of wandering, they would flee this awful ant mound."

"Shhh!"

"No, Anand. They should hear me. If they are chosen to leave, they should welcome it as a blessing."

"What will you do all day? Come with us."

"I can't," she said without a hint of remorse. "I'm not a subject of the King and Queen . . . thank Lord Roach."

Yormu descended the ladder from their shelter, then whistled for Anand to join him as Keel accounted for every member of every family using his talking knots to certify the number. Once gathered up, all were prodded by a sheriff to march to the stadium on the mound's shady side. They trudged through the rings of shanties, up through the shacks, then past the hovels and houses. Gathering castes of the upper rings turned away as the middenites passed, and parents covered their children's eyes.

Anand's caste was the first to reach the stadium and climb the endless flight of stairs to the pen reserved for them. Inside the pen were two chamber barrels that would be filled to overflowing by the end of the day. Anand and Yormu were pushed to the corner, closest to the barrels. They had no slits in the slats to view the events but Anand found a small opening which allowed them some vision after he worked it with his knife. The displeasing sight, however, was of more ragged laborers arriving with their caste brethren.

As the sun climbed, the crafting and trade castes took their seats on benches, followed by merchants in boxes with cushioned chairs. The soldiers appeared, standing in sections according to rank. The generals arrived on mounts of giant soldier ants that had been roused from their dormancy just for the occasion.

Commander General Batra was the last to arrive on the tallest ant of all.

Bands of drummers preceded a train of carrier ants that stretched as far as the eye could see. At its end were the royals, mounted on draped and bangled ants. The entire crowd rose and bowed as Sahdrin and Polexima dismounted to the platform with the Mushroom Thrones. Before she took her throne, the queen took Pareesha from her nurse and presented the baby to the crowd. They fell to their knees and bowed their heads before the newest descendant of Goddess Ant Queen.

Whirlwinds of fragrant dust floated across the arena, then drifted away to reveal the priests. They wore towering miters and their sparkling robes flapped as they walked on stilts. Their cluster parted to reveal Dolgeeno, raising his arms to command that all rise in prayer.

"Blessed is our mound of Cajoria. Blessed are all the United Queendoms of the Great and Holy Slope." His distant words were passed to the people by the caste of voice relayers. Some of these men changed the words into the dialects of the workers.

As was typical of any assembly, the first events were the public punishments. Carrier ants dragged a wicker cage into the arena. Inside it were two naked, sobbing humans. Their skins were red and raw from multiple scrubbings in the sudsy juice of soap weed roots. Dolgeeno shouted over the anguished screams of the prisoners.

"Before you are Nerinda, daughter of a soldier, and Dulfay, a son of the grain fermenters. They are guilty of copulating outside of marriage and caste restrictions. Their punishment is death by bathing."

When Dolgeeno nodded his head, the fathers of the couple approached the cage and cut the ropes that bound it. The cage fell apart and their unscented children were exposed to the ants that had been chasing the cages.

The boy and girl tried to run to Dolgeeno and beg for mercy, but the ants were far quicker. The girl screamed out prayers when she was caught. Ants sliced off her arms and legs, leaving her to bleed to death. When the boy was captured, his head was lopped off. Smaller ants scurried under larger ones and licked the ground for the human blood. As the ants left with pieces of the executed to dump in the midden, their fathers trudged off, covering their heads with the Red Cloths of Shame.

"Let their deaths be a lesson to all," shouted Dolgeeno, and a great cheer went up from the crowd.

Anand shook his head in disgust.

The sacks containing the lottery chips were then dragged to the sand by trucking ants. At the same time, Princess Trellana was carried out on a palanquin to face the people. She was dressed in a garment made from the rare fuzz bee and her lacquered hair had been sculpted into an idol of Goddess Ant Queen. When a breeze blew, she had to brace her neck with her hands so she wouldn't fall over, which made some in the crowd snicker. "I suppose having to sit in a chair for days getting your hair done is one of the downsides of being a royal," Anand said to his father who hid his toothless smile with his hand.

The sheriffs delivered the lottery sacks to the foreman of each caste. Every subject of Cajoria took an envelope and waited for Dolgeeno's cue. Sun was dying when the last sack was delivered to the midden workers. It made its way to the end of the pen, where Anand took the very last lot among the hundreds of thousands distributed.

Dolgeeno held up a bit of a bortshu leaf. "The gods have decreed that the glory of the Slopeish people should be extended on the Sand. Those of you who draw yellow shards are the new pioneers, blessed with the privilege of accompanying Princess Trellana on her trek to establish a new colony."

Dolgeeno tore his leaf and the envelopes were opened. No one dared to cheer the discovery of a red chip but thousands began weeping when they, or someone they loved, received one of yellow. Yormu collapsed with relief when he saw his lot was red. He turned to watch Anand who tore his envelope in two. But nothing was inside it.

Anand looked at his father and shrugged. He tore one half in quarters and looked in its corners. He did the same to the other half and turned it over. A yellow bit fluttered as it fell. Anand looked at it, this piece of a dead flower, and knew everything had changed.

# CHAPTER 7

# THE NIGHT OF INSEMINATIONS

Anand was elated. At last, he would be on a journey, even if it would be with the loathsome Cajorites of the Slope. His joy vanished, though, when he saw Yormu collapsed against the pen and fighting back tears.

"It's all right, Dad," he whispered, putting an arm around him. "In a few more fattenings of Moon, I can live anywhere I want."

Yormu nodded but Anand could see from his downcast and shifting eyes that his father was imagining every possible danger for his one and only son.

Those who had yellow chips made their way down to the arena, in order of caste hierarchy, where they lined up behind the princess. Sun was nearly dead and bleeding when it was the outcastes' turn. Anand was disgusted to see that both Keel and Tal had somehow also drawn yellow lots, ensuring that they would be running the new midden. *How did they both get yellow?* Anand asked himself. *Did they trade with someone?*

Moon was high in the sky and beginning her descent when the workers were allowed to leave. Anand was sleepier than he had ever been in his life. Keel called his name, and, as he turned, the chamber barrels from the pen were thrust into his and Yormu's arms. "Heard you were thirsty," Keel said and laughed.

Corra had set out an excellent supper, but her son and husband went straight to their mattresses after climbing into their shelter.

"Did you both pick yellow?" she asked, in an all too quiet voice.

"Just me," Anand said.

"Where? How far?"

"All we know is that it is north of here."

"The North is riddled with wasps and lair spiders. And its trees are full of cannibals."

"We were told they sent a scouting party, most of which returned alive."

"Most? I heard fifty workers died. You are *not going*," Corra sputtered.

"I thought you said it was a blessing."

"Not for you! Tell Keel that in six moons you will be a Britasyte man who can leave the Slope and join your real tribe. There's no point in going to a new colony for just a few moons."

"There are no exceptions. I will have to wait for

the idols keeper to give me my sixteenth chit. Then I can leave."

"We'll get you out in secret. We can have you on a caravan to the Carpenters' lands in a matter of days."

"If I run away, they'll kill Dad. If they catch me, I will be killed." Anand sat up, took his mother's hand. "It's all right, really. I will learn the way so our clans can follow. Finally, I will have tales of my own wanderings."

Corra's frown turned to a smile so broad it lit up the darkness. "I've always told you that you were destined for greatness. Now I'm sure of it. When do you go?"

"Some time after the next rain, when the ant queens fly for insemination." Anand sniffed the air. It was heavy with the scent of roaches. "You've had a visitor," he said.

"I have," she answered with a chuckle.

"Are they nearby?"

"They will be soon and just in time. A gathering of all the clans! You'll never guess who's being honored."

**S**even days after the lottery, Anand woke to the happy sounds of a spring thunderstorm. For the castes that labored outdoors, rain meant a holiday spent inside. It wasn't all fun and rest, though, because by late morning, when the storm had passed, the Slope's poorest inhabitants had to avoid pools of deadly mud and try and salvage their shelters.

When it was dry enough, the royal messengers fanned through the mound's flats on their mud skates. One of them came to the midden's edge and rubbed a cricket leg to summon Keel and the caste's idols keeper. The two were given important information to pass to the rest of the caste.

Terraclon was out of his shanty and making mud mushrooms with some midden girls. They were about to eat them when Anand appeared and offered some proper food, a pickled butterfly egg. The girls looked at him and ran off screeching, "Pollution! Polluted food from a polluted boy!"

Anand just shrugged and turned to his friend. "Have you heard the message from the royals, Ter?"

"The ant nuptials are tonight," said Terraclon, his brow ridged with anger. "Princess Trellana's consort has left Mound Kulfi. Once he arrives, Fission takes place. Those who are leaving must gather their possessions and the tools of their duties. That would be you, I guess."

"It is. Why are you so sour?"

"I'm not sour," Terraclon said, taking Anand's offering. "Just wondering why you were so stupid as to pick a yellow lot." Terraclon's father poked out from their shanty to scowl at his son, who dropped his head and turned to his home.

"He doesn't want me eating this," Terraclon said, and lobbed the egg to Anand.

"But . . ."

"I have to go."

Anand nodded sadly. He took the egg back to his own shelter, wincing as he heard his friend being beaten, the sound haunting him all the way home.

"The ant queens mate tonight," Anand told his parents as he entered their dwelling.

"Then you'll be leaving soon," said his mother. Yormu strained not to weep as Corra looked at the rug they were sitting on. It was a skillful depiction of the evening's ritual as observed by a rug maker from a lifetime ago.

"I have always wanted to see leaf-cutter nuptials," Corra said. "But this is the perfect opportunity—we have someplace to go while the Cajorites are distracted." She went to a lidded clay barrel that reeked of roach scent.

Anand grinned when he realized where they were going.

While Yormu held his nose, Anand and his mother laid out the oiled leaf ponchos they wore for secret travel. After night fell, they would sneak off to visit her Roach Tribe, the filthiest people on Mother Sand—who Anand saw as his true family.

That afternoon, Sun emerged, harsh and angry, to dry the sand and bake the mud to a hard surface. When He yielded to His sister, Moon, She rose in a cloak of colored mists.

Deep inside the Cajorites' mound, the blinding castes prepared for the exodus of the virgin ant queens, which were oily and stank of mating-scent. Since their last molting, their wings had unfurled to full size. Outside the chamber, masses of their sterile sisters roamed the tunnels, anxious to push the queens out to their destinies. The night sky was buzzing with swarms of drones from the other queendoms that were eager to inject their semen.

Polexima and the royal family, dressed in evening silks, took seats near the edge of the mound's opening where a feast had been laid out. "Do we really have to be here?" Trellana asked her parents after yawning. She was disappointed that there were few guests from the nearby mounds to see her gown or her latest dazzling coiffure.

"Trellana, this may be the only time you ever witness ant nuptials," said Polexima. "It should be a thrilling spectacle."

"I should just die if I were to miss out on any thrills," said Trellana, and yawned again.

Drones landed and began clawing at the mound's opening, attempting to get at the virgin queens. The priests used poles to shoo these drones and send them back to the sky. Far below, the blinders slid open gates and the virgin ants emerged one at a time. Nooses attached to tethers were thrown around the joint that connected an ant's head to its middle. As the virgins passed, they were splashed with luminous paint. At the other end of the tethers were the human anchors that would retrieve and cage the queens once they had been inseminated.

Cries went up as the first virgin appeared, her wings fluttering above the mass of sterile escorts. She launched herself in the air, her wings a blur of light, as she soared into the cloud of buzzing drones.

A small drone reached her first. While continuing to fly, he clenched her abdomen with his mandibles and rubbed her underside with his legs to inject his seeds. Other drones crowded onto the tether and it came down in a slow crash, sending the priests running. Slowed by her excessive costume, Trellana was caught by the rope and knocked to the carpets. Her coiffure collapsed when it was dragged through a platter of grub dip. Polexima laughed as servants ran to clean off the princess.

"Mother, please!" Trellana hissed.

"It's funny, darling. Why don't you show our subjects that you can laugh at yourself?"

Trellana let out a harsh, mock laugh. She then stomped off to her chambers with her handmaidens and a hundred grooming ants crawling after.

Outside the mound, near a pond marsh, an occasion of far less seriousness was getting underway.

# CHAPTER 8

## THE ROACH TRIBE

It had been several moons since Anand and Corra had seen her people. As they got farther from Cajoria, her heart grew light and she sang. She walked briskly, but still, Anand trotted ahead, turned and shouted, "Come on, Mother, hurry!" They followed stones and plants, which had been smeared with roach secretion, until they reached the edge of a marsh.

From out of a thicket of flowering clover, a massive insect appeared. It was shining and greasy and glimmered with moonlight. It could not fly, but its red-brown body was sheathed in armor-like wings and its triangular head was handsome, like a mantis. It rose up on powerful legs as the shorter of its two pairs of antennae probed Anand for roach-scent.

Slopeites thought roaches were hideous, but Anand saw them as the most beautiful of insects, and this one's legs had the thick femurs of a strong rider. Atop the roach was a human, who looked high and tiny as she halted the insect by tightening then clipping its reins, which drew together the larger antennae. Auntie Glegina dismounted and ran towards Anand to hug him. He saw that she still shaved her head in mourning for the husband who had been murdered years ago. Her arms reached up for Anand from under a cape thick with roach scent. Glegina's head was topped with false antennae wrapped with blue ribbons.

It took Anand time to get used to the odors of his mother's people. When his aunt kissed him, he smelled the acrid breath that was typical of the tribe. It was something he would stop noticing once he had eaten their foods but for now it was still an adjustment. It didn't help that Glegina hugged him too hard.

"Auntie Gleg, you're squeezing the life from me," he gasped.

"Only because I've missed you so much," she said in Britasyte. "Do you want to take the reins?"

Too excited to answer, Anand quickly climbed up the roach which was fitted with a rope ladder. Sometimes a roach took tumbles and they could not be righted, but they were more exciting to ride than ants. It was a strain to wrap thighs around the protrusion on the natural saddle at the backs of their heads, but roaches were fast and nimble and easier to guide than any ant with pulls on the reins.

As they drew closer to the camp, Anand could hear the drums and group-songs of the tribe. The drumming made his heart race until it thumped in unison with the beat. The roach reached the peak of a grade and the riders looked down. Spread out on a dried mud flat and lit up by glowworms were the combined clans of the Britasyte tribe. Surrounding the camp were three corrals with roaches of various sizes. The insects were tethered to each other in elaborate webs.

The clans danced around a cage of lightning flies whose abdomens flashed with the beats of drums. Aphid punch tinctured with Holy Mildew was passed to the crowd by Da-Ma, the revered Man-Woman who scooped it from a cauldron. He/she wore a festival costume fashioned from the spotted wings of the green moon moth and the protuberant codpiece of a Slopeish general. His/her eyes widened as Anand and his mother approached.

"Now comes a boy of mixed blood," Da-Ma said, giving Anand the scoop. "Drink deeply, son of two tribes, for your journey commences."

"What journey?" Anand asked, blinking at Da-Ma who he could see had already entered the Spirit World as his/her pupils were large and shining. Several times Anand had drunk the spirit of fermentation, but he had never ingested the black mildew of the Slopeites' priests. He knew he was freer amongst the Britasytes, but Anand still turned and looked at his mother, who nodded her approval. He took a long drink. The punch was sweetened with juice from the phantom berry, but it was bitter all the same and he shuddered as it scorched his throat. He saw that his mother took but a sip, knowing she was responsible for returning her son.

A moment later, Anand had the sensation that his head had dissolved and blown away with a breeze. His feet grew into the ground like a tuber and his arms were sprinkled with stars. Feeling strong and weak, grounded and dizzy, he heard thoughts from the insides of the heads around him. Paralyzed by panic, he was sure that his quick-beating heart had switched places with his tongue.

"Don't be frightened, Anand," said Da-Ma, with a comforting smile. "No one here wishes you any ill. You are safe in the arms of Madricanth."

Madricanth was the one and only deity worshipped by the Britasytes, though they paid service to hundreds of others. Madricanth had a roach's body and a human head, and like Da-Ma, was both male and female. Anand felt cold and hot and had a sudden vision of the world splitting in two: half was colored with the blue and black of night, the other half with the yellows and greens of day. The two halves appeared as the arms of a warm embrace that Anand entered into.

Anand blinked and the vision disappeared. He was dizzy, but back at the camp, wobbling on his feet. He looked into the faces of his mother and Da-Ma.

"Now you occupy both Mother Sand and the Spirit World," Da-Ma said. Anand nodded in bliss. Everything was the same, but shimmering with an inner light—the spirit that resided within all things. He was lured to the dancing by a tribal song as the clans danced in a fever, pivoting as they threw their arms to the moon. Anand was picked up by the music's five-part harmonies as if they were a wave of water. He felt free, like he was floating down a warm stream, when suddenly he was ripped into a different realm.

A startling vision made its way around the dance circle: a large girl of seventeen. She had broad cheekbones, wide and liquid eyes and an expression both defiant and vulnerable. At first Anand was sure that there were a hundred of her, but a second later, her image had folded back into one—was she real or an apparition? She danced outside the circle in a way all her own. As she moved, her full breasts and limbs had an effect that transfixed him. He was wracked with a painful yearning and a sickness that would forever infect him.

The girl caught Anand staring and stopped dancing to scowl at him. He was devastated. He stared at the ground, then looked up at her with a wounded longing. Realizing he was sincere in his admiration, her pouting lips battled each other, then burst into a smile. Her teeth were large and perfect, and she suddenly had the beauty of the moon emerging from a rain cloud.

Anand smiled, too. He had the overwhelming urge to lie down with this girl and free her from her garments. When he imagined removing his own clothing, he was all too aware of what he was wearing: the crude brown rags of secret travel. He looked at his poncho, looked back at the girl, and saw the dancers had swept her away. His mother tugged at his sleeve and they walked. From the look on her face, Anand could see his mother did not like this female.

And for some reason, that made him want this young woman more.

As a member of the Cajorites' lowest caste, Anand was forbidden to wear dyed cloth or expose more than his face and hands. As he walked with his mother, he gawked at the finery of the Britasyte boys. Their red-brown capes were all the same, made from greased cloth and fashioned after roach wings. But under their capes, the boys' legs and arms were bare. Around their middles were tunics that were tight like a second skin and dyed in brilliant colors.

His envy of finery faded and his desire to see the girl became the greatest need of his life. Her smile sang a melody inside him, and her eyes blazed like a memory of the sun. He reeled and fell when he was overcome by a mildew-induced vision of the two of them coupling on the back of a flying moon moth. He could barely hear his mother when she said, "We must pay our respects to the chieftain," and pulled him to his feet.

The two went to the platform where Corra's third cousin, the fat and jolly Zedral, sat on cushions with the other clan chiefs surrounded by a bounty of gifts. Anand and his mother bowed their heads before she removed an impressive cluster of ant eggs from the jar on her back. Anand wondered where and how she had obtained them since they were forbidden as food to all but Slopeish nobles. Such were her mysteries.

Zedral passed the eggs to his daughters to prepare for the feast. He was suddenly serious as he looked at Anand.

"Boy of Two Tribes, do you know why you were named 'Anand'?"

Anand looked at his mother. "No," he said. "Anand means 'worker' in the Slopeish tongue."

"But in our old tongue it means something else," said Zedral. "It means 'spanner,' a link between two worlds, like the bridge that runs through the Tar Marsh to the Dustlands."

"If I had a choice, I know which world I would live in," said Anand in bitterness and looking back at the revelry around them. The mildew diminished inhibitions and he was surprised by his own frankness. He could see that Corra was crushed with sadness and did not hide tears that came like a sudden rain. She placed her hands on her son's shoulders.

"We know it has been a trial for you to live on the Slope among the Cajorites," said Zedral. "But someday soon you and your mother will return to our fold. You will be our interpreter and inform us of the mushroom-eaters' ways. Because of you, our tribe will prosper and be safer in its wanderings."

"But we could never leave my father behind. He is shunned by his caste. He would die of loneliness."

"My heart is touched by your devotion," Zedral said, then turned towards Corra. "You have raised your son among the Slopeites, but he has the pure soul of a Wanderer."

Zedral was somber as he turned back to Anand. "You know that in the view of the Slopeites, your father is not possessed of himself. He is the property of Sahdrin and Polexima."

"I will never accept that my father can't roam with us," Anand said. "We will find some way."

"If we were to adopt him, we would be accused of sheltering a fugitive. The Slopeites would use that as an excuse to rob us, even kill us. At least with you, as a boy of mixed bloods, they have no claim on you once you reach manhood."

"They will be glad to be rid of me," said Anand, fingering his precious age chits. "And I of them."

"When do you turn sixteen?"

"In six moons."

"That time will pass before you know. You will sit beside me tonight when the feast commences."

"I would be honored . . . but why?"

Anand was mystified. It was usually the richest traders who sat by the chiefs, the ones who succeeded in their deals by clever ruses.

"You will see," said Zedral and smiled. "Now go and dance and work up an appetite and I will speak with your mother."

Anand hurried off without looking to Corra for permission. He knew her face would be a tangle of sadness and jealousy, an image he did not want to bring with him.

Anand reached the dance circle and moved to a song sung in the Britasytes' eighteen-tone scale. The words were ancient and spoke of the beauties of the wandering life—of landscapes yet unseen, of foods untasted and music not yet heard. He was pushed and prodded in the writhing mass of bodies, breathing the scents of sweat, perfume, and roach secretion. He could have lost himself but he was intent on finding the girl.

As the lightning flies flashed, Anand grew punchy. He fell out of the dance circle and landed on his bottom. The dirt did not seem firm and he felt as if he were sinking in a black mist. Something like both the sun and the moon was growing before him, blooming like a flower made of light. It was the face of the girl as she stood over him, looking down and softly smiling. The ground beneath him was solid again.

"First time you've drunk the mildew?" she asked.

"Yes," he said. His felt as if his heart was crawling up his throat on six legs.

"Are you all right?" she asked, her face both chiding and full of concern.

"I am well, thank you," he said, suddenly too formal.

She extended her hand to him and he took it. It was as warm as the mushroom bread his mother pulled from a sun kiln. As he stood up, he dove into the lake of her eyes.

"You are Anand."

"Yes."

"You might ask my name," she said, and playfully pushed him.

"I'm sorry," he said, afraid that everyone was looking at them. He was sure that it was not just people, but the grass, rocks, and stars that were staring. Was anyone? He glanced around. No, they were all dancing or chatting.

"What . . . what is your name?"

"Daveena."

Anand was quiet again, but inside, a windstorm was howling.

"Are they not used to conversing at your ant mound?" she asked.

"They are. But I am not," he said, and lowered his lids. "I . . . I have almost never talked to a girl," he said. She took his cold hand and attempted to warm it with hers. Once she touched him, he saw their future in an instant: their marriage, pregnancies, and grandchildren. He saw her hair turn gray and her corpse fed to the roaches. She blinked at him, wondering, and he knew he must stop staring so intensely but he didn't want to stop. A moment later, the thorn players raised their instruments and broke his gaze when they piped the call to the feast. "Will you follow me?" he said.

"Of course," she said and chuckled.

The drumming faded and the dancers fell away to spread over the ancient carpets woven of human hair. Anand and Daveena passed boys and girls of fifteen and sixteen as they gathered at the platter of the promised couples. Anand felt her stiffening as she pretended not to hear their whispers and sniggers. He heard someone call him "Stinks-of-Ants," a beauty who dyed her hair the color of rose quartz.

"Who's that she-chigger?" Anand asked.

"That's Eturra," whispered Daveena. "Her face is pretty. Her words are ugly."

"Better hide the food if you want some," Eturra was shouting as Daveena walked away. "You know how some of these *older* girls eat."

Daveena pivoted and stared at the pink-haired girl as she gloated among her giggling friends. "Who among you should hide her vicious tongue?" Daveena snapped back while stepping in. "Would it be you, Eturra, that says the cruelest things about your friends when their backs are turned?" she continued, and then stared at each of Eturra's friends. "Who laughs at the mustache that sprouted along with your breasts? Your lack of buttocks? The acne that's spread to your chest?"

The three girls glared at Daveena even as they took surreptitious glances at Eturra. The boys were admiring Daveena's fierceness. Eturra's own young man had shifted away from her.

"I didn't mean to be cruel," Eturra said. "I'm happy for you, Daveena. I'm glad to see they found *someone* for a girl as big as a bumblebee . . . even if it is some low-caste ant boy. What affliction does he have? Is he missing any parts? Perhaps we can pray for him."

Anand looked at the young beauty. She was too thin and arrogant for his tastes. "I found *her*," he said in perfect Britasyte. "If you're going to pray, ask Madricanth to give you a kinder heart." Eturra and the others looked startled by his diction and seemed further intrigued when the two approached the chieftains' platform. To their complete surprise, he motioned them to join him.

Anand's mother had changed into Britasyte costume with a turban studded with mica chips. Her face was frozen as Anand and Daveena stood before her.

"Good travels, my lady," Daveena said, touching her hand to her heart in the gesture of esteeming.

"Good travels," Corra responded woodenly. Anand winced.

As the two women eyed each other, Zedral motioned Anand to follow him into his sand-sled. "I have something for you, young man," he said and winked. "And I believe these women need to talk."

Anand winced again.

Corra looked deep in the girl's eyes, searching for her secrets, probing for her flaws. Daveena met her gaze, steadily.

"I am Daveena, daughter of Eltzer and Gupa of the Pleps," she said and raised her chin.

"I am Corra of the Entreveans."

"May I take a seat, my lady?"

"Please."

The two turned to a polite discussion of food and its preparation as the chefs brought in the dishes. Platters of toasted lice were the first to arrive, followed by oil-popped aphids and piles of steamed damselfly meat.

The longest and most glorious dish was carried on the shoulders of several men, a spinach-stuffed caterpillar with a mosquito's egg tucked under every foot.

"I prefer to stuff a caterpillar with basil," said Daveena.

"So do I, if it's fresh," said Corra, "but I would also mix in some green onion."

As the two discussed herbs and spices, Corra's objections and suspicions vanished. She sensed that this was a young woman who exemplified the virtues of the tribe: resilient, playful, modest, but brave. She was struck by how familiar Daveena seemed. At first Corra thought this large and imposing girl resembled her sister, then realized, no, Daveena looked like herself. At one moment when the words ran dry, the two continued to look at each other and Corra was sure Daveena had also seen the same startling reflection.

Upon their return, Zedral was grinning as he stepped from the sand-sled, motioning Anand to follow him out. Anand appeared with his shoulders thrown back, dressed in his first Britasyte costume. On his head was a spangled turban that added to his height. He elbowed back the oiled cape and revealed a tunic of rich orange. His arms and legs were shiny with roach grease.

A wave of murmurs rolled through the crowd as they turned to Anand. No one recognized him as the visiting ant-boy. The young man standing with the Entreveans' chieftain had a penetrating beauty. Anand heard women make the "mmm" sound that accompanies good eating. His broadening smile was both toothy and toothsome, rendering him like some living confection. Daveena stared at him and looked suddenly frightened, as if she could not believe this boy had chosen her. It was her turn to be wordless as he took his seat and looked into her unblinking eyes.

The thorn pipers stood before the platform to sound the melody that silenced the tribe. Zedral's eldest son, the tall and powerful Bejetz, handed a headband to his father. Attached to it were four long and dramatic antennae decorated with ribbons of purple, red, orange, and blue—the colors of the four clans.

"Good travels, Britasytes," shouted Zedral to the thousands. "Tonight we honor a man who has made great sacrifices for our tribe, who has suffered for our safety, our prosperity, and our right to roam. In his other life he is treated like a louse. In our world, he shall be a teacher, a trader, a master of the tongue of the *sedites.*"

The crowd chuckled. Zedral had used the Britasytes' name for Slopeites that likened them to something that was dead and stank and could not move, like a corpse. He turned towards Anand who for a sad moment was returned to the outskirts of Cajoria, reminded that among the corpse-people of the Slope he was a hauler of corpses.

"Rise, Spanner. The Britasytes dedicate this feast to you."

Anand felt a sudden heat in his face. His mother and Daveena nudged him until he stood. "Why didn't you tell me, Mother?" he asked.

"It was just arranged," she said with a grin, "when I told them you would miss your manhood rite because of this stupid Fission." Her smile stretched wider. "And I *did* tell you they were honoring someone special."

Stunned, Anand walked slowly to Zedral who attached the headband to his turban before turning him to face the crowd. As the people cheered and clapped, he realized he had never been applauded before. Under the strange influence of the mildew, the applause appeared like a thousand flowers blooming and closing. He saw that the only person not applauding was the pink-haired Eturra. She suddenly scowled and looked at Daveena who stared back at her with a vengeful smirk.

Anand gasped when he felt a powerful surge through his legs. Bejetz had thrust his head through Anand's thighs to lift him on his shoulders. He was pivoted to face the crowd as their applause reached a pitch. He sensed the vaguest of shadows over his head as the cheers and claps turned to a sudden silence— and then to screams and panic.

He saw the faces of the tribe as they stretched in fright. "Night wasps!" came the shouts. Anand's joy turned to dread as he looked up into the face of the most feared predator in all creation as its antennae whipped out and lashed his chest.

# CHAPTER 9

## PROMISES

Daveena's mouth was open, but she was too stunned to scream.

Bulging from the wasp's head were monstrous eyes as dark and deep as death itself and as wide as Anand was tall. The wasp hovered with two pairs of orange wings, more garish than the dying sun. A long and sinister stalk connected its middle to a black abdomen with indigo stripes. At its end was the long and notorious stinger.

A dozen wasps had landed silently at the camp's edge and were crawling into its center. The tribe flipped over their carpets to expose undersides encrusted with crystal razors. The people scrambled under the carpets and curled themselves into balls. Atop the chieftains' platform, Daveena and Corra were both hesitant to take cover, staring at the wasp descending on Anand. The men grabbed the women by their ankles and yanked them down and under.

Atop Bejetz's shoulders, Anand had been the easiest target. As the two of them dropped, the wasp lunged at Anand as he scrambled for the carpet. He gasped when the wasp caught him, then cried in pain when its leg needles pierced his skin. Daveena looked out as Anand groped for the carpet's edge, only to see him jerked into the wasp's crushing embrace.

"No!" she shouted, as she popped from the carpet and threw herself at the insect's forelegs. She banged against them but caught the hem of Anand's cape. When the wasp rose in vertical flight, it took both Anand and Daveena.

"Let go, Daveena," Anand wheezed, struggling to stay conscious. "Let go now or you'll die!"

But Daveena would not let go, though her clutching hands were fatigued in an instant and slipped from the oiled cape. She caught the ankles of Anand's boots and swayed below him like a kite's tail, swinging left and right. The wasp wobbled in its flight as its antennae picked up her scent and probed downwards.

As they ascended toward the wasp's nest in a distant tree, Daveena shrieked when the wasp's abdomen curved under and towards her. At its end was the clear, sword-like stinger with its inner needle pulsing inside. As if she were on a rope swing, Daveena pumped her legs, rocking herself and Anand. She avoided the stinger as it stabbed and missed and stabbed again.

Because Anand's clothing and skin were coated with oil, Daveena could feel the wasp's grasp slipping each time she swung. The grasp shifted from Anand's chest to his shoulders and she heard him suck in air as his lungs were freed from the clasping legs.

"Keep swinging! Don't let go!" he shouted to her and she pumped even harder.

She had no intention of ever letting go.

Anand felt the wasp's leg needles rip out of his shoulders as he squirmed himself out, dropped, only to be caught again. His cape had flown up and the wasp had snatched it in its mouth. The collar gagged him when he remembered he had his knife, which he took from his sheath and brought to his neck.

When he cut the collar, the two of them plummeted. Anand shut his eyes. *Save us, Sweet Roach God*, he prayed. He/she must have heard him because the two fell to a cluster of pitcher plants, bounced on the bumpy mouth of one, then slid down the chute of its cylindrical leaf. They splashed in a pool of sharp-smelling goop at the pitcher's bottom.

"Come on," said Anand as he swam to the wall and used his knife to slit open the pitcher. They squeezed out, landing in a bog where they struggled over the springy loam and fell in its fetid puddles. When Daveena tripped, Anand pulled her up and they faced each other, close enough to feel each other's heat. "I have chosen well," he said, holding her with his eyes.

"Who says *you* were the one who chose?" she said, her eyes glorious in the moonlight.

Lost in her gaze, he had forgotten the horrors of just a moment ago.

Taking her hand, the two stumbled through the bog's tangled threads until they reached the edge of the dried mud flat. They were unsure which way to walk until their noses picked up roach-scent. As they got closer to camp, they heard the keening of the Britasyte women. The wasps had left and a funeral had begun—which Anand realized was for them.

The tribe had gathered around Da-Ma at the idol-sled. "Benevolent Crawler, bring them into your Heavenly Caravan," he/she prayed, "to wander in eternity." The tribe was silent when two filth-covered figures wove through them, then took the stairs to the altar.

"Anand? Anand!" shouted Corra, as she and Glegina rushed the altar. They were followed by Daveena's parents. All of them screamed in joy.

"Stay back!" shouted Da-Ma as the parents lunged for their children.

"We are not spirits," said Anand, understanding her/his suspicion, for who had ever escaped a night wasp? "We are Britasytes who bleed red blood," he continued, showing Da-Ma the bloody punctures from the wasp's grip.

The parents hugged their children in teary disbelief. Da-Ma took the two into the sand-sled and rubbed healing extracts onto their cuts.

Anand felt heavy with fatigue, but he rose to his

feet to address Daveena's parents, Eltzer and Gupa, as they knelt at their daughter's side. From a mattress, the girl looked up at Anand with a faint smile.

"I will not have this chance tomorrow," Anand said to Eltzer, "and must speak to you now, sir. My fate is with your daughter. If she agrees, I wish to take her as my eternal wife." Eltzer looked to Gupa. She nodded with enthusiasm.

"Of course," said Eltzer, who rose and bowed. As he looked at the floor, he smiled, in evident relief that his large and intimidating daughter was betrothed to an extraordinary boy.

"There is one problem," Anand said. "I am the property of the Cajorite royals for six more moons. I have been pressed into a colonial expedition, far to the unknown North, and I am unsure of when I can return. Daveena must wait for me, no matter what happens."

Eltzer was silent before speaking, but his face filled with apprehension.

"I cannot do that to my daughter . . . she is not a young girl anymore. What if you are killed on this trek? She will be eighteen in a few more moons. After that, we will be lucky if we can match her with an outsider."

"If you have no word from me in seven moons, she is free to find another. Until then, I ask that she wear her hair in the braid of one who is spoken for. I am a poor boy with one thing to give her as my betrothal present: a promise to love and honor her all our days together."

Eltzer took Anand's hands in his own and nodded. Anand felt as if his future was the brightest star in the heavens. He turned to Daveena and smiled, and when she smiled back, Anand knew that even if Eltzer went back on his word, Daveena would stay true well beyond seven moons.

Zedral arranged to return the boy and his mother on a speed-sled drawn by their fastest roach. As Bejetz drove the unhobbled giant, Anand and his mother slept on a cushion in the sled's back.

Anand fell into a dream as they rode. He dreamt of the moment he could leave the Slopeites' new colony to find Daveena in the Pleps' caravan. He dreamt that on his route through the wilderness to find her, he was attacked by fleas, trapped by spiders, and pursued by a swarm of night wasps. At the dream's end, he found Daveena, but she burst into tears and stood to reveal she was pregnant with the child of a Slopeish outsider.

Anand awoke from this nightmare to find himself back at the midden. It was just a dream. He had seen inside her, seen the commitment in her eyes. *Yes, just a nightmare. Now the next nightmare of Fission begins*, he thought.

Yormu was awake inside their shelter, looking relieved to see his family's safe return. Anand patted his dad's arm, then stumbled to the mattress. Anand's own assurances did nothing to keep him from tossing and turning until daylight.

# CHAPTER 10

## DEPARTURE

Anand was sick with hatred at the idea of donning his usual rags and facing another day at the midden. Before he left, he helped his mother butcher a drone that had landed near their tent. Before he and Yormu departed, she filled their bowls with fresh ant-flesh. It was something so forbidden Yormu would not eat it.

"It's all right, Father," Anand said as he scooped up the rich jelly with his fingers. "It's been decreed."

"For one thing, they want to fatten up the pioneers for the Fission," said Corra.

But Anand could barely eat it himself. Soon after he tasted his food he pushed away his bowl and clutched his stomach. "I'm stomach-sick," he said.

"It happens after you leave the Spirit World," said

his mother. "You must eat something, and drink as much water as you can today." She released a terrible sigh.

"Something wrong, Mother?"

"Just the usual sadness of returning to this place."

"It won't be forever," Anand said in Britasyte. It was the first time the thought of leaving the *sedites* didn't make him happy. He looked at his father and wondered—how would he live once they left?

At noon, during a water-break, Anand clustered with other middenites that had drawn yellow lots.

"I have told you, I will not go," said Pleckoo the Noseless. He was tall with the lightest skin in the midden but a disfigurement had left him with a bone that poked through gaping nostrils.

"Don't be a fool, Pleckoo," said Keel. "If you don't go you'll be executed!"

"There are far worse fates," Pleckoo said, then spat in defiance. The wad landed on Anand's foot. When Pleckoo realized he had spat on his half-breed cousin, he didn't bother to apologize.

"The sheriffs will kill your parents if you run away," said Keel.

"My parents have lived long enough," said Pleckoo, "and I weary of sharing my rations with them."

"Where do you plan to go, idiot? Will you run away with the roach-eaters? Will you climb a tree and take up with cannibals? If you leave the mound, you leave the protective spells of the priests. How long will you live then?"

Pleckoo snorted, stood his most erect, and said in full voice, "I have my own magic. And with it, I will find and settle in Bee-Jor."

The crowd was shocked into silence . . . followed by a roar of laughter. Even Anand chuckled in disbelief—Bee-Jor was the name of a land from a children's song, where edible mushrooms grew in abundance in fields outside its mounds. Bee-Jor's ponds were filled with honey and its stream gushed with cold berry-wine. It was never hot or cold and all were welcome to live there if they worshipped Bee, the honey goddess.

"And just where is the Land of Endless Honey?" sneered Keel. "Aren't we to wait for the Dark-Skinned Son of Locust to lead us there?"

"The Locust's Son has led many to Bee-Jor," answered Pleckoo. "It is far to the south, past the Dustlands, a long and dangerous journey. But it is no more dangerous than the one all of you are about to take."

Impy, a hairless old man considered a fool by everyone, piped up with his squeaking voice. "You are wrong, Pleckoo. Bee-Jor is past the land of lair spiders. It is where we are going . . . far to the north!"

Now it was Impy's turn to be laughed at and he shrank under the assault. "To the north!" others repeated and clutched their sides.

"You've been talking to *them*," Keel whispered. "Those *traitors* defecting to the Dustlands, the ones tempting Slopeites to termite worship."

Pleckoo was all too silent. Keel pressed in, poking his finger into Pleckoo's chest. "You will be among the pioneers, Pleckoo. If you are not, you'll be hunted down and dragged back for bathing. Are we understood?"

"We are," Pleckoo answered. And then he spat in Keel's face.

"You shit!" said Keel. "Take him to the whipping pebble!"

Tal and some of the other boys grabbed Pleckoo and stretched him over the whipping pebble. His rags were ripped off as Keel raised his whip with its lashes tipped with crystal razors. He lashed Pleckoo's back and buttocks until they were bleeding. Anand turned away. He suffered nearly as much as the victims when he watched.

While the other middenites gathered to snicker, Anand remembered when everyone had loved his cousin. When Pleckoo the Handsome was fifteen, he risked beatings to stand at full height with squared shoulders in imitation of the nobles. Now everyone was savoring Pleckoo the Noseless's suffering. When he was released, they watched as he tried to stand, then fell. He wobbled as he crawled to his shelter on the far side of the midden.

"Where do you think you're going, Pleckoo?" screamed Keel. "Get back to work!"

Pleckoo fell on his face. Anand ran and turned him over.

"Get away from me, roach bastard!" Pleckoo shouted. Anand stared into the disfigured face as Pleckoo's lips twitched with rage. "I said get away from me," he cried and then beat Anand's face with his fists.

Anand's nose was bleeding and his mouth had been cut, but what pained him most was his pity. *Why is this sadness so familiar?* he asked himself. An old wound inside him was hemorrhaging again, a memory so painful, he tamped it down to the furthest end of his mind.

He had to find something to distract him. *Bee-Jor.* Pleckoo seemed so sure it was real. If there was such a land, the Britasytes knew of it—he would ask his mother about it. *I would follow Pleckoo if he let me,* Anand thought, *and bring my parents and all my tribe . . . and then we could wander in peace.*

Polexima was almost dancing as she supervised the packing of her trunks, when the king's servant sounded "creet creet" like a cricket, through the portal.

"Enter," said Polexima, unhappy to be removed from her reveries. The king's manservant crawled through, yanked in the king's crutches and false legs, and then pulled in Sahdrin himself. Once the king was righted, he hobbled to his wife and saw the trunks.

"Polexima! Are you planning on accompanying Trellana?"

"No. I'm going to Palzhad. To see my family."

"*What?* When?"

"In the morning."

"Just after the pioneers leave? Why can't you wait?"

"I've no choice but to go now. I have fourteen days to show my parents their other female grandchild. I have a sister I have met but twice in my life. I should like to know Lamalla while she is still a girl."

"Is it wise to travel so soon with the baby—with the female heir to this mound?"

"In Palzhad, I saw laboring women take their babies into the weeds and out to the Tar Marsh and down to the chambers with the ants. I am sure Pareesha will survive a fortnight's journey with a retinue of hundreds."

"I shall miss you," the king said.

The queen looked up from her trunks to address the servants. "I need to speak with His Majesty in privacy," she said. The servants bowed then crawled away, backwards. Polexima sat on the bed and signaled Sahdrin to join her.

"I don't know what you're about to say, but it's already saddened me," he said.

"I plan to raise Pareesha part of the year in Palzhad."

Sahdrin readjusted his false legs to hang over the mattress.

"Impossible, my dear. Everything would collapse."

"It would be during the months of hibernation."

"Polexima, even during hibernation a descendant of the goddess must be present in the mound. Perhaps you have forgotten, but this is Cajoria, and it would be unseemly for the most influential mound on the Slope to be without its queen. It's an invitation to chaos!"

"We will return well before spring."

"You know we shall have to speak with Dolgeeno about this," said the king.

"It is my decision to make. I have given you twenty-one sons and two daughters and have been a most dutiful queen. This is not a request I make of you, it is a demand."

"A demand?"

"If you know what is best for our mound and our little girl, you will let me raise her in my way. She will not be a catastrophe like Trellana."

"*Catastrophe?* Trellana?"

"You are the only one who doesn't see it."

A sigh escaped through his nose and Polexima accepted this as his concession. She took his hand.

"There is one other thing."

He looked at her as his good eye rapidly blinked. She hesitated, knowing her words were about to stab him.

"When I return from Palzhad, I should like to move into Trellana's chambers."

"Polly, why? We have far more room here. I don't see . . ."

"I should like to move into them by myself. With the birth of a second daughter there is no longer need for me to share your bed."

The king looked away from her.

"I see."

"You have your concubines."

"But I won't have you." He looked on the floor and then back at her. "Then again, I suppose I've never had you."

On a bright, sunny morning, Prince Maleps and his spectacular retinue from Mound Kulfi arrived on schedule for his wedding. His train of ants and human attendants seemed to stretch to the horizon, then back through time. After the ceremony, the tents, supplies, and gifts of his caravan would be turned over to the Cajorite pioneers and loaded onto their pack ants.

"I'm a bit fearful," said Maleps to his twin brother, Prince Kep, whose duty it had been to accompany him.

"Really, Maleps?" Kep said. "Why fear any woman?" Though the two were identical, it was Kep who was considered the handsomest man on the Slope. Women were drawn to the attentive glimmer in his eyes and men liked the scars on his cheeks inflicted by the swords of jealous husbands.

"Last time I saw Trellana, we were children," said Maleps. "I don't remember her as being that pretty."

"I'm afraid I don't either," said Kep. From Kep's grin that turned to a smug smile, Maleps assumed his brother was glad he was not the one getting married that day. The two dismounted at the opening of a vast tent pitched on Cajoria's ant riding course. They were escorted by priests to a makeshift altar where the cathedral's idols had been washed, dressed, perfumed, and bejeweled. As they waited for the bride to arrive, the priests prayed and polished Maleps's ceremonial armor until they could see their faces in it.

He did not appreciate how much focus they had placed on his codpiece.

Trellana sulked under her veil flapping over her towering coiffure as she made her way to the wedding site atop a gold-powdered ant she shared with her parents. She had wanted a wedding in the cathedral with a weeklong feast and thousands of guests from the other mounds, but omens insisted that the pioneers depart after an abbreviated ceremony in the outdoors. After her descent from the ant, twelve of her handmaidens helped her dress in the bright pink and voluminous Cloak of a Virgin, then held its heavy edges as they trudged with her to the groom. She knelt next to Maleps who she was surprised to find stank from a common grass liquor. His profile was perfect but for his pouting lips stained with green.

Dolgeeno sang a chain of prayers and passed them a chalice of honey that they licked, then offered to the idol of Ant Queen. They bit a consecrated mushroom, then set its remains before Grasshopper. The priest used his knife to prick the couple's fingers, which they pressed together after smearing their blood on an egg chip offered to Mantis.

As their two bloods mixed, Dolgeeno looked toward the heavens and awaited the words of the gods. Cricket-drums beat slowly. Finally, Dolgeeno's head fell and his eyes opened.

"The gods bless your union and accept this marriage," he said. "You are bound forever, husband and wife."

She watched Maleps gulp as he rose to lift the veil

over her hair, then returned to look in her turning face. His hand was cold when it took hers.

"May our children never know famine," he said. She sensed his disappointment and was silent.

"Repeat after him," prodded Dolgeeno.

"May our children never know famine," she mumbled.

Maleps thrust an egg-cake in her mouth. She was wounded and her mouth did not make enough saliva to chew.

"You . . . you look lovely," he whispered. "I'm stunned."

"Thank you," she said through the cake, eagerly accepting what seemed a belated but sincere compliment. It was enough to get her mouth water going, at least, and she was able to swallow. Dolgeeno summoned Sahdrin and Polexima to approach and complete the ceremony.

"We entrust you with our daughter," Sahdrin said.

"I will not betray your trust," Maleps responded and bowed towards the couple.

Just moments after he had paid her a compliment, Trellana noticed Maleps looking at his mother-in-law in a way that she had hoped he would look at her. A second later, Trellana was sure his eyes had wandered from her mother to her handmaidens as they released her from the virgin's cloak.

"Congratulations, Trelly," said Polexima as they exited the tent. "He is as handsome as they say. Such . . . inquisitive eyes."

Trellana reminded herself to breathe and willed herself from being sick.

In the near distance, the parade of human pioneers had gathered by caste. They stood with their belongings and the tools of their trades packed into sand-sleds.

Thousands of soldiers led by General Batra were at the head of the line in a circular cluster, anticipating predators. Trellana and Maleps donned royal-yellow wedding capes, then mounted grand and glittering ants. For some of the journey the royals would ride, but later they would be pulled in a great sand-sled covered with a furnished tent.

The privilege of dragging the caged ant queens was given to the youngest soldiers. It was a taxing labor and their faces showed both strain and delight. The priests followed them, led by Dolgeeno, who carried the sacred relics he would need to consecrate the new mound and anoint the new queen. With him were the priests who had picked yellow lots. They rode atop the tallest ants which had prayer cloths tied up the length of their legs.

It would be late in the morning before Anand's caste finally joined the parade at its rear. Anand heard Yormu sniffling behind him as he stood with his hands on his shoulders. He turned Anand to him, pointed to his nose and shrugged his shoulders.

"Are you asking me where Pleckoo is?" Anand asked and Yormu nodded.

"He slipped away, Dad. At least a hundred have defected from different castes. They've been sentenced to death by bathing if they're caught."

Corra arrived, out of breath, and gave Anand a pack she had stuffed with food and articles he could trade. She saw that Yormu was weeping and took his hand.

"Yormu! Bitter tears do not commence a sweet journey."

Yormu nodded his head, but like rain collecting in a leaf, his tears gathered to spill down his cheeks. Anand was touched by his father's display. "I will see you soon, Father," he said and stroked his back.

"I have something for you," said Corra, "a present from someone."

The way she said "someone" stirred something in Anand. Corra handed her son a bit of folded straw. Inside it was a gossamer sash, the present offered to boys from admiring girls. Someone had labored over its delicate weaving for days.

"Is it from . . . ?"

"Daveena, of course. She thinks only of you."

Corra was tying the sash around Anand's tunic when a crude doll sailed overhead and landed atop the seed comb of a stinkweed.

A tiny girl of five summers ran into the area set apart for middenites. Anand and his family looked at her and were charmed. She had chubby cheeks and tear-filled eyes. Her hair was a tumble of dark curls.

"They threw my doll over here!" she gasped.

"Who did?"

"Those mean boys over there. Have you seen her?"

The girl had an endearing lisp. Anand and his parents smiled.

"It's up there," Anand said, and pointed to the top of the weed. She ran to the plant to climb its slippery stalk but fell on her bottom. She stood and rubbed her seat and cried.

"I'll get it," Anand said, and he shimmied up to the seed comb. He dropped the doll to the girl and she hugged it. When he slid to the ground she asked his name.

"Anand. What's yours?"

"Elora," she said. "My doll is named Geeta. My father says we're going somewhere to build a new mound."

"We all are. Is your mother going, too?"

"Yes. We all picked yellow lots. Mommy says that at the end of the journey they will give us some aphid candy."

"Elora!" someone shouted.

Anand turned to see the girl's parents were approaching. They wore palm-sized blades around their necks to signify the scraping-caste. It was their duty to remove mites and other parasites from the older ants.

"Elora, get away from that boy!" shouted the girl's mother.

"Get away from him now!" the father shouted, then ran to her and swatted her behind. The mother grabbed the doll and threw it towards Anand.

"My doll, Mommy!"

"I will make you a new one. That one is polluted."

As her parents dragged her off, Elora turned to look at Anand over her shoulder. "Good-bye, Anand."

"Shh!" her mother hissed.

Anand felt an unbearable ache in his chest as he watched her go. She was the first Cajorite girl who had ever talked to him in a way that acknowledged him as a person. Corra shook her head and muttered curses against the Slopeites. At last, a guard with a nose pin called out, "Midden caste."

Anand went to his father, who clenched his son. His mother did not hug him so hard. "My sadness is small. My heart is brave," she said. He nodded, but he did not believe her sadness was small. She gritted her teeth to stop from sobbing. Over her shoulder, he saw Terraclon running towards him, panting and sweating. His eyes did not leave the ground to look into Anand's own.

"Ter! I was hoping you would say good-bye."

"I did not come to say good-bye," said Terraclon reaching into his bulging tunic. "I have come to repay you for all the food you have given me."

"Don't be stupid. That was just sharing."

"I have come to *repay* you," insisted Terraclon. He handed Anand a package wrapped in cocoon shreds. Anand removed the wrapping to reveal a new knife. The blade was a whetted shard of quartz and was embedded in a handle of sun-baked resin. Anand knew from the handle's design that Terraclon had carved it himself.

"I can't take this!" Anand gasped. "You have labored over it for moons."

"I told you . . . it's a repayment," Terraclon insisted, and he wiped at his eyes. "My father's calling," he said, though it was not true. He ran off after he burst into tears.

Anand sniffled as he added the knife to his pack, then joined the others. A harness was fastened over his chest that was attached to the first of the middenites' sand-sleds. When Keel cracked his whip, they took their first steps.

Corra watched in silence as her son trudged off. As she and Yormu walked back to the midden, she remembered when he was a baby, a sweet and tiny creature who laughed with delight at every new discovery. She tried hiding her tears from Yormu but as her crying turned to sobbing and her body shook, he placed his arm around her and she leaned on him. She tried and failed to dismiss the fear that she would never see her son again.

## CHAPTER 11

# ROYAL JOURNEYS NORTH AND SOUTH

The rear pincers of earwigs made good daggers. Yormu was removing the pincers from some dead earwigs whose misfortune had been to wander into the path of some returning foragers. The ants halted their parade, dropped their leaves, and tore the earwigs into pieces they then picked up before dumping at the midden.

Yormu hated this work—a sheriff had used this kind of dagger to cut off his tongue. He was drenched with sweat and worrying about Anand when a sentry approached. As custom dictated, he pointed to the first middenite he saw.

"You," said the sentry, "are drafted to serve Queen Polexima on a trek to Palzhad."

Yormu showed the sentry that he had no tongue and led him to speak with Corra as she hung her slug sausage to cure in the sun. The sentry winced at the woman's color.

"Your mate is needed for Queen Polexima's journey," he said while looking away from her eyes.

"Palzhad? How long will he be gone?"

"Twenty-eight days. It is your decision to accompany him if you choose."

"Of course I'm going," she said.

Yormu stood, blinking at her in fright.

"Don't worry, Yormu. You'll like it there. It's older and almost empty these days and they aren't so stuck in the Slopeish ways."

For the first time since Anand had left, he saw her smile.

---

With happy thoughts of her trip, Polexima returned from a Sacred Wetting to the sunlit chambers that had belonged to Trellana. The queen would leave behind a supply of the precious fluid that the priests could set before the ant queen. The divine urine had to be fresh to be effective, but Queen Mother Clugna would arrive in time to assume her daughter's duty.

The Royal Chief of Protocol, Zembel, supervised the final packing for his monarch. He was completing his task when Polexima pulled herself into the room.

"Good morning, Zembel. Any message from the pioneers?"

"No, Majesty. No messengers at all."

"That's the third day in a row."

"Yes, Majesty, but the pioneers have ventured deep into unfamiliar territory. The messengers may have fallen prey to any number of things."

Polexima's mood turned dark. She imagined the steaming corpse of her daughter, dressed in her most indulgent costume, being pulled from a sun kiln and unwrapped for eating. Pareesha cried from her crib.

"Would you bring her here, please?" Polexima asked, as she pulled down the top of her garment. The nurse brought over the baby, who was dressed in thirteen gowns that bound her arms and legs. Her face was a frightening red.

Polexima shook her head. "Nurse, Pareesha is not hungry. She objects to being baked. For this journey, one gown will do with a simple slip."

Polexima sighed and reminded herself that this daughter would be raised differently. *This one will not be tutored by gray, fat eunuchs,* she thought, *and she will play in the outdoors with children from many castes.*

On top of the mound, the procession bound for the southernmost queendom had been assembled since the night before. Polexima insisted that no more than a thousand soldiers, four priests, and fewer than fifty servants accompany her. The queen and her infant entered into a large sand-sled and climbed a winding staircase to its throne. The procession lurched off with summoners at its head who rubbed cicada wings so that the people would draw to the side and bow.

**T**hough he hated being used as a draught animal, Anand loved travel by day. He had the bad habit of looking out at the passing landscape when he should have been keeping his eyes to the ground. In his travels with his mother, Anand had to wander under cover of night. In daylight he saw new vistas of intense beauty that were almost unbearable.

Two days after the rain, poisonous mushrooms had exploded into fat towers with light spews of stinking spores. The procession trekked through thickets of these mushrooms, stopping when they grew too dense and had to be uprooted. A day later, they collapsed in their own slime and gave rise to smaller blue mushrooms that were clear, like water. Ahead of the pioneers was a terrain of trees that were stripped, but whose upper branches sprouted leaf buds. The mysterious canopy tribes who attacked and ate leaf-cutter ants protected these branches but they gave the procession no trouble.

Later, the pioneers entered a sunless territory with thriving trees that smelled damp and sweet. Anand had never seen a tree that was not a victim of ants. He sniffed the pleasant decay of leaves that trees had dropped by themselves. Under these trees, the sunlight took on a greenish color. In a few places, it poured down pure and yellow on patches where weeds flourished and bloomed.

The journey continued under ferns, a plant unknown on the sunny Slope. Orange powder misted down from ribs of buds on the leaves' unfurling undersides. Progress was slower, as the leaf-strewn ground was springy with loam that clogged the sleds' scale-lined runners. Also blocking the path were fallen logs rotting under moss and teeming with termites.

A hundred kinds of forest insects, many of which Anand had never seen, scurried or flew as the procession marched. When they stopped to rest under a bortshu sapling, the pioneers were captivated by chalk-and-jade butterflies as they emerged from a cluster of chrysalises. Young girls, briefly freed from their harnesses, ran over to wish upon the butterflies, who might take their dreams to the gods in their tree palace.

Anand was making a wish too, when his ear was split by the soul-rending scream of a child. The scream ignited more screeches and shrieks as the pioneers turned and saw it: a monstrous lair spider. She had erupted from her trap door and targeted a child, snatching her with a web-snare stretched between her forelegs. The victim was a spinning blur as she was wrapped in a silk cocoon. Anand's knees went weak as he saw the spider sink her fangs in the squirming bundle before slipping under the door to her lair.

The girl's mother screamed without control as her father sputtered in panic. Hundreds of workers had seen the girl's capture and were too stunned to move. They watched as the victim's father fell out of line to plead with a sheriff. Unconcerned with the child, the sheriff was angry that the march had slowed.

"Please, Good Sheriff, help me rescue my daughter!" begged the father.

"Keep moving. Nothing can be done."

The father got closer to the sheriff, who turned away to avoid making physical contact with someone of the low scraping caste.

"But my daughter! She's . . ."

"She's at the bottom of a deep hole and so will you be if you attempt to rescue her. If she's lucky, the spider's poison is melting her flesh and it will drink her soon."

"But it could be laying its eggs in her. She will suffer for days!"

"Pray to Grasshopper," said the sheriff, "and get back in your harness."

The father ran to the spider's trap and fell to his knees.

"Elora! *Elora!*" he cried as he dug with his hands.

Anand felt as if his heart had been ripped out of him as it dawned on him that he knew this man. The victim was the girl with the doll.

"Do you want to die, too?" the sheriff asked the father as he pawed the soil. Panic deafened him to the sheriff's words. They were not a warning against an attack of the spider, but the sheriff's own blade. The father's arms were reaching through the flap when the sword came down, chopping his head off. Anand and hundreds of others went still with rage and fear.

The sheriff rode toward them on his ant. A scowl was on his face and blood flew from his sword as he waved it.

"Keep moving . . . if you don't want to be next!" he bellowed. He traded his sword for his pole and used it to knock on the people's heads until they were roused into marching.

Anand watched as Elora's mother fell on her back and screamed. Her relatives ran to cover her mouth for fear she would further provoke the sheriff. Since the trek began, the lower castes had seen predators pick off several of their own, but not a child. Anand stole a glance to see skull-flies descend on the father's corpse to lay their eggs. These had no chance to hatch, for soon, carrion roaches crawled from under a log to eat it all.

That night, as he used his pack for his pillow, Anand wept. He was haunted by the image of Elora's smile. He felt he was drowning in water, surfacing and gasping, only to sink again. Not for another second could he tolerate knowing the girl was in the spider's lair and might be alive and suffering with eggs inside her whose spiderlings would hatch to drink her blood as their first meal.

He knew what he must do.

# CHAPTER 12

# THE LONGEST NIGHT

**O**nce he was sure that everyone was asleep, Anand pushed off the dead leaf he rested under to hide himself from night wasps. He grabbed a sharpened fly pole and a water bladder and raced into the night. An avenging spirit would not allow him to consider the aches that plagued him. Aiding his sight were luminous bark fungi that glowed soft blue.

Anand looked for the sapling whose branches were hung with empty cocoons. When he found it, he treaded softly to the spider's lair. His ears pounded with his heart's thumping. The sky, the trees, and the air all seemed to pulse around him.

Circling in back of the trap, he was uncertain as to whether he could rouse the spider. If she was making a meal of Elora, the spider might be too content to take another victim. He probed the door with his pole by simulating beetle steps. Nothing.

Anand tapped harder on the door, then harder still. No response. A breeze picked up a leaf and scuttled it over the trap door. Anand blinked and when he opened his eyes, the spider's back was to him, her rear-eyes taking him in.

She pivoted and Anand saw the snare stretched between her legs. She sprung at him on her hind legs, but he ran forward, not away. He thrust the pole through the threads of the net and between her fangs . . . but he missed. The point jammed in the side of her head, but did not kill her. Though she was blinded in two eyes, it did not stop her from leaping again.

Anand dove over her snare and into her spiny legs. He scrambled to retrieve his pole as her legs batted him about. Plucking out the pole he held it flush against his chest. Pushing against the spider's legs, he flipped her over. He turned to see her claws wave in the air. Before he could stab her, though, she pulled herself tight, rolled on the sand and was on her legs, at him again.

He crouched and waited as her forelegs stretched the net and her fangs parted. Just as she lunged, he leapt up, thrusting his stick between her fangs.

This time he struck true and the point pierced the spider's head. She collapsed on him, her legs still twitching as blood seeped down the stick in oily globs. Anand felt her fangs as they grazed the skin of his neck and he shuddered at the thought that, were she alive, he would be dead right now. He gingerly shimmied out from under her to avoid the glittering poison. After finding the edges of the trap door, he folded it back, but could see nothing down the black cavity.

Shaking and coated in cold sweat, Anand crawled down the hole anyway. He hurt himself when his knee jammed in something round with cavities on its surface. He handled it briefly and realized it was a human skull. As he crawled over more bones, he wondered how much deeper he would have to go. Sand grains fell on his back when he heard a faint wheezing.

*Elora?*

He sank down farther until his hand touched a warm body. He stroked her hair, touched her warm skin. The girl was alive! He did not know if she could hear him in her paralysis, but he spoke.

"Elora, it's me, Anand. I'm bringing you out of here," he whispered. Anand tucked her frail chest under his arm and began his ascent. Crawling up with one hand, a rain of dirt fell on his head until, suddenly, the lair's walls collapsed. With his face and arms buried in loose dirt, he pressed the girl to his chest and squirmed up.

When he heard the chirping of crickets, he knew they would make it out—but he also heard the whipping of long antennae. Poking his head out, he saw white insects, three times the size of a man, tearing at the spider's corpse. A pack of moon roaches had converged on the dead spider, but their antennae were far more alert to Anand. They hovered over the lair, excited by the scents of ants and humans.

The moon roaches' forelegs were strong and lined with sharp hooks. Anand knew they could clutch his body and chew his head off. After surviving the spider, he wasn't about to let that happen. Thinking quickly, he let a baby roach approach and fall on top of him. Grasping his knife, he thrust under the insect and slit it to its head. As blood oozed down his face, he used the carcass as a shield and pushed his way out. As the larger roaches attacked, he slashed at their antennae, watching them fall, twitching on the ground. The now-senseless roaches wandered without aim and butted heads before stumbling away.

Anand pulled Elora out of the hole and set her on the ground. He freed her arms and limbs from the spider silk, revealing a raised bruise on the front of her thigh that spread to her back. When he turned her over, he saw where the spider had pierced her and laid its eggs in a bulging chain. The eggs' transparency revealed the living spiderlings that twitched inside them. These tiny monsters were more revolting than their giant mother.

After scraping lichen from a nearby rock, he dampened it for a poultice with his water bag. Then, taking a deep breath, he used his knife to excise the eggs. It was delicate work as he did not want to pierce the sacs and free the spiderlings to prick the girl with their fangs. He was sweating by the time he removed the last one and knew he had to stanch the bleeding soon. He pressed the lichen against the bleeding wounds and bound it with grass fiber. Her eyes were glazed and unmoving but then he saw her blink.

"You're going to be all right," he said and tried to smile. "I'm bringing you back to camp now. You will be with your mother before Sun is reborn."

Anand took her limp hand and held it, unsure if she could hear him until he saw a tear well in the corner of her eye.

Elora's mother was lying outside her camp, muffling her weeping with a wad of cloth. In the dim light, she saw the figure of a boy carrying a limp body over his shoulder. Anand set Elora down. Then he collapsed. He looked as if all the aches and pains in the world were weighing on his limbs.

The mother dropped the cloth from her mouth and shrieked. Other mite scrapers surrounded Elora and felt for her pulse. They saw the poultice that Anand had applied and looked at his spent figure.

"She's alive!" said one.

"This boy went back and rescued her! And he's cut out the spiderlings!" said another.

"Who is he?" asked the foreman, stroking the long mustache that indicated his authority. Elora's mother rocked her daughter and could say nothing. All she could do was sob in relief.

"He's from the shit caste," said a sneering boy who was Anand's age. "Let's kick him back to where he belongs."

Other boys were ready to take up the suggestion and surrounded Anand to stomp on him. He had heard their threats but was too weak to move.

"No!" screamed Elora's mother, throwing herself over the untouchable.

"You are polluting yourself!" screamed the woman's sister. "He's polluted your daughter!"

"He *saved* Elora! Kick me before you kick him!" she shouted. The foreman stepped towards her, and for a moment it seemed he was about to do just that. Instead, he gave her a sharp yank and looked down at Anand.

Anand gazed up wearily. "All I ask is that if you're going to kill me, be quick about it," he said. His eyes then closed and he fell into a deep sleep or death—no one was sure.

# CHAPTER 13

# THE GHOST ANTS OF HULKREN

At the halfway point of her journey, Polexima met her mother's more modest caravan on its way to Cajoria. Polexima and Clugna chatted happily in the shade of a daisy plant and doted on the baby Pareesha before resuming their treks.

Riding inside Polexima's sled was a brilliant orator from Mound Loobish, the seat of learning. His specialty was history of the Wars of Unification, the conflict that forever bound the tribe of light-skinned warriors with the dark-skinned primitives who had first settled the Slope. After four days of narration, he was about to end his recitation for the queen.

"Locust and Mantis had commanded that the tribes become one, and yellow-skinned soldiers were given access to brown-skinned women. Thus all future peoples of the Slope, no matter how low-born, are related to each other and descended from Ant Queen."

The orator left the trance that enabled him to sing the vast chain of words. As he slumped a bit in his seat, Polexima lifted up the flap of the sled's tent to speak with her attendants. "Please, bring us refreshments," she commanded. A sentry scurried back on his ant to the royal provisions-sled.

"Thank you, learned one. Will you join me for a repast?"

"I would be honored," said the orator as he adjusted a necklace that dangled the jar which contained his pickled testicles.

When the food arrived, the orator did not join Polexima in eating the bitter wafers proffered to her by Pious Kontinbra, the haughty priest that accompanied her on journeys. The wafers were mixed with dried fruit, but she knew they contained roach eggs, something she usually consumed in her morning tea. She still wasn't sure why they were required in her diet, but she had gotten used to the taste to the point she almost enjoyed them. Kontinbra watched Polexima eat the wafers, then excused himself and let his ant fall back. Without a priest to eavesdrop, she probed the orator as he smeared grub jam on a mushroom cracker.

"Learned One, do you know the histories of the roach peoples?"

"No, Majesty. The Britasytes are a secretive tribe."

"It's why I asked," she said ruefully. "Maybe you can tell me this, then—how long have the Britasytes been granted freedom to travel on the Slope?"

"Since the time of the Wars of Unification."

"Do they trade roach eggs?"

The orator was quiet as he searched his chains of words. "The Britasytes do not trade roach eggs with Slopeites, only the cured goods made from them." After a moment he added, "Roach eggs are known to be poisonous to Slopeites and can result in death after ingestion."

The queen sighed, certain she was not being poisoned. What the orator had told her did nothing to assuage her curiosity—after thirty years she was still longing for the end of this mystery. Her frustration was forgotten when she sighted her home. Palzhad was larger and more impressive than Cajoria, but it was far less significant. She could see that even more of the lowest castes were squatting in spacious dwellings within the mound's closest ring, a condition that made Palzhad ridiculous in the views of other Slopeites. She noticed that even the workers of the midden had moved up to occupy large and lacquered houses.

*And why shouldn't they have nice houses if it's possible to provide them?* she thought. She also noticed that since her last visit, the outer rings had become denser with weeds too poisonous for the ants to mulch. The tall grasses smelled sweet, and at the top of their stalks were spittlebugs coating themselves with meringue. She thought the weeds were pretty and gave the mound a luxuriant quality, but she knew others viewed the growth as further evidence of Palzhanite decline.

Only trickles of ants were climbing up and down the mound. A few dropped their leaf pieces to run their antennae over the arriving Cajorites. The humans who were at home ran outside to see the queen they knew as a child. Polexima knew the faces of many of them and waved the arm of her newborn daughter. The queen could see the deliveries of abundant torches to the feasting halls as well as fragrant blossoms to shred and sprinkle on the floor. She smiled as she imagined her father was in the royal kitchens taste-testing her favorite dishes before he was girdled and dressed in his finery.

*It's so very good to be home.*

**C**orra and Yormu were housed with the Palzhanite midden caste in their fragrant dwellings set among the weeds. It was Yormu's first time in a house and he sat in his first chair. Both were astonished when a torch, a bag of berry-wine, and worm fudge were delivered. They were gifts from King Kammut, who wanted all in the mound to celebrate.

The Palzhanite untouchables invited the strangers into their largest house for a gathering but they were frightened by Corra's darker skin. Some of them looked for the poisonous stinger above her buttocks that Britasytes were said to possess. She lowered her skirt and laughed as she showed them she possessed no such thing. They were won over with her gifts of damselfly bangles, and by the liquor that had them giggling within minutes of imbibing. She didn't tell them it was enhanced with what their priests called the Holy Mildew, something they were never supposed to know about, much less sample.

The moon was high in the sky as the middenites enjoyed a third squeeze of liquor. They asked Corra to perform her Mantis Mating Dance for a second time when they heard a commotion of insects outside the shelter. They stepped out slowly to see leaf-cutter ants, scurrying wildly, crawling down from the mound with their eggs and larvae clutched in their mandibles. Corra saw Yormu's panic when he smelled the *alarm/disperse-scent* they were spraying.

"Why are the ants abandoning the mound?" she asked.

Her hosts had no answers, but it didn't take long to understand what was happening.

A strange and meaty smell of alien insects was crawling up their noses. They turned to see the surrounding grass bend with the weight of coming intruders. Corra saw the first of some massive, see-through ants with scissoring mandibles crawling towards them. She didn't know what they were, but she was sure she needed to run and hide.

**R**aucous laughter and orchestras throughout the mound were drowning the ears of the Palzhanites. In the royal feasting hall, His Most Pious Ejolta stood with the other priests near the quartz viewing window, sneaking sips of fermentation as they looked out at the frenzied ball. Their raised eyebrows were a reminder not to abandon all propriety.

The window suddenly darkened, and the high priest turned to see what had blocked the moonlight. He looked out and down and was astonished to witness their queen ant being pushed and pulled down the mound by attendants. Her fat body used weak legs to stumble over man-made structures and she tumbled down more precipitous slopes. When she reached the bottom, her clustering attendants attempted to push her beyond the weeds and to safety in the sand fields.

It was far too late.

A swarm of alien ants, some with human riders, had surrounded the mound and were gobbling up the leaf-cutters. The priests could not absorb the invaders' appearance which was so eerie it was paralyzing. Pious Ejolta looked out and could only ask himself, *Has a ghost army erupted from the Netherworld? It has to be an apparition!*

Surrounding Palzhad was an army of enormous, transparent ants, an insect no Slopeite had ever seen, and half of them mounted by humans. They were a few hundred at first, then suddenly as innumerable as the leaves of a tree. The soldiers riding on them were white as chalk and clad in transparent armor. Pious Ejolta clenched his eyes closed. When he opened them, the army on ghost ants had not faded like a mirage, but instead continued its advance up the mound.

"Priests, do you see what I do?" he asked.

None answered him, though, as the priests watched in stunned silence as the invaders slaughtered the leaf-cutters, their massive pincers piercing the leaf-cutters' heads and lifting them to be guzzled whole. Eggs and squirming larvae were taken from the leaf-cutters' mandibles by smaller ghost ants. These little raiders raced with their living prizes to a trunk trail going south.

Ejolta, in turn, raced to King Kammut, who rocked Pareesha as his daughters whirled in a dance circle.

"Majesty, we are under attack! A great army so numerous our ants are fleeing instead of fighting."

Kammut rose to his feet. "Seed Eaters or Carpenters?"

"Neither. They appear to be . . . ghosts."

"Ghosts?"

Kammut ran to the window and reeled from the bizarre vision. He jerked himself away to displace the orchestra's conductor on his platform. The room quieted.

"I regret to inform you we are under attack and our ants have fled," the king shouted. "As quickly and quietly as possible, you are to walk to the tunnels and down to the shelters. Our guests from Cajoria need your guidance. We do not need panic."

The king's message was relayed quickly through the tunnels and to the other castes. The Palzhanites had rehearsed shelter drills years ago, but after years of peace the practice was unfamiliar. In the feasting hall, children and women of childbearing age exited in a daze. The military scrambled through the barracks and fumbled for their weapons.

*What brazen fools would attack a mound of the most powerful nation on the Sand?* thought Kammut. He looked again at the phantom insects, whose insides glimmered with moonlight. "Slopeish armies will gather in an instant to confront these attackers. They'll butcher them and send the rest running," he said to Ejolta, with an imitation of bluster.

Ejolta said nothing. They watched as an enemy sand-sled was pulled towards the Palzhanites' ant queen. The egg-layer made a pathetic attempt to crawl away, but her swollen gaster slowed her down. Her clustered retinue tried to protect her, but they were picked off or crushed and then swallowed by the ghost ants. The human invaders then had to fight back their own ants to protect the leaf-cutter queen. In an instant, the panels of a cage were erected around her to protect her from further assault.

*They wanted her alive!*

Kammut panicked when he realized these marauders were abducting the Palzhanites' egg-layer. Just then, an unmounted ghost ant reached the feasting hall's window. It was three times the size of the largest leaf-cutter soldier ant and so frightening that Kammut staggered. *I'm a soldier,* he reminded himself and regained his composure. "It's best we disguise the crown princess as a boy," he said, and Lamalla was swept away and re-dressed. The other Palzhanites tumbled down to shelters designated by caste.

Below in the weeds, Yormu, Corra, and the Palzhad middenites awaited the moment they should flee. Ghost ants were surrounding the house they had gathered in and were sawing through its walls with their mandibles. "What do we do? They won't let us in the mound," Corra shouted as she paced with her satchel of jewelry.

"Our hiding place is in the nearby weeds," said the midden elder. "You must follow us. Leave your satchel!"

As ghost ants' heads poked through the walls, the middenites fled into the low weeds and ran under them to avoid attackers. Yormu stood in a daze, then jerked Corra by the hand and yanked her outside. She would not abandon her satchel, though, which slowed them as they ran through a maze of battling ants. She stumbled and fell and they lost sight of the others. Yormu looked up to see grass blades bending from the weight of climbing leaf-cutters.

Setting its sights on one leaf-cutter, a ghost had crawled up a barley stalk to engage the smaller ant. The two tangled and fell. Yormu tried to pull Corra away from the falling ants, but he was too late. Yormu strained as he dragged her crushed form out from under the fallen ants and prayed she was unhurt.

She was not.

A gush of blood soaked her clothing, where a thorn of the ghost's petiole had pierced her lung. She was weak and in pain and could barely breathe. Yormu urged her on as human foot warriors advanced through the weeds, but she could not rise. Yormu was lifting her into his arms when the blade of a human soldier sliced out and into her chest. The warrior took aim at Yormu, who was blinded by blood. The weight of his wife's body pulled him down and away from the deadly swipe.

Foot warriors trampled over Yormu and then he felt the claws of ants. He was torn between the fear of dying and the desire to join his wife in death. He was giving in to death when someone grabbed his ankle and dragged him through a hatch to the middenites' underground shelter. In the moment of safety, Yormu surfaced from his despair, attempted to shout his wife's name, and climbed out of the hatch to grab her ankles. But her body was jerked away and hoisted up by a ghost ant that swallowed it whole. Yormu watched from under the hatch to see her as she slid down the gullet of the transparent invader. He saw her face and realized she was still alive as she thrashed and drowned in the ant's fluids before it crawled away. He blacked out in grief.

In the upper stories of the mound's barracks, Palzhanite soldiers futilely shot their arrows. The archers were too far away to take aim and their arrows fell like so much mist. Retreat was called for the first time in centuries. The mound's defenders fled to the military's shelters, where their wives and children waited. The soldiers entered in humiliation, and their presence deepened their families' panic.

Ghost ants reached the top of the mound and destroyed the living gate of leaf-cutter sentries before pouring down, killing and eating the crippled, aged, and lost men and women. The human warriors came in the next wave, mounted or on foot, and grabbed at the wall-torches to light their way. They fanned out through the royal compartments, uninterested in the abundant treasures. They journeyed instead downward through the rectories, the barracks, the merchants' apartments, and the shelters of the laboring castes.

The warriors splashed an X in glowing paint over every searched chamber. They took tunnels to the depths of the mound and spread through the mushroom chambers, the cathedral, the larval and queen chambers, the food stores, and the water tanks.

Tiny ghost ants sniffed out the clusters of humans through the shelters' seals, signaling a find with whirling antennae. Foot warriors broke the walls with mallets and entered with their swords. They slew the males and crones within moments. Young women and children were bound and gagged.

One warrior, scrawnier than the others, was central to the mission, albeit inexperienced with his weapons. Beneath the transparent chitin of his helmet, his nose had been deformed, cut off to create two gaping nostrils with a knot of protruding cartilage.

The Palzhanites were most frightened by this man with his skull-like face. When he came close to examine the dress and faces of the women, they saw his white skin was dark under its cracking paint. He shook his head before leaving on a new search, but not before he smashed a filled eggshell to release a noxious liquid.

The warriors scurried out and left their victims to die from the liquid's fatal fumes. The ghost ants were impervious to the gas, however, and rushed in to eat the fallen or the fleeing. Palzhanite children and young women were doused in the kin-scents of the invaders and thrown in sacks dragged over the tunnel's floors.

Inside the royal shelter, Polexima sat with her baby, King Kammut, Princess Lamalla, sixteen of her brothers and their wives and the priests. The air tube was clogged and all were sickened in the poisoning atmosphere. Each attempted to suppress their panic when Pareesha's tiny fists flailed and she cried out. Polexima quieted her with a cupped hand, but it was too late.

The wall crashed in and outside it, Polexima could see a stream of the monstrous ants crawling through the tunnels. Some foot warriors walked over the rubble, set down their mallets and raised torches to the royals' faces. The man with the missing nose examined Polexima. She looked in the jagged cavity of his face when he scowled, nodded his head, and pointed.

"Didn't expect *you'd* be here," he said to the queen in the low tongue of the Slope. "You'll be coming with us."

Polexima wondered how he had recognized her. Had he been a Cajorite? She went rigid with dread.

"Wh-where are you taking me?" she asked.

"You know the place as Hulkren."

"H-Hulkren! What? Why?"

The skull-face turned from her when another warrior of Slopeish stock alerted him to something in their own tongue. The warriors backed away and bowed their heads as a magnificent figure rode up through the tunnel on the largest ghost ant Polexima had seen yet. The ant's rider dismounted in the swirls of his gossamer cape.

"Your *Majesty*," the noseless man sneered, "may I present you to Commander Tahn, the Warrior Prophet of Hulkro."

Tahn looked to be a man of forty summers with a high and noble forehead. He was covered in white paint, and Polexima thought he had a disturbing beauty with a jutting chin, sharp and high cheekbones, and a full mouth. His eyebrows were knitted in anger, like twin caterpillars battling for the same morsel. Tahn eyed her up and down, with a hungry look that made the queen clutch her child even closer. He directed his Slopeish convert to ask the queen a question in a tongue that was not completely foreign.

"Is this your infant?" asked the skull-face, scornfully imitating an upper caste accent. "Would this be the Princess Pareesha whose birth was celebrated just before her sister Trellana left on a Fission trek?"

"No! I mean . . . who . . . who are you? Where are you from?"

"Do not ask questions," he said, exaggerating the harsh accent of his caste. "I am Pleckoo, a soldier for Hulkro, and disciple of his prophet."

Pleckoo examined the elaborate dress of the baby and when he held a hand torch closer, Polexima could see he had discerned a family resemblance. He spoke with Tahn, who responded with an order.

Pleckoo reached for Pareesha. "The brat comes, too."

"No! Take me, but leave my baby with the priests!" she screamed.

"The priests will all be dead," Pleckoo shouted, and then boxed her ear. "You can give me the baby, or I can take the baby."

Polexima would not give the baby up. Pleckoo

signaled the others. They rushed the priests, King Kammut, and the princes. The men's chests were slashed open and their rib cages were pried up. Those who tried to run were stabbed or shot with arrows through their backs. Princess Lamalla's disguise as a boy had worked too well, and her head was lopped off her neck. The older wives of the brothers were beheaded while the younger ones were thrown into rough sacks that were cinched and hooked to the ghost ants' saddles.

The men turned their swords towards Polexima and surrounded her. She felt a lump in her throat as big as Palzhad as she handed Pleckoo her baby. Someone grabbed her hair and dragged her out to the tunnel. She screamed as Pareesha was tossed in a circle like a ball.

Ghost ants converged on the corpses of the royals. Polexima collapsed at the horrible sound of crunching that could only be the snapping bones of her family. Children stuffed in sacks wailed as they were dragged past her. She was stripped of her clothing. The baby, also stripped, was given back to her just before the moment both were forced into a sack reeking with the kin-scent of ghost ants. The sack was cinched and Polexima gasped as she felt it being hoisted up and left to swing from a hook.

As Polexima hugged her baby, she could hear the commander as he shouted his next orders, and her blood chilled when the harsh translation came from the malformed warrior. "Back to Jatal-dozh and hurry," Pleckoo interpreted for the other warriors of Slopeish descent, "before the leaf-cutters at the nearby mounds pick up our scent."

The ghost ants were large *and* quick, with tall legs that took powerful strides. They herded the smaller raider ants that had stopped to lick their prizes of eggs and larvae in order to coat them in the ghosts' kin-scent. The raiders crawled with their captives onto their giant sister ants before they all raced south.

Breezes with the scents of the invaders slowly roused the sleepy ants at the southern mounds of Bentilamak, Rinso, and Caladeck. A few leaf-cutter soldiers were out and marching with their gasters held high as they sprayed *recruiting-scent* to call out their numbers. The human sentries of Rinso rode their ants to the tops of rocks to look south. They witnessed the uncanny sight of transparent ants racing through the Petiole, the narrow channel between the Tar Marsh and the Great Jag that led to the Dustlands.

It was far too late for the Slopeish commanders to rally their armies and ants to attack. Like wraiths, this new enemy seemed to have faded back to the Netherworld. Not that it mattered—even the ants that had mobilized to enter the Dustlands kept losing the invaders' trunk-trail. The scent of the ghosts had vanished as quickly as they had.

# CHAPTER 14

## THE ANOINTING OF
## QUEEN TRELLANA

When Anand woke, he was lying on his back on a soft mattress of cocoon skins and looking up at the underside of a magnificent and leafy bortshu. When he raised his head, he realized he was in the sand-sled of the scraper caste. Beside him were a water bladder and a bowl of dried mushrooms. He squeezed some water on the fungi to reconstitute them and drained the rest to quench a vicious thirst.

Finished, he sat up to see Elora's mother and the female kin of her caste marching behind the sled, pulling a smaller one of their own. They were smiling at him and, in defiance of all rules, the mother spoke and made eye contact.

"How do you feel?"

"How long have I been sleeping?"

"Two days. When you are ready, you must rejoin your caste, Anand. But for now, rest."

*Anand.* She had called him by name!

"Someone wishes to say something to you," the mother said. Anand turned to see Elora swinging in a hammock behind him. She weakly raised her head and managed to smile.

"I have something for you," she said in a faint voice. She offered him a new doll of woven grass fibers. He took it and looked at the faceless head.

"Thank you," he said and returned it. "Will you take good care of her for me?"

"Yes," she said and smiled. "But he's a boy. His name is Anand."

"Oh."

"I heard you, Anand."

"Heard me?"

"In the spider's lair. I wanted to say thank you, but I couldn't. Thank you."

"You are very welcome."

He wanted to kiss her cheek, but instead he had to jump off the sled. He appreciated that they had risked so much by carrying him the last two days, but he knew he should not stay long among a caste above his own. He was walking away, sore and stiff, when Elora's mother called after him.

"Good-bye, Anand," she said, and he saw that she was weeping with gratitude.

As Anand passed the other castes, they whispered and pointed at him. Some even smiled and he realized news of his deed had spread. He approached his own caste with trepidation. Sure enough, Keel, Tal, and the others looked as grim as ever as they lugged their load. Both father and son shot angry looks at him.

"Get into the harness, hero," Keel said and spat. "Some people will go to any length to steal a couple days' rest."

Anand shrank, expecting Keel to lash his face, but instead he saw a faint smile. Once Anand had resumed the harness, he saw that the others, even Tal, regarded him with a quiet admiration. Anand's position in the harness had changed as well—he was no longer on the far outside of the arrangement, but closer to the middle.

*Change is possible*, Anand realized. Which got him thinking, *How* much *change is possible?*

The day came when the procession slowed for good. In the distance, Anand could see sheets of sunlight on the edge of a clearing. They were leaving the forest for a meadow, but were halted by its dense grasses. Sentries relayed the orders down the tail of the parade until they reached the midden caste. All were told to set down their burdens and bring their axes and saws. "This is the place," Dolgeeno had said. The royal tents were erected quickly on stilts above some open sand. Trellana went into a tent to prepare for her Anointment as Queen the following morning, whereafter she would make the first of her Sacred Wettings.

The laboring castes hacked at grasses and plants and heaved with lever-shovels to hoist up roots to extend a clearing and their temporary plots. The midden caste was assigned to create their own separate clearing with a path to the center. As they worked their way out, Anand watched flushed-out grasshoppers leap up, then plummet when they were targeted by idle soldiers with bows and arrows. He looked over to see Prince Maleps and his hunting party making their way up the new path, the sun-kiln caste following after him to retrieve and haul off the grasshoppers to roast for the next day's feast. Anand's mouth watered at the thought of a crunchy roast, but he knew the best they might hope for were some barley seeds. He patted his growling stomach and went back to work.

Once a path to a temporary midden was completed, the caste was summoned to collect a neglected pile of commodes. "Back to our usual work," said Keel. "But if we get done in time, we've been permitted to construct a pen tonight we can hide behind if we wish to witness the anointing tomorrow."

"Imagine, everybody . . . a day off," Anand said, and nobody boxed his ears for impertinence.

On the morning of the Anointment, the seeded ant queens were released from their cages, although they were still leashed to stakes in the sand. Within the radius of their confines, the queens began digging burrows that would eventually become the first mushroom chambers. Soon, they would drop their fungus pellets in the moist sand and lay the first eggs, so it was urgent that Trellana be anointed and begin her most important function. When Sun neared his zenith, drumbeats summoned the pioneers.

After a light bath in some captured dew, Anand walked with the midden caste to the Annointment and allowed himself a tiny bit of pride in membership to the Slopeish nation. All were in a rare good cheer as they carried their barrier in segments to the clearing, even as delicious smells of roasting insects and green onions wafted their way. Setting up at the back of the crowd atop a flat rock, the middenites watched through slits as the pioneers gathered before the royal tent.

Glittering on the royal platform were the new Mushroom Thrones of carved and jewel-encrusted amber. The priests arrived on stilts, lugging an upright drum of quilted human leather. As they pounded it, a thick puff of mist went up and Dolgeeno appeared on the platform in a glistening, honey-yellow garment and his tallest miter. His arms were smeared with drone semen and his face was powdered with golden pyrite.

"Your queen and king," said Dolgeeno in the common tongue. Maleps appeared from the tent in great finery: billowing trousers and a broad-shouldered jacket of sun-colored silk. His antennae were wrapped with threads of gold. He held out his hand and Trellana appeared. She was in a simple gown of pollen-stained cloth that was slit up the sides and wore short, functional antennae. Her hair was combed to fall down her back and her only adornment was yellow face powder. The crowd bowed before them as she and Maleps crossed a bridge to the platform.

A priest set a basin bulging with an amber drop on a stand before Dolgeeno. "Behold Queen Trellana," he bellowed, "direct descendant of Goddess Ant Queen."

"You may look upon me," said Trellana, and the crowd raised its eyes. She sat on her throne. Dolgeeno presented the basin to her.

"*Ag kwilkshus, bok kwilkshus,*" he sang in the holy tongue and she thrust in her arms and coated her hair. Combined in the oils were the individual scents of the surviving ant queens.

"Behold Trellana, Sorceress Queen of Dranveria, a New Colony of the Great and Holy Slope," sang Dolgeeno. Anand joined the crowd in falling to their knees as Trellana descended to the new burrows.

Trellana turned her back to the first burrow's opening and waited for the young ant queen to appear. The ant did so promptly, roused by the intense scents of the anointment. She ran her antennae over Trellana's body and accepted her as the first of her "daughters," and allowed her to squat at the entrance.

As the priests held the panels of her dress, Trellana

urinated. She had drunk a great amount of water and was happy to release some of it, but she had to save enough for the other burrows. She was ready to stop in midstream when she gasped in pain and continued to piss it all away. Dolgeeno went to examine her.

A dart had hit her naked shoulder.

Trellana fell on her side, her eyes glazing over as a dart pierced Dolgeeno in the neck. He stumbled as a hard rain of darts poured down on the crowd.

**B**ehind the barrier, Anand watched in confusion. He realized the pioneers were under attack, but from where? He turned and saw movement near the surrounding grasses, only to realize something had pierced his chest.

It was a dart. He tried to pluck it out but his limbs went dead and he fell off the rock and rolled to the ground.

Anand felt as if his bones had been ripped out of him. His breathing was shallow and his eyes could see, but he could not blink nor move his limbs.

Around him he heard screams of panic as the pioneers fled into the grass only to encounter new flanks of attackers. From the corner of his eye, Anand saw a faceless army of humans riding in on blood-red hunter ants. Seeing the crimson insects, Anand couldn't help but wonder if his powerless body would be roasted alive in the sun-kilns of these attackers.

Were these the legendary Dranverites?

Cajorite soldiers attempted to group and fight back, but the attackers' darts pierced their armor and they fell with the rest. Some pioneers escaped the ambush and scrambled south to the trail, but as they slowed to catch their breath, darts poured down from hidden shooters at the tops of ferns or saplings. In less than a few hundred heartbeats, every last pioneer had been subdued.

One of the attackers' captains supervised the destruction of the inseminated queens. Soldiers on foot arrived with clusters of smaller hunter ants on leashes whose mandibles and stingers were free. They were given enough rope to descend into the burrows and sting the leaf-cutter queens to death. When the leashed ants reemerged, it was with pincers full of blood, a leg, or other pieces. Afterwards, the human soldiers went into the burrows to make sure the egg-layers were lifeless, and the few eggs they had laid were severed in two. The royal and priestly tents were looted and, once emptied, their ropes were cut and their panels disassembled and piled into wagons.

Within the passing of a breeze, all that was left of the Cajorites' presence was the clearing they had cut, the Cajorites themselves, and the platform where the Mushroom Thrones had sat.

Anand had landed in a painful position with his head on a rough sand grain. He could not shift his eyes, but was positioned to watch the attackers as they scuttled over the paralyzed bodies sprawled through the clearing. The mounted officers gave orders atop their sleek and gleaming ants. These ants were not steered by lures, but by manipulations of their antennae with the rider's gloved hands. The mandibles of the mounts were sheathed and their stingers were muzzled.

He could hear the attackers speaking to each other through grills cut in their visors in an unknown tongue. From the number of high-pitched voices, Anand was sure that some must be boys. But he couldn't tell, as each soldier wore a skillfully linked armor that covered every part of their bodies. Dangling from a cord around their necks or in their hands were repeating blowguns with soft magazines that were pulled through a slit in the barrel to align their cartridges.

A large hunter ant, painted with stripes, crawled over Anand on its way to the platform. On its saddle was someone he assumed was their commander as the helmet was different, topped as it was by a tall rod with a yellow banner. The commander rode onto the platform, removed the visor . . . and revealed herself as a woman with deep brown skin.

Anand would have registered shock if his face could register anything. *A woman as their commander, and one as dark as any Britasyte!* he thought. *How could someone of such low caste end up in such a position?* He soon realized that the high-pitched voices he had heard belonged to women, not boys, and that this was a mixed army of males and females. As the commander spoke in her strange language, Anand felt the authority of her words even if he didn't understand them. When she finished speaking, her soldiers slapped their chests to acknowledge her orders.

Each of the red soldiers chose a Cajorite. Anand saw a faceless soldier approach. As the soldier unsheathed the thinnest of swords, Anand appealed to his maker before entering the Spirit Realm. The soldier used the heel of his boot and tipped Anand's head back to expose his throat.

The blade did not come down in a deadly swipe. Instead, it started below Anand's tunic and ripped it open. The headband that held his antennae was snapped. His sandals were removed, and once Anand was completely naked, he was lifted over the soldier's shoulder and brought to cages of very foreign design.

The cages had arrived in a train pulled by creatures Anand had only heard of: enormous weevils, round and fat in appearance, with thick and powerful legs. Their long, curved snouts followed mating scent in the turbans of people whose translucent ears were larger than their heads. Underneath the cages, Anand saw four orbs that were connected in pairs by a rod that the cages floated upon. These round objects rolled in the way that a ball did.

Anand was laid out on finely shredded hay on the cage's floor. Other paralyzed Cajorites surrounded him. All he could do was listen and stare at the ceiling. When the floor was covered with bodies, the cage moved off in a fluid way. It would have been pleasant to Anand if he were not terrified. Next to him was what sounded like it might be an older pioneer who rasped as he or she struggled for breath. A man inside the cage walked towards the rasping and into Anand's view. The man had skin that was as blue as the iris flower and a cone-shaped head with yellow sprouts at the tip of its crown. He shifted the head of the rasping pioneer to normalize the breathing.

The blue man then took oiled rags and set them over the prisoners' eyes. Strangely, at the moment Anand's vision was blocked, his fear abated. Perhaps he would not be killed and eaten. Whoever his captors were, they were concerned about his eyesight.

*Maybe they want me to see their world.*

# PART 2

# A PRISONER OF THE PEOPLE OF THE BLOOD

# CHAPTER 15

## THE LIVING DEATH

Over the next uncountable days, the train of cages rolled and rolled. Twice a day, the blue man—who Anand came to think of as the cage keeper—would make his rounds among the paralyzed and raise up their heads in order to squeeze diluted insect-blood down their throats through a tube from a feeding bag. Once a day he came by to reset the rags set over their eyes. Every other day, the soiled hay was replaced.

With an inability to move, talk, or see, Anand experienced tedium so extreme it was more excruciating than the sting of any insect. Sleep and wakeful times became indeterminate from each other. His inner-mounting anguish turned to rage and violent fantasies against his captors and the Cajorites that had forced him on this trek. He imagined reaching into the mass of Dolgeeno's face and ripping out his skull. He wanted a pair of stone boots to crush Maleps and Trellana into a bloody pulp.

Finally, on what might have been the thirtieth day, Anand felt something different in the cage's movement. The round objects were rolling over a surface of some regularity, perhaps a terrain of smooth, dried mud. He knew it was night from the chanting of crickets. As the train slowed, the sound of a human crowd increased until it gushed like water in a stream. Finally . . . they had arrived somewhere!

The cage keeper removed the cloth from Anand's face. In the periphery of his sight through the cage's bars, he made out torches of tiny cages with glow-worms squirming inside. The light was faint, but hurt his eyes which had been in darkness so long. It was joyous to see again, to see anything, and the light illuminated strange faces with stranger features. Some of these strangers entered the cage.

Two women lifted Anand and set him on a canvas stretched between poles. The purple-skinned woman at his head had four breasts with orange nipples. Her second pair was set symmetrically under the first. Her green-skinned partner looked like a Slopeish woman, but her costume was completely foreign. Her hairstyle was a hundred thin braids and her garment was made from flatworm leather. Like the Slopeites, these women wore pairs of false antennae, but they were well fashioned, almost like jewelry.

When the four-breasted woman was asked a question, she nodded her head and used the Britasyte word for "yes." Anand heard her use the Slopeish words for "penis" and realized they were talking about his genitals, something that made them smile. Their discussion about his body continued as they pointed to his thighs, his arms, and chest.

They brought him to a bathing station where he was set in a tub made from a weevil abdomen. If he could, Anand would have smiled at the four breasts of the one woman as they swayed in unison with her gentler movements, then battled each other when she scrubbed in circles. In the water, Anand smelled the kin-scent of red hunters.

As the women dried Anand, he caught glimpses of a growing crowd. The event had the feel of a festival as they gathered to look with fascination at the invaders from the land of yellow ants. The red ant people were no less strange to Anand—their faces and body shapes were far beyond type, and their skin as varied in color as the spring flowers of a meadow. The females stood among the males, the children among the adults, and the dark walked with the light.

Strange!

Anand was moved back to a cage and set on its straw. Aphid syrup was trickled down his throat and he was left with another cloth on his eyes. Other

Cajorites were laid next to him. When the cage was filled, Anand heard its gate being closed and a new sound—the gate was being lashed tight with ropes. *Why?* Anand asked himself. *To keep something out?*

Outside the cage he heard humans and ants patrolling, but further off was a gathering in song. The distant music was eerie and intricate, rich with harmonies. From the clatter of ankle bangles, Anand knew these were a dancing folk, like those in his Roach Tribe. One of their tunes sounded like a Britasyte song that celebrated the end of a trek.

*Who are these people?* Anand asked himself. He was suddenly sure that the reason they had washed him, then examined his body was because they intended to roast and eat it. They had lashed the cage's door so that "the meat" would not be stolen or escape. As Anand thought of them carving him up, he trembled. It was the first movement his body had made in a month.

# CHAPTER 16

## A SLOPEISH QUEEN IN THE LAND OF GHOST ANTS

**F**ar to the south, and deep inside a ghost ants' mound, Polexima was sick with rage and fear. She could barely eat the revolting food thrown to her in the darkness, but she knew she must consume it to have milk for her baby. Most of the food offered was the regurgitation of the ghost ants, and it likely had human as well as insect remains in its gritty gel.

Pareesha cried without end in the black chamber she shared with her mother and the Palzhanite ant queen. The layer-of-eggs was listless for several days, then died over several more. For all her life, Polexima was raised to never consider the death of any ant as a sad event, but the passing of this ancient egg-layer deepened her anguish. Contrary to the hopes of the Hulkrites, the queen ant had not eaten what smelled to Polexima like her usual predigested food. But Polexima knew the egg-layer would not open her mouth unless the food was offered by daughters prompting her with their antennae. *At least she won't lay eggs for these demons,* thought the queen.

One day—or perhaps it was night—she listened as the stone at her chamber's portal was pushed aside. Some ghost ants, summoned by *death-scent,* entered and carved up the corpse of the ant queen with their long, sharp mandibles. Unlike leaf-cutters, ghost ants apparently ate their enemies and did not drag their dissected corpses to middens. Polexima listened in the darkness as the ants commenced their noisy mastication. Others ants followed, and soon after, every bit of the ant queen had been removed and consumed.

A few days after that, the stone to Polexima's chamber was pushed aside once more. Pleckoo stood before her with a fungus torch under his chin illuminating his skull-like face. He had already visited several times with other defectors from the Slope. They had taken a heated pleasure in belittling and beating a royal. Polexima no longer resisted these assaults, and they soon lost interest.

"Rise, oh Queen," Pleckoo snarled at her while curtseying. "A special treat for you today. An outing."

"Where are we going?" she asked in a demanding tone.

"You're going where I say you're going," Pleckoo answered. "And if you don't want my sword thrust through your precious one, you'll pull yourself through that portal. Leave the brat behind."

Polexima set down Pareesha and kissed her forehead. She pulled herself out to the tunnel, which was poorly lit with shriveling fungus torches. She was weak and her ankles were shackled with cuffing grass that cut her skin as she trudged. Pareesha cried in the distance.

"You are from the Slope," she said to Pleckoo.

"I was a Cajorite," he answered. "But I'm a Hulkrite now. As a boy in your queendom, I cleaned the nobles' shit pots. Why, your own probably wafted under my nostrils on occasion. But that is no more. Among these people I am a warrior in an army, one just promoted by our Prophet to captain."

"What do the Hulkrites want from me?"

"Your holy piss, Your Majesty, so we can grow our own mushrooms and an even larger army. Soon every low-caste laborer in every Slopeish mound will be liberated to worship Hulkro."

"Hulkro? Our people will never bow to the Termite God."

"They will when they hear His words through our Prophet. Hulkro is the One True God. He fed us in the time of the Trial, and bestowed the ghost ant upon us at its end. Now He sends forth His warriors to liberate all peoples."

"You are a son of the Slope, a descendent of Ant Queen. Why abandon that privilege and take up with these monsters?"

"The privilege of cleaning up your shit?" Pleckoo's laugh was short and cutting. "No, there was no privilege in serving you and your false gods. There has never been and never will be a Goddess Ant Queen. The One God rules the Sand, The One God moves the sun and moon, and The One God created all men, insects, plants, trees, and fungus."

When they reached the opening to an ant's chamber, Pleckoo turned to Polexima and looked strangely reverent and gentle. "All men are equal before the Termite. Hulkro blesses those who praise His holy name."

"Hulkro!" said Polexima, and bit her lip to stop from grinning. "The Termite is the deity of decadent primitives . . . the sub-humans of the lands abandoned by Slopeites."

Pleckoo was enraged. He grabbed Polexima by her arms and threw her into the ants' chamber. She fell on her face and was stunned, then dizzy.

"Get up!" Pleckoo shouted. "Behold the power of Hulkro!"

Polexima rose slowly and looked out at the chamber which had been richly lit for her. To her horror, she saw leaf-cutter ants scurrying across a carpet of shredded leaves to take leaf shards from arriving kin. Oblivious to their enslavement, the leaf-cutters took food from the mouths of tending ghost ants.

"Your ants from Palzhad have been absorbed by our ghosts, just as your people will be absorbed by Hulkrites," Pleckoo said. "During the Great Trial, our people lived in forests destroyed by the Slopeites' leaf-cutters. Your ants chased them into tunnels of termite-ridden wood where Lord Termite sheltered us. The Trial is over and we are unstoppable—as Hulkro is unstoppable."

"Mantis will show us how stoppable you are," said Polexima, turning away from the terrible sight of leaf-cutters living with ghosts. "Your body will be thrown to Her in sacrifice. Hulkrites will be slaughtered before they can retreat to their tunnels or these old Slopeish mounds."

"*Mantis!* Mantis is an idol, nothing more. You will grow to worship our god, grow to love him. Hulkro will forgive you once you abandon the little dolls on your altars."

Pleckoo came up from behind her, clamped his hands over her head and forced her to face the back of the chamber. "Look over there, Majesty. A gorgeous sight."

She saw a winged ant with a bulging gaster, one that was likely a newly hatched leaf-cutter queen. Pleckoo turned Polexima to face him, grinning into her face.

"Yes, Queen. An egg-layer—one that thrives—has been seeded and will soon be laying eggs. Now piss, Urine Sorceress of the Cajorites! Bring forth your magic water!"

"My urine is holy," she said. "But it may have no power in this evil place."

"The nature of your urine is part of some grander design. It is just a coincidence that this potion lies within you. Your daughter's daughters will possess this ability and those children will worship Hulkro."

Polexima lifted up her garment and squatted, but nothing came.

"I cannot," she said.

"Piss," he said, "or you won't be able to suckle that brat of yours."

She breathed out and emptied her mind until a trickle came.

"Kind thanks," Pleckoo said, and jerked her back up.

"Was it so awful for you in Cajoria?" she asked as she stood and looked closely into his disfigured face. Her defiance vanished as she confronted the twisted cartilage that jutted through the flesh of what had been his nose. She turned away from him, nauseated.

"What do you think? Why can't you look at my face?" he asked, grabbing her by her shoulders. "Keep looking!" he shouted. "Look at what was once my nose!" He shook and shook her, then pushed her to the ground.

"I had never seen a mirror. But I knew how ugly I am from the expressions of others as they passed me. When the Hulkrites found me dying in the Dustlands, they fed me, taught me their language, let me ride on a ghost ant. When I was ready to apply the

White-Paint of Submission, they handed me a mirror. Only then did I know how truly gruesome I am."

"If your nose was cut off, you committed some crime," said Polexima.

"A crime? *A crime?*" he bellowed at her. "I did *nothing* to no one!" He began crying, turned his face away from her in shame. Polexima went hot and her head throbbed. She looked at Pleckoo as he relived some terrible moment and wiped the sweat from his brow. He turned back to her, grimacing.

"Should I cut off your nose, Majesty, so you'll know how I have suffered? *Should I?*"

He removed his knife, grabbed her nose and gouged the skin of it. She felt a drop of blood well up.

He did not do it. He threw her to the ground once more and kicked her ear. Overriding her fear and pain was an insufferable pity for this man as she imagined his life.

"Get up. Starting tomorrow, you will see how hard life was for me," he said as she trudged after him in the tunnel.

"Wh-what do you mean?"

"No one eats for free in Hulkren."

# CHAPTER 17

## ROYAL INSULTS

When Anand woke, he realized he was on his side and the cloth on his face had fallen away. The morning sunlight was rapping on his eyelids, which had been closed of their own accord! Remembering he had been paralyzed for days, he opened his eyes and was blinded by Sun slicing into the cage. His body was stiff and achy and his head throbbed with pain. His arms reached in a great stretch as he yawned. He felt the shoulders of someone next to him as his arms extended. Then he heard a piercing scream.

The woman Anand touched jerked up from her mat and kept screaming. He sat up and realized his face was a finger's length from Queen Trellana. She was backing away, trying to rise, staring in horror at the missing earlobe that identified him as polluted.

"Get away from me, you brown-skinned maggot!" she shrieked. Trellana backed into an old woman from the cocoon-chewing caste. In an instant, over one hundred Cajorite pioneers, emerging from paralysis, were violently roused in the cage. They were surprised to find themselves so close to their monarch. She was as naked as the rest of them and attempting to hide her body with hands shorn of jewels.

"Don't look at me," Trellana screeched at them. "On your knees, faces to the ground!" Everyone complied except for Anand and an old, fleshy man with mottled skin.

"Your Majesty," he said, "it is I, Pious Dolgeeno."

Indeed, it was His Most Pious, unrecognizable without his dusting of gold-powder and a grand costume. Anand could see he had lost weight on the journey and skin that used to stretch over his girth was hanging in ugly folds. Trellana turned her spiteful gaze to Anand, who continued to meet her eyes.

"How dare you stand there and look at me! How dare you touch me!" she shouted. With a subtle defiance, Anand slowly assumed a position of subservience.

"It was an accident, Majesty," he said. "I had no intention of touching you."

"How dare you address me!" she screamed, red in the face with fury. Her high-pitched ranting pierced every ear as well as those in the cages nearby. "I am polluted!" she shouted at Dolgeeno.

"I will begin prayers to reverse it at once," Dolgeeno responded even as he cupped his shriveled genitals to hide them from her and the others, "but we have no potions to complete the rite."

"Our captors must be the most disgusting primitives on all the Sand," Trellana ranted. "When we are rescued, I will have this filth-collecting boy executed by bathing before the entire mound."

Anand's body was trembling with a rage beyond his control. He raised his head, then rose on his feet as the queen stared in disbelief. He looked her directly in the eyes.

"Allow me to look on your hideous face, Trellana, for that should be the greatest punishment of all."

Trellana gasped. Anand could see her knees weaken and she struggled to stand erect. The others in the cage held deathly still, in total disbelief.

"The gods will punish him if we cannot," said Dolgeeno finally. "And when he is dead, his soul will be flung down to the Netherworld, where night wasps will sting him for all eternity."

"Your gods will do no such thing," Anand said. "I spit on your stupid gods as I spit on you." And Anand did exactly that, spraying the priest's face who stumbled in horror and fell on his ample backside which sent tremors through the cage.

Trellana gathered herself and turned to the others. "No need to wait for assembly! I command you, my subjects, to seize this boy, and tear his limbs off. Throw his pieces out of this abominable cage!"

The others looked to each other in confusion. How could they obey this order and touch an untouchable? Anand decided that if he were going to die, he would have the last word.

"Very well. When I am torn into pieces, Holy Queen, my hope is you will dine on this."

Anand grabbed his penis and shook it at her. She went into a paroxysm of screams, ran about the cage and tripped over her low-caste subjects. They did not dare to touch or right her when she stumbled and fell in the crowded confines. The screech-filled chaos continued as she ran around, her backside covered in little curls of shredded straw, when she tripped over one of her subjects and fell facedown.

"You heard me," Trellana shouted as she spit out straw and rose from the floor. "I command you to *kill this boy*! Isn't there a soldier in this cage?"

There was not. It seemed the Cajorite soldiers were the one group that the captors had sequestered in separate cages. A man with the splotchy skin of the tar worker caste spoke to the priest.

"Holiness, please remind Her Majesty we are forbidden to touch a boy of such low caste. And he's a half-breed, a son of the roach-eaters. His blood will pollute us—could blind us and eat our skin—if we tear him to pieces."

When Trellana heard this, her wailing climbed to a pitch that was unbearable. It summoned a cadre of guards to the cage, covering their ears. Trellana screamed at them in the servant dialect.

"I am Queen Trellana," she huffed, "of Mound Cajoria of the Great and Holy Slope. If you do not wish for your own extermination, you will release me and my priest now."

The guards did not understand a word, but they certainly looked irritated. As she ranted, one of them covered his mouth with a finger and made a shushing sound.

"Do not shush me," she screamed. "When my father's soldiers descend on this place, they will hang you from rafters and cut off your feet. You will bleed to death while watching your families get thrown to the ants for dismemberment. Others of you will be baked to death in a sun-kiln while . . ."

Trellana continued to list a series of tortures as the guards made their decision. They stood in a circle, shrugging their shoulders. Finally, they departed from the huddle and unlashed the cage's gate. Trellana exhaled with relief, regaining her poise as she prepared to step out.

"Step aside," she said to the guards as she cocked back her head. "You will bring me suitable clothing and take me to whomever is in charge." Once Trellana had set foot outside the cage, a guard raised her blowgun. The dart landed in Trellana's forehead and she slumped to the ground. Her subjects watched as her free leg popped up and twitched.

*Not very queen-like,* Anand thought as he watched

her body go all too still. He felt a twinge of relief, a moment of amusement, and then pure dread for her when he considered the depth of her torment if she were to be paralyzed for another moon. *Still*, he thought, *it's better her than me.*

*Not to mention that at least she's stopped screeching.*

Sometime later, bowls and boxes of strange foods were brought to the cages as well as bladders of drinking water. Anand noticed that the foundation of the cage had removable drawers on its sides that were pulled out, loaded with provisions, and then re-inserted to reach the prisoners. Anand watched as a cheerful youth with a pink complexion and pink eyes set down platters of ant eggs. Anand looked at him through the bars and said "Thank you," first in Slopeish, and then in Britasyte.

The second "thank you" caught the youth's attention. He spoke in his own language to Anand, who shook his head and shrugged his shoulders, then repeated the strange words. The young man pointed to himself and said what Anand assumed must be his name: Dwan. Anand pointed to himself and said "Anand." They grinned at each other, but soon the Cajorites were pushing in to get at the meal.

"Stop," said Dolgeeno with an imperious wave. "I will distribute what appears to be food. I don't believe our captors meant to give ant eggs to common laborers." Turning to Anand he said, "And *you* will not be eating."

Anand's hunger was painful and to see food was

taunting. He reached for a water-bladder when Dol-geeno shouted at him.

"No! Touch that bladder and none of us can drink from it!"

Anand's mouth was as dry as sand in a rainless summer. "Then it is all mine," he said, and sucked. "Though I would gladly share," he added after wiping his mouth. He held out the bladder, but all in the cage turned away. Anand chose that moment to grab an ant egg, bite the end of it and suck out its jelly before munching on its rind.

He looked over at Dwan who seemed fascinated and disturbed by what he had witnessed. Dwan cocked an eye, smiled at Anand, and then ran off. Anand had the sense he would be returning with others.

# CHAPTER 18

## POLEXIMA THE SLAVE

The Hulkrish recolonization of forsaken leaf-cutter mounds resulted in a crude imitation of life on the Slope. The mound of Zarren-dozh was structurally sound, but the ghost ants had done little more than clear the sand-filled tunnels. The human slaves were set to repairing the exterior, patching and repitching the rain shield, and making the chambers habitable again after two hundred summers. When they were cleared of their ancient dust, the walls and floors were reinforced with cocoon skins soaked in resin. Before the resin was dry, Hulkrites moved their barrels of war booty, their families, and their slaves inside.

One of the Hulkrites' slaves was the Cajorite queen who had thought of herself as compassionate.

She thought she appreciated the daily ordeals of those whose stations required them to spend their days in labor, many in the darkness of her mound's interior or in the dangerous wilds of its weeds. But like others of her immediate kin, she thought the laborers were not suitable for anything other than drudgery and had been born with a constitution for it. She believed they embraced their work as a sacrifice to the gods and carried it out as a happy prayer.

How little she had known—how little she had *wanted* to know.

On her first day of working with slaves, she understood that the most prayerful of them could not possibly find joy in repetitive tasks that lasted from sunrise to sunset. Her back was a throbbing tangle of aches, as the only way she was allowed to keep her baby was in a pouch strapped at the chest. The sole pleasure in labor was the promise of sleep, a promise sullied by the dread that it all started again in the morning.

Before Polexima was set to work on the renovations, her morning task was the cleaning of chamber pots, which she and other Palzhanite nobles emptied into a vat. Pleckoo and the other Slopeish defectors took particular delight in watching Queen Polexima carry out night soil. As she did, she prayed that the gods would soon reveal the plan for her rescue.

In the afternoons, Polexima immersed sheets of cocoon skins in resin, a rare substance in a treeless region. The smell of resin was sickening and made her lungs ache and her head throb. Her thoughts were torn and disconnected, like a nightmare, and when darkness fell, she could not remember who and where she was. Pareesha suckled lightly at her mother's breast as the milk had the taste of resin. The baby was losing weight.

One morning, the queen awoke unable to rise. She was too ill to eat the rancid chunk of slug that was her breakfast, lunch, and dinner. The overseers kicked and poked her with their swords and urged her to fulfill her urination duty. She preferred to risk further beating than stand. Pleckoo was summoned.

"Rise, you lazy she-flea," he said and kicked her. "Your subjects await your heavenly secretion."

"I cannot move. A hundred demons eat me from the inside."

"If you cannot work, you cannot live. Everyone contributes to the Empire."

"Then kill me. Let this mound succumb to the Yellow Mold."

"We don't need you, Polexima. We have your daughter's urine."

"Her urine is of no value until she is a woman who bleeds between the legs. Perhaps in twelve summers."

"We can capture another Slopeish queen."

"Then that is what you shall do. If you wish to kill me, I've no objection. I know I am already dying."

Before sleep or death took her, she managed a last request. "Take good care of my daughter, please."

# CHAPTER 19

## THE CHOSEN ONE

**A**nand was seated on the floor, looking out of the cage in hopes of distracting himself from the anger that churned inside him. The place was a darkly beautiful land of cool shadows and intense greens, with trees so tall their tops could not be seen. The moss-mottled boulders had steep and rugged faces like those of the Great Jag.

From around a rock came a covey of men and women in flowing blood-red robes. Dwan was among them, leading them to the prisoners. The Cajorites recoiled in fear as guards opened the cage and entered. Dwan followed the guards in, stepped over Trellana, and approached Anand. He rose to his feet and backed against the bars, staring sideways.

Dwan bowed, smiled to reveal his teeth, touched his heart, and extended his palm. Anand was not sure how to respond. He watched as Dwan's other hand offered him a roll of parchment. Anand unrolled it and saw a portrait of himself standing on a two-headed arrow. At one end of the arrow was a drawing of a mound with yellow ants and brown and yellow people. At the other was a mound with red ants and multicolored people.

"Well, well," said Dolgeeno, looking over Anand's shoulder. "You have been given an invitation."

"They're giving me a *choice*," said Anand.

Dolgeeno pursed his lips and squinted. "Go, traitor," he said. "And take your stink with you. We've learned your mother is a roach-eater. It was probably Britasyte scum who alerted these savages to our mission."

"I know nothing of these people or what I've been chosen for," said Anand. "But I will take a chance they will let me live. Your queen wanted me torn to pieces merely because I brushed her arm."

"Not just a queen," said Dolgeeno with a snort. "You have polluted a direct descendant of Goddess Ant Queen."

Anand stepped over Trellana at that moment. He wrinkled his nose.

"The descendent of Ant Queen has just polluted *herself*," he said and left Dolgeeno, the only one suited to touch the queen, with a most unpleasant task.

Anand had assumed his captors would bind his

ankles and wrists with strips of cuffing grass, but instead they let him walk freely as if he were joining them for a pleasant stroll. Dwan bowed a second time, and with a curl of his fingers, signaled Anand towards them. For a moment he thought about running, but he quickly realized it was pointless. He was weak from a month of paralysis.

*And just where would I run to?*

Dwan grinned as he placed a pair of red antennae over Anand's head. He could not help but grin in return. Dwan may have been his captor, but his smile was like sudden sunlight on a cold day. *How much I'd like to trust him!* Anand thought.

The party stopped as they encountered a parade of hunter ants which probed the humans with their slender antennae that danced like ribbons in the wind. As Anand watched the others get sniffed/touched, he noticed these ants were not blinded. He liked their ruddy sheen and long, graceful bodies. They were so unlike the tubby leaf-cutters, with their pockmarked chitin. Anand was even more charmed by his captors and the casual way they chatted while ambling. The entire party stopped to admire the shadow of a bee dancing inside a drooping slipper orchid before it crawled out, its head spattered with yellow powder and its hind legs bulging with pollen baskets.

The sounds of civilization grew louder as they rounded a boulder. Anand had expected to see a human-inhabited ant mound, like Cajoria. Instead he saw an enormous bivouac with thousands of troopers and attending civilians. Their houses, like the cages, were set on wagons, and Anand was reminded of a Britasyte gathering.

They strolled past a clearing where children were involved in some pleasant commotion that involved a ball being kicked on a grid with nets on either end. Smaller children were spread across the velvety carpet of a violet leaf. They looked like little gods as they occupied themselves with tiny replicas of ants, people, trees, and wagons.

Dwan brought Anand to a circle of elders inside one of the wagons. Upon seeing him, they rose and also touched hands to hearts and extended their palms.

"Illen," said the eldest, pointing to himself. His skin was green and yellow, like the stripes of a weedmelon. Anand said his own name, pointed to himself. The others returned to seats behind tables to do the strangest thing Anand had seen yet: they dipped sharp sticks into red ink and made ugly little drawings.

"*Kwak,*" said Illen, pointing to his hand.

"*Kwak,*" Anand repeated. Pointing to his own, he said "hand."

This went on for a while—Illen pointing to an object and saying a word, and Anand giving the Slopeites' term for it. At one point, Illen pointed to everyone in the wagon, and said "Dranverite," smiling. Anand felt both relief and a moment of trepidation when his guess was confirmed. The hearsay about Dranverites seemed at odds with all he had seen . . . but perhaps this was just an elaborate trap. Maybe they would cage him for life and put him on display in a traveling show. Perhaps they would hobble him and make him the exotic pet of a royal.

Sometime later, the cage suddenly lurched—the caravan was heading off. Anand looked out the bars, to the south toward the Slope. He felt an abrupt sadness soaked in fear. He longed for his parents, wished for Daveena, and wondered again what these strange people wanted.

**T**he Cajorites were pacing as the Dranverites wrapped the cages with bark cloth that allowed light in at the top. Moments later, the cages were rolling. "Where are they taking us, Pious?" asked a woman from the palace servant caste. "What don't they want us to see?"

"I believe they are returning us," said Dolgeeno, "and don't want us to know the way back." Dolgeeno was seated near Trellana, nursing her paralyzed body in a corner. "Yes, Majesty," he cooed to her. "And if we are returned, we will unite the soldiers of the Slope in war. Your children's children will rule this place. Leaf-cutter ants will strip these trees and beautify the land with mounds and sunlight. Every last Dranverite will be sacrificed to Mantis and quench Her bloodthirst for a generation."

As he finished his words, Dolgeeno knew he was lying to the queen as well as himself. Slopeites stood no chance against these red armored demons. Among the first things he would do at home was ingest the

Holy Mildew. Perhaps the gods would inform him how they could defeat these savages in a war that would be the Slope's greatest triumph. *And that, finally, might insure my succession as the Ultimate Holy*, he thought, smiling for the first time in weeks.

# CHAPTER 20

# A SCOLDING

Commander Tahn was returning from his greatest victory yet, the conquest of Bulkoko, Land of the Honey Reapers. Some thought Bulkoko was the legendary Bee-Jor, but far from being a paradise, it was a highly stratified nation whose degenerate rulers lived in trees near beehives, but whose masses toiled in slums on the ground. The laborers immediately took to the Prophet-Warrior's promise of a sword, riches, and multiple wives for all who worshipped Termite. Hundreds of thousands of them took the White Paint of Submission to battle their way up a labyrinth of rope bridges and relish in the slaughter of the masters. The rulers were thrown from their tree palaces to be trampled and cut to pieces, while some were drowned in their hoards of honey.

Pleckoo set out on a speed ant with good news he knew would please his commander at Mukaz-dozh where he had stopped midway for fresh ants and rest. He arrived to find Tahn preaching to the masses on a speaking rock at the base of the mound. Near him were sleds full of unending booty and massive honeycombs that attracted fruit flies.

"Hulkrites of Mukaz, the Termite wants his people to have honey, not just in the next world but in this one," said the Prophet to the masses. As he spoke, warriors shot the flies out of the air which were added to a spontaneous feast. Tahn blessed his followers, then went to peruse the cages of captured maidens in their bee fuzz gowns as Pleckoo rode up and dipped his head.

"Commander, we bring good news from the capital."

"Yes, Pleckoo?"

"Not only have a few mushrooms spiked and fruited, but some of the leaf-cutter nymphs are winged. One of them, a queen, was seeded by her brother after a recent rain and is already laying eggs."

"Excellent. And how is our Good Queen Polexima?" Pleckoo hesitated.

"Yes?"

"For the moment she lives. Her brat lives."

"For the moment? Is she not well?"

Pleckoo was silent.

"Pleckoo, we must have these mushrooms! Not just as food, but as a means of increasing fertility in Hulkrish women. In order to do so, we must have a healthy Slopeish queen. Is she being well fed? Exposed to sunlight and air?"

Pleckoo hesitated. "Commander, we have treated her as we treat any infidel—she refuses to . . ."

"She is not *any infidel*! She is the source of a power our faith needs if it is to grow in new lands. You will coddle her, Pleckoo. See to it yourself that she thrives. We can't risk another raid against the Slope without igniting total war, a war we are not yet prepared for."

Pleckoo nodded and felt heat in his face. For some strange reason, he was reminded of the welts on his buttocks when he had been whipped in Cajoria. He looked into the commander's face, which was searching the heavens. Pleckoo was plunged from shame into envy as he watched Tahn commune with their god. Pleckoo was wondering why Hulkro had chosen this man, already so gifted and beautiful, as his conduit to men when Tahn's eyes blinked open.

"Hulkro will save Polexima if we treat her well," Tahn said. "Her daughter will make a faithful Hulkrite. So say I."

"Then so says Hulkro," said Pleckoo. "If the commander will forgive me, I should make a quick return."

"Why?"

Pleckoo hesitated.

"To . . . to prepare for your celebration."

"You are dismissed, Pleckoo."

Pleckoo reached for the roots of his ant's antennae and clutched them with his scent-gloves. As the ant picked up speed, Pleckoo promised Hulkro a sacrifice of ten thousand wood chips if Polexima were alive by the time he returned.

# CHAPTER 21

## THE CITY OF PEACE

Anand had never seen spinach that grew like this. Outside the Dranverites' capital, spinach was flourishing in neat rows to the exclusion of any other plant. It was followed by a field whose only plants bore pointed berries with seeds dotting their skins.

Relieved from his exchanges with the translators, Anand walked with Dwan beside the wagons. Dwan had bathed and his skin was now as red as the berries they passed. Other Dranverites had changed their skin colors as well as their clothes and from their laughter and chatting, seemed ready for a celebration. Night was falling when Anand heard the distant scurry of thousands of ants and the hubbub of uncountable humans.

The procession reached boulders with carved caves in rows, each with a faint glow and a human family inside. Just past the boulders was a tree with dwellings hewn in its bark, each connected to the ground in a dizzying system of ladders. The inhabitants stepped out on ledges and shouted down greetings.

Anand's heart thumped when they veered around a boulder to a sudden revelation of the capital mound and its massive, luminous beauty at the center of a great clearing. The spectacle made him stagger. As the caravan entered the main artery, Dranverites poured out of dwellings painted in a riot of hues. Perhaps more than anything, Anand was dazzled by the clothing. Red may have been the only color of their cloth, but their garments were of an astonishing variety. They wore short tunics, long gowns, loose and tight blouses, capes, towering headdresses, tiny caps, or—in some cases—almost nothing at all.

As the caravan rolled up the mound's grade, the people followed it and beat hand-drums while dancing and singing. Fragments of flowers were thrown from the windows and sent up a heady perfume. Candied worm and salted berry were thrust in the mouths of soldiers while bowls of frothy acorn beer were circulated. Girls set garlands of flower clippings around the soldiers' necks and boys smeared glow-paint on the weevils. The main artery was teeming with humans when a parade of red ants threaded through them with the bits and pieces of a slaughtered mantis.

Anand was astonished that the streets surrounding the mound were bright with the light from lamps on poles. Inside the lamps' crystal bowls were glow-worms. Open areas had mushroom lamps of yellow and orange growing from pots of fermenting grass. Around these pots were benches where Dranveri-tes chatted and ate and moved tiny sculptures over checkered boards.

Anand slurped some acorn beer and was imitating the whirling steps of the dancers when he stumbled into a thick-limbed woman in what looked like Brita-syte costume. He excused himself in Dranverish. She was smiling in forgiveness when he was struck by her resemblance to his mother.

The squalid flats of Cajoria rushed into his mind and felt like a knife in his heart. He imagined Corra as the first to see the pioneers returning in humili-ation. She would run and grab Yormu, happy that their son would be at the tail of the parade. Anand was wrenched with anguish as his mind's eye saw the moment when the midden caste reached his parents. Corra would wildly pace, then run after Keel scream-ing, *"Where is my son?"*

Dwan turned from the festivities to see Anand's despair. Unable to express his sorrow, Anand had never felt lonelier. As soon as he could express it, he would tell his captors that he must return to the Slope.

Eventually, they reached the astonishing dwell-ing where Anand was to stay. The house was a hand-some multitude of cubes made of sand-bricks glued with resin and its interior was divided into spacious chambers. The walls inside the house were covered in thin sheets of a fragrant wood and the windows were slices of quartz that invited in sunlight. Dwan led him to a chamber with two sleeping cushions— one for each of them! Next to Anand's cushion on a chest of drawers was an outfit of red cloth with tight leggings, a loose tunic, and a cape. There was also a tall hat with a sun visor and the fluffy antennae of a sugar moth as decoration. Best of all was a pair of red boots made from the egg casing of a roach.

For only the second time in his life, Anand would have clothes instead of rags. He fell asleep with a smile on his face that would last until morning.

Anand's new clothes made Dwan smile, too.

When he brought in their breakfast, the young man burst out laughing. Through gestures, Dwan showed Anand that he had put the undergarment on over the leggings. Sweating with embarrassment, Anand quickly fixed his outfit and then joined Dwan for the morning meal, which consisted of a porridge of sweetened leaf-cutter mushrooms.

*Where did they get mushrooms?* Anand wondered. *They certainly don't trade with the Slope.*

Every moment in this place brought a new mystery.

When the boys were ready to depart, they bowed before Dwan's mother as she reviewed maps in the house's parlor. Anand looked at her face, wondering where he had seen it. He was looking from her to a crystal case that displayed Dranverish armor and a helmet with a banner at its top when it all fell into place: this was the woman commander who had led the Dranverite army! She nodded to the boys, smiled, and returned to her maps. Dwan's father handed each of them a hollowed seed pail that, upon inspection, contained their lunch.

In the daylight, Anand and Dwan hiked to the top of the mound where there was a cluster of crystal palaces, far more beautiful than those that housed the Cajorite royals. Atop the roof of one, Anand was stunned into reverence by the vast sprawl of the city which stretched to the distant mists.

The two ambled down the mound and into the streets. Vendors pushed carts loaded with foodstuffs, clothing, shoes, and oddities. Anand saw what looked like rough-cloth for a coat, but it was torn into strips and then dunked in a sauce to be eaten. Something wet and gooey, which looked like food, was tried on as a hat. Outside a large and impressive dome of twigs, Anand saw merchants selling leaf-cutter eggs and mushrooms.

As Anand got closer, he saw the dome was a cage and inside it was a completely enclosed leaf-cutter ant mound. Some were clinging to the underside of the dome to provoke the red ants patrolling the outside. Men and women carted in leaves that were seized upon by yellow foragers. Some human workers with mushroom lanterns on top of their helmets emerged from the mound with harvests of eggs. In a separate area, dead leaf-cutters were cut up for food and their blood was scooped into barrels. Looking out across the city, Anand saw similar domes and wondered what insects lived in them.

Dwan nudged Anand to a market in the shade of a tall column where bees darted in and out of a cube-shaped hive at its top. In a nearby stall was a trough of honey. No attendant presided over the stall, and passing Dranverites scraped the honey into crocks. In gratitude, some bowed before a wax statue of Bee in a nearby shrine. Others took honey but ignored the deity.

Anand scooped up some with his finger then licked it. *The old fool in the midden was no fool at all,* he thought. *Bee-Jor is real and it is in the North. From now on, I will worship Bee as an equal to Roach.*

Anand fell to his knees, bowing before the statue. Without a knife, he bit into a bulging vein on the back of his hand until it bled. He scraped a doming drop of blood on the post of the altar to Bee and signaled for Dwan to join him in worship. Dwan's face darkened and he shook his head. Anand wondered what he had said or done to make Dwan look so disdainful. "I see now," said Anand in Britasyte. "You want me to save my blood. You're giving me the best day of my life before your priests drag me up to some altar, rip off my head, and then offer my life to some thirsty god before you attack the Slope."

Dwan could only shrug and shake his head.

It did nothing to make Anand think he was wrong.

# CHAPTER 22

## A MYSTERY SOLVED

Without explanation, Polexima and her daughter were carried to a sunny chamber near Tahn's own dwelling and set to rest on a mattress. Her food was also improved. She was brought berry leather and abundant mushrooms as well as clear, sweet water. Best of all, she was not summoned to work. She wondered at the change in treatment, but knew not to ask her captors why. For the first few days, they did not talk to her or meet her eyes, but later the Slopeites, including the noseless one, glowered at her when they brought her food, as if she had somehow betrayed them.

For the time being, she could care less.

It was a late summer afternoon when Pleckoo and other Slopeish defectors gathered outside the Prophet's chamber to bring him unwelcome news. He was in the midst of inseminating one of his thousands of concubines.

"I am assuming this is an urgent matter," said Tahn.

"Forgive us, Prophet, it is. It appears that Polexima fails in her duties. You may have noticed that since the leaf-cutters have restored the chambers back into working farms that a smell like fresh mud has turned into a bitter stink. We would like to show you something."

Tahn joined the men on passing ants and rode them down to the spiraling tunnels. As they approached the chambers, Pleckoo held his torch to the wall.

"If you please, look there, Prophet."

Clinging to the walls were veins of gooey, yellow fuzz. Inside the mushroom chambers, the stench was even worse. The mushrooms were wilting under a yellow mold or had melted into a slime.

"Has she been pissing here?" Tahn asked.

"Every day. We watch her."

"Bring Polexima and her child to my chamber."

Moments later Polexima and her baby were pushed through the portal to Tahn's chamber. She sat on the floor, clutching Pareesha, defiantly meeting his gaze.

"Come forward," Tahn said.

Polexima rose to walk when Pleckoo pushed her to the ground. "On your knees before the Prophet," he shouted.

Polexima walked on her knees as the baby cried.

"Are you enjoying your stay?" Tahn asked, slitting his eyes. Polexima did not answer.

"I asked you a question," said Tahn. She had noticed he was wearing a foreign robe of tinted gossamers and elaborate weaving—hardly an austere choice.

"No. I do not enjoy my captivity," she said.

"A very good answer, Majesty, because it is an honest one. Answer me this. Why does your urine fail to protect this mound from the Yellow Mold? All our ants and tunnels are threatened."

Polexima was silent. The truth was, she did not know. She had heard of queens on the Slope who had lost their magic. The priests had to intercede with Ant Queen in order to return it.

"I do not know," she said, her eyes locked with Tahn's.

"Lying she-flea!" Pleckoo shouted.

Tahn quieted Pleckoo with a brief glare.

"Perhaps you do *not* know, Majesty," Tahn said. "But perhaps you might consider what it was that your priests fed you or put in your drink . . . something special, maybe, which combined with your water to make its protective essence?"

Polexima was silent, but images, scents, and tastes were spinning in her mind.

"Captain, what is it they call the King of Cajoria?" Tahn asked Pleckoo.

"His Highness the Legless," said Pleckoo as he and a guard grabbed the queen. A third guard took Pareesha and set her on the floor.

"Perhaps your daughter could be legless, too," said Tahn as he removed his sword and set its blade on the child's legs. Polexima jolted. As much as she hated helping these loathsome primitives, she had no choice—she wouldn't let them harm her daughter. *Think*, she urged herself.

She gasped and then shook her head in self-contempt. *Of course*, she thought, *I've been so stupid!* Tahn smiled at her.

"Well?"

"Eggs," she mumbled.

"Ant eggs?" Tahn asked.

"No."

"Then *what*?" Tahn shouted, raising the sword.

"Roach eggs," Polexima blurted out. She broke away and crawled to her baby and realized she had always known.

"Very interesting. But from which kind of roach?" Tahn asked. "And more importantly, where do we obtain them?"

# CHAPTER 23

# THE SILENCE OF THE GODS

When Trellana woke, she looked up from the cage's floor at the faces of Slopeish sentries. Though their skin was fair, and their armor was made from leaf-cutter chitin, she panicked. She backed away from them, screaming and stumbling over the bodies of her subjects. She scrambled out the gate and saw Cajoria in the distance. "Father, help me!" she called, until she could run no more and collapsed on the sand. Priests arrived with the task of setting her royal body over a pack ant for return to her old chambers.

The pack ant turned and antennated Trellana with its abdomen up in a defensive posture—she had no trace of kin-scent. The ant sprayed *alarm-scent*, then attacked her, pinning her with its claws as its mandibles parted to sever her waist. "Kill it!" shouted the priests.

But the ant was not to be deterred. The sentries hacked at the back of its head, attempting to sever it. The pincers closed and Trellana was pierced. Her blood gushed and she fainted. The soldiers' struggles intensified, and the ant was slain just before its pincers could gouge through her rib cage.

But that was just one ant. A hundred others converged on Trellana and the foolish returnees who had followed her out. The sentries made a barricade of themselves, and as their swords flashed and thrust, the priests covered Trellan with their own clothing. As the ants gnashed their mandibles, the sentries cut off their antennae which sent them racing in spirals and colliding into streams of soldier ants spilling down from the mound by the thousands to counter what smelled like a red ant invasion.

The pioneers raced to the people in the outer rings and begged for scented clothing. They threw themselves into whatever tubs of water they could find until an idols keeper could bring them kin-scent. For an unfortunate few, it was too late and they lost limbs or their lives.

Yormu had been tired and weak ever since his long and winding trek home from Palzhad. He was back at his old tasks in the corpse piles and praying to Mantis for the end of the day when a stream of ants arrived at the midden to dump human corpses and severed limbs.

"Yormu, those are the pioneers!" Terraclon shouted, running towards him. They examined each body to make sure that none was Anand. They ran to see Keel who was recovering outside his old dwelling where his wife tended a gash in his arm. He had not been wounded by a leaf-cutter, but had been stabbed by the man his wife was in bed with.

"Where's Anand?" asked Terraclon.

"Dead," said Keel, avoiding eye contact.

"*Dead?*"

Terraclon clutched his neck, struggling to breathe.

"Dead to us anyway," said Keel. "Went off with the Dranverite demons, from what we heard. He's a traitor to the Slope."

As everyone watched, Yormu grabbed Terraclon and embraced him without shame. Terraclon did not resist and used Yormu's chest to hide his sobbing.

**S**ome days after what came to be known as the Cajorite Repulsion, the priests of all the Slopeish queendoms convened at Venaris. They were instructed by his Ultimate Holiness Pious Ennochenzo to imbibe the Holy Mildew and seek the god's counsel. Chanting and pacing continued in the Ultimate Cathedral until the priests dropped from exhaustion. When they awoke, no priest reported contact with the gods but Dolgeeno, who claimed to have had an audience with Mantis. Ennochenzo conferred in private with Dolgeeno, then released the priests to gather in the feasting chamber.

Kings, princes, and generals from all the mounds arrived for a conclave, anxious to hear the conclusions of the holies. After an austere meal of raw mushrooms, Ennochenzo emerged from his chambers to address the nobles. The Ultimate Holy was too weak to address the thousands directly, so his words were relayed by a young and strapping novitiate.

"The gods are hungry," the novitiate shouted, as Ennochenzo rasped the words in his ear. "Mantis wishes for blood and in her desperate thirst, failed to protect our pioneers from the northern demons of Dranveria. She grows weak in her own fights with the ghost warriors of the Netherworld, who have invaded the Heavenly Plain as well as the Dustlands south of our borders."

Sahdrin rose on his wobbly legs. Summoning all his energy, he addressed the Ultimate Holy.

"Holiness, are you saying it was *ghosts* that captured my wife?"

"The accounts we have cannot be trusted as they come from a low-born folk. But border patrols confirmed the attackers from the south in Hulkren are Netherworld spirits on mounts of ghost ants."

The novitiate hesitated before relaying the next chain of words, and blinked nervously as murmurs rolled through the hall. His voice cracked as he relayed the gods' pronouncement.

"In order to defeat these new enemies," he said, "we must commence holy wars on our neighbors. From the Carpenter peoples of the west, blood sacrifices must be secured. East in the Seed Eaters' country, we will annex the border mound of Xixict and convert it to a Slopeish colony."

A low rumble ran through the kings and generals again. Sahdrin spoke for all when he addressed the priests.

"We have fresh treaties with our neighbors. Moreover, a war on two fronts is foolish."

Ennochenzo set eyes on Sahdrin as he rasped to the novitiate.

"We will let the gods tell us what is foolish," was the response from the Ultimate Holy as Sahdrin looked from him to his mound's own Pious Dolgeeno, who avoided all eye contact and busied himself with his prayer beads.

# CHAPTER 24

## THE POWDER BATTLES

**A**nand's arrival in Dranveria coincided with its highest festival. He awoke on his second morning, sick from stuffing himself the night before with food of unbelievable tastes. Dwan's family had invited neighbors to the house, and each had brought a platter of glowing pastries in the shapes of the Dranverish deities. First they were hung on a sprig as the Dranverites sang songs. Afterwards, they danced around them in the dark before they were eaten. Anand had thought it odd that a part of this ritual was to eat the pastry head first, reviving the rumor that the Dranverites were the cruelest of cannibals. He couldn't help but wonder if the eating of real humans was the next part of the celebration.

Dwan was still asleep when his father, Hopkut, entered the room with the morning's garments. Anand was disappointed in them. They were white and new, but still resembled the rags of Slopeish workers. Instead of boots, there were flimsy white sandals that might last a day. *Better than bare feet*, Anand thought and put them on.

Dwan woke and dressed in the same clothing. When Anand tried to speak to him, the young man pressed his finger to his lips. Anand accepted that for some reason there was no talk this morning. Dwan's mother, Belja and Hopkut nodded silently to him in the eating room, and all that was offered for breakfast was a scoop of water.

Sun had yet to climb in the sky when the family left the house. In silence, the people of Dranveria walked through the crowded streets. All were dressed in white and carrying bundles on sticks slung over their shoulders. They wound their way to great stadiums carved into the slopes of boulders.

Anand assumed that Belja's status as a commander would entitle them to enter first and that she would assume a place of honor. Instead, the family joined a long queue and waited their turn. They took no seats of honor, and since they had arrived late, they were seated some distance from the impending ritual.

When the stadium was filled, gates opened from opposite the spectators. Troopers mounted on ants scattered to stand as guards. Drummers and musicians marched through the gate with their great instruments rolled in on wagons. The drummers climbed ladders to beat on two-sided barrels that were thirty times the height of a man. Men and women played giant wood horns, with some working bellows at one end while others pressed valves for the different pitches. Lutes that were forty times as tall as a man were plucked by individuals at the base of each string who obeyed a conductor.

Since the music was somber, Anand wondered if they were at a funeral. Maybe the body of a royal personage in a funerary sack would be presented to carrion beetles for destruction. Perhaps the feast the night before was a celebration of the dead noble's passage to the Heavenly Mound. With so many questions in his head, one thing was sure: he was determined to learn Dranverish.

A party of thirteen men in priestly robes entered the arena. Puffs of white mist exploded in noisy bursts as harnessed women dragged in a sand-and-resin statue atop a narrow pedestal. When the mists subsided, Anand saw the statue of Goddess Bee. In her six arms were cones of honey and on her back were pairs of golden wings. When the idol reached the edge of the arena, the crowd stood and bowed before it. Dwan nudged Anand to rise and do the same. He was more than happy to worship.

A second idol was rolled in as more mists exploded and the musicians' tune changed. Anand's heart soared when he recognized the statue as Madricanth, with its breasts of a woman, protuberance of a man, and body of a roach. He/she was set on the same kind of narrow pedestal. Yipping excitedly in the way of the Britasytes, Anand was shushed by Dwan as the crowd rose and bowed to the Roach God.

The mists exploded again and Anand's heart sank when two idols appeared one after the other: Mantis and her consort, Grasshopper, the Slopeish gods of war and prosperity that Britasytes held in contempt. Everyone bowed, but Anand stood in erect defiance. Dwan placed his hand on Anand's neck to bend it. He pushed Dwan's arm away and grimaced.

More idols flooded the field and were set close to each other in a spiral pattern. Deities from the Slopeish pantheon included Mite—the goddess that Yormu prayed to—Locust, the blue sky god, and Hulkro, the eyeless termite god whose statues had disappeared in Cajoria but whose image Anand knew of from ancient Britasyte carpets. Anand was astonished at the strangeness of idols from other lands. Among them was a spider god, a moth god, various plant, flower, and mushroom gods, as well as gods of stars, trees, sand, and rain. There was a scaly god of a lake monster that had no limbs but had flippers to fly through water. Strangest of all was an invisible god represented by an empty tent whose flaps were open to reveal the nothingness inside.

The final idols entered. They were statues of a human male and female whose clothing had been dyed red, like that of the Dranverites. The last statue was of a great ant with a human face painted in what looked like blood. The people bowed three times to these idols when they were set in the center of the spiral.

The north gate closed and the drumming intensified. The east gate opened, and a thousand children poured onto the field in their white rags. As the children ran around the outer track and waved to their friends and families, they cheered to break the silence. The orchestra played a festive melody as the troopers threw the children ropes and rigs.

Anand was shocked when the children climbed on top of the Bee idol, set at the beginning of the spiral. One girl was beating the others to the top and in her climb, broke off one of the idol's wings. The crowd laughed and then it cheered. Anand was horrified. When the girl got to the top, it was apparently her privilege to catch the ropes and set them around Bee's neck. After the girl climbed down, Anand stood in alarm as the children, squealing with delight, yanked down the statue and smashed it into Madricanth. The entire spiral of idols tumbled in succession to the ground.

The people jumped to their feet and cheered themselves into ecstasy. Anand was nauseated. He looked to the heavens expecting falling boulders to crush them all. None came, but from the western gate, young men and women appeared with mallets over their shoulders. As the cheering grew more frenzied, they attacked the idols and smashed them into powder.

Then the south gate opened. On a towering cart drawn by weevils, the honored aged of Dranveria appeared. Most were white-haired and some too infirm to wave, but the crowd cheered as their cart was pulled over the rubble and into the center of the arena. The people bowed towards them as the aged poured blood-red powder over the smashed idols.

From above, Anand saw what looked like an archless rainbow stretch across the sky, thinking that the gods had finally responded—especially when he realized the colors were mists being trailed by a formation of blue-mottled locusts.

"Locusts!" Anand cried in Slopeish. "Run! It's the vengeance of the gods!"

The crowd stared at him in curiosity, then laughed. Dwan giggled and patted Anand's back as the locusts landed in a thick mist. When it cleared, Anand saw there were human pilots seated on natural saddles at the back of the locusts' heads. His heart beat hard, first from fear, then in excitement as he watched the pilots rub different patches of tendrils between the locusts' eyes to send them into flight. The pilots flew in circles, dropping sweets on the crowd. Dwan unwrapped a candy and gave it to Anand whose mouth was too dry to chew it.

With the sounding of thorn trumpets, the crowd untied their bundles to reveal sacks of colored powders. Anand looked in curiosity as Dwan cupped purple powder, held his hand flat, and then blew it into Anand's face. He gasped, sneezed, and then realized the powder was an edible candy. All around him, people were hurling, blowing, and sprinkling powder on each other. Decorum had blown away in a breeze as the Dranverites ran onto the arena, their skin and clothing changing hues as they tossed powder and danced on the crushed idols.

Anand was shaking as he climbed to the back of the stadium to look down on the destroyers of gods. In the distance, he saw other stadiums where the same rituals were in progress. *Did these people kill their gods to let demons rule?* he asked himself. Then he realized that couldn't be true, since demons like Scorpion, Flea, and Night Wasp had been destroyed in the arena, too.

The revels continued. Belja and Hopkut had joined the crowd and were dancing on the rubble of Madricanth! They were signaling Anand to join them when the celebrants poured out of the stadium and into the streets to hurl their powders, changing their colors again and again. Dwan grabbed Anand by his arm to bring him to the streets to continue the powder battles.

Anand looked to the clear sky, and realized that he was still quite safe—and completely unsure of what this bizarre festival commemorated. What he was sure of, though, was that someday—when the Dranverites allowed him—he would make a glorious return to Cajoria on the back of a flying locust trailing colored mists. He smiled at that vision only to be plunged into deep apprehensions.

*Will the Dranverites let me leave? Will I ever see Daveena again? Has her father promised her to someone else?*

*Has she forgotten me?*

# CHAPTER 25

## A BAWDY SPECTACLE

**D**aveena could never forget Anand. She breathed him in with every breath and, in endless prayers, beseeched Madricanth to hasten his return. She had heard he was forever lost in some distant country and was seen as a traitor by the Cajorites. In her heart, she knew he was establishing relations with a new trading partner, but her parents were not so sure.

"Daughter, you must savor the journey you are on now, not dwell on the one behind," said Gupa, knowing why Daveena looked out their sled's window so intently on the route to Palzhad.

"I am, Mother. It is a good, bright journey."

But journeys were less appealing to Daveena since her status as the betrothed of a spanner had vanished.

She still felt the sting from the night before, when she had been shooed from the platter of the betrothed girls and boys.

"You are good with languages," said Eltzer, her father, looking over his shoulder as he prodded their roach forward. "And you can see into people, figure out what they want to hear. You should apprentice with your Cousin Silka and learn the fortune-telling trade."

"Yes," said her mother. "Fortune-telling is a good way to meet an outsider looking for a bride. Their mothers will come to you looking for hope and you can offer yourself to a boy you might fancy. You could give birth to a spanner, Daveena. What glory that would be for you."

"I already have a spanner," she said. "We have seen our destiny."

Her parents sighed as she returned to the window and saw builders from all over the Slope that had been assigned to the outland of Palzhad. She had heard its people had been killed or abducted by some mysterious ghost tribe and its mound was being renovated for the returned pioneers of Cajoria. Near the borders of the Dustlands, workers were rebuilding the border walls of pebbles and ant droppings or renovating the neglected warning and observation towers. Lush weeds on the mound's perimeter were being sawed and mulched or uprooted.

"Time to dance," said her mother when Zedral, the chieftain, blew his thorn trumpet at the head of the caravan. Sighing, Daveena stood up, and mother and daughter donned dark shrouds and stepped to the back of the sand-sled as they neared the camps of the laborers. At the back of the clan's parading sleds, the mothers beat drums as their daughters danced in black sacks that obscured all but their eyes. The builders and their overseers, crushed with boredom and fatigue, looked from their labors to the dancing women at the back of the glittering sleds. Daveena could see the men's eyes fill with wonderment as they pondered what gorgeous mysteries shimmied inside the dark cloth.

When the Plep clan reached a quieter area near the border with the Dustlands, they made camp and disassembled the repaired wall to bring their sleds into a thicket of virgin weeds. During the day, the men busied themselves with hunting and gathering in the game-rich wilds feared by Slopeites. In the camp, Daveena and the women beautified each other, for later it would be their work to gather the treasures of the *sedites*. In the land of the starving Slopeites, Daveena and other girls of girth would be put forth as the main attraction that night. That day she did not gossip or sing with the thin girls as they went to work on her. "What's made you so sad?" asked the pink-haired Eturra as she mercilessly plucked at Daveena's underarm hair. "You'll feel better for sharing," she said, openly smirking as she petted the braid that marked her as spoken for.

"You know what's made me sad," Daveena said. "And it's sad that you find such joy in it."

As ever, a slight wind blew from the north, but in a circling current, Daveena caught a vague scent of something acrid from the south. She heard the roaches bucking left and right in their pens on a sand clearing. The chieftain's tallest and eldest son, Bejetz, walked towards the women with his father's orders. "Wandering women, my father believes it is best to leave here before tomorrow's sunrise," he said. "The roaches know something."

After a Britasyte caravan approached a Slopeish mound, their first business was trading roach eggs for the Holy Mildew in secrecy. The priests went out to meet the roach people in the weeds, ostensibly to counter their pollution with rituals. In reality, they transacted crucial and necessary business. They knew the Britasytes used the mildew to contact their two-sexed demon, but such was the price the priests paid to maintain their own powers. On their return to the mound, they warned the people to "stay away from the impure visitors," which always worked as more of an advertisement than a true stricture. Men of all but the lowest stations left during the night in simple disguises to indulge in the roach people's carnival and its spectacles of dancing women with their dark, forbidden beauty.

That night, it was a larger crowd than the Britasytes had expected. Among the laborers were reinforcements from the border patrol who had tethered their ants and abandoned their posts. Shrouded women wandered through the crowd and passed out leaf-cones of free aphid liquor. The punch, colored a bright pink with hymen fruit, was something the women never drank themselves—for good reason. Those who did drank it would pay for it later.

Several group dances were performed first in the shrouds, and then in a variety of outlandish costumes that incorporated wings of moths and butterflies. The dancers' faces were obscured with masks of demons and gods from foreign lands. Later, they switched to translucent veils.

The roach-men played music described as "demonic" by the Slopeites with a variety of drums, scrapers, and singing as they swayed to their rhythms below the platform. As the performance continued, the dancers shed more clothing and, eventually, the veils. For the final number, a hollow statue of Madricanth was floated onto the stage. The idol opened to release almost naked dancers, their skins coated in the glowing lymph of lightning flies.

Released from their cycle of dread and monotony, the Slopeites were caught up in a frenzy of indulgence. Each woman on the stage seemed especially beautiful, and the musicians—intoxicated with a potion of cannabis—lifted the crowd above the Sand with their playing. Aches and pains, worries and troubles, all parted, it seemed, forever.

The last of the Slopeites' money was taken from

them to enter the tents. Here, in the darkness, they spilled their seeds around platforms where the Britasyte beauties rested above them, bathed in the light of glowworms. Overcome, some men even took this chance to indulge in behaviors forbidden between men. When it was all over, most were too drunk to return to camp. They crawled into weeds to sleep on their leaves or made beds of blades of grass.

Tired but contented, the Britasyte men gathered in a clearing of the circled sleds to count the take under weakening torches. After dividing it, they trudged off to their mattresses. The clan was so fatigued they did not have trouble sleeping even though the summer cicadas screeched by the thousands in the dying trees. Some of the clan stuffed their ears with wax plugs.

None of them heard the clicking of the roaches or their antennae whipping the air.

When some roaches rammed their pens and snapped a plank, though, Bejetz woke and shouted a chain of warnings through the sand-sleds between sharp blasts of his thorn trumpet.

"We're leaving! Now! Something's coming!" Bejetz shouted.

But something was already there. Like a great moving wall, thousands of spectral foot soldiers pushed out of the weeds from the south. Each soldier was poised with a bow and arrow, all aimed at the Britasytes popping from their sleds.

**Z**edral and his wives looked out to see Hulkrites, the rumored ghost warriors. Their ants had been left behind, as not even ghost ants would come near roaches. It made little difference as a multitude of Hulkrites without their insects seemed no less threatening. At the army's head was Tahn, shouting his commands from a gilded throne carried on the shoulders of his men. Zedral knew what he must do and shouted hasty orders to his clan.

The men went to the stores of treasure in their sand-sleds. The women and children stripped to their maggot disguises before they went into hiding. They slipped through trap doors and crawled to the roach pen where they wormed under the largest roaches, then nestled within their belly scales.

As Daveena and the other women waited in darkness, Zedral led his men to the Hulkrites' leader. Each Britasyte male carried a barrel of treasures. They were silent except for a fearful shaking that made rattles of the barrels' contents. Zedral bowed to Tahn and greeted him in Slopeish.

"Mighty Stranger, you command a great army. Please, take all our treasures and leave us our lives."

"It is your lives I am interested in," said Tahn through his interpreter, a noseless man with a low Cajorite accent. "Your lives and those of your roaches."

"Our roaches are our livelihood. Without them we would suffer and die."

"You are already suffering. You live in darkness

and worship a demon. The Britasytes will remember this day as a happy and holy one: the day they were brought into the grace of Hulkro."

"We had heard you are ghosts."

"We are obviously not. Do *you* wish to be?"

Zedral shuddered. In the distance he heard the rustle of a swarm of ants tied to weeds.

"Mighty commander, we honor all gods of the people we trade with. We will worship your god, too."

Zedral could see that this statement infuriated Tahn, who shouted his response. Pleckoo shouted in turn.

"No! You will not defile Hulkro by including him in an altar of your demons. You will worship Hulkro *alone.*"

The Britasytes had been in this position before, but not facing so many soldiers. Zedral prayed to Madricanth to bless him with guile.

"We surrender to your ways," Zedral said and bowed. "Hulkro is mighty to inspire such a great army."

Tahn sneered and spat out his words. "Your words are as false as your god," said the translator. "But we will make honest and happy converts of all of you. Where are your women?"

"Our women? They have moved onto Mound Bothomp where . . ."

Tahn did not listen to the complete translation.

"You would not allow your women to travel alone," Pleckoo interpreted. Tahn's next instructions were not translated at all. More Hulkrites arrived, lugging massive containers of woven twigs on sand-sleds which they pulled to the clearing between Tahn and the Britasytes.

"Tahn the Prophet demands that you herd your roaches into these containers. You will follow them inside."

Zedral was astonished. Roaches repulsed everyone but Britasytes. *What do these ghost soldiers want with them?*

"If you do not comply, you may meet your deaths now."

Zedral feigned fainting and fell to his knees. Bejetz caught his father and righted him. Zedral stammered as he concocted a plan and whispered to the men in Britasyte.

"Lead the roaches into their cages," he said, "but allow those with women and children hiding under them to escape. It must look like an accident. Shout after them."

The men went to the pen and untethered the roaches as gates of the twig boxes were raised. A roach hiding women and their children was allowed to race off. Tahn watched and was furious.

"You let that one go!" Pleckoo shouted.

"We . . . we do not have complete control of them," Zedral shouted back.

Tahn gave a command to the archers behind him. They took aim and their arrows found targets in Bejetz's face. His head splattered like a crushed berry. Zedral fell over his son's body and wept.

"All roaches and all your people are to enter the cages," shouted Pleckoo.

Zedral gave orders through his tears, and roaches and Britasytes entered the boxes. Once inside, the women and children emerged.

"The Prophet is as merciful as Hulkro," said Pleckoo to Zedral, the last to enter a box. "But Tahn informs you that the next time you lie to him, you will be slain and your body fed to our ants."

The twig container was dark and windowless and the people and roaches inside it shuffled in confusion. The Britasytes heard the hard scrape of sand as they were dragged off toward Hulkren, a place beyond the Dustlands. It was a place they had never desired to wander.

# CHAPTER 26

# A MISSION FOR THE CAJORITE

One morning in the library of the sand and lacquer palace, Anand wandered about as the linguists debated a translation. The Slopeites' word for butterfly was the combinant "floating-flower," but their word for moth appeared to be "folding-*flying*-flower." While they attempted a clarification, Anand spotted a series of scrolls whose labels read *The Britasyte Tongue.* Excited, he unrolled the pages and found he could read them.

"Who speaks Britasyte?" he asked. The linguists looked delighted. A short time later, a man of forty-six summers was brought to the temple. Though his skin was covered in lavender paint, his physiognomy was familiar. Anand rose and greeted him in the Britasyte fashion.

"I am Anand, a Britasyte wanderer, son of the Entreveans."

"Good travels. Pizhyot of the Pafentu," he said smiling sadly. "I was a man-child the last time I heard another Britasyte speak my first tongue."

Anand was surprised and distressed. The disappearance of the fourth clan of Britasytes had been a mystery for years.

"How long have you lived here?" Anand asked.

"Since my twelfth summer."

"When were you captured?"

"I was rescued."

"Rescued?"

"Our caravan was raided by renegades of the Zulzict mound of the Seed Eater people. They killed our roaches and then my clan. I was saved at the last moment by Dranverish defenders."

"Why haven't you returned? There are other roach clans."

"I did not want to. I was grateful to these people and taught them the Britasyte ways and language. I was ready to return when I fell in love with my interpreter. We have two daughters."

Pizhyot wore amber amulets about his neck which he held up. Carved upon them were portraits of his wife and daughters. Anand was marveling at the craftsmanship when he realized the linguists had been following the conversation. One of them, a woman with a tower of hair in sunset hues, addressed them in Britasyte. "Our tasks will go very quickly now. Pizhyot, will you join us in our efforts to document the language of the Slopeites?"

"It is my duty to peace," he said and bowed.

"To peace?" Anand asked.

"To peace. On its edges, our great nations . . ."

"Nations?" Anand asked, emphasizing the plural.

"Yes. Our Dranverite nations border more than a thousand others."

"You exaggerate. *A thousand* other nations?"

"More than a hundred nations inhabit the treetops alone."

"What do these people want from me?" he asked Pizhyot. "Are they learning the Slopeites' language before they conquer them? Will they kill me when they are done with me?"

"Killing a human is forbidden in Dranveria. It is only done in self-defense and as a last resort. Were any of the Slopeish invaders killed when they violated our borders?"

"I don't know."

"I assure you they were not. You could be our emissary, Anand, like a spanner. One day, should you choose, you will return to Cajoria with a gospel for both the slaves and masters of the queendoms of the Slope."

"The slaves and masters?" Anand blinked in confusion. "Define this word, 'slave.'"

"I will Anand-shmi, it means . . ."

"What does this suffix 'shmi' mean?" Anand interrupted.

"Beloved citizen," said Pizhyot. "A member of a nation."

"Like a subject," Anand said.

"No, Anand-shmi. There are no subjects in Dranveria, for no man or woman here subjects himself to any other."

"Who is the ruler here?"

"We all rule. We choose our leaders."

Anand was very suspicious of that notion. What if the Slopeites, as stupid as they were, had the chance to choose their king and queen?

That night Pizhyot and his family dined at Dwan's house. His daughters stared at Anand for a good, long while before they asked any questions. Once they did, they spoke in Britasyte which Pizhyot's wife interpreted for Dwan and his family who mostly sat back and watched the encounter. The eldest daughter, Lasku, was of marrying age and wore a red skin paint that matched her baggy pants and top. Her sister, Valoha, had just reached womanhood and strangely, she painted her brown skin with brown paint and was one of the few in Dranveria who liked to wear green.

"Might you know of any relatives of ours?" Lasku asked. "Of anyone from the Pafentu clan?"

"I did not know many Panfentus," Anand said. "They had vanished before I was born. Some of their women married Entreveans, of course. I believe we knew a Cherra, married to Kilgot—he was a good drummer and she was known for her carpets which had good likenesses. Cherra had all daughters, if I remember, and her sister, Mexantee, was a dyer who made cloth that sold well among the Carpenter people. Mexantee had all sons, and one of them, Somby, was a celebrated hunter—he was good at drawing out earthworms."

"Cherra and Mexantee, yes. I believe they are your fifth cousins," said Pizhyot to his daughters.

"And were they dancers?" asked Valoha, somewhat snidely.

"All Britasyte women are dancers," said Anand.

"So their fathers put them out there, naked, to dance in front of strangers in these traveling shows?"

"If a girl is pretty and talented, she can gather a lot of treasure dancing for the outsiders. The girls are never completely naked. And they are well protected."

The daughters' stiff faces said that they disapproved. Their father smiled, but looked somewhat uncomfortable as a silence fell across the table.

"I've seen dancing in this nation," Anand said, looking to Dwan's family. "I don't believe it is discouraged."

"It is not discouraged," said Hopkut.

"Nor is nudity," said Dwan.

"Did any men dance in the spectacles?" Valoha asked.

"Men? No," said Anand with a chuckle.

"And why not?"

"Women on the Slope and in the Barley and Pine countries are not allowed to attend the carnivals. Even if they could, women would not pay to see dancing men."

The daughters looked at each other and giggled. Belja had been following the discussion with great interest when they heard a rap on the window. She opened the pane to accept a scroll tube from a grave-looking messenger wearing a startling white bonnet.

"From what father has told us," said Lasku, "the women danced and made the costumes. They also prepared the food and drink the men sold to the people they called 'sedites' as well as the jewelry and handcrafts. Is that correct?"

Anand felt mildly under attack. His anxiety was mirrored in Belja's face as she read the scroll.

"And is it not the men who keep the money?" Valoha asked. "While the women are at work all day, don't the men play music and go off hunting and lounge around drinking cannabis liquor while making all the big decisions?"

"I . . . I believe you already know the answers to these questions," Anand said. "It has always been as you describe."

"But should it be?" Lasku asked, cocking her head.

Anand was rescued when Dwan spoke up. "What's the matter, Mother? Bad news?"

"I'm sorry," Belja said, rolling up the scroll. "It's an invasion again, to the northeast. A thirty-four day journey. Some unknown tribe is crossing the Salt Flats, a people with sand-covered ants and very hostile. They raided the Tegenet nation on their way here. We must leave tomorrow."

Anand figured he must have looked sad as Pizhyot rose to pat his shoulder.

"Please, stay with us, Anand, and you won't be lonely. My house would be graced to have a Britasyte guest."

"Thank you," Anand said in Dranverish. "But I should like to go to this war."

Everyone was quiet. Dwan broke the silence.

"Anand, we do not war on anyone. As is often the case, we are taking a defensive measure."

"Then I should like to go to the defensive measure," Anand said and puffed out his chest. He was deflated when everyone chuckled.

"It is not a good idea," said Belja. "The learned elders would miss you. Your best contribution is in teaching them your language."

"I suppose," said Anand, but his head dropped. When he looked up, it was with pleading eyes. "I've worked hard with the elders and we've made some good progress. Wouldn't you agree I have been very cooperative . . . so far?"

Dwan squinted in suspicion. "Yes, Anand, you have been very cooperative. Are you implying you may not be?"

Anand didn't answer right away, and instead took a bite of his mashed gnats. "Certainly not," he said, making eye contact with no one. "Though a break from our studies might be . . . beneficial. Is that the right word?"

"Yes, that's the right word," said Lasku. "He's a clever little Britasyte, this one."

Belja folded her arms and stared sideways at Anand before speaking. "Perhaps Anand is right," she said. "Maybe the linguists will agree to accompany us on this latest measure and serve as its documentarians. On the journey there, Anand can continue to impart his knowledge."

Anand took that as a yes— which meant he was going off to war. Remnants of the vision that had appeared to him months ago were returning again in greater clarity. Would the Dranverites teach him their military ways, cover him in their armor and grant him his own weapons?

Would he ride upon a red hunter?

# CHAPTER 27

# THE SAME OLD ENEMIES

Atop the Cajorite mound, Trellana stretched in her favorite lounge chair wearing a gown so soft and light she could barely feel it. Her toenails were being clipped and buffed and at her side, the kitchen servants were presenting her with over fifty choices for breakfast on fine platters of rainbow quartz. She was taken with a damselfly larva which had been delicately butchered, colored with poppy extract, then rearranged to look like the adult it might have become.

"I'll have this," she said and a silk bib was set around her neck. The servant was hand feeding her with tongs when they heard *creet-creet* through the portal.

"The hairdressers!" Trellana said, clapping her hands excitedly.

"I'm afraid not," said the voice of an old woman. Trellana's face fell when servants helped in her Grandmother Clugna. Was she more stooped than the last time Trellana had seen her, or bearing some inner weight? Clugna made no attempt to smile at her granddaughter or pretend any warmth.

"Good morning, Trellana. May I join you for breakfast?"

"Certainly, Grummy. This is a surprise."

The servants ran to an amber lounge chair and pushed it towards Trellana's own.

"We are so very relieved that you've been returned safely. I understand your ordeal was trying," said the old woman.

"*Trying?* Grandmother, I was tortured. We must retaliate against these Dranverites immediately. I should like to leave them all limbless and unable to squirm while we pull out their livers through a tiny puncture."

"I know you have been traumatized, but I must tell you what's befallen your mother and Palzhad."

"Whatever it is, it could not be as awful as what happened to me."

"And to the other pioneers, Trellana. You were not alone."

"But I am a royal. The indignity was unbearable."

Clugna frowned and pushed away her strained pond scum.

"My dear girl, your mother has been captured, perhaps killed."

It entered Trellana's mind in an instant that she could

become Queen of Cajoria, the most envied mound on the Slope. Clugna frowned when she saw Trellana smiling. "Well, Trelly, I can see you're just . . . destroyed."

"Destroyed, yes, many times over," said Trellana. Just as she was imagining the glories of her second anointing, a runner brought news from the emergency conclave at Venaris: the mound's custodians were to dye new banners to fly over the queendom. The cloth would be dyed with human blood.

"War! Wonderful! When do we march on Dranveria?" Trellana asked.

"No, my dear," said Clugna. "They will march south into Hulkren. That is where your mother is."

"No, Your Majesties," said the messenger. "The wars will be in the east and west."

Trellana pouted. Clugna gasped.

**Y**ormu wanted to die. Ants were piling up aphid corpses in tall, sticky towers in the midden, all of which would have to be scraped for their syrup. With a new war on the east, he knew that the aphids would be replaced by piles of human and ant corpses. He turned in the direction of Ganilta, The Holy Tree Top, where the gods looked down on their mortals. Yormu thought about a scrubbing bath in unholy water so that the ants might take him.

Keel noticed Yormu's desperation and had seen his pondering the suds of the tool-washing basin and sent him to Glurmu, the caste's idols keeper. He tended the altar on the fringe of the weeds where he received offerings of food for the gods. Since Glurmu was the fattest of all in the midden, it was no mystery to Yormu as to where the food ended up.

"Don't commit the ultimate sin, Yormu," said Glurmu as he took Yormu's mushroom ration and set it before the dolls on the midden's altar. "If you kill yourself, you will go straight to the Netherworld. Roaches will eat your heart out every day and drag you by your own intestines over hot and jagged sands. The next day you'll be whole again, and it will start anew for eternity! Fulfill your duty, Yormu, especially at this time of war."

Yormu got on his knees, bent his head in prayer, and then offered his arm. Glurmu jammed a tube of razor grass into Yormu's artery and pumped it until his blood filled a bowl which was set before a woven doll of Mantis.

Yormu stumbled back to work. He had begun the dissection of an aphid when he smelled the noxious war-scent from the harvester ants of the Seed Eater nation. Without a breathing filter and weak from blood loss, Yormu fainted and fell.

"Get up, Yormu," said Keel, winding his whip. "No faking your way out of work." The whip lashed over Yormu's chest and he twitched in agony. Watching from the vats, Terraclon ran over. He bowed his head towards the foreman, using his antennae to brush his face and halt the whipping.

"I will bring this man back to health," Terraclon

said, "and have him back soon at his duties. If you whip him again he will die."

"He is already going to die," Keel said. "It's a waste to give him rations."

"Then I will share mine with him," said Terraclon. "Please, sir. I will look after him and keep his shelter."

"So you'll be like his wifey?"

"No," said Terraclon, hanging his head in shame as Keel gave out with a bellowing laugh. "I will be like his nephew."

"Go ahead, take up with him," Keel said between guffaws. "I hope the two of you will be very happy."

Terraclon picked up Yormu and carried him back to his shelter. Terraclon returned a short time later with his few possessions. Yormu was shamed that other middenites might assume Terraclon was sharing his mattress, but the boy had made a show of bringing his own bedding by carrying it on top of his head in a roll.

"I'll look after you as best as I can," said Terraclon as he chewed Yormu's mushrooms for him and spat them into a bowl he could slurp from. "But you can't die. You can't let Anand come back here to find that both his parents are dead. Will you promise me?"

Yormu tried to nod but he also wanted to shake his head. He had no desire whatsoever except to be rid of the hundred pains that crawled over his skin and gnawed him from inside. He shut his eyes to remember Corra's face the first time she nursed their newborn son and looked at both of them with her warmest smile.

# CHAPTER 28

# UNLEASHED DEMONS

**A**nand assumed the habit of bowing to a scroll tube before uncapping it and pulling out its pages. He had wondered if the Dranverites held books sacred, then remembered one of the statues destroyed at the parade of idols was the Book God which had also been smashed into powdery bits. Dwan and Belja were reviewing maps as the scholars readied ink and paper in an academy wagon making its way out of the city. Anand looked up from his reading as they passed the stadium.

"Scholar Babwott, what was observed by the ritual at the stadium—when all the gods were destroyed?" Anand asked in Dranverish.

"You mean when all the *idols* were destroyed,"

said Babwott, as he tucked the ends of his long mustache into his collar. "It is called the Celebration of Colors. To answer your question is to tell you the history of the Collective Dranverite Nations and United Peoples."

"Is there a book of this history?"

"There are a hundred thousand books of this history."

Anand slumped. "No one could read that many books in ten lifetimes."

"No. But perhaps it is time you read one book on our journey north. It is titled *The Loose Doctrine of Dranveria*. It is what we read in public gatherings in lieu of religious scriptures. It contains a concise history of Dranveria and the Code of Moral Conduct."

"I should like to read it today."

"It will take you many days to read it, especially as you have one obligation when you do so the first time."

"Yes?"

"You must make a legible copy of it."

"So that I may keep it for myself?"

"No. So that you may destroy it when you are done."

Anand frowned, then shook his head. "One day I hope to tell everyone of the wonders of this place and the kindness of its people, but . . ."

Dwan looked up from his map, cocked his head. "Speak freely, Anand," he said. "It is the Dranverish way."

"Your customs are so strange." Anand felt heat in his face.

"They are strange to *you*," Dwan said. "We learned long ago that people's beliefs and customs are rooted in their circumstances. We may like, dislike, or even object to their customs, but we never judge anyone as wrong unless they wrong others."

"What do you find strange about me?" Anand asked.

"Everything," Dwan answered and smiled warmly.

"And have I wronged you?"

Dwan hesitated.

"No, but . . ."

"You obviously object to something!"

"Anand-shmi," Dwan said quietly, taking him to a corner. He bowed towards Anand and then continued. "The concept of cleanliness and what is proper varies from people to people. Perhaps next time we go to the latrines I can show you how most people here clean themselves afterwards. Your habit of using your heel to wipe yourself and then dragging it through the dust is . . . unfamiliar to us."

Anand was dead still. He had wondered why Hopkut had been washing his right boot from the inside out every day. Under his paint, the color of new grass, Anand felt as if the sun were burning his face. As the wagon continued down the main artery, they passed the cage of leaf-cutter ants and their tiny mound as men and women exited with carts of sterile eggs.

"Who is your sorceress?" Anand asked. "Does she live in that cage?"

Babwott consulted the Britasyte dictionary.

"Our sorceress? We are not possessed of one."

"Your urine sorceress—the one that leaves her magic essence that enables leaf-cutters and humans to live together without fear of Yellow Mold."

"We have many women in the Leaf-Cutter Union who provide the anti-fungal you describe."

"*Many* women?"

"Yes, Anand. Though it cannot be explained, the urine of some women—never men—is a destroyer of the Yellow Mold fungus."

"These women are not considered the descendants of Goddess Ant Queen?"

"No one is a descendant of any god."

The academy wagon reached the outskirts of the city where it joined with the military caravan. It was almost evening when the wagons stopped in an area of few plants and no insects that was very far away from trees. In the distance, Anand saw a great pit, the walls of which were coated in black.

"What is this place?" Anand asked.

All were quiet and turned to Hopkut who had been silently sitting in the corner, reading.

"A fire pit. I am a fire master," Hopkut said. "Before we deal with the human invaders, we must deal with an invasion of venom sprayer ants."

"Venom sprayers?"

"Venom sprayers have never been domesticated by humans. When attacked, they spray a poison so toxic a human will be blinded and paralyzed and likely eaten. We will need fire to make a poison to kill these awful ants."

"What is this 'fire'?" Anand asked.

Babwott met Anand's eyes and translated the word into Britasyte.

"Fire!" Anand whispered, and his head was pumped with hot blood. "Fire is real?"

"It is very real," said Dwan.

"Fire can be made? Why would anyone do so?"

"We celebrate those who devote their lives to making peaceful fires, for it provides us with many gifts," said Babwott. "Hopkut is an honored citizen of Dranveria." Hopkut looked both pleased and uncomfortable to be the focus of so much attention.

"Is it hard to make fire?"

"Not so hard," Hopkut answered. "But it is both hard to keep going and hard to control."

"We will all be participating," said Dwan. "Making a fire is not without dangers. If you wish to join us, you have been advised."

A short time later, men and women descended on rope ladders that unfurled to the fire pit's floor. Wagons loaded with finely shredded twigs backed up to the pit and dumped their contents. Afterwards, wagons with chips of wood were unloaded on top. Down in the pit, Hopkut supervised the arrangement of the chips on shreds. When he liked the composition, thick twigs and then branches were arranged on top as the final layers.

A strange contraption made of wood was lowered

after that. It looked like an enormous bow and arrow whose point spun in the divot of a block. Above the pit, barrels with mysterious contents were perched on the rim.

Eighty men and women grabbed the bow from handles along its back. Anand joined Hopkut and Dwan at one end as they started a chant. The men and women rocked back and forth in what became a dance. As the speed of the chant increased, so did their movement. Suddenly, a white and fragrant vapor arose from the divot.

"What is that?" Anand asked. "It smells good!"

"Smoke," Dwan replied. "No questions, we can't stop now."

As the smoke increased, Hopkut and several others left the line and forked shredded hay on the smoke's source. The hay caught the smoke and its edges glowed with a brilliant orange that spread to the bottom of the woodpile. Men and women ran over and waved fans of green leaves that spread the glow deeper. The smoke built upon itself, then spread like fog. As the chips caught the glow, Hopkut stared and gauged the moment to call for escape.

"Now!" he shouted, and the fire builders ran to the ropes and climbed them in a quick but orderly fashion. Hopkut and Anand were the last to go. Anand was captivated by the strange beauty of erupting flames, which flickered like windblown leaves in autumn. He felt a heat that was painful as fire leapt out and licked the air around him. "Anand! We must go!" Hopkut shouted. He grabbed Anand and yanked him toward the ladder.

The fire spread to the wood on top and the smoke turned an ominous black. Hopkut, Anand, and the others ran to the pit's rim to push over the barrels. Anand was alarmed to see they were loaded with a great fortune of silver pyrite. Everyone ran from the pit and stood downwind. Only Anand remained behind, astonished that so much wealth was being thrown into this strange and beautiful thing called fire which appeared to be destroying it.

"Anand," screamed Dwan. "Get away from there! If you breathe that smoke, you could die!"

It was too late. The smoke was overwhelmingly sweet and Anand inhaled a sudden thickness of it, then felt suddenly ill and collapsed. He looked at Dwan whose eyes bulged in panic as he held his breath, ran back for Anand and threw him over his shoulder.

Blackness . . . . an empty, soundless void, a place of abject loneliness. Anand was a dead leaf floating on a cold wind. Who had ever felt like him? Who knew what it was like to be a stranger to everyone and at home nowhere? He sensed he had been almost dead for days but was finally returning to the living world. Suddenly, he saw something floating towards him, glowing in the dark: a scroll with the title *The Loose Doctrine of Dranveria*. He opened the tube and pulled out its thickness of pages, looked at them with awe as they lit up like fire and dispersed the darkness.

As light filled the void, Anand realized he was in a place of comfort, on a warm mattress, waking from the longest dream. Beside him were Dwan and his parents and another woman who peered in concern. She wore a tunic of bright pink over her red leggings. Anand tasted something bitter that had been squeezed in his mouth while he was unconscious.

"Drink as much water as you can," said the woman in pink.

Dwan raised Anand so he could suck his water. "What happened?" he asked.

"You breathed in the fumes," said Dwan.

"But it smelled sweet."

"We told you to run. The smoke was full of arsenic."

"Arsenic?"

"Poison. To all creatures."

"And who are you, Holiness?" he asked the woman as she looked through her bag with assorted jars. "I have never met a female priest."

"I am not a 'holiness.' I am the physician," said the woman.

"I don't know this word."

"She's a healer," said Dwan.

"Yes, but what temple are you from?" Anand asked. "Which god has healed me so that I might make an offering?"

"I am not from a temple," said the physician with

a chuckle, "and I bring no magic potions. I have given you medicine."

"Medicine? What is that?" asked Anand.

"You must be all right if you are back to asking questions," said Dwan, laughing. Anand noticed Dwan and Hopkut were dressed in tight clothing that was embedded with what looked like beeswax. Their hands were inside bulky mittens and around their necks was the type of breathing filter that Slopeish soldiers used when they fought the Seed Eaters.

"Why are you dressed like that?" Anand asked.

"To protect ourselves when we walk through the ashes today and gather the arsenic," said Dwan.

"I want to gather arsenic, too," Anand said.

"No," said the physician. "You are to lie in bed and recover. That is all."

"Perhaps we can bring you something to read," said Belja.

"I dreamt of reading *The Loose Doctrine*," said Anand. "I should like to read that."

The silence that followed had a majestic richness as Dwan's family looked to each other, then back at Anand.

"We would be ecstatic to bring you a copy of *The Loose Doctrine*," said Belja. "And paper and pen to copy it."

"You'll need to make your own red ink," said Dwan, "and add a couple of drops of your own blood."

"Blood? Why?" Anand asked.

"Because our history is a bloody one."

# CHAPTER 29

## THE LOOSE DOCTRINE

As the Dranverites' troopers rolled toward the latest incursion on their distant borders, Anand read and copied *The Loose Doctrine*. The preface of the book reminded the reader that the history of any people was slanted by the views of the writers and nothing was to be completely accepted as fact. The first chapter of the *Doctrine* apologized in its heading for being a long and monotonous list of the thousands of peoples known to have inhabited the area currently occupied by the Collective Nations. One tribe of people would establish a kingdom, a republic or a military state that was absorbed, chased off, or destroyed by invaders.

In the last five thousand years, converging nations attempted to share the land with borders that respected racial, religious, and linguistic divisions. The vast majority of conflicts were over territories and their resources, but their causes were attributed to demands on humans from their deities. The deities never stated their desires directly to the masses, but chose prophets to speak for them. Problems arose when different prophets of the same or different gods presented different messages. Some prophets called for peace and tolerance, some for holy wars, and some presented gibberish that was interpreted by others for their own purposes.

Most prophets sought converts for their religions, but some tribes hoarded their gods and neither proselytized nor forced conversions. These tribes saw their own races as descending from gods, or they believed they were chosen by a god to fulfill a mission. These racist tribes had periods of ascendancy in which they enslaved other peoples they deemed inferior. The slaves broke away to rally around their own prophet whose goal was to destroy the over-class and obtain their own slaves.

The last two thousand years of Dranverish history was little different than the previous. Waves of monotheistic religions swept over the land with conversions made at the points of swords. Implementations of a single idol were subverted by internal movements to resurrect old gods. Saints of one universal god were eventually worshipped as new gods. A single god or goddess eventually called for a different sexed counterpart or an alternate demon that ruled from a punishing netherworld. Tyrants came to power who banned all religions but ended up being worshipped themselves.

The Unholy War of Near-Annihilation ended with the Destruction of the Idols, which marked year one of the modern era. In the center of the Dranverites' plain was the Great Holy Rock, which had been warred over for ages. The Rock was a massive dome of pink quartz and its magnificence inspired religious awe. Five nations laid claim to it as the center of their faith.

An ascending power, the Koozhi Nation, believed the Rock was an egg laid by their Red Ant Goddess and at its center was their warrior-savior, Ebwum. A Koozhi prophet demanded the destruction of all temples and their idols on or near the Rock and then the destruction of the Rock itself. It was a massive labor that chiseled the Rock into glittering rubble in order to release the Third Coming of Ebwum and commence The Thousand Year Peace. No savior was inside the Rock, and instead of peace, a conflict was ignited that pitted all the nations against each other. Hundreds of millions died.

A council of interfaith clergy from the five nations convened during a truce to urge the re-forming of the Rock. They demanded that all who had stolen its shards and fragments return them to be pieced back together or face death. Others, including a coalition of scholars, wanted the Rock to remain destroyed so it could never inspire another war. They suggested its fragments be used in the creation of a five-sided Hall of Peace.

The demand for a Hall of Peace was clear. Rising up in all the lands was the idea that the gods were dead and it was pointless to worship them. Others posited the notion that the gods had abandoned mortals. Stronger still was the growing belief that there had never been any gods, and if they did exist, they did not intercede in the affairs of humans. The Koozhis' prophets had been wrong. So were those of the other religions who predicted the end of the world with the destruction of the Rock. The conclusion was accepted that all prophecies originated within men and women, not from a god.

As new conflicts threatened to break out, a Great Consortium gathered to create an edict. The following laws were enacted:

No one may kill another human under any circumstance other than in self-defense. All those who have killed must be removed from the fellowship of humans so they may never kill again.

All individuals must be held accountable for their actions. No one is allowed to take the defense of violating another to honor the requests of a god or gods or the creeds of his or her god or gods.

All men and women must be allowed to worship as they please. No one may force his religious beliefs on another or persecute a worshipper of different beliefs or persecute one who worships his god or gods in a different manner. The decision of those who choose not to worship must be respected.

No one may steal from, cheat, harm, or enslave another, especially when these actions are justified as being permitted by one people to do to another with the permission of a god or gods.

No man, woman, or child will be restricted to a permanent status or occupation because of the circumstances of his or her birth.

All men and women are not created as equals, but all must be treated equally.

**A**nand needed twenty-eight days to copy the book. He was devastated by its contents, excited by its vivid descriptions of wars, confused by its jumble of information. Dwan and the scholars watched Anand as he set down his pen and capped the ink-mixed-with-blood.

"You have finished, Anand-shmi," said Dwan.

"I have."

"And what do you think?" asked Babwott.

Anand paused. "I think I should like to become a citizen of your Collective Nations and join in your latest defensive effort."

"Not permissible. You are not trained as a soldier. And you must be inducted in a rite before becoming a full citizen."

"But I wish to help."

"Certainly. You can prepare food. Or bandages. There are many other things you can do, but for your own safety, you will not be allowed near the battlefields."

Though it filled him with dread, Anand knew exactly what he wanted to do. "Who will take care of the prisoners?" he asked.

# CHAPTER 30

## THE DEFENSIVE MEASURE

**A** few days later, Anand became a sworn citizen of the Collective Nations. He completed the rite before Dwan and his parents, Babwott and the Learned Ones. On a dais set under a blooming, blood-red poppy, it became his turn to read aloud the daily passage from *The Loose Doctrine*. He promised to abide by its laws and swore loyalty to its principles. Afterwards, he took his copy of the *Doctrine*, tore it to shreds, and then plunged it into a basin of water where its ink dissolved.

"No idol, book, word, place, or relic should ever be held sacred," he said. "Only human life is sacred."

Next, Dwan and his parents presented Anand with three deities he had selected to be made out of candy. They were Madricanth, Goddess Bee, and Goddess

Ant Queen. Anand took a mallet and smashed them into pieces. "Today you are a Dranverite," said Dwan.

The congregation stood and clapped and the candy was distributed. Afterwards was a feast and the opening of gifts. The first gift was a compact version of *The Loose Doctrine* that Anand could keep on his person along with a magnifying glass he could use to read its fine print.

The feast came to an early end when flying-scouts on locusts returned to camp with detailed reports of the invaders, who the Dranverites had taken to calling the Sand Tribe. Anand was given a printed agenda describing the invaders that came from a device that could manufacture as many copies as desired. He was amazed by the amount of information the Dranverites had already accumulated on the Sand Tribe without making contact.

**T**he assault on the Sand Tribe was nothing like the maneuvers on the Cajorite pioneers. Sand people were bizarre in appearance and fierce foot-warriors that herded ants too small to ride. The sand ants were half the size of men, but they were quick and could overwhelm insect or human prey with their poisonous stings. Like the humans who had domesticated them, they were covered in glue, then fine sand, which allowed them an effective camouflage. Opponents would wander into an ambush to see clusters of sand suddenly rise and hurl tethered spears that were jerked back to be hurled again.

The Dranverites had surprises of their own, though. On top of their red ants were hollow dummies stuffed into armor. The legs and arms of the dummies were filled with beetle maggots to give the appearance of moving limbs. The deception was only needed for a moment, for it roused the Sand Tribe and their ants into battle mode.

The Sand Tribe were facing the fake warriors when the Dranverites converged in overwhelming numbers on their rear. In less than sixty breaths, their blow-darts found every target. Anand was called in with others to gather the paralyzed. He marveled at the efficiency of the Dranverites, of the thoroughness of their plan. As he spaced the captives throughout the wagons, he looked at them with pity and wondered, who were these invaders? Were they forced to emigrate by cruel rulers? Maybe they were a band of criminals who had been expelled by a people as just as the Dranverites. Whoever they were, each and every one of them was suffering the Living Death.

Dwan, smelling the breath of a small girl, said, "Apparently they eat their own ants."

"And other humans," said Babwott, noticing that most of them wore necklaces of human teeth. "This loincloth is made of human leather."

Anand became less sympathetic when he learned they were cannibals, but he was impassioned about bringing relief to them on the trek back. With a piece of parchment, he ticked off the thirty days and showed the marks to the glazed eyes of the paralyzed. Each night he fell into bed ragged with exhaustion.

On the eighteenth evening, Dwan was in his own bed when he heard Anand enter the wagon, drop onto the mattress and moan.

"Will you spend all of your time with the captives, Anand? We have missed you. The scholars want to know when they can resume their exchanges."

Anand was silent. As tired as his limbs were, his mind was active.

"I swore to Madricanth I would massacre those responsible for sentencing me to the Living Death. It was thirty days, but it felt like thirty years."

"I know your agony," said Dwan.

"How could you?"

"I have suffered the Living Death, too. It is a part of every soldier's initiation—the worst time of my life."

Anand was silent for a moment. "But you knew that after thirty days you would have your limbs back and live. We suffered not knowing . . . not knowing how long this spell would last, or if we would become the dinners of cannibals."

Anand writhed as he recalled his torment. It was Dwan's turn to be silent.

"It is a horrible thing to do to anyone, but that is precisely why we do it."

"Why?"

"To put fear in invaders. This is how we have avoided wars with the outside for over five hundred years. The Slopeites will be very reluctant to wander north again. If they do, we will repeat the process until they stop coming."

"There must be an alternative," Anand said.

"There is. We could have killed you."

Anand was aware of the crickets chirping. Their noise cut his ear like a blade.

"Dwan, I've been told that at some point I will be sent back. When?"

"You can go back at any time. We would prefer you went back as our informed emissary."

"And to tell what to whom?"

"Two things. First, you will warn their leaders not to bring themselves or their tree destroying ants into our country. Slopeites, like all ants and humans, have what we call a territorial instinct, an innate desire to expand, to conquer new territory. Ants cannot be dissuaded from their instincts, but humans can be. The Slopeites must accept that they cannot expand here. Nor should they do it elsewhere."

"And the second?" asked Anand.

"The second mission is more complex. We wish for you to spread the ideas of *The Loose Doctrine*."

"They will not consider your ideas. The Slopeites are certain they are the only civilized nation on the Sand. And they do not read."

"Very likely some do. Perhaps the priests . . . in secret. Every people, including your Britasytes, believe they are a divine race. Most believe their country is at the center of the world . . . until they are conquered."

Anand had heard this all his life from both his tribes. "And what if the Slopeites spurn your advance?" he asked. "As a half-breed, I would be killed before they allowed me an audience with priests and royals."

"We can provide you with some impressive trappings, some well-trained troopers, and gifts to make them receptive. More importantly, we hope you will bring our message, not just to the enslavers, but to the slaves. It is among them that our ideas will take deepest root."

Anand shook his head. "Unless the priests decree it, no one will listen."

"We want them to stop listening to priests."

Dwan got up and looked at Anand before he covered the torches for the night. "We gain much from contact with other civilizations, but we do not sustain relations with any nation that abuses its people. If you choose not to return to Cajoria, we will send another emissary once we have mastered your language. Good night, Anand."

As exhausted as he was, Anand could not sleep that night as fantasies raced in his mind. He saw himself on a finely appointed riding ant, surrounded by a dazzling entourage. His brown skin would be concealed by a fine gold-powder and his perfume would waft through the royal chambers. Trellana, Sahdrin, and Queen Polexima would extend the most glorious of welcomes . . . to the son of a roach woman and a shit-scraper!

# CHAPTER 31

## MASTERING THE LOCUST

When Anand looked in a mirror, he was in mild disbelief that the strong and confident man looking back at him was none other than himself. He had always been the best-fed boy in the midden and in the last months, he had eaten nutritious foods that further aided his growth. His voice had deepened, his beard grew thick, and he never again assumed the stoop of the low castes but stood with a fierceness that accentuated the width of his back and the narrow contours of his waist. In the fashion of the Dranverish military, he wore tight clothing that accentuated his musculature. An unexpected consequence of wearing body paint for months was that his skin had become lighter.

No one in Cajoria would ever recognize this tall and imposing figure as one of their own.

Anand was grateful to the Dranverites for showing him a thousand other worlds as well as a world of possibilities—and for that he was committed to the scholars in their passion to document his knowledge. But he knew, like others who chose soldiering as a career, that he had a lust for battle that went beyond reading about it in books. He yearned for the chance to fulfill the vision he had seen in a dream: to fight atop an ant for glory. He spent more and more time with troopers and imitated their ways but when he inquired as to how to become one of them, he was always politely discouraged.

"Am I not a Dranverish citizen?" he asked one night at the evening meal.

"You are," said Belja as Anand unrolled pages from a scroll.

"And is it not the right of every Dranverish citizen of sound mind and body to serve in its military?" asked Anand while reading exactly that from a page. Dwan grinned and pinched him under the table.

Belja was quiet. "How old are you?" she asked.

"I have seen eighteen summers," Anand lied.

Belja was lost in thought as she sucked lymph out of a spider leg. "I shall speak with the Learned Elders," she said.

The following day Anand struck a deal that promised all his evenings to the inquiries of the scholars in return for permission to train as a trooper in the Dranverish National Defense during the day. With Belja's reluctance, he was sent to a training camp atop the towering rock-formation known as Rainbow Lichens.

Anand eased into military life. He found its rigors exciting and its austerities comforting. He was quick to learn the crossbow and the blowgun and was adept at operating the Dranverites' war devices. Though he was good with a sword and shield, he was frustrated by challengers in the mock battles who had the privilege of training with them since childhood. He gorged on books of history, ethics, and comparative religions in addition to the required text, *The Dissection of Magic and Other Superstitions.* But military science was his favorite subject. He marveled at the Dranverites' creative responses to each new enemy, their absorption of superior techniques and their dedication to minimizing casualties on both sides.

A few moons later, Belja was reviewing the new graduates. "I'm not surprised to see you here—well ahead of schedule," she said to Anand.

"I didn't have to undergo the Living Death again," he said. She smiled, then informed the fledgling troops of a recent conflict in the east. She was reluctant to send Anand into battle, but it was not the Dranverish way to renege on agreements. The following day Anand went off to his first armed conflict in a new suit of armor with sharpened weapons.

A fortnight later, Anand felt his hands shaking

as he steered his ant into formation. Fear gave way
to excitement as the troopers reached the troubled
area. The campaign was against a clan of raiding
Aphid Milkers who wandered down from their thorn
shrubs. The Milkers had been stealing goods and
food and abducting women from Dranverish pond
settlements while their men were in floating ves-
sels, hunting the strange, water-breathing creatures
known as fish.

A locust-scout alerted the troopers to an imminent
attack by the Aphid Milkers at a settlement farther
north where fishermen had returned to shore with a
catch of the limbless, oily creatures. Anand's division
was called forward and they rode their ants under
pickerel weeds towards the pond's edge. Anand's captain signaled them to wait in the shade where they remained hidden but able to view the fishermen. They
were gutting the fish and scraping the hard, translucent plates from their skins which sent up a strong
smell in the air, a lure for the Aphid Milkers.

Anand's heart was thumping when he saw the
Milkers emerge by the hundreds from out of the
rushes. The raiders had no mounts, but they wielded
bows and arrows as well as maces and slings, and all
of them made a trilling howl that pierced the ear.
They were abruptly silenced when the "fishermen"
raised up blowguns from around their chests and targeted them with darts. Half of the raiders fell to the
ground while those in the back shot arrows which
lodged in the fishermen's hidden armor. The raiders

attempted to turn and retreat when they encountered mounted Dranverish troopers weaving through the rushes. The raiders ran south towards Anand and his division who rushed to attack. Anand urged his ant forward and used his shield to collect the first of an enemy's flying arrows. He smiled to himself. At last, a battle!

As he had always suspected, war was what he was created for. His joy rose to higher heights each time the darts of his blowgun found their targets. He no longer considered his enemies' torment as they fell to the Living Death, but lusted to bring down more. The standing Milkers were weaving through the pickerel weeds and back to their thorn bushes. Anand's division pursued the last of them when they reached a thorn shrub and crawled up the ladders on its stems. His captain raised her helmet and twisted it as a signal to make a vertical pursuit. Anand hooked himself to the horn of his ant's saddle as she went vertical to chase the climbing raiders.

Anand targeted the man furiously climbing above him who dropped from the ladder and fell to the ground. When the last of the raiders had been subdued, Anand went to retrieve his target and saw he had downed what must be the tribal elder. He wore a spectacular jewel on his forehead, a purple amethyst with an inner cloud of white quartz. Anand looked both ways, pulled off the jewel and stuffed it in his backsack. One day, he would present it to Daveena. As duty bound him, he examined the man to make sure he was positioned to breathe freely and not folded upon his limbs.

The man was not breathing at all. When Anand lifted him, his head fell too far back. Upon further examination, it was clear that his neck had crashed on the edge of a sharp pebble that snapped it in a fatal break.

Anand was ashamed of his previous joys. Here was the real face of war, the corpse of a man who was a chieftain. He was a raider but he was also someone's son or brother, father or husband, and those who survived him would live without him all their days.

On the return from the campaign, Anand joined Dwan and the scholars in their wagon. Though they exonerated him of any misconduct, they seemed strangely unsympathetic to his misgivings about the dead chieftain. Later, they were short in their answers to his questions and initiated no conversation. Unused to their silence, Anand concentrated on his books or stared out of the wagon at the scrubby landscape.

As the Dranverites finished their defensive measure, so did the Slopeites complete their wars on their neighbors. Caught by surprise, the Seed Eaters' Emperor ordered the abandonment of the mound of Xixict. Its inhabitants fled into the country of the Stink Ant people, displacing its inhabitants who took refuge in Dranveria's Buffer Zone, drawing the Dranverites into the conflict.

In the West, the Carpenter People in their border colony of Eth were even more vulnerable to a sudden attack. The Slopeites did not want their land, which had few leafy trees and was seen as unfit. What they brought back were thousands of men for a blood sacrifice to Mantis. They sent a demand to Emperor Sinsora in his tree stump capital of Gemurfa that a thousand of his subjects should be sent as human tribute each new moon to be sacrificed to the Slopeish gods. Sinsora agreed, but consulted his priests of the Beetle God to divine the time of retaliation. One priest tore out his eyeball, and as he staggered in pain screamed, "We must wait for an enemy to bring us victory."

Two moons after their return to the City of Peace, Dwan woke Anand and said they were to bathe and dress in proper attire for a meeting with the People's Agent, the elected official who presided over all Dranverites. They would also meet the Council of Rulers, the five men and women who governed the united city-states. Anand was painted in yellow-and-black bee stripes and Dwan was shimmering in an iridescent blue-and-white cloud pattern. Both were wearing new cloaks and boots and the uniforms of government service.

Anand was nervous to meet the Council and the People's Agent at the Great Hall of Peace, a building erected from shattered pieces of what had been the Holy Rock. Flecks of pink quartz were used as currency in all nations, but this was a building made from blocks of it. Its vaulted ceiling was as high as a berry bush and its interior was flooded with an unreal and rosy light.

Anand had expected to meet with six men and women that day, but when he walked into the Chamber of the Peoples, thousands rose to their feet to applaud, and it poured into his ears like a pleasant rain shower.

"They're clapping for me!" Anand said to Dwan, who coyly smiled as they headed for the dais. He watched as Anand waved.

"Actually, Anand, they're applauding me," Dwan shouted in Anand's ear.

"Oh." Anand felt himself blush under his paint. "Why are they applauding you?"

"Because I'm the one who picked you."

"Who are all these people?"

"The elected representatives of every population center of Dranveria."

Anand and Dwan sat behind cones to amplify their voices. Across from them on a raised platform were the Council and the People's Agent. Bound to her chin with a strap was a ceremonial beard of the five colors of the collective nations. Just below the platform were scribes at desks who recorded every word.

"Welcome, Dwan, beloved citizen and trooper of Dranveria," shouted the People's Agent. "Welcome, Anand, son of two tribes and new citizen and trooper."

"Thank you," Anand said.

The People's Agent left her chair and hobbled on a cane to Anand. She bowed her head to him, then spoke into an amplifying cone.

"We thank *you*, Anand. We have learned much from you about the Slopeish peoples. We are greatly indebted, for after life itself, we hold knowledge to be the most precious of things."

"I have learned far more from the Dranverites. I have been given new eyes and seen a world of possibilities."

The Agent nodded approvingly. "Anand . . . we understand that the Cajorites treated you poorly. Do you wish ill on them? On all the Slopeites?"

Anand grimaced. "I wish knowledge upon them, a complete reformation. Among the Slopeites are my father, who I love . . . and one friend."

"Your other tribe is the Britasytes, of whom we know much already. Is it not true that the Britasytes are allowed to steal from those they believe are not descended from their own god, Madricanth? That Britasytes who steal from Slopeites and other tribes are celebrated for their crimes?"

Anand was silent for a moment. "That is true," he said, "but if you knew the Slopeites, their cruelty, their thirst for blood . . ."

"Would Britasytes be allowed to steal from *us*? We have only one account of Britasyte life. We wish to verify our knowledge."

Anand nodded his head. "We . . . we . . ."

He stopped to clear his throat, aware of a heavy silence.

"We Britasytes believe our god permits us to take from his lesser creations."

"Lesser creations. Indeed."

Everyone laughed but it was more of a murmuring snigger. The Agent held up her hand to quiet them. A page appeared with a plain box and presented it to Anand. He opened it to see the tourmaline he had taken from the Aphid Milkers' chieftain.

"Do you recognize this?" asked the Agent, getting closer to Anand. He looked into her eyes, cloudy with age, and realized she had little sight. Anand looked at Dwan. He did not avert Anand's gaze, but stared steadfast.

"Yes."

"You stole this?" asked the Agent.

"I . . . I didn't take it for myself."

"You stole it for another?"

"Yes."

"But you did steal it."

"Yes."

The Agent hobbled back to her chair, which took some time. Whispers rolled through the chamber.

"Stealing is never allowed in the Dranverite nations," she shouted through the cone. "How can we expect moral behavior from our neighbors if we engage in transgressions against them? Until further notice, you are suspended from all duties in the National Defense. Do you wish to make amends?"

Anand gulped. He felt the eyes around him like a soaked blanket on a cold evening. "I do," he choked out.

"How will you do so?"

"I will return what I stole."

"That's a good start. We have initiated something like a treaty with the inhabitants of the Thorn Shrub People, also known as Aphid Milkers, who are expecting the tourmaline's return. They remain quite hostile to others outside their tribe and at this time are uninterested in an exchange of ideas. We have invited one of them to stay with us, as we invited you, in hopes of learning more about his people and their language."

The Agent looked hard at Anand, coming closer to look into his face. She lifted a stemmed panel of quartz to her eyes and stared as if she might see inside him.

"We have invested a great deal of time and effort in you, Anand, to be our emissary to the Slope. Not all of us are convinced you are ready for this mission—or might ever be."

"I have made a mistake," Anand said. "I have violated the code of the Defense as well as the laws of Dranveria. I have tried to excuse my poor behavior as a result of my tribal indoctrination."

"Fine words," said the People's Agent. "We want to put our trust in you, Anand. The peace and safety of nations are at stake in this mission, as well as the potential uplift of millions. Are you the one we can trust to fulfill this objective?"

"I am," said Anand. "It is my only mission. It would be the greatest fulfillment of my life."

Anand had not known how true that was until he had said it.

"Our message may ignite turmoil among the Slopeish masses. It may do little or nothing to relieve them from the tyranny you have described. Is this still a message you want to deliver?"

"Yes," Anand said. "A thousand times, yes."

She paused and fingered her beard.

"It will not be a mission without danger. You could lose your life."

"I would gladly risk my life to liberate the Slope from suffering and darkness."

She was quiet a moment before speaking. She turned to the Council who were nodding.

"Before you return, we recommend that you learn all you can about the ranching of leaf-cutter ants. From what you have told us of the Slopeites, their priests and royals wrap this discipline in a veil of superstitions to preserve their own powers."

"Gladly, yes," said Anand. "I will learn all I can. I have one request to make before returning the tourmaline."

"Yes?"

"I wish to become a locust pilot."

Everyone laughed. Dwan tried not to.

"My dear sir, you have been suspended from military duty. You will not learn to ride a locust."

"Not at government expense," said Anand. "But there are private pilots, yes?"

"There are."

"I do have some wage credits from my time in the Defense. I'd like to spend them learning to fly. And for my first lesson, I wish to take the tourmaline back to the Thorn Shrub people. I could do this . . . tomorrow."

The Agent looked to the Council, who nodded their agreement.

"Very well, Anand," said the agent with the slightest chortle in her voice. "Rise, citizens. This is Anand, bearer of *The Loose Doctrine of Dranveria* to the people of the Slope."

Thousands of representatives in red costumes of every settlement in Dranveria rose to their feet to applaud. Anand looked at Dwan, who was smiling again for the first time since the stealing of the tourmaline.

"This time they're applauding *me*," Anand said.

"And so do I," said Dwan and clapped.

**T**he following morning Anand hitched a ride on a red hunter ant who brought him close to a private airfield on the edge of the City of Peace. He checked his backsack to make sure that the stiff paper certificates that amounted to eight hundred wage credits were still inside it with the tourmaline. Surrounding a paved clearing were rows of roomy cages filled with molting nymphs. Next to these were crowded cages where adult insects transformed from green grasshoppers to blue locusts with shorter antennae and a greater capacity for flight and steering.

"That will be four hundred," said Lentop, the airfield's operator, a man of about fifty summers with a handsome but weathered face. His complex wrinkles reminded Anand of the map he had brought with him and its coordinates. As Anand surrendered four of the certificates, he pondered all the good food and drink he might have bought with them. He had known feasting . . . but he had never known flight.

*I can do without for this chance.*

"Is this your first time on a flyer?" Lentop asked, as they entered a smaller launching cage where a locust had been fitted with reins. Anand was taken with the insect's startling blue eyes and its splendidly mottled body.

"Yes," said Anand. "But I know how to ride two kinds of ants as well as grass roaches."

"That won't help you much here. Locusts are much trickier to ride but much more fun. I do need you to sign something."

"Yes?" said Anand as he was handed a stiff sheet of paper and a stylus.

"Signing this means you acknowledge the dangers of locust flight and hold no one other than yourself accountable for what may happen to you."

"What might happen?"

"You could fall. You could get thrown. If you are high enough and land on the wrong surface, you could plummet to your death. If you do get thrown, it might take you days to walk home if you can't hitch a ride in a trunk-trail. Other than surveillance, this is why locusts have little use in our military."

"Were you in the Defense, sir?"

"Yes. All our pilots served in the military."

Anand was using the stylus to scratch his name into the bottom of the sheet when he heard the smaller of the two gates swing open.

"Your teacher's here," said Lentop. "My daughter, Jidla."

Anand turned and his breath was stolen from him. Jidla walked slowly towards him, wrapped tight in pilot's gear. She was terrifyingly beautiful with round, voluptuous thighs and the tiniest waist. Her lips were thick and fruit-juicy and parted into an intoxicating smile that revealed sparkling teeth. As skin paint she wore deep violet with spatters of yellow stars. *Why am I afraid of her?* Anand asked himself.

"Let's get you some gear," she said, pointing Anand towards the back wall where she helped him select the hooked boots, paneled suit, tight cap, mouth prod, and the scented gloves he would need.

"This is . . . where . . . where we are . . . going," he managed to get out of his mouth as he handed her the map and its circled destination. She glanced at the map as he dressed but he was sure she was looking over it to study his naked body. When he was dressed, he turned to face her and she looked approvingly at him, smiling as she cocked her head.

"You won't be able to dismount until noon," she said. "Are you ready?"

"I am," Anand responded, trying not to stare. Her eyelashes looked long enough to tickle his own.

"You are just to ride today, to observe and ask questions," she said.

"Yes," said Anand. He was lost in her blue eyes, which seemed like pieces of the sky they would be flying in. Her beauty was so intense it was painful, but he did not want to stop the pain. As she crawled up the leg of the locust, he looked up at the muscles of her haunches as they shifted in a way that made his heart beat even faster. He was more excited than the first time he had seen Daveena, but with this woman he had no sense of an unalterable destiny.

*Daveena!* Inside him now was a pain that he *did* want to end. He longed for Daveena, felt hurt for her, was deeply worried for her well-being. He never imagined he could be drawn to someone else until this elegant creature walked into a cage and cast the spell of a sorceress. When Anand climbed onto the saddle, he hooked a short rope from his chest plate to Jidla's armor.

"Grab my waist," she commanded. It was the one part of her that was naked and her skin was as warm as a sun-bathed rock. Anand marveled that he could ring her waist with his hands. The connection between them was a radiant magic she acknowledged by smiling coyly over her shoulder.

Lentop opened the larger gate and the locust leapt

out and up. Anand lost his breath, felt punched in the stomach, and his vision darkened as his head swelled with blood. As the locust climbed up air, his discomfort was displaced by a pounding excitement and an uncontrollable need to laugh.

The sun poked through patchy clouds and lent a dramatic illumination to the ground. Jidla blocked Anand's front view, and the locust's wings blurred his view from below. What he could see confused his senses and unspooled before him like a music for the eyes or a streaming drink of a hundred thousand flavors.

Stopping was a more difficult process than taking off. Jidla released the antennae and cupped the locust's eyes with her hands when she sighted the thorn bush dwellings of the Aphid Milkers. Sometimes locusts suddenly plummeted and fell on their sides before righting themselves. This time the landing was a good one on a large patch of sand the Milkers had stained with orange leaf dye as the area to leave their sacred jewel. Anand looked around, fearful of an ambush, then set down the tourmaline before remounting.

The return ride was less fluid. The locust made several stops to rest and landed on plants at an angle that was not comfortable for Anand or Jidla. She prodded the flyer by rubbing the scents of her thumbs on the stumps of the antennae. The locust responded with a combination of jumps and short glides that were jarring. As it grew dark, the locust was even less cooperative. They were nearing the capital when the locust landed on a large and deep-throated gloxinia flower. The flower was a rich red and its surface was a seductive velvet that demanded exploration.

"I'm afraid we have to dismount and let this locust go," Jidla said, holding Anand's gaze too long. They removed the reins, and dropped to the flower. The locust buzzed off.

"What was the problem?" Anand asked as he stood and found his balance on the flower bobbing in a breeze. Even as his limbs ached, he was fixated by this woman's mouth and the way her fitted armor accentuated the winsome slope of her hips.

"It's night too soon because of the clouds. Locusts don't fly in the dark. Besides, I've been feeling something of yours in the small of my back all day," she said, scolding. Anand felt hot under his paint.

"I . . . I'm sorry . . . I . . ."

"Don't apologize. It's just that I'd prefer to feel it someplace else."

"I'm betrothed to another," he said.

"But you are not yet married."

"I have never done it," he finally admitted.

"Then I shall have to give you those lessons as well."

"But . . . my betrothed . . ."

"Your betrothed wouldn't want an inexperienced man, would she? Don't you owe it to her to be the best of all lovers?" Jidla pulled off her cap and revealed a mass of thick, ginger hair. Anand felt drunk as he watched her shake it out, then pull it behind her ears as she thrust out her breasts.

"If you are at all hesitant, Anand, then, no—we should not do this. Forcing anyone into sex is against everything we Dranverites stand for."

He looked at her and tried to slow his deep, rapid breaths.

"I want to," he said.

"Are you sure?"

"Right now it's all I want."

"I can see that."

They crawled to the satiny throat of the flower. He felt a rush of heat as his hands started at her back, then slid down to grasp what had bewitched him all day. Their mouths pressed in a tongue-clash. He watched as she pulled away, removed her armor, then reached inside one of its panels for a capsule of pollen from the satchu flower.

"What's that?" he asked.

"A contraceptive," she said, smearing it inside her. "I've no wish to bear your child. Would you like to take your suit off?" she asked.

"Yes," he said. His tumescence had made it painful to wear anything about his middle.

That day, Anand had questioned if there was anything better than flying. Inside the gloxinia, he had found his answer. With Jidla in his arms, he relaxed and told her of his coming mission, of his worries, and all about Daveena — which did not rouse anything like jealousy.

"I'll have to tell her about you," he said. "That will be difficult for her."

"I hope not," Jidla said. "In Dranveria, we honor the ideal of fidelity between one man and one woman. But we recognize this is impossible for most people. Perhaps your Daveena is involved with someone on a temporary basis. Maybe *you* will need to forgive *her*."

"Never! It would mean her ruin!"

"So it's like that, is it? Something tells me your roach tribe allows a man more than one wife, but not the other way around."

"Well, of course! For one thing it's a man's obligation to marry his brother's widow . . . if they both desire."

"But a woman would not marry her dead sister's husband, I would guess, and have two men."

"Two women with one man would be impossible! They would kill each other!"

Jidla chuckled to herself. "You strike me as an extraordinary young man, but you've got so much to learn."

Anand was quiet a moment, savoring the warmth between them as they nestled. "Jidla, do you think they'll let me fly a locust back to Cajoria?"

"I don't think so," she said.

"Why not? It would make the best impression—arriving on a bright blue locust, in a magnificent robe of deep red, with a satchel full of matchless gifts for the royals."

"Anand, I'm sure they have very different ideas

about your return," she said, her fingers tracing the sweaty trail of hair that started at his navel. "It will be far more spectacular than anything you have ever imagined."

And before Anand could start his reimagining, they entered into a second vigorous coupling.

# CHAPTER 32

## A MOST UNWELCOME SURPRISE

**M**oons after the pioneers' repulsion from Dranveria, Sahdrin's ailments had grown worse. He had withdrawn from public life and was given the title of "King Father" so that Maleps and Trellana could rule. Trellana was swelling in two ways: with a heightened arrogance as queen of the Slope's most powerful mound and with her first pregnancy. About the mound flew lacy banners that reminded the people of the imminent arrival. While the upper castes indulged in feasts celebrating the next generation of royals, the lower castes prepared for a winter famine.

Trellana's greatest discomfort came with the holding of her water before her visits to the ant queen. It had become even more difficult now that she was urinating for the three or four others inside her. Pious Frinbo accompanied her most days as Dolgeeno was often at Venaris where he waged a campaign to succeed the faltering Pious Ennochenzo as the Ultimate Holiness of the Great Slope.

It was a rainy autumn morning when Trellana appeared before the ant queen and the drop she left behind was larger than usual. At last, her water had broken. After laboring for three days, Trellana gave birth to two boys and two girls. The girls did not survive the sting. The first boy to appear was named Sahdrin the 87th. A celebration was arranged with a spectacle at the stadium for the people. Many far-flung visitors were planning to attend.

Some of them were not invited.

Trellana and Maleps sat on the Mushroom Thrones with their new sons as they watched the entertainments at the stadium. Recently returned from Venaris, Dolgeeno sat next to them, fingering a garnet necklace with matching ear bobs which Trellana regarded with an envious appreciation.

Set on the arena were towering flesh-eating plants growing in basins. As priests uttered prayers to Mantis, the sides of a great cage were pulled apart to reveal the thousand humans sent as tribute. Ants swarmed over the field to attack the Carpenter people stinking of beetles. They were simpletons, the weak, and the old, and some were likely criminals or captives from the Carpenter's western enemy, the League of Velvet Ant Peoples.

The weak and old were destroyed in a moment. Those who were able tried to climb up the flesh-eating plants but the ants followed after them. The first ants to reach the top slashed at the victims until they bled to death. Other sacrifices jumped and fell in the throats of the flesh-eating plants causing their spiky lids to snap shut around them. The victims screamed as the acid made their skin a sizzling pulp before they bled to death.

As usual, Cajorite criminals who had defied caste restrictions were hauled out as the second of the blood diversions. Their crimes were being described when a distant buzzing grew in volume and drowned out the voices. The buzzing grew louder and panic spread when the people looked up and saw a spiral of flying insects.

The spiral lowered over the stadium like a great wheel. A sudden rain of something pelted the Cajorites, and they realized it was wrapped aphid-taffy in all the colors of the rainbow. The people were stunned to see that the insects were mottled blue locusts and seated at the back of their heads were human riders with rippling capes. As the locusts continued to spiral downward, their pilots released powders of brilliant hues. A few Cajorites dared to ooh and ahh but the priests shook with fright. Was it gods or demons descending? Should they run or fall to their knees?

Unable to take their eyes from the locusts, the Cajorites did not realize a procession had entered the open side of the stadium in the north. Weevils hauled festive coach-sleds covered in petals of chrysanthemums, the last flowers before winter.

Soldiers grouped for an attack when the riders of the weevils unrolled white banners with paintings of a downward palm, a signal of peaceful approach. Leaf-cutters ran to the weevils and human invaders to antennate them. The ants crawled onto the foreign coaches, and strangely, identified all the invaders as kin. Instead of attacking the invaders, the ants escorted them in.

Those who had been pioneers in Dranveria were in sudden fear at the sight of the weevils and the humans on top of them, for the latter were suited in red armor. Very prominent in the invaders' hands were Dranverish blowguns held at the ready.

"Dranverites!" went up the cry as the masses broke castes and scattered to escape. The weevils and coaches continued a slow, majestic approach as chaos reigned in the stadium. Cajorite arrows flew at the invaders and skidded off or broke on their impenetrable red armor.

"You are not under attack!" shouted a boy-man through a grand amplifying-cone as he raised his visor. "We are friends come to offer this humble gift." He was seated on a great and golden throne atop the largest coach. His voice was nearly lost in the panic, but the hatch of his coach opened to reveal a giant, pink face. An enormous idol rolled out with a smiling visage familiar to all Cajorites: Grasshopper, God of Prosperity, in the crouching position. The statue was studded with more gold pyrite than had ever been amassed in Cajoria with a face rendered in pink quartz. The crowd was silenced and knelt to the idol loved by all. Those who were running returned to worship.

The man-boy walked to the middle of the arena on stilts, trailing a garment with twenty trains in different shades of red. General Batra raised the back of his hand to the military as a signal to relax their bows.

Anand turned on his stilts in the direction of Queen Trellana and King Maleps and bowed to them. "Greetings, Your Majesties," he shouted, "from the Dranverite Collective Nations and United Peoples. We beg your forgiveness for this intrusion and request an audience."

After some time, Trellana and Maleps descended from their thrones and conferred with Dolgeeno and Batra. Nothing like this had happened in centuries—members of an alien nation had intruded and deflected an ant attack!

Anand waited on the sand, shifting on his stilts, determined to calm his nerves. He reminded himself that if the Cajorites renewed their attack, he was backed up by thousands who were well-stocked with darts and other weapons. In deference to the Slopeites, he wore a bright yellow miter of grasshopper chitin, and around his neck was a spectacular amulet of the purest turquoise. Batra broke from the others to approach.

"What do you want?" the general asked, looking up at Anand, his fingers near his sword as he jutted his cube-shaped chin.

"Peace," said Anand with a slight bow, "and some contact between our governments. We extend our sincerest apologies for the incident of a year ago. This is what we describe as a diplomatic mission. All of the most advanced nations on our borders have engaged in such missions for generations."

Batra snorted. "Are you suggesting we are anything less than the most advanced nation? This is Cajoria, grandest mound of the Great and Holy Slope."

"General, respectfully, I submit that it is time your advanced nation and ours create some channel in order to avoid further incidents."

Anand attempted to use terms and phrasings of the upper castes and was imitating the accent of Dranverites, since his low-caste inflections would render him as Batra's inferior.

"Are you a defector from the Slope?" Batra asked.

"I am not," said Anand. *I am a member of the Britasyte Roach Tribe,* he thought. "We would be most honored if you and your Royal Majesties would join us for a repast of Dranverish delicacies," Anand said. "We should also like to present them with some gifts."

"From which caste are you descended? We do not wish to expose ourselves to the polluted."

"In Dranveria, we have no castes," said Anand who tried not to smile when Batra flinched. The general left again and conferred with the priests and royals.

The crowd was noisy with rumors and speculations as Batra returned. "It would be unseemly for our royalty to visit your camp," he said. "If you wish an audience, you will be welcome to dine with us in the royal chambers. We will retrieve you at the appropriate time."

"We are most grateful," said Anand, nodding his head low enough to conceal his grin. "My religion does not permit me to enjoy the fabled dishes of Cajoria. You will forgive me if I bring my own food and plates?"

Anand guessed from Batra's silence that he had foiled his plot to poison him.

"Perhaps we should forgo dining. If you will remove your party from the arena, we need to continue with our festivities today."

"Pardon our intrusion," Anand said, glad to part. He had no desire to watch the execution of the caste-defilers. Part of him had hoped that the Cajorites would rebuff him. Then he could leave after making a blunt warning about further intrusions into the Buffer Zone.

Before the Dranverites backed away, Anand looked up into the far expanses of the stadium, searching for his father and Terraclon. How soon before he could contact his family?

Late in the afternoon, a Cajorite soldier arrived

at the Dranverites' camp to inquire of the number attending the impromptu reception that evening. Anand and forty men and women he called his "retainers" would attend, but they were *gottallamos*, the most skilled troopers in Dranveria. If needed, they could use their hidden weapons to subdue thousands. The gottallamos' clothing was imperceptible as armor, but it was lined with layers of the thickest wasp-chitin and spider-web cladding. Each gottallamo possessed astonishing reflexes and they were as adept with their feet as they were with their hands.

Cajorite soldiers brought a train of forty-one undecorated ants to Anand, which he mounted with the gottallamos. The ant train proceeded up what was the occupied side of the mound, the side that was sunny during the day. The Cajorites wanted the barbarians to see all their inhabitants, regardless of the masses' poverty. Anand was diverted past the shameful midden, but he could see the vague shadows of its refuse peaks in the moonlight. *"Mother, Father, I will see you soon,"* he thought as the ants crawled toward the peak.

The journey through so many squalid dwellings was astonishingly ugly and distressed Anand as it never had before. He knew that inside each flimsy shelter was an enormous family starving for food, aching with fatigue, itching with mites and deprived of light. As he looked up the dark mound, he saw the first faint torches in the merchants' windows and realized how little the Slopeites knew about illuminating the night, even for their richer subjects. The lights were only somewhat brighter as they passed the homes of the soldiers and priests.

As he neared the top of the mound, Anand remembered being a boy in Cajoria who ached with curiosity to see how the royals lived. At long last, he would enter one of their palaces and see for himself if their splendors fulfilled the fables. His depression lifted when he realized he would engage in deception against the people he hated most. He was still deciding on what to give as his name.

The ant train pulled into a side tunnel and proceeded in weak light to a chamber that Anand knew was not the Hall of Royal Reception. He was being taken to the lesser Chamber of Mercantilism.

Before they entered, several of the gottallamos helped Anand moisten his outer cape with a clear solution that ignited the phosphorous dyes of its embroidery. The gottallamos then pulled themselves through the portal to the chamber, tugging sacks in after them. They lined up in two columns and placed hands over their hearts as Anand pulled himself in and stood. He proceeded toward the thrones, wrapped in his robes of glowing tapestries. The luminous threads of silk outlined skillful depictions of the Hall of Peace, Rainbow Lichens, and other marvels of Dranveria.

At the end of the voluminous room were Trellana and Maleps, seated atop a platform with a hundred and twenty-seven steps, one for each of the mound's different castes. Anand could see that his robes had shocked the king and queen, disturbed Batra, and sickened Dolgeeno with envy. The Cajorite guards who stood on the steps with readied swords stared in disbelief. Anand knew his miraculous garb reminded all in the chamber that the visitors were from a place of far more powerful magic.

"King Maleps and Queen Trellana, we offer these humble gifts," said Anand, who bowed his head, not his body.

"Do you not kneel before royalty?" scolded Dolgeeno.

"It is not our custom," said Anand. He bowed his head again.

"You know our names, but we do not know yours," said Trellana.

"My name is Gwinthuli Hebeth-uk," Anand said with a smile. In Dranverish, "gwinthuli hebeth-uk" meant "lick my testicles." In the corner of his eye, Anand saw the gottallamos shifting uneasily, stifling their responses. When Anand ordered them, each emptied his or her sack, each of which contained one magnificent opal, the most desired of all gemstones. The Cajorite royals leaned from their chairs in open awe.

"If we had more illumination, you would see that each opal was selected for the brilliance of its star," said Anand.

"Are you saying we do not have enough light?" asked Maleps.

Anand was used to the Dranverites' plentiful indoor lighting. He had not realized the Cajorites had gone to extremes to impress him.

"Certainly not. We are grateful to find such a wealth of torches. I am saying that one needs the glory of the sun to truly appreciate an opal."

"Yes," said Trellana. "Sun. Do your people worship Lord Sun?" she asked.

"They are free to worship any god of their choosing."

"Do they know of Goddess Ant Queen and Goddess Mantis and Lord Grasshopper?" asked Dolgeeno.

"We are aware of your entire pantheon. I should like to tell you one thing about my people and our ways. We do not consider it respectful to inquire too deeply of an individual's religious beliefs . . . or lack thereof."

"Religious *beliefs*?" snarled Dolgeeno. "It is not a matter of beliefs. It is a matter of whether a man fulfills his duty to the One Holy Truth."

"Priest, on that point we shall have to disagree. We are a collective of many diverse nations and even more diverse peoples. Though all Dranverites are bound to the same civil code, each is allowed his own religion."

"Ridiculous," muttered Maleps.

"Sacrilege," hissed Trellana.

"You are bound for an afterlife of unimaginable punishments," said Dolgeeno.

"Most certainly not," said Anand. "Some of my countrymen believe their souls never leave the Sand but are invested again in a new being, an unending cycle of rebirth. Others believe that this is their one and only life."

"That's absurd," said Dolgeeno. "We would take such blasphemers, bathe and throw them to the ants."

"You would not be allowed to do so in Dranveria, Pious."

"We are allowed to do as we like with our subjects," said Maleps.

"No one is subject to anyone else in my home," said Anand. Each time he responded, he nodded his head in a humble manner. He could not help but grin, for he was having a very good time.

"How did you enter our queendom without inciting our ants?" asked Batra.

Anand had hoped he would be asked this question.

"General, you are not the only nation which has parasitized the leaf-cutter ant."

"What?" gasped Trellana. "Parasitized?"

"Yes, Majesty. We have many colonies of leaf-cutter mounds scattered through our thousand nations."

"You could not possibly live among leaf-cutters," shouted Dolgeeno. "Not without ordained priests and a sorceress descended from Ant Queen."

"I assure you we do."

"You Dranverites are rather spectacular liars."

"The Dranverites are dedicated to the truth, as elusive as that is. And truthfully, Pious, it is Slopeish priests who immerse their people in lies."

Anand dropped all courtly pretenses as the rage of years gushed from him. "You know as well as I do that you have no godly magic, Pious, and *neither does your queen.*"

Trellana rose.

"Kill this alien bastard!" she screamed at her guard. Before she could finish her sentence, the gottallamos had aimed their blowguns. Before the royal guards could raise their weapons, the darts had found their marks. Each guardsman slumped to the ground. The gottallamos turned the blowguns on the royals, pulling the next cartridge of the magazine to the barrel. Trellana shrieked and slithered out of her chair.

"Kill me and you will bring down the wrath of the Collective Dranverish Nations," shouted Anand. "Hundreds of thousands of my nation's troops are poised on your borders. They have enough darts to paralyze this entire mound and the rest of the Great Slope." Anand said this with such conviction that no one but the Dranverites would know he was exaggerating. "If you insist on aggression," he continued, "we can change our dart's paralyzing sting to something more deadly."

Trellana reseated herself. She could not suppress her sniveling.

"I am a descendent of Ant Queen," she squeaked. "It is my sacred essence which protects this mound. Without it . . ."

"Yes, yes, yes," Anand shouted. "Without your

piss, the very walls of your tunnels would crumble. What is it that you eat, oh Queen, which gives your urine this quality?"

Trellana looked to Dolgeeno, who averted his eyes.

"Do you know? Do you suspect? There are one hundred thousand women in Dranveria whose urine can keep back the Yellow Mold, as long as they eat something that combines to make an anti-fungal. What would it be, Queen?"

"He's lying, Trellana," Dolgeeno said.

"Search your tongue, Sorceress," shouted Anand. "The bitter residues of *roach eggs* reside there still. You are not special, Queen of Cajoria. Hundreds of women in your own queendom have this ability. Your royal brothers and fathers are allowed to rape the lower castes. The daughters of the raped could be as 'holy' as you. That is why you teach your subjects to hate and fear the Britasytes and their insects. Your priests don't want anyone to learn that eating roach eggs is what makes you a holy sorceress."

"What do you want?" shouted Maleps, who was on his feet.

"Let me tell you what we *demand*. We are aware of the wars you waged on your neighbors. It has resulted in the displacement of the Stink Ant people seeking refuge in our country. You will cease to war on your neighbors, quit your expansion, and will end this gruesome demand for human tribute."

"And if we don't comply?"

"Then prepare yourselves for confrontation. We

recommend that you domesticate a different ant than the leaf-cutter and find something else to feed your people besides mushrooms. *Some* of you are aware that the fertility of your women is a result of a constant diet of the leaf-cutters' fungus. That's why your mounds are burdened with starving masses that you force to settle in other peoples' lands. Your leaf-cutter ants must stay out of Dranveria and away from the inhabited trees of its Buffer Zone."

Trellana looked at Dolgeeno who did not meet her eyes.

Anand looked around the room and gave a mild snort of derision.

"My deepest thanks for your hospitality," he said. "Perhaps someday you will welcome us at the Royal Hall of Reception. We will be returning to Dranveria tomorrow, but before we go, we should like to provide some gifts to the people you call your 'subjects' as a token of our good will."

"Gifts?" said Maleps.

"Honey and handcrafts. Harmless items. Enjoy your opals. Good night."

Anand turned to part and his capes swirled around him in a gorgeous eddy of lights. As Anand reached the portal, he turned and saw that Dolgeeno was fixed on him, still staring with envy at his cape.

**T**rellana sputtered in rage. "We'll send messengers to the other mounds," she screamed once Anand had left. "Gather all our armies to crush that flea-spawn and his men!"

"We can't do that," Maleps said. "They're Dranverites!"

"So what! We are Slopeites!"

"You heard what he said. They have an army ten times the size of our own at the border, just waiting for an excuse to attack."

"He's lying."

"Let's not risk that he isn't. Just look at *them*," Maleps said, pointing to the fallen guards spread over the stairs. "Do you want to go through *that* again?"

"I didn't know I was married to a coward."

"I've known for quite some time that I am married to a half-wit."

"If Their Majesties would permit me to advise," said Batra, interrupting. "I *am* in command of the army here."

"Please," said Trellana as she glared at Maleps.

"King Maleps is correct, madame. If we are attacked, then, yes, we should defend ourselves and summon the entire Slope. But we should not wage war on the Dranverites . . . not at this time."

"Or any other time," said Maleps.

Trellana turned to Dolgeeno who was very still before he turned his eyes to her.

"We will have our day against the Dranverites," said the priest. "But it will not be tomorrow."

"But you heard that demon!" Trellana screeched. "He'll be barging in here and luring the people with his gifts in order to fill their ears with trash! We can't allow this!"

"We will allow it," Maleps said. "If we kill him, we've invited a retaliation."

After some silence, Dolgeeno spoke again. "The preservation of our mound comes first. Let us send out messengers at sunrise and warn the people that the alien bearing gifts is attempting to destroy our peace. We'll tell them they can accept his offerings but they should reject the poison of his words."

The ant train was not waiting in the tunnel for Anand and his guards—they would have to walk back. Anand laughed to himself on the hike down, but was sobered when he passed the midden. Tomorrow he would finally see his family. Were they well? How was Terraclon?

And tomorrow, if the Cajorites did not gather forces from the nearby mounds for an attack, Anand would attempt to bring the message of *The Loose Doctrine* to the worker castes of Cajoria.

*But will any of them listen?*

# CHAPTER 33

## REUNION

Trellana looked out the clear quartz viewing window of her bedchamber and thought her prayers had been answered. Lord Grasshopper Himself was crawling up the mound's main artery in the pink light of dawn. She was sure when He reached the top He would rise up and announce in a thundering voice that He had destroyed the Dranverites for their sacrilege and that order had been restored.

As His glittering face reached the platform of the uppermost dew station, Grasshopper did not rise up but instead was turned to face downward. As it grew lighter, Trellana realized she'd been looking at the jewel-faced idol the Dranverites had brought to the stadium. The idol was a wagon, like the sort she was carried in during her paralysis and it had been hauled to the top of Cajoria. Perched on a platform near its head was the Dranverish meddler with the unpronounceable name. This morning he was surrounded by a hundred of his faceless guards.

She fell back on her bed, screaming, sending her servants running in.

"What's wrong, Majesty?" one asked. "What can we do?"

But Trellana could only scream, and as her servants waited nearby, they covered their ears until she was hoarse and exhausted.

The increased number of gottallamos surrounding Anand wore soothing, priestly robes that cloaked their weapons and six of them encircled him on top of the wagon's platform. Anand could see mounted Cajorite sentries maintaining a watch on Lick-My-Testicles, but it was from an uneasy distance. Their ants seemed as nervous as they looked.

Caste restrictions prevented the laborers from entering each other's quarters by more than three degrees. As a result, Anand would have to make his presentation over thirty times at the descending dew stations. Special paints were on his face that day: a stripe of yellow on the left side, red in the center, and brown on the right.

The Dranverites made their first appeal to the stream of servants making their way to work. At first some fell to their knees to worship Grasshopper, and listened to Anand, thinking he was a demigod. More reluctant Cajorites approached because they saw the bolts of bright cloth and the wax-jars of honey. Some liked the jewelry of red-ant chitin.

"I have come to trade," said Anand through an amplifying cone. "I offer you these items in return for your ears. Cajorites, you have heard of Bee-Jor, a land of flowing honey where no one has to labor." He saw hope in their faces at the mention of the mythical paradise.

"Bee-Jor may not exist, but I come from a land of flowing honey, a place known as the Dranverite Collective Nations," Anand said as he opened his cape to display images of the City of Peace. "Cajoria and all other mounds of the Slope could be places where honey is free and plentiful, too." On this cue, the gottallamos tossed jars of honey to the crowd. They were listening now, hushing those in the back.

"Men and women everywhere must work, but they should be rewarded for their labors with ample food, warm clothing, comfortable shelters, and potions from healers when they are sick. This must be the birthright of all humans. No one's labors should rob one of eyesight or limbs or leave them so fatigued they are sickly. All should have rest from their labors and time to spend in pleasures. And all should have the right to seek their own destinies, to be rewarded for their own efforts."

Anand looked out at the Slopeish sentries who

were huddling among their ants to whisper. They still seemed more abashed then threatening.

"I come from a place where there are no castes, where men and women choose their work based on their abilities and desires. We have no nobles who live off the labor of others. We choose our leaders, and if they fail us, we are free to choose again. For all your lives, your priests have lied to you and said that you will spend an eternity being tortured in the Netherworld if you do not carry out the duties of your caste."

The crowd stared at him, terrorized and intrigued. The question was clear on their faces: *Priests who lie?*

"Yes—lies. You have also been lied to about the roles the gods play in your lives, made to believe the royals are something more than humans like yourselves. The royals sustain their privilege by keeping you in fear of their gods. The thing is, these gods are nothing more than the wood or stone they are carved from. One day you must challenge the nobles and reclaim what is yours. The brown-skinned people were here first. It was the yellow-skinned people who stole this land and enslaved your ancestors."

Anand was in a state of ecstatic concentration as he shouted his next words. "You have been told that, just as the ants have castes, so must humans. Listen to me now . . . these are the designs of the Slopeish priests, not the gods. Know this about the land of Dranveria: anyone of any color has the same privileges. The leader of my great and rich nation is a woman and her face is as brown as damp earth."

A murmur of disgust ran through the crowd, even among many with faces that could be described as brown. Anand raised his voice.

"Cajoria and every mound of the Slope are invited to join the Dranverite Nations. In order to qualify, all of you, your nobles, priests, and soldiers included, must prove you are dedicated to a just and sustainable way of life for all. You must stop hating the castes you believe to be beneath you."

At that, many walked off in anger. Some threw the presents back at Anand, some spat at the gottal-lamos, and cries of "polluted!" went up. A few stared in disbelief, while others ran away with their prizes, having no interest in speeches of any kind.

Receptions grew warmer in the circles farther outside the mound where skin and hair was darker, but as Anand reached the lowest castes, the people were too hungry and obsessed with the gifts to hear his words. Some would not get off their knees before the Grasshopper idol. Most did not understand when Anand talked about "destiny" or concepts like '"just" and "sustainable."

Anand began questioning his own interpretation. His voice was growing hoarse, and he bolstered his energy with drinks of kwondle-bark infusion. He was renewed when he recognized Elora, the girl he had rescued from the lair spider. She was with her mother at the ring of the scrapers' caste, but neither looked well. As he spoke, Elora stared then approached. Her growth was stunted and her cheeks were hollow.

"Don't I know you?" she asked, searching his face and his eyes.

Anand smiled broadly, betraying himself. He loaded her arms with gifts. "Yes, you do," he whispered. "I am glad to see you and your mother."

"Where do I know you from?"

"From a spider's lair," he whispered and she began weeping. "Just as I freed you from the spider, I have come to free you from misery."

"You betrayed us, Anand," she said, dropping the presents and running off.

His heart fell and splattered into bleeding pieces. His teachers had warned him that friends and family would reject his message, that most people preferred suffering over the uncertainty of change. Still, his heart rose again as he neared the midden.

The middenites were slower to reach the wagon, always so weary and wary. He looked at those who approached and could not contain his joy when he saw Terraclon. He was still thin but much taller. Terraclon's sadness vanished at the sight of the glittering wagon and Anand's clothing. He looked at Anand's face briefly and failed to recognize him through his beard and skin paint. He resumed the usual cringe of a middenite, always in fear of a fist or a whip from his superiors.

One of the last of the middenites to arrive was a broken man whose head was bowed to the dirt. His black hair was streaked with gray, his cheeks were sunken, and his face was covered with grime. He lifted his head briefly to look at the young stranger on his wagon that sparkled too brightly in the noonday sun.

Anand realized he was looking at his father. Unable to make his speech, Anand fought every urge to wilt. Sadness rolled through him in waves, like a sudden illness. He gathered his breath and bolstered his determination.

"I offer you these presents of food and cloth," he said, "from the people of Dranveria."

Anand knew the middenites might not take anything. They would assume his offers were a humiliating trick. He pointed to Terraclon.

"You, tall and thin boy, come here."

Terraclon placed a hand over his heart in his fey manner. He was astonished to be addressed by someone of such regal bearing.

"Yes, you. I want you to be the first to take these presents. Something tells me you might like this cloth."

Anand picked up a bolt of the shiniest material on the cart, cloth that resembled the mottled-blue locust, and held it out. The gottallamos parted to let Terraclon approach but he was too frightened to move.

"And take some jars of honey," Anand continued. "You!" Anand said, pointing to his father. "Take this food and eat, for you are far too thin. Bring it to your family so that they might feast tonight."

Yormu stood in silence with his head so far down it looked like his neck was broken. The gottallamos were bringing Yormu the items when Keel elbowed his way through the crowd and took what had been proffered. After examining the jars, Keel bade his wife and children to take their share.

"It's all right," Keel shouted to the crowd. "The priests have passed on a message about this outlander. We are allowed to take his presents, but should reject his words. He has come to stir up trouble, to rob us of our peace."

"I *have* come to stir up trouble," said Anand. "For I have come to tell you that all of you are as worthy as the royals. And you must live without a cruel foreman who lashes you with his whip."

Keel dropped his jars. For the first time, Anand pulled back the draping sleeves of his right arm to reveal a blowgun.

"Were you fond of your time in the Dranverites' wagons, Keel, when you suffered the Living Death?" Anand asked.

Keel was stunned. How did this stranger know his name?

"I can arrange to come back and paralyze you," said Anand. "And I will if I hear you're abusing these poor people."

Keel's lower lip trembled.

"Give me your whip now," said Anand. Keel looked around. Though all watched him, none stared directly.

"I said give me your whip," shouted Anand, and ever so slightly, he raised his blowgun.

Keel took the whip, which was clipped to his side. While he stared at the blowgun, the gottallamos parted so he could approach Anand who snatched the whip and cracked it high in the air. In the distance, the Cajorite sentries had gathered now by the dozens. They were still watching, still keeping a distance.

"Remove your garment," Anand said to Keel.

Keel trembled as he pulled his tunic over his head. His body was thick and fat with a belly as big as any royal.

"Why should you be so fat when the rest of your caste is starving?" Anand asked. "Bring him up here."

Anand cracked the whip again.

The crowd was drooling for Keel's public whipping and they snickered as he was pulled up and onto the cart's platform. Midden children who hated Tal and his brothers were snarling at them now as they sweated with shame. Keel braced himself against the coming lashing.

"Turn your back to these people," Anand commanded, and Keel complied. Across his back were the old scars of whippings he had received from the previous foreman.

"Look at your foreman's back . . . it's covered in scars! He knows the agony of a good whipping. But does this make him sympathetic? No! When he became foreman, he was all too happy to inflict the same. In the Dranverites' country, we have no whips! Get off this wagon, Keel, and *never use a whip again.*"

Anand wanted to keep the whip but remembered

the tenets of The Loose Code—no stealing ever. He threw the whip into the crowd as Keel scrambled through it. Most of the middenites were disappointed, but some looked to be warming to the message of the young foreigner. "This is the first of happier days," said Anand, "though I promise you, your struggles against your oppressors will be a great trial."

Terraclon froze as Anand stepped down from the cart and walked toward him through the faceless guards, pressing the blue cloth into his arms. "I chose this for you, Ter. I am sure you will make costumes to imitate the royals," Anand whispered. "That remains our secret for now and so does this: Anand, son of Yormu and Corra the Britasyte, visits this mound. Tell them their son wishes to see his parents at the camp of the Dranverish visitors. You will accompany them, Ter. My guards will retrieve you."

Anand was pulled back onto the wagon as Terraclon dropped the cloth and shook. As the wagon rolled away, Anand turned to wave with a smile that revealed his molars. A moment later, he was sick with worry. What had happened to his father? Was his mother away on a visit?

Inside his dwelling after sunset, Anand laid out food and drink for his parents and Terraclon. When he heard the soft crunch of the gottallamos' boots, he ran outside.

Anand panicked to see Terraclon and Yormu walking towards him with the gravest expressions. Where was his mother? Walking into Yormu's embrace, Anand felt his father's trembling, his boniness. It seemed Yormu might snap in two if Anand hugged too hard.

Terraclon stood by, his face a mix of envy and dread as he took in the beauties and comforts of the caravan's wagons. He was watching Anand hug his father and startled when Anand pulled away to reach for him.

"Anand! You can't hug me! It's forbidden!" said Terraclon, pulling away.

"This is the custom of my new country. We embrace all who wish to embrace."

Terraclon let himself be hugged. When it lingered too long, it was Anand who broke away. "Where is my mother?" he asked. Yormu burst into crying he could not muffle. Terraclon looked to the ground as Anand's heart pummeled his rib cage.

"She . . . she did not return from a trip with your father to Palzhad. The priests have not disclosed all the details, but some say invaders from the south captured or killed the Palzhanites. Others say phantoms on ghost ants spilled up from the Netherworld."

"She's dead?" Anand asked Yormu. "Did you see her die?"

Yormu nodded his head. Anand fell and writhed, then ran into the weeds, tore at them with his hands. His bawling reached the moon and reverberated back.

Sometime later, Anand returned to the wagon. Yormu and Terraclon had waited patiently, savoring the feel of cushioned chairs. "Eat as fully as you like," said Anand.

Terraclon was fascinated by the glowing biscuits. "I can't eat something so pretty," he said. Yormu ate what was familiar, then tried the other delicacies when Anand pressed him to try. Anand felt he might never eat again.

"Ter, have any Britasytes passed recently?"

"Yes, but they were not your mother's clan. Their sand-sleds were poppy-colored."

"The Fallogeths. How long ago?"

"Only a few days. We had other visitors, too. Men from the Dustlands."

"The Dustlands? Who?"

"Some believe they are the riders of the ghost ants. They knew Pleckoo, who lives among them now. They were from Slopeish working castes and like you, came bearing gifts and a message of another way of life. They promise riches, a full stomach and the glories of fighting for their god, Hulkro."

"They worship the Termite?" asked Anand with a scoff.

"Yes. They say he is the only god, and all others are demons. Unlike you, they did not boldly enter the city, but made a secret summons of all those that work or forage in the weeds. One was caught and killed before he could return to the Dustlands."

"Weren't they attacked by the leaf-cutters?"

"No. They killed idols keepers on the borders and stole the colony odor."

"Did they convince many to follow?"

"More than a few. One gave me food and money and told me that if I wanted more, I should wander south to Palzhad, then through the Petiole and past the borders of the Slope. When I reached the Great Brackish Lake to the south, I should wait on its shores to be brought to Jatal-dozh, a Hulkrish mound. When the Hulkrites found me, I should then say, 'I surrender my life to Hulkro.'"

"Why didn't you go?"

"I've been waiting for you. You said you'd return and I believed you."

Anand's tears welled again. He sent Yormu and Terraclon back to the midden tugging a sled of provisions that could last them the year. That night, Anand tossed violently in his bed. While he was on the Slope, he determined to find Daveena and take her and all of the Roach Clans into the safety of Dranveria where they could forever roam in peace.

Before sunrise, Anand wrote two letters which he left inside the wagon. The first was to the gottallamos, telling them their mission was complete and they were to return without him. The second letter was addressed to the People's Agent.

*Your Eminence,*
    *My mission at Cajoria is completed for now.*
*As expected, most of the Cajorites are too fearful*
*to consider our message. Though they hate their*

oppressors, they are loath to unite with those they consider beneath them. Regardless, our invitation has been extended and the seeds of the Slopeites' liberation have been planted. We shall see if they grow at all.

I regret to mention that my mother met her death at the hands of new invaders to these lands, apparently from Hulkren, the wasteland long abandoned by the Slopeites and their leaf-cutter ants. My discourse to the Cajorites was somewhat diluted by a similar message from warriors proselytizing for the worship of Hulkro, the termite god, who has fallen from the Slopeites' pantheon. I am afraid that our own nation and its principles may become confused with those of these new invaders.

I fear too, that one clan of my Britasyte tribe is in danger. I will not be accompanying the gottallamos on their return to Dranveria in order that I may search for the Pleps and the woman who is my betrothed. It is my duty to my nation of Dranveria and to my original people to find out who these Hulkrites are and what threat they pose. Some believe they are not humans at all, but are ghosts from the Netherworld who ride upon ghostly insects. Perhaps our two nations share the same ideals or perhaps the Hulkrites are bloodthirsty opportunists. When I have formulated my own opinion, I will return to Dranveria and add my account to our store of precious knowledge.

I have borrowed something from the supplies of our

*military. On my return I will compensate our treasury
for its replacement.*

*Please relate my concern for the well-being of
Dwan, Belja, Hopkut, and Pizhyot.*

*—Citizen Anand*

Anand came to his father's tent to say good-bye
and to borrow the rags of a Slopeish laborer. In his
backsack was a wealth of rare goods to trade as he
made his way south. Yormu tried and failed to form
words, but it was obvious from his every action that
he was begging his son to stay.

"Father, not only will I return, but when I do, I
will take you with me to a beautiful land. You will
grow fat as a bumblebee and never work again."

Yormu sobbed and wrung his hands.

"I promise I will return," said Anand. "But you
must promise me something. You must eat every day
and stay strong."

Anand presented his father with some Dranverish
remedies he should drink for various illnesses. Before
leaving, he rocked in his father's arms. Under the
shack, Terraclon sat and waited for Anand.

"Thanks for looking after my dad. I'm indebted . . .
forever," said Anand, pressing a bag of pyrite flecks
into his friend's hand. "I want to see both of you thick
and strong on my return."

"I'm going with you, Anand."

"Not this journey. But you will join me and my
father when we leave for Dranveria."

Terraclon rose, looked both ways, and then clasped Anand to his meager frame.

"I will follow you anywhere," he said.

Anand knew that the Fallogeth clan of Britasytes were likely to be east at Mound Bavi. There, they would be allowed to set up stalls on the outskirts of the largest market on the Slope. Anand marched east with a haste fueled by rage. He was heartened to find fresh roach droppings and knew he would soon see the gold-colored sleds of the Fallogeths.

Anand found the clan's spanner, Mereeno, presiding over stalls typical of the Britasytes. The shelves were full of bangles and necklaces that were considered both polluted and showy for anyone above military status. Mereeno looked barely interested in the raggedy Slopeite approaching him.

"What may I interest you in, noble sir?" said Mereeno, thinking his sarcasm would be lost on the man.

"Anand of the Entreveans," he said in Britasyte. "Good travels, sir."

"The Entreveans? Yes, I remember you. The son of Corra, and like me a spanner to the Slopeites. Good travels."

Anand nodded. Mereeno's brow filled with ridges. "What can you tell us of the Pleps, Anand? You were betrothed to one of their daughters, right?"

"I *am* betrothed to one of their daughters."

Mereeno was silent, then gave a great sigh.

"The Pleps failed to show up for the summer solstice. When we arrived at Palzhad, the *sedites* told us the Plep women had danced there one night. The following day, the roaches, the clan, and the sand-sleds were gone . . . disappeared with the morning mists."

Anand dizzied and his knees went wobbly. Mereeno grabbed Anand and righted him.

"But what . . . who . . ."

"The Slopeites saw what they said was a ghost army who walked out of the night. Apparently it was the same army that raided Palzhad and abducted Queen Polexima on the backs of their ghost ants."

"Ghost ants," Anand muttered.

He had no choice now, no indecision. He knew where he must go.

# PART 3

# A WARRIOR FOR THE TERMITE GOD

# CHAPTER 34

## THE DUSTLANDS

The Fallogeths feasted Anand, but in recognition of the Pleps' disappearance, there was no music or celebration. Comely young women joined Anand at his platter, offered their best dishes, and openly flirted. Afterwards several women slipped samples of their embroidery and pickles into his tent. If he wished to bed one, all he would need to do was bite into her bachelor pickle, wrap the rest in her embroidery, and leave it outside the tent. He would not do so. A nighttime encounter with a Britasyte girl meant an unbreakable engagement.

Before parting the following day, Anand was assured by Mereeno that he was welcome to any of their young eligibles. "I am honored," said Anand, "but I must find Daveena. I have seen my vision. She is my destiny."

"Yes, of course, Anand," said Mereeno. But the look on his face betrayed his assumption that Daveena and her clan were dead.

Anand had journeyed south for a day when he reached into his backsack for some worm jerky. That was when he realized he had left his copy of *The Loose Doctrine* in the tent of the Fallogeths. They would not know what it was. What if they dumped it with their trash or sold it as a curiosity? The loss of the book haunted Anand for days. It felt like the loss of his closest friend.

Anand knew he could not look well-fed when he entered the lands of the Hulkrites. Over the long journey south, he limited his food to leaves and roots. The Hulkrites would be suspicious of him if he looked anything other than bitter and hungering.

That was a guise he could easily re-assume.

Oblivious to the Slopeish sights around him, he became a tireless strider, a creature constructed of hate that slept very little each night. It might take him months or years, but he would learn who was responsible for his mother's death. And if the Hulkrites had harmed Daveena or any other Britasyte, he would make them suffer and then destroy them. He set his sights on the Great Jag, the chain of steep-faced boulders that hemmed in the Slope's southwestern queendoms. When he finally reached Palzhad, he smelled the sulfurous Tar Marsh, which stretched across the southeast border. Between these two barriers lay the Petiole, the narrow passage the riders on ghost ants had traveled when they raided Palzhad.

When Anand reached the ravaged mound, border patrollers ordered the young worker to return to his mound and his duties. Anand bowed respectfully and presented each with pyrite flecks. Once the patrollers took them, they allowed him to wander into the thicket of weeds.

Just before the walls of the rebuilt borders was a large white rock with distinctive veins that resembled a spider in its web. Anand took off his rags and his Dranverish armor and put them in a waterproofed sack with the rest of his currency. Last to go in the sack was a jar with leaf-cutter kin-scent. He buried it all near the spider rock to be exhumed on his return . . . if he should return this way.

One thing Anand did not put in the sack was a small, tightly capped tubular jar bound with beeswax he had borrowed from the gottallamos' store of weapons. Under the thick coating of wax, the jar had Dranverish writing that warned of an extreme poison and gave lengthy directions for the handling of its contents. Anand grimaced as he tucked this bottle into his pouch.

Night had arrived and with it, moisture and cold. Whispers of clouds drifted over Moon. To Anand, the clouds looked like ghosts fleeing some calamity, for ghosts had been much on his mind. He looked both ways in search of border patrollers before crawling over the piles of ant pellets, for it was a crime punishable by death for anyone other than a soldier to leave the Slope. He remembered telling the Dranverite scholars that the Slopeish words for border translated to "place where priestly magic ends." He could still hear their clucks of disapproval.

On the other side of the border, it was very much the same: dense weeds that blocked any view of the distance. Clad in rags, Anand carried only his dagger, his pouch and a water-skin. He made his way towards a glowing cluster of lightning-fly eggs on the underside of a blue wort plant. Fashioning a quick torch from them, he continued his hike and disturbed grasshoppers, which flew off with a frightful kick and sprays of their mouth-slime.

Holding his torch up to the thick stem of a tarberry plant, Anand saw a ripe one and ate a drupe to quench his thirst. He knew his water would be colored black the next day, but he savored the tart-sweet delight. Atop the plant were slowly moving thorns that trailed long, diaphanous threads. They were thorn aphids, and Anand shimmied up the stalk to reach them. He wrapped their threads around a stick for later eating, then suckled the end of one for its sugar-rich dew, avoiding the sharp tack that grew on its back.

Anand was frightened to travel in unknown weeds in the dark. When he reached a clearing and could look up, the clouds had parted to reveal a sky that was black and sinister. The stars looked like clusters of dew-spattered spiders, ready to drop on threads to bite him. All around were creaking twigs, rustling leaves, and the crunching mouths of nocturnal hunters.

His heart beat faster and his head throbbed with panic. He felt safer when he walked. The Learned Elders of Dranveria believed prayer was useless, but Anand turned to Madricanth for his/her protection and to the spirit of his mother for guidance. His mother . . . had he told her how much he loved her before he left with the pioneers?

"How did you let this happen to her?" he suddenly screamed to the skies, the place where Madricanth roamed at night. "What kind of protector are you? Will you let me die, too?"

His rant was halted when he heard great gurgling and smacking sounds. Blocking his path were undulating walls that he realized were two great earthworms. They had surfaced to mate and were coating each other in mucous before linking. Anand smiled as he skirted the gentle monsters, for this sight was a good-luck omen to Britasytes.

He slipped in the earthworms' slime and was falling forward when he felt something grab him. Webbing had snapped around his face, his torso, his ankles and he was lifted off the ground. His body was spinning as sticky threads wrapped tight around him and his arms were bound to his body. Dizzy and pulsing with fear, he looked through the threads at the multiple eyes of a lair spider. Its black fangs were parting as Anand went for the dagger in his holster. He could not reach it. The webbing pulled tighter. The spider leaned back, stretched Anand between its forelegs, and readied to sink her fangs as she raised his chest to her mouth.

Anand was drenched in his own cold sweat. Just as he gave himself up to dying, the spider went still. Her legs relaxed and Anand swung between them, as if in a hammock. His sweat had lubricated him, and he was able to squeeze his hand down to his knife. He was sawing at threads when he heard a deep and almost musical buzzing. The lair spider was taking flight! How? Anand looked down at the ground through the webbing. What had come to his rescue? He was higher than he had ever flown on any locust's back.

Anand saw the answer to his question and his dread flared anew. He was being flown toward a nest of night wasps. He must be dead! His spirit was in the Netherworld the Slopeites had warned him against! Soon he would be stung and chewed to bits, and a short time later, he would be whole again and the torture would start all over.

He remembered the Dranverites did not believe in a punishing Netherworld. "I'm not dead," Anand said to himself. He realized that a night wasp had paralyzed the lair spider and was carrying it to her nest to dismember and feed to her sisters and their young. The night wasp was as yet unaware that she had also captured a human.

The wasps' cone-shaped nest hung from a slender attachment to the underside of a tree-branch. The insects' massive black bodies blended into the night, but their garish wings were an obscene orange, as frightening as the flames of a fire. Hundreds of wasps were crawling over the six-sided cells stuffed with their maggots. When the wasps discovered Anand, they would sting him to paralyze him, then tear him to pieces.

The stunned lair spider was dropped on top of the nest, where the wasp's sisters converged on it with an angry buzzing and gnashing of mandibles. The spider's limbs were chewed and tugged until they fell away. Suddenly Anand was freed from the legs of the spider, but not its web. The wasps smelled him as he squirmed away and over the papery top of their nest. He used his free hand to pull himself inside a cell occupied by a maggot.

Struggling to cut himself free, Anand kept at the sticky threads until he could scrape them off his body. The maggot wriggled and turned its mouth to Anand. He was coated in its slime, which helped him to worm out of the last of the spider's threads. He caught his breath, backed into the cell, and braced himself against the maggot. It alternately swelled and grew thin as its mouth-end craned for food.

*What to do now?* he asked himself. He pulled himself out to the edge of the cell and looked down. The height was dizzying and it felt as if his insides were pouring out of him. Up above, the wasps were tearing into the spider's blood-rich abdomen and were lapping up its green jelly.

One wasp was already regurgitating spider blood to the maggots. The wasp flew back to refill her mouth, then targeted the cell where Anand was hiding. He backed away, knowing the wasp could pluck him out with her claw. Instead, her antenna probed the cell and brushed Anand's head. His pounding heart threatened to burst from his chest. The wasp paused a moment, cocked her head at Anand. Her mandibles parted and her mouth opened to reveal spider blood. She expected him to eat. *I have their kin-scent*, he thought. *She thinks I'm a maggot!*

To test his assumption, Anand popped out of his cell. The wasps were crawling all around. One came near him, antennated his body, crawled over him. Anand looked up at its massive body and realized he could pull himself on top of these creatures. He had no choice, no other way out, but to get on top of a dreaded night wasp!

Anand grabbed one by its claw, and then climbed its leg hairs toward the thorax. He slid over her and then crawled onto her head. Between her antennae was an indentation, a natural saddle like those of the blue-mottled flyers. Anand knelt in it and grabbed the wasp's thick antennae with his hands.

The wasp did not respond to his prodding for he had no pilot-scents. Anand looked at a bit of spider blood on his chest and rubbed it on his hands. He pressed his palms to the tips of the antennae and the wasp buzzed its wings. When he pressed harder at the center, the wasp flew off.

Anand thrilled to the sudden flight. The wind blew cold on his skin, but it felt like freedom itself. The wasp did not jerk or skid on the currents, as locusts did. She had a gorgeous fluidity in her flying, a combination of hovering and soaring.

As Anand probed the antennae for different responses, he realized its receptors were much like those of the hunter ants. He slapped its head to slow it, and when he stood and flared out the antennae, the wasp made a gentle spiral downwards.

The night wasp did not abruptly drop and clutch at whatever plant lay below it, but hovered first, negotiated its landing, and set down on all its claws. Anand slid off its head and fell to the ground. The wasp stood quietly, waiting, and then crawled after Anand as he walked away. Thinking he was safe, she suddenly lunged, knocked him down, and he panicked. He turned to see the wasp with her mandibles open but her antennae were drooping as she bowed to nuzzle him.

Anand collapsed in relief. He pulled himself up from some jagged sand grains, then laughed as the wasp pivoted around him. *May as well fly to Hulkren,* he thought, and climbed back on to her thorax. The wasp resumed flight, heading back for her nest, but Anand prodded her antennae until she turned south. Throughout the night they flew over terrain that would have taken days on foot. As the moon was sinking, the weeds below Anand grew sparse and gave way to patches of sand.

At last, he saw a silvery sliver on the horizon. As they flew closer, the Great Brackish Lake spread before him. The water was like a vast and glittering mirror where Moon admired Her own image before She slipped to Her bed below the horizon.

Anand knew he should not approach the lake on the back of a night wasp. If there were other defectors waiting on shore to join the Hulkrites, it would bring him far too much attention. He coaxed the wasp to spiral over a thicket of low-lying *mehta* plants which thrived on sand. These had tall stalks with ugly brown flowers that stank like human corpses to attract flies.

He dismounted and trod softly through the leaves since their undersides were speckled with mites and could hide larger predators. The wasp was still crawling after Anand, tending him. The plants thinned out to reveal a great plain, empty and made more ominous by the dark. Anand's legs wobbled with fatigue. After cutting a broad leaf from a mehta, he examined it for mites, then made a slit at its end. Inserting the leaf's stem into the slit, Anand made a tent and weighed down its edges with larger sand grains.

Inside the tent he lifted and arranged the sand until the floor was somewhat flat enough to lie on. Without a blanket, he curled himself into a ball and dreamt of ghosts again. Streams of ghosts screamed as they floated back and forth from the Sand to the Spirit World, unhappy to be in either place. The wasp waited outside the tent, occasionally nudging it. When the sun appeared, she crawled under a broad mehta leaf and hung upside down to sleep until darkness returned.

Harsh sunlight woke Anand. He left the tent and looked at the arid expanse ahead and saw distant stands of devastated bortshu that were broken, leafless, and gray. Many of the trees had become jagged stumps or logs turning to powder. Farther south there were no stumps at all. This was the Dustlands and all that was left in it were abandoned mounds, trailing back over centuries of Slopeish migrations. Before the sun could take it, he licked the dew on his leaf tent.

Anand took the first step to the Great Brackish Lake. A few times the lake appeared before him, blue and shimmering, but when he ran to it, it was a dream that disappeared. The grains under his feet grew large and rough and pierced the soles of his boots. A gray dust blew over the sands. He filled his mind with images of Daveena and sang her name in every tune he could remember. She was there somewhere in the south, waiting for him, singing his name in all the tunes she knew.

The sand yielded to layers of dried and cracked mud. Sometimes Anand fell through the delicate pieces and coughed on clouds of powder. At last he reached the water's edge where he found other men who were silent at his approach. They looked at Anand in disappointment, wishing he were a Hulkrite bringing food and potable water.

Anand went to the dark yellow water. He touched it with the tip of his fingers, tasted it, and found it was indeed quite bitter. In the distance were great water striders. The insects' elongated bodies and thread-like legs allowed them to glide on the lake. Anand swam towards them, hoping to tear the limb from one and suck at the blood within, but as soon as he drew near, they slipped away in a speedy blur.

The water striders converged at a distance from him, a skittish audience. While in the water, he reached in his pouch for the tubular jar bound in beeswax. This he hid in his most personal place. As he waded out of the water he saw some of the other men on shore were Slopeites, but a few of them were Seed Eaters. Two men were of the Carpenter people and fifteen others were from unknown eastern and western tribes. Anand gasped when a young man with a Slopeish face walked towards him. He looked strikingly like Pleckoo before his nose was taken from his face. His hair was tied behind his neck to reveal intact earlobes that showed he was low caste, but not an outcaste.

"I'm Aggle," he said. "From Culzhwitty. Do you have any water?"

"No," said Anand. He was about to give his name, then hesitated. "How long have you waited?" he asked with a Dranverish accent.

"Two days," rasped the Slopeite. "We can't capture much dew here. Too few plants. One of us has already died. He would not wait and drank the lake's poison." Aggle pointed to a corpse. Anand looked at the others, who were weak with thirst, and knew that sweet, clear water was the only thing on their minds. He looked out at the water striders, their forelegs crouched before them, waiting to strike at something. Anand figured their prey must be wriggle worms or something that lived under water. He got an idea and reached for his dagger.

Holding his breath, Anand swam just under the water's surface, his face up, with his dagger's dull edge clutched in his teeth. He could see little through the cloudy water, but just as he was dying for breath, a dark blur came over him and the sharp claws of a strider's legs clasped his chest. He was jerked up from the water and brought to the strider's mouth. Anand took his dagger and smashed it between the strider's eyes. He felt his fist burst through the chitin of the insect's head. With its claws hooked into his sides, the strider raced and spun with Anand over the water as he fought to mount its head. Anand screamed in pain as the claws dug into his ribs. Pulling himself higher, he reached his arm back and smashed the knife again, this time crushing the insect's brain.

The striders legs stilled, but it continued to float, pushed into an idle twirl by a breeze. Anand yanked the claws out of his bleeding sides and dropped to the water. He grabbed the insect's corpse by its leg and swam with it to shore.

"Help me bring it in," he shouted. The men from the Slope who understood his words jumped into the lake. They dragged the insect's corpse onto the sand where it was rolled onto its back. After Anand rubbed mud on his wounds, he used his dagger to split open the abdomen. Inside its shell was sweet and watery lymph that would quench the men's thirsts and fill their stomachs.

After Anand recovered, he looked about at the men to see that they were staring at him. Their eyes were wide and unblinking. These men had become his followers.

"Let's go farther south," he said and they followed. They trudged and trudged and saw nothing on the horizon. How much longer before they were approached by the Hulkrites, if ever? They kept on.

Finally in the distance, the men saw what might be an ant mound glimmering under a coat of shellac. Just as they turned towards this delicate vision, they heard the faint splashing of something speeding over the water. Anand turned to see a great pack of water striders whose size and number were astonishing. Their legs pumped invisibly fast and they would be at the shore in moments.

"The striders want revenge!" shouted one of the Slopeites, a one-eyed man who looked in fearful accusation at Anand. "Run!"

"Let them come and get me," said Anand. "They won't step on shore."

Anand knew the striders could not run on land, that their legs were designed for water. Aggle and the other recruits looked in his face, borrowed his resolve and stood as firmly as he. Only the one-eyed Slopeite ran away.

When the monstrous water striders reached the shore, the recruits looked up to see Hulkrites riding high atop them. The warriors dived from their mounts and waded to shore, their heavy swords before them, grunting in a foreign language. Anand tried not to smile. He knew he should look afraid at their show of might. Since he was not fearful, he dropped his gaze and fell to his knees as the Hulkrites approached.

The one-eyed man running in the distance was trotting back now, shameful of his cowardice. He dropped to his knees, aware that the Hulkrites were snickering at him and probably planning some humiliation.

The recruits all fell to their knees, too, and as instructed, they made a promise in their different languages. "I surrender my life to Hulkro," they said. Anand said it in Slopeish.

It was the first of many lies he would tell the Hulkrites.

# CHAPTER 35

## JATAL-DOZH

Ghosts were supposed to be made of something like fog. The men who grabbed Anand and yanked him to a distant tunnel's entry had fingernails that gouged his skin. They threw him to the tunnel's floor and cursed him in a language that was somewhat intelligible and shared Slopeish words. The recruits were doused with the kin-scent of ghosts and had antennae jammed on their heads. Prodded by swords, the recruits were forced to run through the black tunnels. The only light was from torches set at distant junctions where crude signs with pictographs indicated different destinations.

The recruits were herded down a tunnel with a sign depicting the primary opening at the top. As they progressed, the tunnel filled with the traffic of ants and humans. Though it was dark, Anand marveled at the size of the passing ants which could support several human riders. Every man he passed was an armored warrior. He did not see any women. The new recruits chugged up a long and exhausting incline, but to their eventual relief, daylight seeped into the tunnel as they reached the top. Anand emerged from the dark to the gruesome spectacle of daily life among the Hulkrites.

Jatal-dozh was a noisy tangle of activity. Its people were living in endless tents on and around the mound, but they were in the process of emptying the sand-and-lacquer dwellings of their ancient dust to make them habitable. Everywhere warriors were practicing with weapons or betting on matches of hand-to-hand combat. Some warriors bid on slave girls and children at an auction. Semiprecious minerals were used as currency, as well as arrowheads and daggers. A few men were openly engaging in intercourse with their new purchases.

Before Anand knew it, a ghost ant was behind him and rubbing his antennae for kin-scent. He stepped back and turned, shocked by his first view of the transparent ants in daylight. Even their legs and antennae were like some living quartz with a vague green tint. He saw tubes inside them pumping with green blood as well as the digestion of the day's meal. Visible in the thorax of the probing ghost was a reddish pulp that might have been the remains of humans. Only the ghost ant's massive eyes had color, a bright yellow-green. Anand surmised that these eyes were excellent for night vision, but were useless during the day, allowing in too much light. The ants looked to rely on their long, always whirling antennae during the day to make their way and seemed sluggish unless prodded.

The ant came closer and Anand knew it was best to submit to antennation. He looked into its hideous mouth with its sharp, crystal mandibles. He thought of what must have been his mother's paralyzing horror when she looked up, then was swallowed by one of these abominations. *Someday I will kill every one of them,* he thought.

The Hulkrish men were painted white and their bodies were covered in armor of their ants' ghostly chitin. Through the transparency, Anand could see this armor left them vulnerable. It was not reinforced with spider-web cladding, nor was it coated with layers of sun-cured shellac. The wearer's joints were naked instead of protected by panels of scales.

As Anand pondered this, a band of warriors sucking from a mead bag surrounded him. They were joking about him and he gathered from a few words that it was about the darkness of his skin. They pointed and laughed at his darker penis. Another warrior appeared who seemed to admire Anand's buttocks. They encircled him and pressed in.

The situation felt all too familiar to Anand, but he was free to respond in a different way. The band guffawed when he crouched to the ground with his hands in a defensive pose and readied himself to spring. The circle pressed in closer.

Anand scurried and spun like a whirly-bug as he kicked at throats and stomachs. As the gottallamos had taught him, he never turned his back on any one of them for long. A tall, stout soldier snatched at Anand and he scuttled to the other side. A second soldier, with a rag covering his face, caught him and pushed. When the stout soldier cocked back a fist to slug him, Anand dodged the blow, grabbed the man's arm and used the momentum to jerk him onto his belly. Leaping on the stout man's back, Anand waited for him to rise, then used the leverage to spring outside the circle. As he backed away anticipating a new attack, the men turned to him in silence.

Suddenly they laughed. Some sank to their knees or clutched at their bellies as their laughter turned to roars. The stout soldier burst through them, his face twisted in fury. He charged at Anand, who fell on his back and thrust his legs into the stout man's belly, kicking him over to skid on his face.

The laughter swelled again and attracted a growing crowd. The stout man rose to renew his attack, when he was ordered to desist by the one with the rag on his face. Anand saw this man's helmet had a third antenna to denote a higher rank.

The man removed the rag to speak to Anand, who tried not to recoil. The man's nose had been grossly disfigured and its pink cavities were more pronounced under a white coating. Even with his face covered in paint, Pleckoo was recognizable to Anand. *All my plans will come undone if he recognizes me,* Anand thought. He steadied himself, knowing that in Cajoria his father and his best friend had not recognized him through the thick beard and thicker hair that hid the clipped lobe of his ear. Anand kept his head bowed, but not too low. It was best to be submissive but not obsequious.

"Can you understand my words?" asked Pleckoo, first in Hulkrish and then again in Slopeish.

"I know the Slopeites' language," said Anand affecting a Dranverish accent. "I also speak Tjamedi."

"Tjamedi? What tongue is that and of what people?"

Anand spoke a few words in Dranverish. He said, "You poor bastard with a cave for a nose." He did not follow up with a translation. Instead, he said in heavily accented Slopeish, "The Tjamedis are a people of the distant northeast. I am the first Tjamedi to learn of the love of Hulkro and the holy war of Tahn the Prophet. My hope is to bring his message to my people."

"Really," said Pleckoo. "You are an interesting young man. I suspect that Hulkro brought you to me for a reason."

*I'm sure he did.*

Soldiers appeared with acorn barrels full of paint made from sap mixed with chalk powder. Pleckoo beckoned Anand to come closer, and when he did, he was suddenly slapped with broad brushes. He gasped as one brush tickled his penis. Another slapped his face and soaked his hair. The last strokes went up his legs and through the cleft of his buttocks. Now he was as white as any of them and reeking of the ghost's kin-scent. As he stood drying, Pleckoo turned to him again with eyes full of both suspicion and admiration.

"From whom did you learn of The Prophet?" Pleckoo asked with a cocked brow. Anand wanted the story to appeal to Pleckoo, but was unsure of what to tell him. A new story with its own life spun in Anand's head. Before he could examine its details, it marched out of his mouth as automatically as ants drawn by *recruit-scent*.

"I was wandering west in search of Bee-Jor through the Red Pine Country wearing beetle kin-scent I had bought from Britasyte traders," said Anand. "But I was captured by Slopeish soldiers who enslaved me for their war on the people who ride the wood beetle."

Anand saw his reference to Bee-Jor was not lost on Pleckoo.

"After I was caught, I learned the Slopeites' tongue from the low caste attendants in their camps," Anand continued. "The Slopeites forced me to cart off shit and corpses. From one slave, I heard the legend of The Prophet and his glorious Termite God, Hulkro. We came across the Dustlands together, but my companion was lost to a lair spider on the journey to the Brackish Lake." The details of Anand's story surprised even himself.

"Since when do Slopeites enslave others outside

their tribe?" asked Pleckoo. *He had never been stupid,* thought Anand.

"I was an object of amusement, a novelty," said Anand, "because of my accent and strange ways. I knew they would kill me before they returned home. It was while they were at battle that we freed ourselves and fled."

"Your Slopeish is good," said Pleckoo as he stroked his thin beard with its flaking paint.

"I have always had a skill for language," said Anand, bowing after making a boast. Around another Slopeite, Anand found himself returning to the old manners he detested, the ones that reinforced humility.

"Then you shall learn Hulkrish quickly, as Slopeish is a corrupt descendant of it." Pleckoo was lost in thought for a moment. "The Prophet will be interested in hearing more about Tjamed," he finally said.

"It is a place of tremendous wealth where the mounds themselves are made of yellow pyrite and the ants have a golden chitin. Sadly, its uncountable millions worship idols other than Hulkro," said Anand. Pleckoo's eyes dilated with the mention of mounds of pyrite, then narrowed at the mention of idols.

"Hulkro desires that all the people of the Sand leave the darkness for the light of His holy love," said Pleckoo. "Come. You shall join the other recruits and begin your training. Have you a name?"

"Vof Quegdoth," said Anand. In Dranverish, the words meant truth and vengeance.

*Which I will exact soon.*

The new recruits slept in leaf tents and spent their first days immersed in language lessons. Since everything was done by rote, Anand assumed the Hulkrites did not know of writing. The teachers were warriors who instructed them first in military terms. The first word taught was "sword" which was the same word as in Slopeish. The recruits' duty at night was making weapons, arrows in particular, which they assembled under the dull lights of a torch or two.

Later, the recruits were given ghost mandibles, which they would use to make swords. Anand was unsure of what the binding strips were until he smelled them and realized it was human leather. The Hulkrites' swords were large, heavy, and graceless. Anand was already skilled in the use of weapons, but he pretended some ignorance when instructions began and kept his mouth shut when he disagreed with the instructor.

Other recruits were frightened to mount the ghost ants on the day they trained to ride them, but Anand only pretended nervousness. Like leaf-cutters and hunters, the ghost ants had no natural saddles at the back of their heads where a rider knelt. Instead of man-made saddles, the Hulkrites wore rough knee- and toe-pads that locked with the fine hairs on the crevice between the ants' eyes. Like the Dranverites, the Hulkrites had gloves with fingers that were infused with potions to press to different segments of the antennae.

The Hulkrites' ants were faster and more deadly than red hunters, but less easily controlled. The ghosts could be halted by banging fists on their skulls, but when an ant was incited to war by another insect, or was alerted to a food find, there was almost no controlling it. For this reason, the Hulkrites engaged in battle in the same way the Slopeites did: their ants waged a separate war on enemy ants while the humans fought each other from on top or below.

When they had achieved some measure of control over the ghost ants, the new recruits were engaged in their first exercise. For purposes of military training, the Hulkrites kept colonies of the axe-head ant. Axe-heads were great and fierce and the only ants that posed a worthy challenge to ghosts. The recruits were to face a mock army of seasoned warriors mounted on the dreaded axe-heads. Both sides would have blunted arrow tips, dull twig swords and shields for the mock battle.

Despite his attempts to stay inconspicuous, Anand was appointed the captain of the recruits as he was clearly the most talented member of his cohort and he spoke the best Hulkrish. On the day of the exercise, Anand looked at his men, some only boys like himself, as they braced for the conflict. It was rumored to be a fierce match, with the mock enemy nearly as ruthless as a real one. The recruits understood that they could die if they fell to the spearlike mandibles or knife-sharp skulls of the axe-heads, and no one would care.

Only the strong were respected in Hulkren.

It would take a morning of riding before the recruits reached the battlefield. Before they mounted,

Aggle and some others ran off to vomit or empty their trembling bowels. Anand said nothing, but he did not smirk, either—he understood their apprehension.

The sun was high and glaring when Anand and his cavalry sighted the enemy. He had read about axe-head ants in Dranverish histories, but was not prepared for how ugly and fierce they looked. The ants were properly named, their great heads square in profile and much like an axe with a razor sharp edge at the front. They had long, straight mandibles that could pierce from a distance. Sitting on top of them was a well-trained army who hurled insults at the approaching recruits. Under a tarp on the sidelines were the recruits' instructors, sitting in judgment.

"Look at the women who ride such pretty ants," screamed a distant enemy. "Let's eat these women for breakfast and feed their bones to our axe-heads," cried another. "Let us slay these women and then fuck their corpses on the sand," shouted a third.

From the height of his mount, Anand could see that as sharp and long as their faces were, the top of the axe-heads' skulls were flat platforms. Their riders had to sit low and far in back in saddles on the thorax. Anand searched his mind and recalled his readings. He remembered a description of a Dranverish battle against an army on axe-heads. How had the Dranverites won? His mind kept searching.

Like a true enemy, his opponents weren't going to give him time to figure things out. They let loose with a barrage of arrows with blunt ends to knock the recruits off their mounts. Anand dodged one arrow, but a recruit to his rear took one in the chest and fell. He ran after his ant and tried to remount by crawling up the spikes of its legs, but the ghost was too quick. Anand couldn't worry about one fallen man—it was fight or fall himself. He aimed his arrows with what would have been deadly accuracy but all of them flew over their enemy in their low saddles even as they were urging their ants forward.

"Forget your arrows! Drop the antennae, use your shields!" shouted Anand. "Let the ants clash, leap on the skulls of the axe-heads and use your swords on their riders!"

A short moment later, axe-heads and ghost ants could no longer be controlled. They had smelled each other, and now they raced to battle and become entangled. As he had suggested, Anand and his men deflected arrows with their shields. His own ant locked mandibles with an axe-head who used her sharp face to cleave the ghost's head and kill it.

Anand realized his ant was about to be flipped over and he could be crushed under it. He jumped off the ghost and onto the flat skull of the axe-head, swinging his blunted blade down at its rider. He smashed once, twice, to each shoulder, then kicked the enemy off. Once anyone had fallen, they had to flee the entanglement for fear of being sliced or pierced, so that was one less foe to Anand. He looked about, then leapt to the head of another axe-head. He landed on the skull and thrust his sword at the rider who tried to rise. The man dodged the weapon, but Anand kicked him in the chin and down to the fray to get tangled in ant legs.

The other recruits followed Anand's example, seeing that their opponents were vulnerable at a low angle on their mounts. "Thrust your swords through the axe-heads' skulls!" Anand shouted, and rammed his own blade into an axe-head's brain. The others followed his example, killing all the axe-heads, and then turned their arrows on the human enemy as they fled on foot. It was not at all what their opponents had expected. When a trumpet sounded, the exercise was ended.

Among the corpses of their ants, Anand's men turned to dressing some minor wounds as they waited for dismissal from the chief instructor. He was a distance away with the other warriors from the battle, bathing in tubs of ghost ants' abdomens to wash away the axe-head scent. Anand and his men froze in fear when the chief instructor and his men marched towards them, weapons in hand, as if ready to slaughter them. When they reached Anand and the recruits, they raised their swords as if to hack off their heads.

"Who would have expected that . . . from recruits!" snarled the chief instructor through a mutilated, lipless mouth. The instructor stared at Anand, who tried to avoid looking at the man's eternally bared teeth.

"Did I do something wrong, Instructor?"

"Yes."

"What, sir? I did what I thought was right. We did defeat you."

The instructor's ragged snarl turned into a grue-some grin. "No recruits have ever won this exercise, Quegdoth. You weren't expected to. This was just a trick, boy—a test for cowardice."

Anand smiled and gave a modest nod.

Though they had to walk a great distance, the re-cruits floated back to Jatal-dozh on a cloud of laughter. Aggle walked with Anand, arm clasped around his shoulder, in a display of affection that would have had them whipped on the Slope. Once again, Anand saw ad-miration in these young men's eyes and he gloried in it.

He thought he might like it *too* much.

*I'm not here to become a Hulkrish hero. I must remem-ber that.*

Moon was small in the sky when they reached their tents, but the victory had made them tireless. Anand could not sleep and spent the time savoring his win. It was so sweet, like an everlasting lozenge of aphid sugar. When a shallow slumber came, he dreamt of Daveena and the soft patch between her legs. Just as he was about to bed her, she took out a sharp sword and poked it into his chest.

"Get up and follow me," said a manly voice. Anand awoke and looked up at an officer's messenger.

"Where?"

The messenger just pointed, and when Anand looked up, he shuddered with fright. Anand had been summoned up to the sand-and-lacquer palaces of Jatal-dozh.

Did Pleckoo have a sudden remembrance of him?

# CHAPTER 36

## A GROWING REPUTATION

**T**he ghost ants were running up and down a trunk route on Jatal-dozh's east side with their bodies illuminated by moonlight. Anand and the messenger stood in the ants' path and antennated one for food, which offered its regurgitation. Instead of eating, Anand and the messenger stepped onto its mandible, climbed up the head and made a speedy arrival at the mound's upper chambers.

"This way," said the messenger as he slipped off the ant and climbed down its leg. Anand followed him in near darkness to what was obviously once the mound's royal residence. They pulled themselves through the portal to find a sprawling gathering. The remains of a simple but abundant feast littered the floor. Officers were seated on rugs and eating dinner off of wort leaves.

In the distance, the women sat at their own leaves. Though it was dark, Anand could see the females had none of the restraint their men had when it came to dress. The wives were clothed in the richest spoils of war, and each was clanking with jewelry. Their pendants made them stooped, their multiple nose rings distorted their nostrils, and heavy earrings of amber and pyrite stretched their lobes to their shoulders.

The women's voices were coarse and shrieking, but when the handsome man-boy entered, they quieted to admire him. A few of them had naturally pale, yellowish skin, which was left unpowdered. Others enhanced their color using powders of marigold. *Light skin is valued everywhere,* thought Anand.

Anand roused admiration in some of the men as well who looked on him approvingly. Clad only in a loincloth, he stood with broad shoulders, a prominent chest, and his chin held high. He bent his toes inward to accentuate the bulk of his thighs. Pleckoo was eating with the other captains, slipping food under the rag about his face. Anand bowed his head, then made the gesture of esteeming.

"Hulkro is all powerful," said Anand, "and blessed is his Prophet, Commander Tahn."

The other officers returned the greeting.

"Have you eaten, Quegdoth?" asked Pleckoo.

"I have taken from the gullets of the ants."

"Enjoy some real food," said Pleckoo. "Be seated.

Forgive our poor lights, but we are so far from foraging places."

Anand sat at the leaf, aware that all eyes were on him. The men were silent as he looked at the food and found an abundance of ants' eggs as transparent as the ghost queen that laid them. There was also a sun stew of greens and some shriveled leaf-cutter mushrooms. He reached for an egg and the greens.

"Eat a mushroom, Quegdoth," said Pleckoo. "Don't you like them?"

Anand hesitated. He realized mushrooms must be a delicacy, even exotic, to some of these men.

"I . . . I have never eaten this kind of mushroom," said Anand. "Only the stringy kind that grow like ears on the sides of trees."

"Eat one and grow stronger," said a figure in darkness at the end of the platter. "For the army of Hulkro will march on these mushrooms." The voice was rich and loud and filled the chamber with its authority.

Anand picked up a mushroom and bit into it. He pretended to be disgusted.

"Not to your liking?" said the voice.

"No, sire. I am but a humble Tjamedi of a low caste who does not always appreciate the refinements of the privileged."

"Quegdoth, you are a blessed son of Hulkro," said the voice. "Soon you shall live in the upper chambers of a conquered mound and eat what you please. You will dress your women and children in finery—and your slaves and concubines, too. Come here, boy, and sit beside me."

Anand rose and went to the voice. "Bring me a torch," said the figure to a slave girl. She removed one of the few from a wall. The figure rose and used the torch to examine Anand's face.

"How many summers have you seen?" he asked.

"Seventeen."

"Seventeen! Hulkro has blessed you with many gifts, my son, many of which you demonstrated on the field today. Not the least of your gifts is this capacity for learning our language."

Anand looked at the man's heavy face and then saw his great belly, which flapped over his crotch. He was one of the few Hulkrites that was overfed. His face had the smugness of a Slopeish royal but his gestures were less refined. Anand thought he saw yellowish skin through the cracks of the man's paint.

"Whom am I speaking with, sire?" asked Anand, his heart thumping. Was this the Prophet of the Hulkrites?

"I am Edgeth, a second cousin of the Prophet."

Anand started to prostrate himself when Edgeth scoffed.

"No need for that, Quegdoth. We prostrate ourselves before the Termite and no other. I think it is best you meet my cousin. The Prophet is in need of clever young men to lead his warriors . . . especially men from lands we wish to liberate someday."

"I live to serve Hulkro," Anand said, "and should like to call myself a Hulkrite soon."

"Then you are. For the time being, you shall live here in Jatal-dozh. You are no longer a recruit but a warrior of the One True God. Pleckoo has asked we make you a lieutenant and will conduct your conversion ceremony in the morning. We have prepared quarters for you, Lieutenant Quegdoth."

Anand smiled. Promotions were rapid in this army.

"You will find a torch there and a comely slave girl. She has been bathed and perfumed, so enjoy her. As she refuses to accept Hulkro as her god, she will not be with us after tomorrow."

"My deep thanks," said Anand, but he wondered why he was offered this gift. Perhaps Edgeth, whose age and corpulence would prevent him from enjoying intercourse, would spy on Anand for the chance to live through him. *Or perhaps, they want to make sure I can father children.*

"In a few days you will depart for the capital mound for an audience with Tahn the Prophet."

"A thousand thanks," said Anand, bowing his head. He trembled with excitement. His only worry was that things were going a bit too well. Before crawling through the portal, Anand turned and looked at the men, bowing in respect. He saw Edgeth whispering in Pleckoo's ear—was that suspicion he saw in their faces as they watched him crawl out? He was not sure.

Anand was led to what had long ago been the chambers of a merchant. The rooms stank from a fresh coat of shellac and there was no furniture save the flat sack stuffed with rags that the Hulkrites used for a mattress. Still, it was far more comfortable than a bed of sand under a leaf tent. The mattress even had a blanket, albeit a crude one, of chewed egg-cloth. Under it was a very sad girl. The room was too well lit, with several torches spaced around the bedroom which confirmed Anand's suspicions that he was being spied on through holes in a wall.

"Please, stand," said Anand and the girl rose, slow as the sunrise, avoiding his eyes. Her skin was yellowish with brown freckles.

"Turn around, please," said Anand. She did so with reluctance. Anand's breathing increased as he saw the twin globes of her buttocks. His rapture fled when he saw the incisions at her calves. She had been hamstrung and the scars were only freshly healed. A wave of pity came over him and he slumped.

"I'm sorry," he said. "You may lie down."

He knew it was painful for her to stand. She looked at him in disdain, then crawled over the bed with her rump held high, waiting for him to take her from behind.

"I hope you'll be quick," she said.

"Not like this. Please. I've no wish to hurt you."

"What?" she said, and turned to stare at him.

"Please. Lie down," he said, and she watched in astonishment as he picked up the blanket and neatly laid it over her. Once she was covered, he removed his boots and loincloth and joined her.

"What is your name?" he whispered.

"Durelma," she said, avoiding his eyes.

"Where are you from? Whisper to me."

"I am a Slopeite, from the mound of Palzhad."

He reached for her and felt her cold yet sweaty skin.

"You have no reason to fear me," he said in Slopeish. "My name is . . . Vof." He had almost said his real name. She might be a spy and her hamstrung condition might have been a tragic yet clever disguise.

"You speak Slopeish, but you are not from the Slope," she said.

"I am from the land of Tjamed, very far to the east. A journey of a hundred days," said Anand.

"Why are you so less brutal?" she asked, her upper-caste arrogance returning.

"Less brutal than whom? Slopeites are as brutal as Hulkrites. Their ruling goddess is Mantis. They war to feed her human blood. And their royals rape the common people."

"The gods command us to war."

"No, sister. Your *priests* command you."

"You don't sound like a Hulkrite at all," she said and turned away from him.

Anand turned her to look in her eyes. He placed his arm over her and pulled his body, warm as summer sand, against her own. She seemed unsure at first, but then he felt her relax and accept his warmth.

"Are you going to violate me?" she asked. She could feel his hardened sex throbbing against her.

"No. I do not wish to violate you even though you are an idolater," said Anand, playing the Hulkrite. "I wish no harm to any human as I wish no human to harm me. I place myself inside the bodies of others only when they permit me to do so," he said, drawing on the Dranverites' code.

Durelma was stunned into quiet.

"For my own survival, we need to look like we are making love, though," he whispered in her ear. "I know they are watching us and testing me."

"What do I care if you survive?"

"Because we can save each other. I know they plan to kill you."

"What? When?"

"Tomorrow, but I know how you can save yourself."

Tears welled in her eyes and she bit her fist.

"Keep crying," he said, "till you've no more tears." She found herself suddenly comforted and turned to look at him, searching his eyes and wanting to trust.

"Were you married?" he asked.

"I was. I watched as they killed my husband—lopped his head off, then kicked it around the room like a toy."

"Did you love him?"

"Not at first."

"Can you close your eyes, think of me as him?"

She was quiet, blinking, lost in a memory.

"What did he do that you liked?" Anand asked.

"His . . . tongue," she said and lay on her back.

"Yes," said Anand, smiling as he recalled his golden afternoons with Jidla. "Do you invite me to do that?"

"Yes," she said.

Anand slid out from under the blanket and used his tongue in a soft attack, determined to give her the tenderest experience. Her body shook as he used the raised buds at the back of his tongue on the ceiling of her vault. Only after her hands eased their grip on his hair did he move from where he was.

"Listen to me," he said, climbing over her, and pulling the blanket over them as he whispered. "I will stay on top of you, pretending to be inside. Act as if I *am* inside and cry out, as if in pain or in joy."

"All right," she said.

As Anand thrust above her, Durelma began a rhythmic crying.

"Good," he whispered. "Now shake your head, back and forth."

Anand pretended to climax and decided it was better to do it quietly than make a loud show of it.

"Thank you," he whispered, and kissed her cheek before rolling to her side. She looked at him, mystified.

"Why didn't you just—like these other demons, who . . ."

"Because I am not a demon," Anand whispered. "In the morning, I will tell you how to save yourself. Sleep well."

When the sun came up, he woke and saw Durelma's back was turned to him. He tapped her shoulder and she flinched.

"Listen," he said, turning her to face him and locking her eyes. "This very morning, you must make a show of accepting the Hulkrites' god. If your gods are as merciful as you claim, they will understand when you pretend to worship the Termite."

"I can't do that," she said, and looked away.

"This morning, *to save your life*," he whispered, "you must tell the slave master that Hulkro came to you in a dream, welcomed you into his six arms, and accepted your pledge to abandon all other idols."

He hurriedly tied on his loin cloth, watching as she buried her face in the mattress and cried. "Perhaps they should just take my life," she said.

"The world belongs to those who wait for their moment. Just say *the words*," Anand said after he tied on his antennae. "'I accept Hulkro as my one and only god.'"

But she just shook her head, avoided making eye contact with him, then limped back to the slaves' quarters.

**A** few evenings later, an initiate was going through the conversion ritual that Anand had just completed. Although he enjoyed engaging in deceptions, he did not enjoy his guise as a worshipper of Hulkro. The Hulkrites were genocidal rapists with no capacity for mercy, but their religious ceremonies had a sweetness that was sickening.

Anand had detested the plodding rites of the Cajorite priests but now he realized they were worthy spectacles with an impressive gravity. Slopeish sacred music was grim, but executed by skilled musicians. By contrast, the Hulkrites had simple rituals and their music was a folksy affair, composed for participation by the masses. As Anand entered the cathedral with Pleckoo and the other officers, the "Friendship" song was repeated until all were seated.

> Welcome, welcome
> Show the sign,
> Friends of Hulkro
> Are friends of mine.

Anand made "the sign" to his neighbors, an imitation of termite antennae, made by wiggling the forefingers over the eyes. Termite antennae were short and curly, and when a worshipper made the sign, he shut his eyes to suggest the insect's blindness to skin color.

Anand sat on a bench in the men's section of the reconstructed cathedral. Where a hundred idols once stood, there was now a slice of wood with a termite track to suggest Hulkro's presence. The warriors next to Anand picked up his hands and raised them to sway as they sang.

When the seats were filled, a warrior-preacher, The Robertsah Patezh, stood on the altar in a sheer gown that revealed his armor and weapons underneath. Anand had learned the Patezh was not a priest who interceded between men and Hulkro. His name in Hulkrish meant "The Called Upon" and he was known to be "drunk in the spirit of the Termite." His smile was constant but looked to Anand like something false, like an object he glued to his face each day.

"Welcome soldiers of Hulkro-uh," sang The Called Upon. His accent was typical of the mounds to the south of Zarren-dozh, with a short vowel attached to the end of every phrase. "Joy be upon you in our holy war-uh. Joy be upon those we liberate-uh. Let us throw up our hands and praise almighty Hulkro-uh, for one who was lost is now found-uh. Praise Hulkro-uh — for she will be reborn-uh!"

Anand turned to watch as six women carried a cocoon down the aisle and set it before the altar. A knife poked through the top and the new convert freed herself and stepped out. She was slow to rise and it pained her to stand. Anand recognized Durelma. She was sobbing as she stood before The Called Upon, who opened his arms to rock her in his embrace. The congregation sang:

> *She needs Hulkro like we all do*
> *She surrenders to His will*
> *She loves Hulkro like we all do*
> *For Hulkro, she would kill, kill, kill.*

The Called Upon stepped away and Durelma knelt before the piece of wood. She threw up her arms and prayed aloud. "Take me, Great Termite, I give all that I am to Thee."

Two young men with termite wings on their backs

stepped onto the altar and lowered a garment over Durelma's shoulders. It was sewn from termite cocoons and covered with wood dust. A young warrior brought a freshly hatched termite larva to the altar. The termite was soft and white with no strength. Its little fat legs writhed like individual maggots. The Called Upon took the hatchling and raised it to the heavens.

"Mighty Hulkro-uh, when we were starving and abandoned in the Dustlands, Thou gave us Thy countless daughters so that we might eat-uh. We praise Thee and consecrate this termite to Thy name-uh." The Called Upon lowered the termite to mouth level, bit into its head, then chewed and swallowed.

"Arise, Durelma, partake of Hulkro's sacrifice!"

She rose and bit into the larva, grimacing as she tasted its turpentine. As Anand knew from his own ceremony, she would immediately be plunged into a lucid drunkenness.

"Arise, all, and welcome a new Hulkrite-uh!"

The congregation arose, stamped their feet, and began another hymn. The larva was hurled into the crowd and torn into bits. Its lymph was smeared on faces. Its flesh was eaten and intoxicated the worshippers. Other larvae were brought in so all could eat and imbibe the spirit.

Durelma, supported by two other women, joined the others in an endless dance around the pews. The men danced in the other direction. Anand joined the dance, and at one point, when the worshippers jammed in a corner, he brushed against Durelma and caught her eye. She did not look away from him, but nodded in a way that acknowledged a secret camaraderie.

Afterwards, Anand left for Zarren-dozh on a train of ghost ants that traveled with speed at night. The essence of the termite he had bitten gave color and intensity to his thoughts. The primary thought was a question that buzzed in his brain like a mob of blowflies:

*How should I prepare for a meeting with Commander Tahn, Prophet of the One and Only God?*

The soldiers of the ant train were deferential to Anand and prepared his tent and food. They stopped for fresh ants at several mounds in various states of reconstruction. These other Hulkrish mounds were much the same as Jatal-dozh. The inhabitants were warriors with multiple wives and the women's only occupation was the ordering about of sickly slaves. The outdoor slaves were hamstrung males who carried out drudgeries under overseers who snapped their whips.

Anand had been given a helmet to wear with an amber carving of a termite at the end of a central antenna. The sight of the carving commanded respect from all who passed him and nearly everyone asked him to extend their regards to the Prophet. They proffered their chips of quartz and pyrite for the Holy War Fund, which filled several sacks.

Thirteen days later, Anand sighted Zarren-dozh, a mound that had once been the religious and political center of the Slopeish nation. It was enormous and glistening under fresh shellac. Its ghost ants were the largest Anand had seen.

Strangely, this mound had more resemblance to Cajoria than Jatal-dozh. Not all its inhabitants could live in its chambers, so rings of outside dwellings had sprung up like mushrooms after rain. The rings were not a shamble of shanties, but the dwellings were small and made of modest materials.

What was very different was that there were other kinds and colors of ants that lived among the ghosts and even hitched rides atop them. Among the adopted ants were yellow leaf-cutters who carried grass and leaves from some distant meadow. *So this is where they grow their mushrooms,* thought Anand.

The human slaves were more abundant and just as miserable, but were culled from races in lands unknown or forgotten by Slopeites. Everywhere he looked, Anand hoped to see the people of his mother's clan. He searched the face of every brown-skinned girl wishing that she was Daveena. What if she had been hamstrung or was pregnant with the child of a Hulkrish rapist? When Anand's rage began to consume him, he determined to empty his mind. He knew that rage must wait in hiding, like a lair spider, and spring at the appropriate time.

It took much of the morning to climb to the top of the mound, where Tahn the Prophet occupied a crystal palace. Anand was brought to large, spacious rooms of his own. The interiors conformed to the Hulkrish ethic of austerity, but there were barrels of flashy treasures and the floors were piled with rugs as thick as beds. One of the rugs saddened Anand when he realized it was a Britasyte creation, a skillful depiction of a red scorpion carrying her young on her back. Had they taken it from the Pleps?

For the first time in moons, Anand would sleep on a true bed. He ate from a leaf piled high with sun-toasted cricket eggs. The eggs were surrounded by dunking-cups of different sauces. A servant girl bathed and painted Anand for his audience with the Prophet. The paint was more refined, less sticky, and as pure white as a cloud. He was admiring his startling whiteness in an obsidian mirror when he heard the rustle of someone squeezing through the portal.

Anand noticed the ragged nostrils first and tensed. He remembered to use his Dranverish accent.

"Captain Pleckoo!"

"Quegdoth . . . The Prophet sent me to welcome you to Zarren-dozh."

"I am honored."

"I've just met the commander returning from his conquest of the Thrip People in the west. Such a lazy people from his description—they harvest thrips as food and their silk for clothing. The men spend most of their time eating kiln-roasted cannabis and dancing in worship before some scorpion idol. Their women do all the work."

"Why have they never been conquered before?"

"They live in the west, which the ignorant think is some Land of Death where the Sun dies each day."

"Were they receptive to the Prophet's message?"

"The Prophet said they were too fuddled to hear it. They practically handed us their women who he says are quite beautiful, that he can't fuck enough of them. Our Prophet was disappointed in the battle—he can't savor such an easy victory. But enough of that. He's quite intrigued by you."

"Is he?"

"Of course. He's heard all about this remarkable recruit with a talent for war and languages—from a land of outrageous wealth. Just as I may rule the Slope some day, so may you rule this place called Tjamed."

Anand was imagining Pleckoo in his white paint seated atop a Mushroom Throne. The image was so disturbing he was unable to move any part of him including his mouth.

"I've got to go, Quegdoth. Let your girl here know if you need anything. She's yours for all purposes. Praise Hulkro."

"Praise Him," Anand managed to say.

After Pleckoo left, Anand looked deep in his mirror and labored internally to construct a mask of adoration and reverence for the Warrior-Prophet. Anand wanted to jam his dagger through Tahn's skull, but knew that at their first meeting, he had to win his love.

# CHAPTER 37

## HULKRO'S PROPHET

**A**nand yanked out some nose hairs, which made his eyes tear, just before he pulled himself through the portal into Tahn's chamber. When Anand reached the Prophet, he had the appearance of someone trying not to cry.

"Who is this that snivels before me?" asked Tahn with a grin. "Surely not a warrior for Hulkro?"

"I am indeed a warrior for Hulkro," said Anand, affecting a quiver in his voice. "I would be lying if I said I was not overwhelmed with gratitude at this moment. Before anything else, I should like to say I am thankful, Commander."

Anand looked Tahn in the eyes. Inside them, Anand saw what he really desired: images of slashing the fraud in two and then stomping on his skull until it was a fine paste. Tahn smiled at him, charmed to see him holding back tears.

"For what are you thankful, young man?"

"Never did I imagine I would be here in the presence of the man selected by the One and Only to reveal his desires for mankind."

"What did you think you would become?"

"I thought I was to waste my life as a hungry slave, mated to a miserable wife so that our enslavers would have workers for their own children."

Anand turned away from Tahn and pretended the need to compose himself. "Forgive me, Commander," he said, striking his most manly pose. "But since submitting to the will of Hulkro, I am often overcome by joy."

Tahn nodded his head and rose. "Hulkro is love," he said and opened his arms. Anand had imagined this very moment and summoned up the image of his return to Yormu at Cajoria. When he walked into Tahn's arms, Anand hugged with the warmth he would give his father.

"Now then," said Tahn, pulling away. "I have always planned, as my final triumph, the conquest of the rich and mighty Slope. But perhaps it is just a step to a place more magnificent. Will you tell me about this intriguing land called Tjamed?"

"Of course, Commander. I am just as curious about Zarren-dozh."

"I'm sure you are," said Tahn and patted Anand's

shoulder. "Ambitious men are curious men." Tahn brought Anand to a portal that led to an outside terrace where they looked upon the glories of the Hulkrish Empire's capital.

"Is it true that the ants of Tjamed have a golden chitin?" Tahn asked. "And that the mounds are made of yellow pyrite?"

"Yes. It is so abundant it is almost worthless to the Tjamedis. And so is rose quartz, which is almost as easily sifted from their northern sands. But the greatest treasures of Tjamed are its millions of souls who hunger for the light of the True God."

"Yes, yes," said Tahn, heading for a divan. "Sit and have a bowl of mead with me."

As if he were in a trance, Anand wove a description of Tjamed for Tahn. He was uncertain as to where he had pulled the details, but much of what he recited was from studies and histories of peoples absorbed by the Dranverites. When Tahn asked him how they could reach Tjamed, Anand had a ready answer.

"Tjamed has existed in near isolation for ten thousand summers. A great and violent river, the Malvup, is impossible to traverse and separates the country from other lands. It is only at the height of summer, in the dry season, when the river sinks underground and rocks emerge, that bridges can be laid and a crossing becomes possible."

Tahn began calculating when to make his conquest. "I will have to consult Hulkro on when we might take Tjamed. It may take some time to absorb and convert the Slopeish nation—so perhaps this Tjamed should wait a few years."

When Tahn had no more questions, the two of them faced each other, held hands and gave thanks to Hulkro. A guard escorted Anand back to his chambers, where he collapsed on his bed. The trance he had entered to weave his tale had taken all his energy.

The following morning, Anand was summoned to the top of the mound, where he looked with Tahn on fields full of warriors on ants engaged in exercises. They left to review the troops upon an ant that crawled swiftly down the mound as they ate breakfast from sacks around their necks. Anand pulled out the cap of a fresh leaf-cutter mushroom that was gleaming white.

"Prophet, this type of mushroom is a great rarity. How do you come by such a treasure?"

"After the termite, the ghost ant is the greatest of all Hulkro's gifts, for ghosts can enslave any other ant. Soon we will export a leaf-cutter queen to every mound in Hulkren, and as the mushrooms swell in our mounds, so will the wombs of our women."

Anand was astonished. *So he knows about the mushroom's powers!*

"In Tjamed we have heard of the Slopeites," said Anand, "and their yellow ants which strip trees. The people are said to use magic to grow this fungus. Supposedly their queens are sorceresses."

"Just as the ghosts brought back ant slaves, we brought back Slopeish humans, including one woman in particular. They do what they must to make these mushrooms grow."

"But this woman—is she somehow divine?"

"Only Hulkro is divine. The woman has no magic. It is simply a matter of nature, something her water provides that discourages the mold."

Anand's heart was thumping as he asked his next questions. Would the answers lead to the question that plagued his being: Were Daveena and the Pleps alive?

"But what is it about this woman's urine in particular? It must be special."

"Not so special, Quegdoth. At first, the powers of her water failed and the Yellow Mold threatened to rot our tunnels. Then we forced her to admit she ingests something to give her piss its powers."

"Really! What was that?"

"The eggs of grass roaches. Since this 'sorceress' resumed eating them, the mold has vanished."

"Strange. Are eggs of roaches so easily obtained in this sandy place?"

"We sustain a colony of such roaches on our outskirts," Tahn said, as his nose wrinkled and his voice dropped. "And the human clan that tends them."

"A clan of roach people?" asked Anand, with a derisive chuckle in his voice that didn't completely hide his excitement.

"Yes. They call themselves Britasytes. And a filthy, loathsome bunch they are. Never trust one, for their every word is a lie. They are failing us now, even though we have offered them their lives."

"Failing you, sir?"

"Their roaches are dying and they are producing less of the eggs we will need for other leaf-cutter colonies. We may need to extinguish this clan and abduct some other one and see if they might be more cooperative."

Anand hid his alarm. An idea came to him that he considered perhaps a moment too long before speaking. Tahn was staring at him, wondering about his silence.

"May I confess something, Prophet?"

"Certainly."

"In Tjamed, my family were . . . we were . . ."

"Yes?"

Anand hung his head.

"We were . . . roach slaves."

"Roach slaves?"

"Yes, sir. Please, understand, it was not something we chose. Our caste was confined to an area where it was our duty to raise roaches. We collected and tanned the egg pouches for leather and made boots and other goods derived of them. I was considered polluted—as was all my family and all in our caste."

Tahn was smiling.

"You are not polluted, Lieutenant Quegdoth. Here in Hulkren we have no castes. Hulkro loves all his children and all men are welcomed to soldier in his Army of Universal Love."

Anand nodded, wiped at true tears which had leaked for reasons he wasn't sure of. "Thank you," he said.

"Thank you for joining us." Tahn said, then looked at Anand with a strangely sweet expression. "Would you know then what we might do to revive these roaches—to insure their survival and increase their egg production?"

"I might," said Anand. "I'm interested to see them, as I am interested to see all of Zarren-dozh."

"And you will. As I should like to hear more about Tjamed. Can you teach me their language?"

"Brefok," said Anand in Dranverish. "That means 'certainly.'"

Anand was prickly with guilt. He did not want to teach Tahn the Dranverites' language much less inform him of a great and rich civilization he would lust to conquer. Anand had started a lie to save his Britasytes, and now it threatened the nation he admired. *I will need to end this danger that threatens every nation on the Sand and soon,* he thought even as he mustered his warmest smile for Tahn.

After the inspection of the troops, Anand toured the auxiliaries that sustained the capital and was brought to the termite colony first. Tahn brought Anand to the edge of a great pit where slaves pulled sleds of twigs and wood chips to dump through the hatch of a latticework grate. Below were the termites eating wood from distant pines to enrich their lymph with turpentine.

"Hulkro loves all His creatures," said Tahn, "but He takes the guise of the humble termite, the insect that thrived in these devastated lands. It was the termite that fed the Chosen People when they were lost, that enabled our early victories."

"Why are termites so seldom eaten now?"

"At one time it was all we Hulkrites had to eat. They were gathered to the point of extinction as their own food source, wood, was vanishing. That's when Hulkro ended our trial and sent the ghost ants to save us. Now termites are only eaten in the rituals."

"How did the ghost ants appear?"

"They descended from the heavens," said Tahn. "Just after we prayed for food, an inseminated queen landed before my clan, an ant more magnificent than we had ever seen. She had shed her wings, ready to burrow and raise her first brood. That's when the clouds parted to reveal Hulkro, in His aspect as Flying Lord of the Heavens. He said, 'I offer this ant queen to you and your people, my Prophet. From her, all glories and victories will arise. Take care of her, guard her, rub her scents on your people, and she will provide for you.'"

"She did not attack you when approached?"

"She would have. But then a drone landed just after her, spent from planting his seed. Before he died and exuded the death-stink, I rubbed myself on his undersides to rob him of his odor. My clan did as I did and the queen accepted us. She laid her first eggs near the abandoned mound. The hatchlings grew quickly, were excellent hunters, and brought back food for all of us."

"From whom did you learn to ride the ghosts? To antennate for food and steal kin-scent?"

"The righteous of many nations have fled here and

brought their skills and knowledge. Oh, Vof Queg-doth, now those righteous will prevail. So say I."

"Then so says Hulkro," Anand responded. Both looked to the sky and nodded in submission before turning north. On the breeze, Anand caught a familiar scent of roaches. His heart raced with fear and excitement.

"I . . . I do believe I smell roaches," he said, wrinkling his nose.

"We are close to their pit," said Tahn, looking disgusted and angry.

"Commander, if I may ask, have you given up all hope on these roach people?"

"I have. A few of these Britasytes submitted to the faith and went through the rebirth ritual. As soon as we gave them freedom to move about, they ran off. Most were recaptured—we fed them to the ants."

Anand gulped. "Idiots," he said after recovering. When the ants would crawl no closer to the roaches, Tahn and Anand dismounted and went on foot. They reached a great pit covered with a lattice grate of heavily shellacked wood. Anand looked down and saw the roaches clinging to the grate's underside were failing. He knew exactly what was wrong with them. Their bodies looked thin and small and the mild shake of their antennae indicated a lack of water and proper food. He looked between them and could make out the shadows of the sand-sleds at the pit's bottom.

"These roaches are not doing well," Anand said, "but I would need to have a closer look sometime to figure out what's wrong."

"Perhaps you could accompany one of our faithful who descends now and again to bring up the eggs."

"Of course, sir. It's been a while since I've covered myself with roach muck. But I would do it for our Lord Termite."

"When you do, promise me you will bathe several times afterwards," said Tahn, and Anand joined him in chuckling. It was the greatest performance of Anand's life, for he was stricken with grief. His people needed freedom and wandering as others need food and water. They had to be sick and dying in this dark hole in the ground.

Tahn led them to a trunk-trail of ghost ants to catch a ride and continue the tour of insect colonies. "I'm very interested in bringing more lights to Hulkren at night," Tahn said as they reached an area where lightning flies were being cultivated. Anand watched as a raggedly dressed foreman with a great head of fuzzy hair pleaded for something. His rags were not white and his skin was not painted, nor was that of the other humans in a vast cage imprisoned with the flies.

"What is this infidel's complaint?" Tahn shouted to the Hulkrish overseer who translated.

"He says they need more rotting wood and black soil. They need more water to keep everything damp or the eggs won't hatch. He says the flies won't thrive or reproduce if they can't fly about."

The lightning-fly foreman pounded his fist into his hand and dared to show an angry face to Tahn whose eyes turned to slits and whose lips disappeared.

"He says his people haven't enough food either," added the overseer.

At that moment, a slug, the favorite food of lightning flies, was being eased through the hatch of the grate. The slug landed on its back and writhed with its long, moist sucker to the sky. The scrawny, fuzzy-haired people converged on the slug and tore it with their naked hands to stuff in their mouths. Tahn was furious.

"Why are they eating the flies' food?" he shouted.

The foreman's brow wrinkled in defiance. He addressed Tahn directly in broken Hulkrish. "Because we starve," he shouted back.

"Your people shall be fed," Tahn said, "but no one speaks in that tone to the Prophet." He turned to the overseer. "Kill him."

Without hesitation, the overseer removed his sword and thrust it through the foreman's chest. "Remind these people they are lost without Hulkro," said Tahn. "This man is now doomed for eternity. He will never know the Promised World."

The others in the cage turned away to hide their faces in case Tahn should turn on them next. The sudden murder sickened Anand and he was sure he could not contain his discomfort. He forced his thoughts to somewhere else, anywhere else. He looked out at the sight of the ant parades up and down the mound and tried to count the different ants mixed among the ghosts. The leaf-cutters seemed to be a separate entity with their own leafy parades, but when they antennated the ghosts for food, they ate from the regurgitation.

"Those must be the leaf-cutter ants," said Anand.

"Yes."

"And they are taking those leaf bits inside the mound? As a base for growing mushrooms?"

"Correct. The mushroom chambers are a strange and wonderful sight, full of leaf-cutters of different sizes and all set to different tasks. Would you like to see it?"

"I would!"

Tahn and Anand entered a side tunnel at the half-way point of the mound, then rode down a spiraling gradient in the darkness. Tahn demanded torches from servant girls who poked at the translucent eggs at the end of wands. The visible larvae squirmed in their casings and the light increased. As they descended deeper, the ant traffic thickened.

"We are approaching the ghost queen," said Tahn. "These ants are impossible to steer if they hold food and are passing their queen."

"I have heard the ghost ant queens are the most magnificent insects on the Sand," said Anand.

"See for yourself," said Tahn who looked in a fatherly way at Anand. Tahn relaxed his grip on the antennae and allowed the ant to follow the scent. Soon they were riding in a startling current of ants. The greenish lights of the humans' torches lit up the ghosts with a disquieting luminescence.

Anand was not prepared for the sight of the ghost ant queen. She was perhaps the largest insect in the world. As her gaster pendulated from side to side, it left chains of eggs that nurse ants grabbed in their mandibles to carry to the hatching chambers. Darting among the nurses were humans who snatched a few for the meals of Tahn and his elite.

The ant they were riding approached to regurgitate to the queen ant. When she opened her mouth, Anand marveled at the great, living cave of her maw. It was as tall as ten humans standing on each other's shoulders, and just as wide. She accepted the food from the ant, as well as that of fifty others, before she closed her mouth. After leaving the queen, Tahn and Anand's ant bogged down in the exiting traffic. Smaller ghosts crawled across their mount's head and some were upside down on the ceiling.

In the tunnel, Tahn steered the ant in the direction of a sign with a mushroom drawing. As they ventured down, Anand's nostrils were filled with the dank scent of rotting leaves and new mushrooms. Around them, the stream of leaf-cutters and their leaf shards increased.

Tahn halted their mount before one of several mushroom chambers and descended into it on foot. Anand followed him inside and saw it was well-illuminated. Palzhanites were in the process of cutting the mushrooms at the base of their stalks to pile in sleds. Anand had eaten mushrooms his entire life, but to see them shooting up by the thousands from a springy loam was eerie.

"This is the original chamber," Tahn said, "where

the mushrooms have fruited for some time now." Just at that moment a Palzhanite slave girl dropped from exhaustion into the mushrooms, crushing some. "Get up!" screamed a Hulkrish overseer as he lashed at her back festering with sores.

"Whip her again and she may die!" screamed a woman in Hulkrish, who staggered over on crippled legs and threw up her arms as a shield. The woman had a crying baby strapped to her back. The overseer lowered his whip, looked worried, and turned to Tahn. Anand realized the overseer had orders not to harm this slave. Whoever she was, Anand admired her, as he admired anyone who fought against the infliction of pain.

"Good day, Majesty," said Tahn with mock courtliness as the woman helped the girl to her feet. As the two walked back to their tasks, Anand saw that both had been hamstrung and that the woman had an expanded belly.

"Majesty?" Anand asked Tahn.

"The Sorceress Queen Polexima of Cajoria . . . my greatest prize," he said.

"A Slopeite?" Anand said, trying to conceal his surprise.

"Yes. She was visiting Palzhad when we raided. Look at her now, laboring with the people who worshipped her as a goddess. And she is pregnant! Her children shall worship Hulkro."

Anand's former queen was unrecognizable and as haggard as any Cajorite worker. He had heard Polexima was one of the few royals who treated her servants well and he saw now that it might be true. She turned to see Anand was staring at her. She stared back, unable to hide her hatred for all who wore a Hulkrish uniform. *She may have been Queen of the Cajorites, but I hate seeing her like this,* he thought.

Sleds arrived with a long thin bench to return the Slopeites to their sleeping cages in the mound's outer ring. Polexima and the others looked to be in pain as they trudged to the rough bench and straddled it. They collapsed on each other in exhaustion as the sled was dragged off.

"Vof," said Tahn with a curious smile. "I should like to invite you this evening to one of our strategy dinners."

"I'd be honored, Prophet, but I know so little about strategy."

"Oh, don't worry about that," Tahn said with a smirk. "The warriors tell their women that we'll be discussing our next campaigns. What actually takes place are conquests of a different kind."

"I see," said Anand, trying not to gulp.

"You strike me as a responsible young man, Quegdoth. I should like you to join the guards tonight and train as a monitor. And when you become a captain—and I know you will be a captain soon—you'll be able to join us in what is our just reward for fulfilling our holy duties."

"Ah, of course I'll be there," said Anand as dread crept over him.

## CHAPTER 38

## CONVERSION OF THE MUMMIFIERS

It was dark when Anand was summoned to the feasting chamber. He had been instructed to wear his armor and bring his sword. When he arrived, he saw the Hulkrish elite were dressed only in loincloths and lounging over a vast floor of crystal tiles covered in carpets. In the back of the chamber was a broad flight of stairs that was dark at its peak, but had a well-lit platform at its bottom. Anand was directed to stand guard by the portal with a cluster of other promising lieutenants and one of them handed him a chaw of kwondle bark. "You'll need this to stay awake," said the thickset man known as Toothless whose tongue often protruded through the gap in his teeth to enunciate his words.

With hands clasped behind their backs, Anand and the guards watched Tahn and his captains feast from leaf platters and imbibe spirits from bowls large enough to bathe in. Even from a distance, Anand could smell that it was a strong, distilled spirit mixed with turpentine and flavored with sweet alyssum—just its aroma made Anand feel a little drunk. He tucked the chaw between his teeth and his cheek and soon felt its mild stimulus.

The officers finished their meal—a rich roast of pregnant katydids in a sauce of crushed garlic—which was followed by more drinking, a burping contest, and raucous laughter that sent the stink of garlic and turpentine into the air. Tahn led the men to a row of carved and gilded nut-shell tubs where servant girls waited to scrub away their white paint with a solvent. Other servants were rolling up the remains of the feast as still others were setting out silken floor cushions.

Anand wondered what could possibly be offered here that the men could not get at home with their multiple wives and endless concubines.

From the corner of his eye, Anand watched as Tahn, Pleckoo, and the other captains emerged from the final rinsing tub, scrubbed clean of their white paint. Ten or so of the men were as pale and yellow as Tahn and from the same stock. The other forty men, from newly absorbed nations, were brown men of various shades and a few were an almost purple-black. Pleckoo's own skin had lightened from wearing the sun-blocking paint.

"Why have they removed their white?" Anand asked Toothless.

"To enjoy the pleasure of flesh without paint," Toothless said with a broad smirk. "You'll like what's coming next."

Male slaves, whose eyelids had been sewn shut, were guided to a bandstand with a variety of acorn drums that played different pitches. They were followed by a naked trio of gold-dusted women who stood before some amplifying-cones to sing. The musicians commenced an exotic music that was primitive but haunting with harmonies that fell into a strange and occasional dissonance. The music grew more intense, then slowed to something quieter at Tahn's signal.

A buxom, yellow-skinned woman descended from the shadows at the top of the stairs, perhaps in her fiftieth summer. Her ankles, her wrists, and her neck were ringed in thick strands of beads. Her hair was longer than her body and trailed behind her. When she reached the platform at the bottom, Tahn walked to her with beads of turquoise which he added to the bulge around her neck. After accepting his payment, she clapped her hands. The music spiraled, got more frantic.

Over one-hundred women descended from the stairs in single file, fanning out as they reached the platform. They were naked and completely unadorned except for red paint on their pouting lips and a bright powdering of satchu pollen between their thighs. Each was full and curvy and all had naturally pale and yellowish skin. Most were quite beautiful, but some had the close-set eyes of Slopeish royals.

*Light skin!* Anand thought. *In his color-blind world, Tahn rewards his men with light-skinned women!*

The women gyrated in unison to the music, left then right, staring with harsh expressions into the men's eyes while they planned their selections. Tahn was the first to step forward, pointing to three different beauties that followed him to his floor cushion. By rank, the rest of his officers pointed at their pairs. The newest captains, like Pleckoo, got one woman apiece.

"At this point, it's best to look up," said Toothless, "if you don't want a smack across the face."

"For how long?" Anand asked, as he joined the guards in an upward gaze to the crystal ceiling where they could see the fractured night sky beyond.

"Well, you know—as long as it usually takes. Once the men pass out—and they will all pass out—we can sit and have our own feast. No girls or spirits, mind you—not until we're captains. But the leftover food is ours for the taking."

Though his head was tilted up, Anand looked down and saw a mass of activity that was in no way intended to bring more Hulkrites into the world.

The guards parted to allow servant girls to enter with fresh bowls of spirits, which they lugged in by twos and set among the revelers. Once the bowls were set down, the girls sprinkled the tops of the drops with powdered aphid sugar. Some of those who had completed bedding their prizes entered into drinking competitions, and were cheered for taking the longest drafts. Some men were already so drunk that they leaned too deeply into the drop, which adhered to their heads and shoulders and had to be scraped off and back into the bowl as they coughed.

Tahn, to Anand's surprise, was among the first to pass out from too much drink, and as the evening wore on, the rest of his men followed him into unconsciousness. The music ended and eventually, all the officers were sprawled and sleeping on the floor. The brothel mistress appeared again, clapped her hands, and herded her workers back up the stairs and out to the night.

Toothless yanked one of the passing servant girls by her tender arm, pulling her arm from its socket. "We'll have our dinner," he said to her crying face. She ran off and a short time later, fresh bowls of kwondle-bark tea were delivered as well as a leaf platter covered in food. When the food was consumed, Toothless went to the wall where the backsacks were hanging and returned with a purse of currency and a six-sided top to spin for wagers.

"Who'd like to lose some money?" Toothless asked, and the men went for their own purses. Anand had not brought any money but as he watched the game, his mind was spinning faster than any top—he was making plans.

The following morning, as Tahn and the others

were rising in a painful head fog, Anand paced with the other guards in a circle as a means to stay awake. "Vof Quegdoth," Tahn shouted from his mattress and Anand trotted over, heavy with sleepiness.

"At your service, Commander."

"I should like to send you to war, boy," he said, standing and shielding his eyes from the bright light entering the chamber. "But before you go, let's see if you can figure out how to save these roaches."

"I'll do my best, sir," said Anand, feigning indifference.

*Thank Madricanth*, he screamed inside himself.

For the first time in moons, Anand was wearing rags smeared with roach scent. He was accompanied to the roach pit by a one-eyed, hunchbacked overseer whose unfortunate task was to descend to the pit with bales of hay for the roaches and return from it with a supply of eggs for the Cajorites' queen and her people.

Anand studied the pit's confining grate and its hatch lashed with knots in eyehooks. Several Hulkrish guards cracked open the gate and lowered Anand and the overseer on a platform with ropes.

"First time we opened this gate, some of these people tried to escape inside their roaches," said the hunchback. "They crawl under their bellies and insert themselves in the scales, just like the roachlings do."

"I think I'm going to vomit," said Anand, in Slopeish.

"What's that you say?" said the overseer.

Anand repeated himself in Hulkrish. *Good, this man knows no Slopeish and would surely know no Britasyte,* Anand thought to himself.

"Yah . . . the smell of these monsters makes everyone sick."

As the platform descended, the roaches scurried away, then sensed a different presence. With their long, whip-like antennae, they antennated the two.

"This is the part that sickens me—when these demon insects brush me with their feelers," said the hunchback.

In the poorly lit pit, Anand saw that roaches weren't the only ones to scurry away. The Britasytes had retreated to the shelters of their sand-sleds, where he could hear them whispering prayer-songs to Madricanth.

"Do they always hide?" Anand asked.

"Always. Thank Hulkro."

"I was wondering what they look like."

"You'll regret it. Their women aren't bad-looking, if they weren't covered in this muck. They proudly wear it, like it was a bee-fuzz coat."

"In what tongue do you speak to them?" asked Anand.

"Not Hulkrish, which they are loath to learn. Some of 'em speak Slopeish, others know the Seed Eaters' or Carpenters' tongues."

"I know some Slopeish," Anand said. "Beautiful wanderers," said Anand in Britasyte filling the pit with his voice. "Come and look at me, your son and brother and cousin. I have come to rescue you. The Hulkrish idiot with me does not know I am speaking our language. Is Zedral there? Is my Aunt Glegina?"

No answer came. The roaches seemed particularly loud as they scurried around the pit.

"You know me as Anand, the spanner of two tribes, son of Corra of the Entreveans. I am in the guise of a Hulkrite and cannot stay or speak long. One of you must come forward. You must look as if you do not recognize me. Look fearful."

From out of the shadows of the sled wagon, Zedral appeared. He was haggard and his arms were as thin as spider thread. Anand started to laugh, a malevolent, condescending laugh for the overseer's benefit.

"You are right," he said in Hulkrish to the overseer as he searched for roach eggs. "This one is as ugly as centipede droppings."

The overseer laughed as Anand unsheathed his sword and talked to Zedral in a scolding tone. "Forgive my tone, beloved chieftain, but this Hulkrite must think I am chiding you. In some days' time, I will return to set you free."

"Is it really you, Anand?" asked Zedral.

"Yes. I must leave now, but when you see me again, perhaps in one or two moons, we will leave this place. Is my betrothed well?"

"Daveena is . . . she has suffered much. As we all have."

"Can she come out? Let me see her."

Moments later, a dark figure stepped out from behind Zedral. She was wearing a cloth over her head. Anand could not see her face.

"Daveena?"

"Yes," she said, barely able to speak. "Are you well, Anand?"

"I am now, after seeing you. My heart has ached for you every moment we have been apart. We cannot talk long—must not rouse this Hulkrite's suspicions."

Anand wept. The overseer looked at him with his one bulging eye as he hauled an egg casing up to the platform with the hook of his prod.

"This foul air stings my eye," Anand said in Hulkrish. "Can we go?"

"Gladly."

Anand stiffened himself and resumed shouting in Britasyte.

"You will not suffer much longer, beloved clan. Come closer, Zedral. I do this to you only to fulfill my guise."

When he came closer, Anand used his sword to scrape open the skin of Zedral's withered shoulder.

"They bleed red blood. They are humans!" Anand said to the overseer. "They can be saved."

"Not this lot. The Prophet's given up on them. As soon as we learn the secrets of raising roaches, we'll just fill up this pit with sand and bury the whole stinking bunch."

The overseer slit open the casing so Anand could see the eggs inside. "Look here," he said. "These are for the feasts of Queen Polexima. She was used to eating her eggs mixed into lovely little biscuits, she was, but now we feed 'em to her just like this. We make her subjects eat 'em, too."

"Disgusting," Anand said as the overseer tugged on the ropes so they could be hauled up. "Be prepared to escape," Anand shouted in Britasyte as he rose on the platform. "I will inform the Hulkrites that they need to make a daily delivery of fresh, green grass and fly larvae over the next moons so you can grow the roaches to their fullest and strongest. Make sure the riders are fitted with reins and steering bates. Pack your supplies."

The overseer gave Anand a sideways glare.

"What did you say to them?" he asked.

"I warned them. I told them to accept the Termite's love or submit to death and an eternity of torture."

"You are a good Hulkrite, Vof Quegdoth."

"And so are you, brother. I'll inform the Prophet of what we'll need here if the roaches are to thrive and give us a good supply of roach eggs. He'll need to keep these Britasytes alive in the meantime."

The Hulkrites had already conquered the Silk Moth and Bitter Ant People . . . or so the Hulkrites thought. Pleckoo's Silk Moth concubine had learned enough Hulkrish to communicate that the colony that had been subdued was not their capital, but an outpost of criminals, debtors, and other undesirables. One morning, Tahn summoned Pleckoo and Anand to his chambers.

"Faithful Hulkrites," said Tahn, "I received a prophecy this morning. Hulkro has made it our holy duty to return to the Silk Moth lands, which we know are far more rich and populous than first imagined."

"I pledge my heart and soul to the battle," said Anand, who stood tall and puffed his chest.

"I pledge my life, if Hulkro demands it, to this cause," said Pleckoo, not to be outdone.

"Good, Pleckoo. But I have a more demanding task for you. I wish you to stay at Zarren and be the guardian of my followers in our absence. Quegdoth, Hulkro has blessed you with a gift for languages. You will make the Silk Moth concubine your own and learn what you can of her tongue."

Pleckoo had been pleased with his promotion, but his joy went into sudden reversal. Anand saw the resentment in his unblinking eyes.

"As you command, Prophet," said Anand. "And I shall return good Pleckoo's property on my return and desist from intercourse with her."

"Pleckoo has nine wives and many more concubines," said Tahn. "Surely he can part with this one."

"The Silk Moth woman does find favor in my eyes," said Pleckoo. He was thinking of her beauty, of her thick lips in particular, and her exceptional talents in their use.

"As you wish," said Tahn.

Anand turned to Pleckoo and nodded towards

him in deference. "Good Pleckoo, if I am to indulge in women on the march, my seed will land only in the patches of the war trollops."

Pleckoo smiled, happy that Quegdoth did not forget the debt he owed him.

**D**ays later on the march to mulberry country, Tahn invited Anand to his mess to check on his progress in learning the Moth People's tongue.

"*Yakku shunjo ulem.* It goes well, commander," said Anand. "This mission seems very important," he added, modestly probing.

"It is. We have one real mission among the Silk Moth people—to cleanse their souls of idolatry and bring them to the true love and light of Hulkro. In return for the gift of eternal life, they will deliver a steady supply of the shellac we need to strengthen our mounds and conserve them through the centuries as we extend our righteous and eternal empire."

"Shellac, sir?"

"Yes. The Moth People's mounds are thousands of years old, preserved by a fine shellac mixed with natron. It's something they extract from the lac bugs that live on the bark of their mulberry trees."

"Mounds that are thousands of years old?" said Anand.

"Yes, and watertight and free of dry rot. Some people know this nation as the Mummy People because they do not feed their dead to the ants but cover them in shellac.

We are told that hundreds of thousands, perhaps millions of mummies, are embedded in their walls, forcing their ants to build greater, higher mounds. The tallest of them are ten times the height of Zarren."

"Why do they preserve their dead?" asked Anand.

"To worship as ancestors, we have heard. We will break them of this ridiculous sacrilege and will convert them to belief in the True God, but they will never have the blessing of ghost ants here."

"Why not?"

"Our ghosts can only enslave other ants—they attack the silk moths' caterpillars as well as the lac bugs."

"Are these Moth people fierce warriors?" Anand asked.

"The Moth men are poor warriors. They are an effeminate tribe and let their bitter ants do most of their fighting for them. Bitters and their eggs are too poisonous to eat but they are effective in battle—each ant possesses an internal potion that makes them explode when they are attacked, destroying themselves as well as their attackers. That's why we have gathered so many of our own ants in order to subdue this mound of Theb-Thebe."

At the end of the meal, Anand joined Tahn and his captains in prayers and drinks of kwondle-bark tea to keep them alert for the night. With a stop at the mound of Sterlitz-dozh, the army combined forces and grew to an uncountable number. Surrounding the cavalry was a crawling sea of unmounted ghosts, massing towards the mulberry trees.

The army passed the first Silk Moth mound, the outpost of exiles that had already been subdued. Thus far it had yielded little of the desired shellac, for its people were inept or drunkards. After venturing for two more nights, the Hulkrites reached the vast outskirts of Theb-Thebe, which had been abandoned by its laboring castes who had fled to shelters deep in the sand.

"We are to make an example of this mound," shouted Tahn to his officers. "Once they have refused the Message of Hulkro, we will attack." Tahn nodded at Anand as a signal to send the concubine with the Prophet's message. Anand urged his ant forward to a place the concubine had identified as a bathing station.

"You do know what to say?" he asked her.

"You've made me repeat it a hundred times," she said, climbing down the ant's legs. As she stepped into a scenting tub, she turned and looked at him with a look both flirtatious and arrogant.

"What's my name, Hulkrite?"

"Your name? It's . . ."

"You've never asked my name," she said as she covered herself with the kin-scent of bitter ants. "No one's ever asked my name. And no, it's not Moth Whore."

"I . . . I'm sorry."

"So am I," she said, removing herself from the clinging bulge of water in the tub to the excitement of Anand's ant who suddenly identified her as prey. "And you might have asked me if I care what happens to the hundreds of thousands who live at this mound—and if they might accept or believe the words of a trollop who gave her wet-box to hundreds of Hulkrish savages."

She turned and ran deep into the darkness as Anand fought to keep control of his ant. He was sure she was not running to the mound and to its leaders, but away from it. Anand rode back to the army with a crushing sorrow, wondering if the Silk Moth people were no less cruel than Hulkrites or Slopeites.

As the Hulkrites awaited a response, Anand looked up at the enormous black mound, which impressed him with its height and mass. It was an almost perfect cone covered in dark shellac. Around its southern outskirts were fields of cages full of silk cocoons, vats and looms for the dyeing and weaving of silk cloth. On its northern outskirts were vast sheds where Anand saw barrels and grindstones for extracting the precious substance from the lac bugs. Theb-Thebe had windows in its dwellings, but the lights shining in them were dimming as the inhabitants waited to be attacked.

Tahn allowed the release of a few ghost ants to climb up the mound and initiate the battle. The smell of approaching ghosts forced the first wave of bitter ants and their riders out of the mound. Tahn then employed his usual strategy, which was considered cowardly by his enemies: he parted his living barricade of mounted ants to let thousands of unmounted ants make the first assault.

The bitter ants allowed themselves to be over-whelmed, for when they were pierced, their bodies exploded and tore the heads off of the ghosts. This left a stench that made breathing difficult for humans and soon reached Anand's nostrils in the distance. Riders of the bitter ants jumped off their mounts to fight on foot before their ants exploded, but the Theb-Thebans were overwhelmed. Waves of ghost ants picked the men up and swallowed them whole.

Streams of bitter ants poured out of the mound and exploded thousands at a time, sending up blue flashes that looked like the ants' souls rising to the heavens. Thousands of ghost ants died in turn, but they easily replaced their casualties and pressed up the mound. When the moon was at its zenith, nearly all the bitter ants had burst.

The remaining human soldiers fought the ghost ants within a maze of insect corpses, hiding behind them to shoot their arrows. That was when Tahn called for his cavalry to attack. Anand and the other warriors stopped pounding on their ants' heads to let them race into the fray. The Hulkrites aimed arrows at the scattering enemies whose call to retreat back inside their mound was too late.

Anand dreaded what was coming next: the pil-laging and enslavement. Giant bitter ants with enormous heads guarded the mouth of the mound. Unwise Hulkrites smashed their swords into these living gates that exploded with a force that shred-ded the men and sent their blood flying. Once these guarding ants were destroyed, the Hulkrites poured down like water.

Being part of this attack was a nightmare-come-true for Anand. To squelch his suffering, he entered into a kind of living-sleep, a place of detachment where the atrocities whirled around him like so much vapor. He glanced at Tahn, who regarded the carnage with amusement. Anand's impulse was to surprise Tahn by shooting an arrow through his forehead. But retainers surrounded him and Anand had no choice but to carry out the commander's orders.

After grabbing a wall-torch, Anand led a patrol through tunnels connected to the outer shell of dwellings. Each chamber they broke into had endless mummies encrusted in the walls. Behind Anand, young women and children were collected while men and old women were slain.

Anand reached a large, open sanctuary where the nobles of the mound were cowering, praying to the thousands of royal corpses that surrounded them. "You will live," he said in their language. They were tossed crude brown rags stinking of ghost ants to pull over their silken gowns. Anand gave them Tahn's demands, which they were to present to the Silk Emperor in the capital mound of Kair-Kairfu. "You will send a delegation tomorrow to receive the terms of your surrender or risk a more devastating attack on all your mounds, including your capital," Anand shouted. The nobles acknowledged the commands by getting on their knees and bowing to Anand.

As Anand returned to Tahn at the base of the mound, he surveyed an unimaginable carnage of ants. Not a human corpse was in sight as the ghosts were uninterested in eating the exploded bitters. Anand fought his urge to weep. He reminded himself the raid would still have happened even if he had not participated. *I swear to my beloved Daveena, to the spirit of my mother, and all my loved ones in the Dranverite nations, I will right these wrongs.* When he was sure that no one was looking, he allowed himself a single tear.

Women and children were crying inside the bags as they piled up in the sand-sleds. Anand resumed his persona as he reported to Tahn.

"Commander, they have been informed to send their delegation to our camp tomorrow."

"Quegdoth, I have to entrust that meeting to you as I must leave now. Tell these silly infidels we will return in fourteen days for the first thousand barrels of their best shellac."

"Yes, sir. Where do you go now, Prophet?"

"An insurrection at Mukaz-dozh. A former Hulkrite is making his own claims as a prophet of his old god. It will not take us long to slaughter him and the backsliders and restore the Faith. So say I."

"Then so says Hulkro," Anand said as Tahn smiled, held his gaze. The Prophet looked pleased with his new favorite. But while Anand was being admired, he was deciding how he would kill Tahn and grind his empire back into dust.

# CHAPTER 39

## A SPINNING TOP

**A**s Anand and his troops waited for the Silk Emperor's delegation, he wandered into nearby weeds where he had sighted dried milkweed to saw and stuff into his backsack. In his chambers at night, he had worked in utmost secrecy on the reproduction of a Dranverish blowgun. It had a flexible magazine of tempered roach egg leather that could be loaded with seventy darts into its cartridges and pulled with precision to the blowpipe's barrel. Now he had the hard, straight twigs he needed to cut into slivers and sharpen with a bit of obsidian. Soon he could coat them in shellac supplied by the newly conquered Theb-Thebans.

Late in the afternoon, an exhausted and fearful Silk Moth delegation arrived. They dismounted from their ants and continued on foot, their heads bowed in submission. They wore deep colors with much lace at their necks and brought a variety of crafts as well as the requested barrels of shellac, all of it lugged in their travoises. The Hulkrites openly laughed and called them "flower girls," though all of them were men.

Anand laid out the demands of the Hulkrites and the schedule of delivery for the shellac. When they were dismissed, the delegation bowed before scampering off backwards. The Hulkrites were fascinated by the skillful embroideries, bangles, and necklaces. Also left were rare flower seeds that completely mystified the men concerning their value. When the garrison returned to Zarren, Anand had the tribute brought to his chambers until Tahn could examine it.

In privacy over the next few nights, Anand perfected his darts and practiced on targets. One fearful evening he dipped them in the concentrate he had secretly held for so many moons. That same night, Tahn returned from Mukaz-dozh with sled-cages full of the rebellious heretics who had revived their cult of Scorpion the Sun God. Anand had heard the rumor that the Sons of the Great Stinger were communing with their god through injections of His diluted venom, which brought them visions of resurrecting their old nation and casting off the Hulkrites.

The following afternoon Anand was among the masses at a public event in the stadium to watch the backsliders denounce their idol before Tahn. The

Prophet looked kindly and forgiving and offered a quick death to those who immediately confessed. Others of the apostates were tortured by slow slicing until they admitted their heresy and earned their execution. Each confession was politely applauded and when all the heretics were dispatched, Tahn looked to the heavens, announced the rebellion was over, and blessed the loving followers who had joined him in the stadium. He ordered the corpses to be covered in shellac and returned to Mukaz-dozh to be hung from poles near the markets. Anand was exiting the stadium, anxious to get away to the privacy of his chambers, when Pleckoo approached him with a chiding smile.

"Quegdoth . . . we're holding a strategy dinner tomorrow. We'll need your service."

"Yes sir."

"You might have been able to join us in the fun— as a captain yourself—if you had returned my Moth Whore."

"Again, I apologize, Captain Pleckoo. And I will look for her on my next return to mulberry country. We heard she may hiding in a brothel-nunnery in the mound of Shank-Shankua where . . ."

"Yes, yes, you may find her someday. For tomorrow night, though, you will join the other lieutenants as a sober guard."

"It is my duty, sir. I look forward to it," Anand said.

It was the first truthful thing he had said in moons.

Like a good Hulkrish warrior, Anand arrived early at the feasting hall to fulfill his duties at the strategy dinner. Toothless gave him a chaw of kwondle which Anand placed in his mouth, then secretly removed as he feared it would increase his anxiety. He hid the chaw in the right pocket of his backsack which hung on the wall with those of the other guards, its opening cinched extra tight. Anand took some dried, sweetened hover-fly maggots from the left pocket to present to the other guards. "In case you can't wait for dinner," he said, taking a large chewy bite of one. The others accepted his offer, then leaned against the wall to eat as the officers rambled in for their paint-removing baths.

The night's musicians were also dancers of a sort—they wore hard, ball-shaped shoes and hopped on different lengths of wood set across a flat box as a tuneful percussion while others sang and plucked at tall, taut strings for a thumping sound. Anand thought he might like their music under other circumstances, but at the moment it sounded like the rattling of skeletons.

The evening seemed different, off somehow, than the last strategy dinner. As the officers drank from their bowls, Anand sensed a quiet tension between them and their laughter was infrequent. An occasional loud boasting was not followed by a boast in return, but calls to shut up. Commander Tahn was circulating in a way that seemed to chastise the men rather than encourage their revelry. The spirits that were usually drunk so quickly were slower to be consumed. As Anand looked through the darkness of the chambers, he was reconsidering his plans, sure that something was amiss.

**P**leckoo was regretting having drunken and eaten so much. He had enjoyed the spicy sun stew of sprouted, speckled bush beans, crimson chile pods, and minced scorpions brought from Mukaz, but it did not agree with the night's drink which had too much turpentine. "Bring more from a different cask," he shouted to the servants. "This batch is bad!" He looked around and saw the other officers were pursing their lips, holding their stomachs and experiencing something of the same discomfort.

"Drink has nothing wrong," said the man next to him, the tawny-skinned, orange-haired Captain Kraznoy formerly of the Seed Eater nation. "Maybe people who come from Slope can't hold liquor."

"We're all Hulkrites now, brother," said Pleckoo. "And I can outdrink you or anyone else."

When the servants returned with new bowls from a different cask, Pleckoo made a show of taking a long, loud slurp from a darker, even stronger liquor. After an eye-stinging, chili-scented burp, he looked straight at Kraznoy and drank a second slug.

"Slow down, good Hulkrite," Kraznoy said, both impressed and irritated. "Let us leave some for rest of us."

"They can bring us plenty more," Pleckoo said, but even as he sat up straight and did his best to look lively, he felt as if the scorpions he had eaten had reassembled inside him and were trying to get out. The others resumed drinking from the new batch, which they found more palatable. The music quieted and the Brothel Mistress appeared at the top of the steps wearing a new arrangement of her precious beads. Pleckoo had looked forward to this moment when the women would begin their descent with the new beauties saved for the end of the procession. But as he stood to join the others, a sharp, radiant pain stabbed at his gut and spread through his limbs. His mouth began to water excessively.

Pleckoo stepped quietly back from the others as the music started up again. He was dry heaving and afraid someone might see he was sick from drink. He backed into a dark corner of the chamber near a flap portal for the servants and slipped out. He stumbled in the darkness of the tunnel crowded with ants, falling on his knees to vomit. He hoped some passing ant minims would remove the evidence of his weakness, but their antennae sensed poisons in the acrid mess and they scampered off. A large foraging ghost crawled towards Pleckoo to antennate him, but he had left his antennae in his chambers. The ant sniffed him and found the colony odor, but knocked him over in the process. Once Pleckoo had fallen, he passed out and slept at the edges of the tunnel floor.

**A**nand stood looking at the ceiling, waiting for the moment of the Brothel Mistress's return. The music had ended and in the quiet, Anand's mind was racing in a noisy spiral as he reviewed his plans. Tahn, as usual, had been among the first to pass out and his captains took it as permission to follow him into slumber. It seemed to Anand an aching eon before the Brothel Mistress returned to herd her workers back to their quarters in the weeds. Some of them were asleep on the mattresses, but most were sitting at the bottom of the steps, blankly chewing on stems of toasted cannabis.

When the guards were brought their dinner, Anand forced himself to eat, laugh, and make conversation as he swatted at the doubts that overwhelmed him. It was likely his plan would fail, that he would be attacked and subdued by great numbers who would kill him in an instant. *I have no choice,* he told himself, *whatever the odds, I must succeed. Madricanth will help me.* The servant girls returned to roll up the leaf platters and their remains. "Will you be needing anything else?" asked the one whose arm had been twisted from its socket, keeping her distance.

"No," said Toothless and the servants were dismissed. Toothless went to his backsack and brought out his top, which signaled the men to take out their purses and set out the first wagers. Anand took out his purse, too.

"Oh, planning on losing some money, Quegdoth?" said Toothless.

"No, planning on taking all of yours," Anand said.

"Take the first spin and make the first bet," Toothless said.

"Termite," Anand said, referring to the drawings carved into the top's sides. He spun the top but "beetle" came up and he lost the first of his flecks of pyrite. As the game stretched on, Anand waited for the moment that the guards grew sleepy. When Toothless yawned, it set off a chain reaction. Anand yawned himself, then stood and stretched. "Let me get some more kwondle," he said and went to his backsack. In the most casual way possible, he pulled out his blowgun and straightened the magazine.

The men with their backs to Anand went suddenly still, then fell forward while the top was spinning.

"What's this? Wake up, men!" Toothless shouted, scolding them. He looked over their slumped bodies to see Anand with the pipe in his mouth. A dart ripped through Toothless's armor and he fell backwards, his legs popping up and jerking before going still.

With great care, Anand tiptoed through the sleeping bodies of Tahn's captains and targeted every man. A few jerked at the initial pain but could not cry out. Anand saved Tahn for last and was ready to shoot him when he rolled over and onto Anand's feet. Tahn woke. He smiled to see his young favorite, then realized something was amiss.

"What are you doing, Quegdoth? What's that in your hand?"

Anand hesitated. He looked in Tahn's eyes and saw fear in them for the first time. Anand set the gun in his mouth, blew and missed when Tahn jerked away. Through the haze of his intoxication, Tahn rose, tripping over the paralyzed as he lunged for Anand.

"Surrender that weapon!" Tahn shouted, extending his palm.

Like some great infection throbbing to release its pus, Anand's hatred gushed from him. He stepped back as he raised the blowgun to his lips. This time the dart landed between Tahn's eyes. He fell on his back, his four limbs twitching, before he went still.

Anand leaned over Tahn's unblinking face. "I know you can see and hear me, Commander. Your body cannot move, but your mind is alive. My name is Anand, son of Corra of the Entrevean Clan of Britasytes, a woman killed by your warriors at Palzhad. I have come to free my people. I know you are praying to Hulkro to help you, but your Termite God is as deaf as a termite is blind. You will kill, rape, and plunder no more, Tahn. I piss on you, and I piss on your powerless Hulkro."

Anand looked at the small plug of wood Tahn wore around his neck, a bit that had come from a termite colony and stank of its scent. The plug was considered holy, a dwelling place of Tahn's deity. Anand set the plug in Tahn's mouth before pulling out his own penis and pissing on the prophet's unblinking face.

Immersed in a lake of fury, Anand felt like some other being, as if he were outside of himself and watching his actions. He removed his dagger, tipped back Tahn's head and slowly sawed at his throat. Blood surged in little waves and bubbled over the slit. Placing his ear against Tahn's chest, Anand waited until his heart beat no more.

Spinning around the chamber, Anand slit the throats of all the men—everyone that might succeed Tahn. Recently hatched ghost minims squeezed through the service portal to lick at the growing pond of red. Something gnawed at Anand, and forced him to return to Tahn's corpse—he could not risk even the slightest chance that this so-called prophet could rise again. He jerked his dagger up Tahn's rib cage, then cut out his heart. Anand impaled it on his dagger, then threw it down to the ground and crushed it to a pulp under his boots. Tahn could never be resurrected now. Never.

Anand heaved with exhaustion. Emerging from his trance, he staggered under the deepest anguish before falling to his knees in a faint.

He floated through the blackness of the Realm of Death for what seemed like forever and no time at all. When he eventually came to, he wondered if he was better off in the empty blackness. Looking around, he took in the gory spread of corpses leaking blood, remembering each of these men as a living human like himself. He alone had killed these men, and with their deaths, he questioned what had driven him. As he went about his murderous business, he remembered his resolve, then surprised himself when he burst into tears.

He thought of Dwan and Belja and Hopkut in their distant, civilized land. Would they see him as a murderer, or a hero who had dispatched the worst kind of monsters? The unknown answer almost crippled him, but he shook himself free of the thought. It was pointless to ponder it now. Daveena and the Pleps must be freed.

Anand entered the tunnel and hitched a ride on an exiting ant. His boots smeared blood on the ant's head. He passed Hulkrish guards who were helping a man up from the tunnel floor, a messy drunkard whose hair fell over his face. Anand worried the guards would see the blood on his person but they were too busy to notice.

After reaching his chambers, Anand cleaned himself and touched up his white paint. As the paint dried, he reloaded the blowgun and stuffed a rope ladder into his backsack. He placed an obsidian handsaw in the inside pocket of his cape before he exited into the tunnel where he saw and smelled ants with gullets full of predigested crickets. He grabbed a wall-torch and climbed on a ghost as she waded into a stream of her sisters pulsing towards the queen's chamber.

When his ant reached the great egg-layer, Anand waited for her to shut her cave of a mouth, then shot a multitude of darts in her head. The queen's great mass resisted the potion, but slowly her legs gave out from under her. She dropped on her belly, crushing the little ants that groomed her from below. A hundred of her daughters crawled over her, and some looked as if they were propping up her antennae which wilted and made no response.

Anand prodded his ant's "forward" segments on its feelers, but the ant would not obey. He abandoned it and was forced to slip and slide over the crush of ants until he found a stream of them exiting. His heart pounded in excitement as he pondered his next destination. At last he would be with Daveena. Her image was blazing before him now, as if she were ringed by sunlight. She would sit in back of him with her warm arms around his waist as he rode their roach out of this place of infinite darkness.

Mounted guards were patrolling the mound's exterior. When they saw the termite carving on Anand's helmet, they slapped their chests in respect as he passed. No one dared to ask where one of the Prophet's favored was going—why would they? He looked at the sparse beard of one of them, younger than himself, and imagined the moment this boy had bravely taken up with the Hulkrites to defy his abusers. Anand was almost feeling bad for him, wondering if he would be punished for letting him escape when he realized something: Who was left to punish him?

The thought added to Anand's confidence and he rode a touch higher as he forced the ant off the trunk-trail, then down to the pits and cages of the slaves. The blood pumping in his ears deafened him to the rest of the world. Tomorrow the servant girls would be the first to find the carnage, but they would not find "Vof Quegdoth." Once more he wondered, who would the servants run and tell?

In that moment, a painful heat flashed through Anand as thoughts of jagged nostrils and brown skin filled his head. Pleckoo's scowling face had come alive and burned in Anand's mind. *Where was he?* Anand could recall the face of every man he had slaughtered. *Pleckoo was not among them!* The heat that flashed through Anand's body turned to a sudden wave of cold.

Somewhere on the mound, Pleckoo was alive.

# CHAPTER 40

## AN AFTERTHOUGHT

**A**s Anand steered the ant to the pit of the Britasytes, he looked behind him to make sure he wasn't followed and got a full view of Zarren-dozh. From a distance it was beautiful in the moonlight, like an enormous pile of black bee-velvet. The trains of illuminated ghost ants marching around it were like a living sapphire necklace. As he passed the cages and cages of miserable slaves, he was sharply reminded of his mission. The last cage he passed had a crude sign with a mushroom painted on it to designate it as the quarters of the Slopeites and their humiliated queen. Anand felt a strange moment of pity for them that lasted until he neared the roach pit. When the ant he was riding was repelled by roach scent and halted, he dropped to his feet and ran.

As usual, the roach pit was unguarded. Anand heard the scurrying of the roaches as they crawled upside-down on the grate's underside, stimulated by moonlight. Anand looked all ways to make sure no one was watching.

"Wanderers," he shouted down the pit in Britasyte. "The time has come. Are you ready?"

A moment of silence passed. "We are," Zedral shouted back at him and in a moment, Anand heard the Britasytes scurrying from the sleds, gathering their possessions. He saw that the roaches clinging to the gate's undersides were large and lively and fitted with reins and saddles. Anand removed his handsaw from his cape and cut through the ropes that bound the grate's twigs before rolling them away. He took out the rope ladder from his backsack, tied it to a plank, and let it unroll to the pit's bottom.

"One at a time," he shouted.

The children were the first to crawl out, children who were as thin and bug-eyed as damselflies. The women were next to struggle out, including his Auntie Gleg, who ran to hug him. She stank like a demon and her face was like a berry left to wrinkle in the sun, but he couldn't have been happier as they worked together to help the other matrons out.

Next were Zedral and the old men, all of whom had long and scraggly beards. The young women climbed out next, and as each one popped up, Anand's heart beat louder in anticipation of Daveena.

His heart was shredded when the young men emerged too soon.

"Zedral, where is Daveena?"

The old man hung his head. "She is below. Someone will have to carry her. None of us are strong enough."

As soon as the last of the men were up, Anand dropped down the rope ladder to the pit's bottom.

"Daveena! Daveena!"

He looked about the foul place where the Britasytes' glorious sleds were covered in dust. The roaches were aware of Anand and converging for an attack when he remembered he was without their scent. He leapt onto the rope ladder and unsheathed his sword.

"Daveena, come here now!" he shouted.

Cloaked in a poncho, she stepped from a sled, sniffling as she came. He could just make out her wet and lovely eyes in the darkness. Her mouth was concealed by her shawl, which she wrapped tight around her head.

"Can't you climb?"

"I can barely stand," she said.

She opened the poncho and Anand tried not to react. She was thin from malnutrition, having eaten little but sparse roach eggs for moons. She dropped the shawl from her head and he saw her hair was falling out. The shock of her appearance kept him from noticing when a roach probed him from the wall, lashing his face with its antennae, ready to attack. As it lunged, Anand's sword flashed, snipping the antennae and sending it to writhe upside down on the pit's floor.

"We've got to climb," he said running to her. "Grab me tight and clutch my waist with your legs." She complied and Anand strained as he took the rungs, yet his burden felt all too light. The two reached the opening and were pulled out as the roaches gnashed below them.

"I need roach-scent, Auntie," Anand said, "and antennae." Glegina handed him her filthy jacket, which Anand pulled over his armor as his aunt set her antennae on his head. He sawed at more ropes to make an opening large enough to release the roaches for mounting. The first of them poked its head through, and using the natural grease of its body, it wriggled out.

"We will gather in the southern weeds of Palzhad, in the land of the Slopeites," Anand shouted. "The Hulkrites will be looking for us. We must head east, then make our way north through the unknown grasslands. The Hulkrites will not follow us there. Good travels, beautiful wanderers, until we meet again."

He added this last part because he knew of the unreliability of roaches as mounts. Members of the clan would essentially be on separate journeys. Anand worried about the withered elders as they rushed the roaches, sliding onto their heads and grabbing at reins as the insects squeezed out the grate. When all but Anand and Daveena had departed, he sawed again to make a larger hole so that the largest roaches could exit. While they waited for a suitable ride to push through, Anand took his betrothed by her waist and kissed her.

"I have dreamt of you every night," he said. Her eyes glistened. In them Anand could see reflections of the full moon before her tears bulged, then spilled. The bones of her face were so prominent now that they gave her a haunting beauty.

"Why are you crying?" he asked.

"It is my joy that cannot be contained," she said. He smiled at her, knew her relief must be as overwhelming as his own. "You must eat," Anand said, and he reached into the bottom of his pack and gave her a flattened, sugared ant egg he had saved just for her, which she gladly accepted.

He turned back to the insects' progress. Squeezing through the opening was the largest roach in the pit. Daveena got on first and Anand followed, grabbing the roach's reins. He pulled out the lure stick tucked under the head scale, took the sheath off the lure, and unfolded the stick to full length. Leaning his body over the roach's head, Anand had a strange and unstoppable stream of thoughts. The memory of the slain in the feasting chamber came back to him, and with it a remorse that scalded like fire. A moment later, he had a vivid remembrance of the Slopeish queen who charged over on crippled legs to shield her subject from a Hulkrite's cruelty.

Anand made an abrupt decision that he knew was right but he was not sure of the reasons why. "We have something to do first," he said to Daveena, and steered the roach towards the compound that contained the Slopeish prisoners. He dismounted behind a grass clump and tethered the roach to it. "Wait here," he said to Daveena, giving her his roach antennae to hold. He approached the cage on foot after fastening his cape. The foot guards at the Slopeites' cage were pacing to stay awake when they noticed him and reached for their swords.

"Hulkro is great," Anand shouted as he walked towards them.

"And Tahn is his messenger," responded the first guard. "Who comes here?"

"Lieutenant Quegdoth," Anand said. "With orders from the Prophet."

The guards looked confounded as Anand got closer.

"Why aren't you on a mount, sir?" the first one asked.

"I stepped in roach dung," Anand said, "and the ghosts will not come near me."

"Where are your antennae, sir?" asked the second one.

"Why, they are right here," Anand said and opened the cape. He raised his blowpipe and targeted the guards' chests. As the guards twitched, Anand looked into the cage to see the Slopeites and Queen Polexima were awake and staring at him in fright. He took out his handsaw and went to work on the gate's lashings.

"Your Majesty," said Anand to Polexima after he opened the gate and entered. "I have come to return you to the Slope."

"*What?* Who are you?" she asked, backing away on her bottom.

"We have no time. Please, come with me."

"I cannot go. My child, she is . . ."

"Bring the child with you," Anand said. "Command your subjects to remain in this cage for their safety. For some while longer, they must do the bidding of the Hulkrites. While they are here, though, they are not to eat of the ghost ants' regurgitations. They contain a slow-acting poison I used to kill their egg-layer and the ants of this mound. Ask your people to spread this warning to all who labor for the Hulkrites."

The Slopeites stared in disbelief as Anand addressed them in Slopeish with his natural accent. As they wondered at him, he pressed on. "When the Hulkrites ask how your queen escaped, you must tell them Mantis took her up to the stars to confer on a plan to defeat the Hulkrish infidels. This story will shake their faith, especially that of the Slopeish defectors."

Polexima looked quizzical, then nodded her head. "Very well." She turned to a young woman standing attentively near her. "You heard this man, didn't you, Geweth?"

Pareesha's wet nurse, Geweth, nodded her head. She repeated Anand's story for him and then seemed to sink in a trance as she mulled over its details. Pareesha cried as Polexima limped out with her. "Remember," Anand shouted to the rest as he left. "No eating from the ghost ants' mouths!"

Anand walked ahead, then turned to see the pain in Polexima's face as she was hobbled *and* pregnant *and* carrying her child. "Allow me, Your Majesty," Anand said and took the royal baby into his polluting arms. He stopped and hunched his back. "Climb on, please," he said. She stifled her cries of pain as she wrapped her legs around his waist and her arms around his neck.

"I will return shortly," he said as he set down the queen behind a pebble tall enough to hide her. He bowed before running off.

"Excuse me," shouted Polexima, and Anand halted. "Yes?"

"Why are you doing this?"

"No time to explain, Your Majesty," said Anand, running.

Polexima tried to calm herself. What had just happened to her? She was putting her trust in a stranger painted and armored as a Hulkrite. Could he be a prankster leading her to torture, then death? She didn't fear death anymore as the darkness of life in Hulkren was all too constant, but more torture or beatings? She heard an insect's approach and assumed it was a ghost ant, but when it came into view, its chitin was dark and it stank of something else.

"Roach!" she screamed and tried to run. She fell and was squirming on her side as the giant roach lashed her with its antennae. Pareesha cried as she was shaken about in her mother's arms. A head peered down between the roach's mandibles.

"Your Majesty, pull these on immediately, and wrap your child in the cloth," the young Hulkrite shouted, throwing some roach-scented clothes to her. He looked about in fear, and she realized he was worried that patrol guards were in the vicinity. Polexima set down the crying baby and did as Anand commanded and the roach was pacified.

"You are a Britasyte," Polexima said, lifting her baby.

"And . . . a Slopeite," he answered, with some hesitation.

"I cannot get on a . . . roach," she said, spitting out the last word as if it were a spiderling that had crawled into her mouth.

He was smiling at her, tight and grim, as if he shouldn't share his thoughts. "Luckily you won't have to ride on the roach as we have no more room for you on the saddle."

"Thank the gods," she thought, assuming he could produce a sand-sled or something.

"You will have to get *in* the roach."

She stared at him and clutched her heart.

"Get *in*?"

"Yes. Crawl under the belly. You will find scales on

the underside. Pull the center one down, chase out any roach hatchlings, and pull yourself in."

"I could not possibly!" she said, rising on her wobbly legs.

"Then you are welcome to return to the Hulkrites," the young man said. "Decide now. My safety and that of my woman is threatened with every moment we wait."

"This I do for my child," Polexima said, as she crawled under and through the insect's legs. She pulled down the belly scale and pushed Pareesha inside before hoisting herself in. There were no baby roaches in the insect's fold, but she screamed when a multitude of eight-legged mites, like tiny spiders, crawled over her and inserted their fangs. She shrieked as she yanked and then flung them out.

"You'll need those," shouted the young man from above.

"Need what?" Polexima shouted back.

"The mites. To eat. Just tear off the heads. We won't be stopping anytime soon."

"Where are we going?" she shouted.

"To the Grasslands. The Hulkrites won't follow us there."

Pleckoo had been carried to his chambers by the guards who had found him drunk and asleep in the tunnel. He awoke the next morning in a painful haze with a demanding thirst. He rattled the tongue of a wooden bell to summon his slave girl, then sucked from the bowl of water she set on the floor with his breakfast. As his head cleared, he remembered that Tahn expected him at his chambers late that morning, where they would discuss the invasion of the Slope.

Pleckoo smiled at the thought of the imminent offensive and his final revenge. It was assured now that Pleckoo would become governor of the Slopeites in return for his unerring service to Tahn. He hoped the Prophet would rename it Pleckoo-dozh. He imagined himself sitting on the Mushroom Throne of Cajoria, completely naked to enjoy the feel of its silken cushions while drinking Sahdrin's best liquors. He would invite Keel and his overfed sons into the crystal palace for a royal audience so they could marvel in envy at all its wonders. They would tremble before him when they recognized Pleckoo as their new king. "Fear not," he would say, as he lashed them with Keel's own whip. "I won't kill you. I need someone to clean these floors. Using their tongues. On your knees, infidels, and lick!"

Pleckoo was broken from his reverie when he heard the *creet-creet* of Soput, a mound guard with heavy, drooping facial features, calling outside his portal.

"Enter."

Soput looked ill as he pulled himself through and stood. His mouth and eyes looked ready to drip off his face. He barely slapped his chest plate.

"Favored One . . . there . . . there has . . ."

"Yes? Speak, Soput."

"Perhaps it is best you come for yourself. Be prepared, Captain. It is a devastating sight."

Pleckoo followed the guard and was surprised when he led him to the entry of the feasting chamber. He pulled himself through the portal and was assaulted by the sight of his butchered comrades. The stench of death smashed his face like a mallet. The subordinates of the dead men stood about unable to move, unable to weep, unable to act. Pleckoo covered the cavity of his nose as he staggered among the corpses.

"Where is he?" Pleckoo asked. Soput gulped and pointed him to Tahn's corpse. He saw the slit throat and the jagged hole in his chest. Bright sunlight poured in through the wall's crystals to illuminate the massacre in all its crimson gore. Pleckoo was dazed as he stumbled through the dead and he shook his fists at the sunlight.

"How could you let this happen to the Messenger of Hulkro?" he bellowed to the heavens. He did not expect an answer as he felt himself falling and blacking out.

He was immersed in darkness giving way to light when he got one.

# CHAPTER 41

# HULKRO

"Wake up, Pleckoo! You are being called upon," said an angel who flapped her silvery moth wings.

Pleckoo returned from the blackness into which he had crashed. He lifted his eyes from Tahn's corpse to see the angel, a cloud-white beauty with sweet, round breasts. She flew away as the Termite God winged through the sky, then hovered outside the window. Behind Him squirmed His human-faced wife, Hulkratash, the Termite Queen, who laid clutches of spirit eggs in the sky.

Hulkro's voice was as sweet as warm honey. "Fear not, beloved Pleckoo," He said. "I so love the world that I gave it My Most Favored Son. He has returned to Me." Hulkro opened one of His six hands. Perched on the edge of His fingers was the warmly smiling ghost of Tahn.

"My Father has taken me to test the faithful," said Tahn. "Those who loved and followed me must love and follow you. You must turn the idolatrous of all the Sand to worship the One True God."

"Me?" said Pleckoo. "My face is ugly. Beneath my paint my skin is dark."

"In the box of treasures behind you is your new face," said Hulkro.

"A new face?" asked Pleckoo, his heart thumping.

"I care not what face you have. All who love Me are beautiful in My sight. You will keep your old face, always, as a reminder of the Slopeites' cruelty, and wear this new one, as testament of your faith."

Pleckoo was crying. He wiped at his tears, which felt hard on his fingers. He looked at them and saw they had turned into faceted jewels. "What am I to do, Lord?"

"The Slopeish idolaters are an abomination I can bear no more," said Hulkro, and His words shook like thunder. Behind Him, lightning flashed in a blood-red sky. "Feed the bodies of the fallen to the ants. Their spirits reside in the skies with Me, where they look upon My face. Make our empire strong again, then tear the Slope to pieces and rebuild it as Our own."

"Who killed you, Prophet?" Pleckoo asked Tahn.

"He gave his name as Vof Quegdoth. But that is not his true self. You knew him as Anand the roach boy."

Pleckoo felt as if he had been stabbed in the heart.

The vision was disappearing and all was turning back to a cold and silent black.

Soput and the guards went to Pleckoo and lifted his head from the drying puddles of blood. They had heard him mumbling questions in a one-sided conversation.

"We must feed the fallen to the ants," said Pleckoo as he rose. "Hulkro has demanded it," he shouted, his voice growing stronger.

"Hulkro?" Soput asked.

"I am His newly chosen. I saw His True Face. Tahn was seated in His upper left hand."

"Captain Pleckoo, sir . . . we saw no vision, heard no voices but your own."

"I am now Commander Pleckoo, the Second Prophet. Such are Hulkro's mysterious ways that only I have been allowed to see His True Face."

The guards watched as Pleckoo rose to full height and transformed from shocked and weakened to someone radiant with a godly strength.

"Let us break down these walls so the ants may eat our dead and pass us their blood and flesh in communion. So say I."

"Then so says Hulkro," said Soput as his gloom lifted.

Pleckoo searched first for the hardened tears of his vision but did not find them. Next, he went through the pile of corpses to look for Anand but knew he would not be there—he needed to look down and away to hide the shame that pulsed behind his face. *How completely he deceived me!* he thought, as his hatred for Anand blazed like the sun. Sweat burst from Pleckoo's brow and stung his eyes.

Remembering Hulkro's command, he looked in the box of treasures. Atop the piles was an elegant mask of turquoise with inlaid rose quartz in the shape of a termite. Underneath it were tear-shaped crystals like the ones he had shed. Pleckoo picked up the mask and tied it around his head, then turned to a mirror and for the first time ever, he didn't see his noseless visage. He looked fondly on his reflection and saw a leader, a military commander, and a father of holy kings.

**A**s commanded, the walls of the feasting chamber were broken open, but the ants were slow to enter and slow to consume the corpses. Those that did were soon dead.

All over Zarren-dozh, the ants were listless or expiring. The Second Prophet's meditations at the top of the mound were disturbed by a request to visit the queen ant's chamber. When Pleckoo arrived on a sluggish ant, he saw the chamber was empty.

Horrifyingly empty.

"Good warrior, where is this mound's queen ant?" Pleckoo asked the chief gatherer-of-eggs, whose face was wet with tears.

"Died during the night, Prophet. The ants have already shredded and eaten her."

"Where is the new queen?"

"Doesn't appear to be one. Usually before the old queen dies, her replacement is swelling and laying eggs."

"But with the old one dead, a new queen will hatch from the larvae soon," said Pleckoo, aware that panic was creeping into his voice. "The nurse ants are gorging the larvae, yes?"

"Prophet, that should have happened, but they are plagued with some ill spirit, including the nymphs and pupae. Only foragers returning from distant hunts appear unaffected, but soon all of them will die."

*"All?"*

"The nymphs and pupae are the digestive caste of ghost ants. They process the final stages of food before passing it. Without them, all the ants will starve to death."

"Yes, of course. We will weather these trials," said Pleckoo. "Hulkro sends them to test the faithful. So say I."

"Then so says Hulkro."

The head guard of the mushroom chambers arrived and slapped his chest.

"Reporting, Commander Pleckoo."

"How are the leaf-cutter ants and queen?"

"They are well. Their egg-layer thrives," said the guard.

"Seal their chambers so they may not exit or have

contact with other ants. Allow them to eat from their own mushrooms so that they stay well and multiply. So say I."

"Then so says Hulkro."

An angry guard with gnashing teeth approached Pleckoo while pushing Geweth, the Slopeish wet nurse, before him. She stumbled to the floor, lost in some inner world. Though she was in danger at this moment, she was grinning in her milk-soaked garment.

"Prophet, Polexima is missing and so are the Britasytes and their roaches," said the guard. "Tell the Prophet what you told us, infidel."

"Her Divinity, Polexima the Sorceress Queen, was rescued last night," Geweth said in a sure voice.

"Rescued by whom?" asked Pleckoo.

"By a goddess," said the woman.

Pleckoo spat. "Which goddess is that?"

"Mantis, the Queen of War."

"Heresy!" Pleckoo shouted. "You are lying!"

"I will tell you what I witnessed only if you promise me my safety."

"Hulkro is merciful, so is His Second Prophet," said Pleckoo.

"Then swear by your god," said Geweth.

Pleckoo seethed behind his mask. "By Hulkro, your safety is assured."

"Mantis descended, sliding down a moonbeam. She lifted up the cage and took our holy queen to the World Beyond Stars. Mantis sang to us, 'Be not afraid! I will confer with Polexima and the other gods on a plan of vengeance against the Hulkrites and their apostasy.'"

Pleckoo was silent, guessing that Anand had taken Polexima. He realized Anand's mission had been to free his people, but what did he want with the Cajorites' queen? An alliance? Pleckoo's shame at being deceived blazed again. He was the one who had sent the little roach-eater to Tahn and had even hosted Anand's conversion feast. *That shit-collecting bastard has somehow killed our egg-layer and all the ghost ants at this mound,* Pleckoo thought, quivering with rage. *Vof Quegdoth indeed!*

He hated this Slopeish wet nurse, just as much, with her crazed expression because she seemed as convinced of her recent religious vision as much as he was convinced of his own. She had turned his mind back to the idols of his youth and his fear of them. Pleckoo was plunged back into that moment when he was chosen to become his caste's idols keeper, when the demi-priests had herded him and some other untouchables to view the holy relics passed from gods to humans.

Oh, how the demi-priests had praised him for his intelligence, for his quick absorption of all the damaging myths that enforced the caste restrictions! That was the first time Pleckoo had seen the paintings of the tortures in the Netherworld for disbelievers. All of his life Pleckoo was tortured by these images of night wasps using stingers to puncture their victims, blind them with sprays of venom, then drag them to their nests to be torn apart and eaten throughout eternity.

Pleckoo came back from his dreadful reminiscence. The old Slopeish myths would not curse his life.

"Nonsense, woman," he said to Geweth. "You are a weaver of stories, and that is all," he said to her, looking full of pity. "Good Hulkrite, pray for this woman's conversion on the return to her cage."

Pleckoo knew what he must do next. He would summon all the mound's lieutenants and promote them to fill the positions of their slain captains.

"Alert the tunnel guards throughout the nation," ordered Pleckoo from what had been Tahn's chambers. "We must find the young man we knew as Vof Quegdoth. He may be returned to me as a recognizable corpse but I would prefer him alive to exact his confession before the True God. We must also find Polexima and her daughter. They must be returned alive and well."

A scout coming back from the roach pit made his way to Commander Pleckoo.

"Commander," he said, after slapping his chest. "From the roach droppings we have found, the Britasytes appear be running east, towards the grasslands of Dneep."

*Dneep!* Pleckoo thought. It was a country so fraught with dangerous mysteries that neither Hulkrites nor ghost ants would go near it. *But a Britasyte bold enough to kill the Prophet of the Termite would probably not hesitate to enter it.*

"Then that is where we will go," said Pleckoo. *Where I will hunt you down, Roach Boy, and to pay for your sins against Our God, I will extract the bones from your limbs and peel the skin from your body . . . yet leave you most alive.*

# CHAPTER 42

## INTO THE GRASS

**A**nand and Daveena had yet to sight other Pleps or their roaches fleeing east. He sensed Daveena's dread, which increased his own. He had no plan other than the hope that the grasslands of Dneep were more hospitable to roaches than they were to ghost ants. And if they could make it through, they would then have to travel in the lands of the unpredictable Seed Eaters who might let them journey west to Palzhad.

Anand knelt constantly on the roach's head, jerked at its antennae, and over three days, he let it rest only long enough to drink. Daveena, strengthening with nourishment, took over for him when sleep could not be resisted. The mating-scent lure had been effective, but now, as the roach grew hungry, Anand peeled open the stick's opposite end. This lure stank from fly larvae, the roach's favorite food.

After days of open sand, the roach was steered into stretches of weeds where they traveled more slowly but stayed hidden from human view. The thickness of weeds came to an end at the moment Anand was about to succumb to exhaustion. Before them on a rise lay a new stretch of sand, and in the distance, a land of dried grass that rolled away in yellow hills. Was it a refuge, or did the low murmur of chirps portend something predatory? Above the grass at the moment was a twisting cloud of locusts. They seemed unable to decide on a direction as they dropped and scattered, then rose again, chased off by mysterious ground predators. Anand felt just as indecisive but he knew they needed a rest.

**T**ucked inside the belly scale, Polexima had been nauseated for what had seemed an eternity. She savored the few moments of sleep that came to her, sleep with its slippery dreams of comfortable beds, palatable food, and her legs restored to full powers. "I promise you this, Pareesha," she whispered to her child. "I have suffered much, I may suffer much more, but I will return you to safety."

Breathing had been difficult for the queen and little princess. When the roach climbed up rocks or inclines, it pulled its belly scales close as if to contain their usual contents, the roach's own young. The scales had small holes punched through them for breathing, but Polexima lay panting until the insect was horizontal and the scale could open again. The insect was crawling to a slow stop when she heard Anand drop from the saddle.

"We're resting," he said and pulled down the scale. "We just have to get off this roach."

"And I'd really like to get out of it," she said and handed him Pareesha.

The mounds of Hulkren received notice that muck-covered infidels had escaped atop roaches. It had taken less than three days for the runners to spread the news through the network of tunnels that linked the Hulkrish mounds and their distant outposts. Warriors were to patrol for and kill all roaches and examine their undersides. They were to kill and preserve the corpses of the Britasytes, but were not to kill the yellow-skinned Slopeite or her toddler.

Days later, roach corpses on the empire's peripheries piled up high, but no Britasytes had been retrieved. Mounted sentries on the grass frontiers had brief sightings of roaches speeding towards Dneep, but they were just as quickly lost. Roaches were swift and ants would pursue them only so far, but Pleckoo knew how to overtake them.

The Second Prophet led several regiments through ancient and neglected tunnels to Dneep. Without wall-torches, the journey was dark and tedious but the route was mostly unobstructed. For days, Pleckoo and his men lived atop their ants. They slept, and ate and performed all functions as the insects raced without resting, a speeding shadow parade. When his men grew tired, Pleckoo led them in chants that celebrated all of Termite's holy names. "Each step we take brings us closer to Hulkro," shouted Pleckoo. Nothing would stop them until they reached the tunnel's eastern end.

**A**nand and Daveena woke from a too-short nap to resume their flight as the red sun rolled down a graying sky. The grasslands would not be reached until early morning. The roach, which had been tethered to a grass clump, was standing still with its wrapped antennae drooping on the ground. Polexima, clutching her stomach under a daisy leaf, agreed to reenter the belly scale and continue, but when the moment came to pull herself inside, she fell on the ground in deepest fatigue. Pareesha wailed and crawled on top of her mother.

"Perhaps it is best we sleep here one night before entering the grass," Daveena said, looking at the queen's face.

"Yes," said Anand. "Perhaps that is best."

"I am grateful for your compassion," said the queen who looked charmed when Anand and Daveena held hands. As Anand assembled a leaf tent for Polexima, Daveena searched for a pebble where she could make a lean-to large enough for the both of them.

"Thank you," said Polexima, as she watched Anand

cut and shred a second leaf to line the bottom of her tent as a cushion.

"You are welcome, Mother," Anand said, then saw her wince.

"It suddenly shames me to realize that I do not know the name of my rescuer," she said.

He chuckled. "I am Anand. Do you need some water, Mother? Some food?"

"Why do you call me 'Mother'?" asked the queen with a chuckle in her voice.

"It is the way of my adopted nation. 'Mother' is a term of esteem for all women who have achieved a certain age."

"Why have you stopped addressing me as Your Majesty, though? I am your queen," said Polexima as Pareesha crawled towards her and reached for breast milk.

"Respectfully, Mother, I had my reasons then. But I am a free Britasyte as well as a citizen of the Dranverite Collective of Nations. I am not a Cajorite, nor a subject of any mound on the Slope."

Polexima was silent. "Dranverites? Our priests insisted there was no one but tree cannibals in Dranveria."

"Like so many things, Mother, your priests were wrong about that. And not all tree dwellers are cannibals," said Anand as Daveena returned, lugging a rotting grass seed that had succumbed to a delicious blue mold. Polexima looked thoughtful.

"Anand, I should like that you stop calling me that. My name is Polexima."

"Very well, Polexima. This is my betrothed, Daveena."

Daveena touched her hand to her head, then her heart, then bowed in the sign of esteeming. Polexima imitated her as best as she could, but it appeared to be the first time she had ever bowed to anyone. Pareesha took the moment to crawl away. Polexima looked astonished when the baby crawled to a pebble, then used it for leverage to stand on two feet.

"First time she is standing?" Daveena asked in broken Slopeish.

"Yes," said Polexima, "I had feared she never would." The roach girl and queen smiled as they shared the tender moment. It didn't last though, as Polexima looked uncomfortable to have been so intimate with Britasytes.

"Sleep, Polexima, for we will rise well before the sun does," said Anand as he finished the rigging of her tent.

"Morning always comes too soon in Hulkren," said Polexima.

"Every morning is a blessing," said Anand, "when you consider the alternative."

He was walking away from her when she erupted with a question.

"Anand, what do you wish of me?" she asked. "I will not go a roach-step farther until you tell me why I have been rescued. Will you ransom me?"

Anand turned and pinned her with his eyes. He sensed her growing respect, even admiration, but more than a remnant of fear and revulsion.

"I wish for several things," he said, being as measured as possible. "First, see for yourself what life is like among your subjects when you return. Stain your skin brown, wear the rags you wear now, and see the unending misery your nobles impose on their subjects. You will know that life for common Slopeites is as miserable as it was for you as a captive in Hulkren."

Anand watched her swallow and clutch her head as if it throbbed with the worst ache. "We . . . we are not possibly so cruel as the Hulkrites," she said. "We don't hobble our people by cutting their tendons!"

"There is no need to cripple your subjects, Poleximated," said Anand. "They are already crippled—with the lies of your priests that confine them to poverty. If your subjects did escape, where would they go? The insects of enemy nations would eat them, or human foes would kill them. It is only if they reach Hulkren that they might find a different life."

She was breathing hard and he knew the truth of his words was a torture. "Polexima, listen," he said, softening his words. "You have the power to change the Slope, to end the suffering of millions. Do not lament the past but live to change the future."

"But there is no better way. We have the leaf-cutters and the most abundant food supplies of any race."

"No, Polexima. The yellow ant and its mushroom are the most powerful of all the tools of the nobles' oppression."

"How could that be?" she asked, shouting at him.

He fixed his stare on her. "Why did the Hulkrites want your mushrooms, Queen?"

"To eat, of course. To grow strong."

"The Hulkrites have plenty to eat. They are willing to take from the ants' mouths, permitted to eat the dead ghosts and hunt other insects. I ask you again . . . why did Tahn want his *women* to have mushrooms?"

"I don't know that he did!" she gasped. Her breathing grew shallow.

"Listen to the voice within you. Nowhere but on the Slope are families overburdened with ten, twenty, thirty children. They are a wealth of humans to the nobles, but the vast majority of them are fated to poverty and painful labors."

"Fertility is in our race! Our blessing from the gods!"

"No, Polexima. Fertility is in your mushrooms."

"Mushrooms?"

"In the Dranverites' country, mushrooms are eaten by barren women. The Hulkrites want more children to make more soldiers. With mushrooms, Tahn was seeding his women with multiple pregnancies."

Polexima clutched at her belly, at the three or four offspring of some Hulkrite kicking inside her. Anand was quiet and allowed her to recover. "I know you have suffered, Polexima. But if we survive, I will tell you more about my other country, one that strives every day to become a Promised World for all. Will you hear my tale?"

Anand's sincerity pulled the queen out of her bewilderment.

"A promised world for all," she said, suddenly calm.

**A** short time later, Anand dragged a pink clover flower to the lean-to and used its petals to cover the floor. Daveena returned from the weeds, clean and fragrant after using the sliced flower bud of a soap plant to scrub herself and freshen her mouth. Sleepiness weighed on the two like a great rock, but they were more inspired to partake of each other.

The full sight of Daveena, gaunt, balding and imperfect, filled Anand with a new wave of pity. He wanted his love to spread like a balm and end her suffering, to suffuse her being like a warm drink of the sweetest fermentation. Every kiss and caress and touch of his tongue was to banish all thoughts of the pit in Hulkren. She lay beneath him, relishing the ache of her broken hymen, and succumbed to the torrent of warmth that pulsed through her with his every thrust.

The two became one creature that was inseparable from the fabric of the universe. She wanted to give herself fully. When Anand tugged at her ankle, she turned and kneeled and set her head on her arms so that he might fill her to her fullest. As he cupped her breasts, she savored the cry in his voice and thought he would splash his seed inside her. But he did not want it to end.

He fell to his side and pulled her into the curve of his body where they sank into the petals, wet and tangled. He was still inside her, firm and throbbing and aching with joy. Both were certain they had never been this exhausted . . . but they repeated themselves a short time later. Now Anand could not hold back. With his release, it felt as if he had issued all the clouds of the sky on the first morning of Creation. The young lovers wept tears of happiness, grief, madness, and relief before sleep crept over them.

Later, Anand saw his mother in a dream, standing over the two of them. "You should never have stopped here," Corra scolded. "You should have kept going, straight to the grasslands before you rested! Now you have endangered all your charges." Anand woke from his dream and saw Sun was rising and stretching His pink arms. Anand roused Daveena with a kiss. She saw the worry in his face and it ignited her own.

The two scraped dew from the leaves for the day's drinking water, then searched the roach's belly scales for a breakfast of mites. Polexima was still in her tent, lying on the ground, her face full of peace. Pareesha, tethered to her mother's ankle, had crawled outside the tent and was smiling at the Britasyte couple when they approached. They stretched their mouths with their fingers, which made Pareesha shriek with laughter. This woke Polexima, who poked out, her face wreathed by matted hair.

"Make haste, Polexima," said Anand, lifting Pareesha with his right arm. Polexima leaned on the other as he led her to the roach and helped her inside the belly scale.

After a long patch of sun-bleached sand, Anand surmised it was still half a day's travel to reach the golden slopes in the distance. Spread over the sand were the corpses of ghost ants and roaches alike. Anand realized this sand was a Dead Place, a barrier of some kind, probably a source of what the Dranverites called borax, which slowly dried insects from the outside in until they died of thirst. Anand steered the roach closer to living plants and away from the sand as Daveena clasped him, occasionally dropping her hand to stroke his constant erection. The memory of their first and perhaps only time together was wet and fresh in his mind but he knew he should not dwell on it—among the weeds there might be Hulkrish foot soldiers.

When the sun was at its highest, they reached the mouth of a dry creek winding gently down from the grass. On the creek's sides were sandy banks leading to impenetrable grass that was tangled and noisy with other insects. It did not look habitable for humans. The only route was on the sand of the creek, which was tightly packed and would be easy for the roach to travel if it wasn't poisoned with borax.

Anand was not sure at first, but a trace of something made him sniff the air. The roach's antennae were whirling. Anand smelled men . . . and then the more vague scent of ghost ants. Should he risk a rush to the creek bed?

As usual, his mother was right.

# CHAPTER 43

## THE GRASS PEOPLE

Ahead on the dry creek were more rocks and islands of grass with stalks that curved in the breeze. When the grass bent, Anand spotted the Hulkrites jammed at the base of the blades.

"Hide," Anand whispered in Daveena's ear. She slid across the roach's head and down its greasy side, then slipped into the belly scale with Polexima. Anand lay flat across the roach's head. The Hulkrites pushed out of the grass.

In a moment, the air above Anand was thick with arrows that skidded over the roach's oily body. The roach lurched after the humans, hungry to eat them. Anand slipped into the cavity under the natural helmet of the roach's head. In darkness, he reached for the blowgun under his cape, then peered out again.

Hulkrites surrounded the roach as it pivoted towards one target, then reversed itself to chase another. The soldiers tried to leap atop the roach, but their boots slipped off the greasy chitin. Unable to attack it from above, they chose to bring it down to their own level. Using swords, they hacked at its thick legs. As concerning as that was, though, what caught Anand's attention was a man in a jeweled mask that appeared from out of the grass, running with his sword held high.

"Shoot its eyes! Cut its feelers!" he shouted and Anand recognized Pleckoo's voice. The soldiers rose on each other's shoulders and severed the lashing antennae. The roach went into a frenzy as its eyes filled with arrows. It climbed over the Hulkrites and up a sandbank. As it neared the top, though, the sand crumbled. The roach fell and slid on its back. Unable to right itself, its legs jabbed at the air.

Anand was jostled, but looked out from under the roach helmet in fear of his woman's life and saw that the females had stayed locked inside the belly scale. But the Hulkrites were climbing up and slipping about the roach's greasy belly and Pleckoo followed them on, trailed by a man in a captain's helmet that Anand realized was Aggle of Culzhwitty. Both of them slipped on the grease and into each other, falling again before they righted. Pleckoo shouted orders through his jeweled mask and the soldiers attempted to open the scales, but all they accomplished was cutting their own palms on the sharp edges.

"Cover those holes," Pleckoo shouted as he stood, "until they scream for release."

Anand panicked as the Hulkrites stepped over the vents. He crawled up and rose with his loaded blowgun held under his chin. "If they aren't already dead, you will kill Polexima and her child," he shouted. "This roach will not open its scales while it lies on its back."

Pleckoo stared at Anand as silence fell. The wind blew through the straws and made dissonant tunes on their raspy flutes.

"Cousin Anand."

"Cousin Pleckoo."

"My, how you've grown," Pleckoo said in Low Slopeish. He signaled his men to step off the vents.

"And how you've grown powerful," Anand responded in Hulkrish as he wanted all to hear. "You've done well for a collector of night soil."

Aggle looked over at Pleckoo, puzzled.

"It is you who are so special, Anand. Hulkro chose you to test the faith of His followers, which has held, cousin. Indeed, it has grown stronger."

"Is that what your wood-infesting god told you?"

"He did. For I am the Second Prophet."

"You told it to yourself, Pleckoo, for no one is a prophet. Your god resides in no place but inside your head. If Hulkro wants us to know something, why not tell us all instead of speaking through one man?

You kill, steal, and rape in his name, but your crimes serve no one but you."

"My *crimes*? Is it a crime to free people from ignorance and slavery and turn them to the will of the One True God? If you want to speak of crimes, let's talk about those of the Slopeites whose queen you've rescued, Roach Boy, in hopes that she will break you from your caste."

"I am already free of my caste without having to murder the innocent. I rescued Polexima with the same hopes you have: to show the Slopeites a better way."

"The way of roach people? We can't all be thieves and dancing whores."

"Listen to me. After the Fission, in the country of the lair spiders, we learned of a free people, the Dranverites. They have no castes. Peace and knowledge are their passions. The welfare of all is their greatest aim."

"Do these Dranverites worship Termite as the One True God?"

"They allow everyone to worship any god."

"Men cannot be united as brothers until all accept Hulkro as their only god and Tahn as His First Prophet."

"Hulkro is no truer than any other deity," shouted Anand. His fury blazed like a pit fire. "Why must it be your god or nothing?"

"Because Hulkro says so."

"So say we all," his soldiers intoned.

Anand shook his head, laughing through his nose.

"I say piss on Hulkro, shit on Hulkro, for Hulkro does not exist! Let him smite me himself for denying his existence."

A dread-filled murmur rolled through the Hulkrites. Some looked to the sky in fear it would crumble apart to fall and crush them. Pleckoo opened his palms to quiet his men.

"Hulkro does not comply with the summons of a blasphemer," said Pleckoo. "Warriors of Hulkro," he shouted to his men. "Aim your arrows and shoot this worshipper of roaches."

Anand would not die without some attempt to foil Pleckoo. *At least the Living Death for him,* Anand thought. He raised the gun to his lips and the dart pierced Pleckoo's neck. A moment later, a crude spear knocked the gun out of Anand's hand.

To his surprise, the spear was not a Hulkrish weapon. Another flew at Pleckoo's limp body and entered his thigh. Anand turned to see an army of alien soldiers, in armor of straw, as they filtered through the grass, dozens at first, and then hundreds. Their flying weapons cut down the Hulkrites. They attempted to retaliate, but the men pouring from the grass had shields before them, from chin to shin, which they locked together in a wall to make their advance. The men behind them had bows and arrows, which they shot over their advancing front to pour down on the Hulkrites.

Coming from the east on the dry creek was a train of mounted roaches. From the soldiers' armor and the color of their faces, Anand knew these men were not Britasytes. Whoever they were, he welcomed them as the enemy of his enemy if they weren't shooting arrows at him. Pleckoo's men knew they were over-matched and those that remained raised their proph-et's body over their shoulders and ran off, even as Anand slipped under his dying roach's head to avoid the spears and arrows hurtling over him.

Anand peered out once more to see fleeing Hulk-rites that fell to the rear get captured, lifted and eaten by roaches that tore off their screaming heads. He turned to look at these strange Grass Men with their fair-skinned faces. They did not pursue the Hulkrites once they fled the creek, but laughed while watch-ing them run. A few of the grass men scaled the dying roach with spiked boots and headed for Anand. Using their spears, they pried back the head shell and yanked him out by his feet. He was dropped to the ground and surrounded by curious soldiers.

The Grass Men looked disgusted to see his white skin and Hulkrish armor, but were confounded that he was wearing a roach-scented garment and had spikes on his footgear like their own. Their confusion was made even greater when some realized that the white on his skin was cracked and revealed a different color underneath. One of them sniffed him, then yanked on his ear and Anand smacked him with the back of his hand. The man responded by stabbing him in the leg. Other Grass Men grabbed Anand and tied him to a long spear they could sling over their shoulders.

Riders on roaches gathered three in a column and plowed into the dying roach, turning it over. The belly scales fell open and out rolled the three. Daveena landed on her bottom and looked at Anand in panic as he swung on the spear. The attackers were intrigued by her brown skin and curious about her baldness. They did not touch her.

Polexima rolled out, face down, clutching her daughter all the while. The queen shrieked when someone tried to right her and see her face. She rose to full height, became her most queenly and shouted, "Please, do not touch me or my child," in her noble dialect. The attackers looked very confused now— this woman had skin and hair as fair as their own and they seemed to understand her words. They stared at Polexima in awe and one of them ran for their leader.

Anand was stripped of his armor and underclothing as he dangled from the spear. The attackers tugged his hair and beard and poked and prodded as if to see if he had the same things they did and in what proportion. "Stop it, please! You're hurting me!" he said in Hulkrish, Slopeish, and all his other languages.

They didn't stop.

"**U**ntie that young man," commanded Polexima and the Grass Men followed her order. She was astonished to look at a people who had complexions and hair like her own, colors that matched the surrounding grasses. Their eyes, like her daughter Trellana's, were close to their long, thin noses. For reasons Polexima could not fathom at the moment, it was most disturbing that they spoke the same language.

A man she assumed was a leader stepped forward with a cube-shaped miter spangled with silver pyrite. The front of the hat featured a spiky wheat head.

"Who are you, Child Bearer?" the leader asked.

"I am Polexima, queen of a great and powerful country who can bestow many riches. Who are you?"

"We have expected you for a thousand moons, Queen. I am King Medinwoe of the Dneepers."

"We have suffered much as prisoners. Can you give us refuge?"

"Of course, Majesty, but that termite-worshipper must be killed," said Medinwoe pointing to Anand.

"My servants are harmless and will remain with me. You must treat the wound of the boy. He is not a Hulkrite, but is like the brown-skinned woman, a Britasyte. They are also roach people."

"Perhaps we have misunderstood you. Brown skins who live with roaches? What odd country is that?"

"The Britasytes and their roaches are wanderers in our domain."

The Dneepers laughed. "Next you shall tell us that the yellow people live among ants," said Medinwoe.

"Why, of course they do," said Polexima. This only renewed the laughter.

"We should like to learn much more about your country, and discuss when we can leave for it ourselves."

Polexima was not sure how to respond to that. It was best to ask those questions later. For now, she simply said, "Will you take us to your capital?"

"Just as the gods have destined, Majesty," said Medinwoe with a bow of his head.

# CHAPTER 44

## DNEEP

**A**nand smarted inside and out as the grass people returned to their city. Polexima was sitting on the lead roach's head with Medinwoe who had given her soft cushions for her bottom, a bladder of barley liquor, and sugar crystal suckers for her and her daughter to lick. Anand and Daveena were riding behind the roach in a travois that bumped along the path. He resented that Polexima's royal bluster had impressed these strangers and turned them into her submissives. *Who is she but a lame woman of few abilities whose accident of birth was to be a queen?* he thought. *Some lesson is to be learned here.*

The dry creek and its sands were but a brief memory as the Dneepers went deep into their grass country, a rigorous journey that included long and fatiguing inclines on narrowing paths. The grass seemed like an ever-stalking wall and the air was like breathing seed gruel. The strangers to the land were bored by the lack of scenery, for the charms of Dneep were few. After his leg wound sealed over, Anand and Daveena took relief from the monotony by retreating deep inside the roach's belly scale to lose themselves in long and furious lovemaking.

The Dneepers feasted Polexima and her "servants" in the evening, but their diet was simple. It included the dreaded, bitter roach eggs, grasshoppers, and a few of their swarming cousins, brown locusts. These were followed by a salad of the tender shoots of sweet-and-sour grass mixed with minced green onion. The most palatable food was saved for last, seed kernels that had swelled in barley syrup.

After the meals, the Dneepers piled up eggs of lightning flies in tiny clearings. The people squeezed tight around this light to chat and make music. Anand could hear distant singing through the grass in innumerable villages and surmised this country was more populated with humans than any other on the Sand.

One night Medinwoe quizzed Polexima about the glories of her homeland. Anand, intent on mastering Dneepish, frequently interrupted to demand definitions of unknown words.

"Why are the Dneepers so attached to this grass? Wouldn't you prefer to occupy some of the Hulkrites' open space?" he asked.

"We yearn for that open space but we cannot cross to it with our roaches. The Poison Sands are all along our eastern borders and they dry the blood from our insects. The roach you were riding would have died by morning if it hadn't been killed. For thousands of moons, we have attempted to take back Hulkren from its shifting occupiers. The Termite worshippers are our latest obstacle."

"But I saw you defeat them," said Anand. "And quite soundly!"

"We are invincible near our grass, but without our roaches we are vulnerable to their ants in open spaces. Our Promised Clearing is coming, but it is not without battles," said Medinwoe, nodding towards the queen.

"The Promised Clearing?" Anand asked.

"Yes. Finally, as promised, our queen returns to lead us. Is the Clearing so truly beautiful?"

Polexima looked to Anand for guidance. He made the vaguest nod of his head. "Yes," she said. "It is beautiful."

As they spoke, Polexima and Anand became more attuned to the nuances of the Dneepers' language. It was close to the Slopeish that Polexima spoke among royal kin, but was even closer to the Holy Tongue of the priests.

"Medinwoe, would you tell me the names of your gods?" she asked.

"We love Grasshopper the most," he said. "He is our provider, the one we go to for mercy and protection."

"Do you honor Madricanth?" asked Anand.

"Not all conversations are meant for your ears, Anand," said Polexima. He sensed her real objection was the mention of the roach god.

"Respectfully, Polexima, you must make them for my ears," said Anand. "I will need to speak the nobles' dialect if I am to persuade the Slopeites of the need to face the Hulkrish threat."

Medinwoe looked at them quizzically. "Is it the custom in your country for royals and commoners to speak with such familiarity?" he asked.

"No, it is not," said Polexima.

"But it will be soon," said Anand. He watched her wince.

"This idea of being equals with . . . *you* is still quite new to me," she whispered to him.

"You'll never get completely used to it," he said with a wry smile while patting her hand. "I still struggle with my impulse not to see you sallow-skinned people as my natural inferiors."

Polexima gasped. Then, for the first time in many moons, she laughed.

Gezhulzha was a vast city of grass weavings. Only its natives could find their way through its shifting mazes of dwellings and its thin and twisty paths that were too narrow for roach-riding. Its citizens did not labor hard for food, but they worked constantly at the rebuilding of their shelters and at the task of keeping the paths clear—far from trees, the Dneepers had no lacquers or shellacs to preserve their walls of grass.

Polexima and her companions were led to Medinwoe's palace in a precious clearing. It was made obvious that such a free area was the most extravagant of all luxuries and the multitude of Medinwoe's staff were constantly engaged in battles against grassy intrusions. In the middle of the clearing was a modest house of scarce pebbles, chiseled to lock together and set on a platform to stay above rainwater. The "palace" was not even the size of Polexima's chambers in Cajoria. In fact, it was one rectangular hall divided into rooms by grass panels.

Medinwoe puffed and strutted while showing off his prized dwelling. As Polexima, Anand and Daveena followed him, they politely feigned admiration for the dim place of little refinement.

"Please let us know if we can add to your comfort," said the emperor, pressed to imagine that anything could be missing.

"I shall be quite comfortable," said the queen as she compared the room to the horrors of Hulkren. "You are very gracious, Medinwoe, I should like . . ." Suddenly, Polexima felt a warm trickle on the inside of her thigh, a trickle that flooded her being with apprehension.

"I do apologize," she said, "for my water has just broken." She was dreading this birth more than any other. Anand looked in her face and could tell what she was thinking: she would be giving birth to children whose faces would resemble those of a Hulkrish rapist.

*And who knows what color these babies might be.*

**T**wo days later, Anand was invited to Polexima's chamber. One infant was feeding at her breast. A Dneepish wet nurse held two more. A fourth had not survived.

"Are you well?" asked Anand, for it was the Britasyte custom to inquire of the mother's health first and then ask about the sex of the baby.

"I shall be better when I am ugly and mustachioed," said the queen, "and unable to bear more children."

"What sex are they?"

"Two are girls," said Polexima, smiling. "And no priests are here to submit them to the sting ritual."

Anand was curious to know the color of the infants and went discreetly to the wet nurse. "May I see?" he asked.

The infant's face was a yellow-white. Polexima sensed the source of his curiosity. "Yes, Anand. They are yellow. I am certain whose children they are—the one they call Prophet."

"The one they *called* Prophet," said Anand.

She clasped her throat.

"Is he . . . dead?"

"Pleckoo, the one who came after us, is his successor."

"Pleckoo? The noseless one?"

"You knew him?"

She paused before answering, grimaced. "I'm afraid I knew him a bit too well."

"I am . . . so very sorry."

"Are you sure Tahn is dead?"

"I am sure. I slit his throat, then crushed his heart beneath my heel."

Polexima jolted.

"And then I slit the throats of the rest of the Hulkrish captains who were visiting Zarren. Some fifty or more of them. All but Pleckoo."

She blinked in silence. "Why didn't you tell me?"

"I didn't want to frighten you. Daveena does not know yet. Let me tell her in my own way."

"Certainly."

"I must congratulate you, Polexima. But I must mention that we need to hurry back to the Slope."

"Why the haste?"

"I know the Hulkrites. I know Pleckoo. They are crippled now, but their rage against the Slope will only make them stronger. We have no time to lose before they gather to slaughter every Slopeite. Daveena will help you care for these little ones on the way back. Perhaps the Dneepers can provide you with a wet nurse for the journey."

"Anand, we cannot bring these babies back to the Slope."

"Of course we can. It will be difficult but . . ."

"No. For their own safety. These are not Sahdrin's children. If my kin and the priests learn these infants are the union of a Slopeish queen and the

Hulkrite's prophet they will be drowned and thrown to the ants."

"You could just . . . leave them here?"

"I *must* leave them here. For now. I have judged these Dneepers a decent folk. This brood will be well cared for." She was silent as she looked at the face of the baby she nursed. "They should never know who their father is. For their own safety."

"Then that will remain our secret."

She nodded her head as tears came. Anand wiped at a few of his own. A dark, sad silence passed, but it was one in which he felt forever linked to her. She reached for his hand and it felt warm in his own.

"I will make my best effort to leave soon," she said.

"It won't be so soon. The Dneepers will need to organize."

"The Dneepers?"

"They're coming with us. It may be an accident, but your coming here fulfills a Dneepish prophecy. At some point, a band of Dneepers left this land to find a new home. They are correct to believe that you are a descendant of those pioneers. They expect to follow you back to the Slope, to a promised land of space and sunlight."

Anand paused, looked at her with utter solemnity. "We must hurry to prepare the Slope for the invasion of the Hulkrish army," he said. "Slopeish military methods will not be adequate. A new army must be trained and its soldiers must come from all castes."

Anand could count six ridges in Polexima's brow

as she accepted the truth—a devastating war was imminent. Pareesha toddled towards her mother, looking jealous of her new sister and desirous of the teat.

"That's a very interesting idea," said Polexima.

Anand shrugged his shoulders. "A foreigner with outside knowledge will have to lead them," he said.

"I do believe you are putting yourself forward."

"Did you have someone else in mind?"

"I don't know. Someone just a bit, you know, more mature and experienced."

"I was a defender in the Dranverish army, the most powerful force on the Sand. And I came to Hulkren not only to free my people but to spy on the Hulkrish warriors—to learn their ways in order to destroy them."

She stared at him, eyes wide and unblinking.

"All right then, Anand. It may be the slightest bit not queenly to ask this . . . but just how did you manage to slit all those Hulkrish throats?"

The following evening, Anand and Daveena dined with Medinwoe and Polexima in the palace. Sitting with them were the summoned princes of the grasslands, all stuffed tightly in the dining hall. Following the final course of soaked seeds, Medinwoe looked directly at Polexima and asked his question.

"Majesty, we should all like to know. When may we leave for the Promised Clearing?"

Polexima was quiet. She turned to Anand and spoke in the servant dialect.

"I have no idea what to tell him. Have you?"

"Yes . . . I think that I do," he said. Images were gathering in his head but had yet to consolidate.

"Well? They are waiting for an answer, Anand."

"Tell them you are asking me about the exact definitions of some terms and will respond in a moment."

The queen did as Anand told her. He could not suppress his smile at the final image that bloomed, fruited, and ripened in his mind. He had mulled over the opulent histories of the Dranverites, of the great and conquering generals who had aspirations that others saw as foolish.

"They are waiting," Polexima said.

"You must tell the Dneepers that you are ready to take half of their soldiers to the Promised Clearing immediately. The other half will remain to defend Dneep and its women and children."

Polexima translated Anand's words, then addressed him again. "And where do you propose to put these tens of thousands and their roaches?" she asked.

"To their new home in the Dustlands, just south of the Slope."

"That is Hulkrish country now, and you know it."

"Of course it is. You must tell the Dneepers that now is the time for the Grass People to unite with the Slope and defeat the Hulkrish menace together."

The queen's eye twitched.

"Polexima, we cannot negotiate with an enemy as to the time of their attack. Please, gather your strength, and tell them with utmost conviction you are ready to take them."

The queen did as Anand told her. Medinwoe and the grass princes stared at her thoughtfully before turning to search each other's faces.

"Yes," said Medinwoe. "It is agreed we will leave immediately and that the Hulkrites must be destroyed for all time."

When Anand returned with Daveena to their chamber, he buried his face in the mattress to hide his laughter. He saw himself perfectly! He would return with the Cajorian queen to the Holy Slope with an entourage of thousands of roaches. On top of the reviled insects would be fair-skinned men with yellow hair whose language and appearance would force the Slopeites to acknowledge their humble origins.

As Anand rollicked, Daveena forced him to explain his vision. As he did so, through bursts of laughter, he saw her stiffen with fear. She sat on the edge of the mattress, her back to him.

"What's wrong?" he asked.

"It's the curse of our tribe. You're one of those that is famished for danger. All the fear that you push aside will be mine to tangle with for the rest of our days."

"We will both live to a hundred."

"I'm not so sure. I could not rebuild my life if I lost you."

"I am determined to live—for you as much as for myself."

He sat beside her and rubbed the small of her back. Wordlessly, they fell not just into each other's embrace, but into each other, like pebbles sinking in a warm and bottomless lake. That evening, the intensity of their lovemaking was so extreme, so deep and dizzying, it plunged them into a separate world. It was a place where they felt suspended in bliss, a place they never wanted to leave.

**"A**nand, I find all this grass rather boring. Will you divert me?" shouted the queen from her mount in the endless caravan of roaches and soldiers making its way north. "I believe you wanted to tell me about— Dranveria."

The queen was not so much bored as she was grieving the infants she had left behind. She clutched Pareesha a little too tightly as she thought of the tiny siblings she had handed to Dneepish nursemaids jiggling with milk.

"Yes, of course," said Anand who was marching with Daveena. He smiled and climbed up the roach to join the queen.

"I should like to hear it, too," said Daveena, squeezing onto the saddle.

Days later, it was Polexima's turn to recite what she remembered of the Slope's history. Anand took sport in identifying the aspects he thought were the fabrications of the light-skinned victors. Daveena focused on the parallels of the two histories. One of the similarities was achieving the uniting of peoples by political marriages, an idea she found fascinating. "Does that surprise you?" asked Polexima. "Why else would you arrange a marriage?"

"Because the two would love each other," said Daveena.

"Marriage for love," said Polexima. "What a charming notion."

When they reached the meadow country of the Seed Eater people, the brown harvester ants retreated from the roaches and hid in their mound. The grass people prepared for a Seed Eaters' army on foot, but to the former's surprise, no military presence confronted them.

Anand looked upon the Seed Eaters' southernmost mound, which was surrounded by wild barley. It was strangely quiet. Britasytes were allowed to travel the Seed Eaters' borders with the Slope, but it was unlikely these southerners had seen roach caravans, certainly not ones of this number.

Anand had Polexima order the men to drape their tunics over their spears and hold them over their heads, the sign of peaceful approach. After some time, a party of tawny-skinned women and old men with white or orange hair arrived on foot. Daveena translated Anand's words.

"Greetings, Tamers of the Harvester Ants," she said. "We wish to pass through your country in peace. If there is a cost of some kind, we can pay it in grain."

"We will accept your grain," said a crone whose naked breasts drooped below her navel. "We require one seed for each human and one seed for each insect passing through. You must travel near our borders on the Dustlands."

"Ask them where their men are," Anand whispered to Daveena.

The crone looked grave when she responded and so did Daveena when she interpreted. "She says her people are at war with the Mushroom Eaters."

"And who started it this time?" Polexima muttered.

Anand knew what his first order of business was once they reached Venaris.

# CHAPTER 45

## THE RETURN OF POLEXIMA

The caravan left a pile of grains that numbered in the thousands, but the Seed Eaters could not marvel at their new wealth for long. Once the roaches left, the brown ants came out to take their share, some of which they buried.

As the roach train continued towards Palzhad, the Dneepers were delighted by the elevations that allowed them to stare in ecstasy at the emptiness of the Dustlands. When the train stopped for rests or to make camp, the Grass men would run out to the empty spaces to hold out their arms and spin. Some were frightened by the vastness. Others removed their clothes to feel sunshine on their skin. A day later, when their skin turned red and felt like it had burst, they thought they had been cursed by some local demon whose home they had trampled over. Polexima had to explain that Sun had burned them and that they must make a gradual exposure to Him.

Four days later, the caravan reached Culzhwhitta, the first of the Slopeish mounds. Not far from the stinking shores of the Tar Marsh, it was as poor as Palzhad but as populated as Cajoria. On its south end was a clearing that led to a series of flat-topped rocks, the natural stone bridge the Culzhwitty ants used to cross the marsh to reach vegetation on the Dustland's edges. Anand realized this was a possible point of attack for the Hulkrites. He ordered the train to halt and make camp.

Anand negotiated with the midden caste to arrange baths for himself and Daveena and Polexima. They could wash off the staining roach-scent that sent the leaf-cutters scurrying and take on the clear potion of ant-scent for the first time in moons. "This is my first time in a midden," Polexima said, looking appalled by the filth, the crowding, the poverty, and the gruesome tasks of the outcastes. "I want to apologize, Anand."

"For what?"

"For doubting your description of life for the poor on the Slope. Why have I never seen this?"

"I'm sure your priests did not want you to see it," he said.

"And why would you want to see *this*?" asked Daveena.

Polexima bathed, as the middenites did, in public, shedding the grime that obscured her skin's bright tones. The middenites were nervous to see a pale royal in their presence, and even more astonished by her ease among them. She ordered a passing sheriff to alert King Caperfid and Queen Fuff of her presence. "They are to send proper clothing and cosmetics before I ascend to the palace," she said, "and do not forget a mirror." She also ordered a robe of royal-orange silk for Anand and two yellow handmaiden's frocks so Daveena would have a choice. Before they dressed, Polexima insisted that the two apply a thick coating of lily pollen to their faces and hands.

"I am not ashamed to be brown," Anand protested.

"Nor should you be. But if you wish to remain in my company without question, your faces and hands must be yellow. You are about to enter a world as treacherous as Hulkren in its own way, so you will take instruction from me."

"How will you introduce me?"

"As a savior. *My* savior, and the savior of this nation from the threat of Hulkrites."

"Some on the Slope may recognize me as an emissary of the Dranverites—and not with any fondness."

"Then let that strike fear in their hearts," said the queen.

Anand took razor grass to the provided mirror and scraped at the beard that had hidden his identity. He left the mustache, which he thickened with ant blood, dusted with brown powder, then pinched in knots to imitate roach antennae. He trimmed his hair, but left it long enough to cover the clipped-lobe of his ear. Daveena was given a dried dwarf poppy to carry as the queen's parasol and was alarmingly charming in all yellow garb. She took the second frock and deftly wrapped it around her head as a bright and shining turban.

The sheriffs brought Polexima and her entourage a pack of riding ants. She was greeted atop the mound by a contingency of wary guards who looked as if they did not believe it was really the Queen of Cajoria come to pay a visit. Anand climbed down from his ant and followed Polexima to a platform where the royals' thrones had been hastily assembled.

"I had forgotten how oppressive royal dress is," Polexima whispered as she trudged under the heaviness of a floor-length coat with a three-tailed train over a multilayered skirt. "It's especially difficult with my recent . . . disability. Anand?"

"Yes, Polexima."

"You must walk ahead of me and allow me to lean upon you."

"Lean on a roach rider? Walk ahead of you? You are a queen."

"I am a roach rider myself, now. If you wish to have authority, do as I say and walk ahead of me."

When they reached the reception of gathered royals, they saw servants making frantic preparations.

"We've no time for ceremonies or feasts," said Polexima, waving them off. "We must send this message to every mound in the nation: Polexima has escaped from Hulkren and returned to the Slope. The Hulkrites gather their ants by the millions to invade and destroy our nation. Every king and his high priest and commander general are to gather immediately at Venaris. Vof Quegdoth, a commander general from the southeastern grasslands, has arrived to combine your armies with his own force."

Polexima bowed towards Anand and turned to the nobles with an expectant gaze. Her cousin, Queen Fuff, followed her example but hesitated before addressing the astonishing stranger.

"Commander Quegdoth, you should know our nation is already at war. My husband and sons battle the Seed Eaters in the northeast. The kings of the west wage war on the Carpenter nation."

"They war in the east *and* west?" said Polexima. "Idiots," she mumbled under her breath.

"Both enemies attacked the Slope at the same time, retaliations for our own recent aggressions."

"Add this to our message," said Anand, surprised by the resonance of his own voice. "The Slopeish armies must capitulate and make allies of their enemies. Not to do so is to invite the extermination of all our peoples."

Anand swelled with new authority in his old nation but knew he needed one individual under his thumb in order to turn the Slope to its own defense. As the messengers raced toward the kings and commanders on two fronts, a strange trio would be traveling to Venaris for a meeting with its Ultimate Holy man.

**D**eep in the new heart of Hulkren, Pleckoo had counted twenty-nine days and nights of deepest despair. He cursed Hulkro and prayed to the Slopeish goddess, Mite, for release from his aching, still, and stinking body. Alternating with his despair was a growing hatred he thought might explode like a bitter ant.

Hope bubbled through Pleckoo one morning, though, when he found he could hum again. His fingers and toes were moving and with his reviving body came a stream of ecstatic visions: the Hulkrites would be victorious when they used the trident strategy to conquer and crush the Slope. Just as Tahn would have done, Pleckoo would time his arrival to coincide with the moon phase that empowered his ants. The sheer number of ghost ants and warriors were likely to suffice. *But what other painful bewilderments can I present to the people of the idolatrous Slope?*

A day later, the slave women who cared for him pulled the oiled cloth from his blinking eyes and ran for the Second Prophet's captains. When they arrived at his chambers, Pleckoo was sitting up and sucking a water drop. His men fell to their knees.

"Thank Hulkro. You've come back, Commander Pleckoo," said Captain Aggle, who had somehow lost his own nose. Pleckoo was startled by Aggle's appearance, so much was the man like a mirror reflection.

"Where are we?" Pleckoo croaked.

"At Ezzen-dozh. It is where we moved while you were . . ."

"Did you think I was dead?" he asked and searched the men's eyes.

"None of *us*, Prophet. *We* had faith . . . unlike some who were better off as food for the ants. We are Hulkrites for Hulkro, Pleckooites for Pleckoo."

Pleckoo studied all his captains' missing noses and realized how sincere they were in their support for him.

"The Promised World is more beautiful than you know," said Pleckoo as he looked for his mask, then tied it on.

"Is that where you were, Prophet? The Promised World?" Aggle asked.

"Yes, with Tahn in the radiance of Hulkro's smile. We must prepare for war, my captains. How many moons before the winter hibernation?"

"Three, Commander." He looked confused, then asked, "War with whom?"

"The Unholy Slope. It is where my cousin went with the Cajorites' queen. In the coming war, we will slay all Slopeites except for a few royal females. No conversions, no prisoners. Death to the Slopeites! Death to Anand! So say I."

"Then so says Hulkro," shouted his men.

# PART 4

# THE SON OF LOCUST

# CHAPTER 46

## A REMEMBRANCE

To divide the Slopeites' forces, the Carpenter Nation and the Seed Eaters had agreed to retaliate on the Mushroom Eaters on the ninth new moon. As their go-betweens they used the Britasytes, who had been happy to take their currency, pass their messages, and then retreat to the center of the Slope for safety.

The Carpenter people overwhelmed and slaughtered tens of thousands of inhabitants at the Slopeish mound of Teffelot on the western frontier. Beetle pellets that contained bones of Teffelan inhabitants were wrapped in Slopeish costumes and set in the walls of the redefined border. That was sure to provoke the Mushroom Eaters' wrath and the Carpenters awaited their reprisal with glee.

When the western half of the Slopeish military returned to the Land of the Red Barked Pines, they fell into a series of pit traps under pine-needle camouflage. Once the Slopeites and their ants had tumbled in, they were attacked in darkness with tridents launched from niches in the pits' walls. The Slopeish soldiers who could retreat turned only to face the bulk of the Carpenters' army atop their impenetrable beetles as they amassed from north and south to complete their slaughter.

To the east, the Slopeites fared better in retaking Xixict, a mound that had recently been annexed, and then lost a few moons later. Not a blade clashed or arrow flew against the Seed Eaters. A token reserve of harvester ants sensed they were outnumbered and fled from the leaf-cutters.

Soon after resecuring Xixict, the eastern armies of the Slope were reassigned to the calamity of the western frontier. They were riding toward the pines when news broke of sudden invasions in the northeast. Seed Eaters had completely subdued the Slopeish mounds of Dinth and Habach. The Slopeites realized they had been lured to Xixict as a trick, leaving the Seed Eaters free to slaughter their scant defenses in the northeast.

The flesh and bones of Habachites were milled into a paste by the harvesters' giant-headed chewing ants. Slopeish priests and noblewomen of Dinth were captured and held hostage. Their severed right ears—

still pierced with jewels—were returned to the Slope with demands for a new treaty. Among the demands was the return of seven mounds and surrounding territories that had been expropriated over the previous centuries. At one time, such a demand would have been considered laughable, but now it had to be considered.

When the Slopeish commanders on both fronts received Polexima's message, all questioned, but secretly welcomed, the demands of the returning queen. It absolved them from the responsibility of having to call for surrender—or die fighting in a battle it was certain they could not win.

The last half of the route to Venaris was the same one Polexima had taken twenty-five years earlier. That trip was a happy one, full of promise. The land had unrolled before her eyes like a honey-sweet dream. Like all teenage princesses of Slopeish mounds, Polexima had been summoned to the annual cotillion of royal eligibles near the end of winter hibernation.

As was custom, a vast retinue accompanied Polexima and her parents. Queen Clugna knew what was needed to make a good match, and she borrowed from the treasuries of her mound's priests. The right husband for Polexima could save Palzhad from falling into the Dustlands, where the Palzhanites would be dispersed and forgotten altogether. Polexima had to have the most stylish of gowns and proper jewelry and arrive on a well-appointed ant. A famous dress-maker from Cajoria had been summoned. When he returned to Cajoria, he leaked to its royal family that his newest client was a lively beauty with hips suitable for bearing thirty children.

With her parents riding behind her, Polexima was most splendid as she approached the feasting hall atop her magnificent ant. Her gown was a deep purple and her long, loose hair was as yellow as the dandelion her servants carted as their parasol. Of all the young women, she made the deepest stir as she was announced and entered.

The princess was instructed to look indifferent, but she was stunned by the whirl of handsome eligibles that did their best not to stare at her. A two-pronged dagger of pity and disgust struck her heart when she noticed Sahdrin. Everyone noticed him, as he was the prince who hobbled on false legs.

In his favor, Sahdrin was from Cajoria, a newer mound of fabled riches. The Cajorites had secretive trading connections with enemy nations. Cajorian territory contained a freshwater pond and a wealth of trees and other resources. Regardless, no princess vied to become Queen of Cajoria for it meant being married to Sahdrin.

During dinner, Pious Padjanago, the blind seer, had quaffed the liquors of fermented bortshu sap and saw a long and fruitful marriage between a "man of hollow limbs and a girl with hair like the noon sun." The following evening was an outdoor feast atop the mound at a massive circular table that accommodated thousands.

Polexima and her family found themselves seated next to Sahdrin and his retinue. The princess saw he had only one working eye and that the other was false. As horror filled Polexima's face, Sahdrin flushed red, and he turned away in shame. Suddenly, she reached for his hand under the table.

"I am Polexima," she said.

"Sahdrin," he replied.

"It appears we are to be married."

"So it appears. I am touched by your pity," he said, "and sorry to invoke it. If we are to marry, I make you this vow—I will never visit suffering upon you."

But suffer she did, as a result of his sending for her three moons later. Her dowry was meager—musical instruments, serving platters, furniture that emptied her parents' chambers. In exchange, Sahdrin sent her parents a bride price so large it took a caravan of twenty thousand trucking ants and ten thousand men to deliver it to Palzhad. The gift invigorated the commerce of the mound for a few more decades and saved it from being abandoned.

Twenty-three children later, Polexima was worshipped by her subjects as the Sorceress Queen of Cajoria, but her husband's family merely tolerated her. She had always thought of herself as the Suffering Queen, but now she knew her problems were the inconveniences of the rich. She may not have been happy, but she had always known comfort, a full stomach and freedom from debilitating labors. In Anand's company, she saw that life among the Slope's low caste was exactly as he had described it: a gray and hopeless enslavement.

The queen had taken up the habit of looking directly in the faces of the brown-skinned workers. They turned away from her, something required by law, but she saw how their features drooped with fatigue and how their eyes saw little but the task ahead. She was haunted by thousands of these eyes on the trip to Venaris. This time she was going to the Divine Mound not as a princess to be bent by priestly will, but as a leader with two missions. The first was to save her people from the Hulkrites. The second was to overturn all the Slope's institutions, including the one that legitimated her own right to a throne.

# CHAPTER 47

## THE NEW ULTIMATE HOLY

**A**fter Ennochenzo died and other candidates for the office of Ultimate Holy were gently poisoned, the path was cleared for Dolgeeno to achieve his greatest ambition. He was inside the Grand Cathedral of Venaris, where he tended its centuries-old altar. The original, dark-faced idols had been crowded off long ago or set in back of the fair-skinned deities. Locust, the dark-skinned sky god, had once been prominent on the altar, but now He was shorn of His wings, gathering dust and hidden by Sun and His consort, Ant Queen.

As Dolgeeno bathed, then redressed the carvings of Grasshopper and Mantis, he thought about his pending meeting with Polexima and the outlander who had freed her from the Hulkrites. Dolgeeno wanted them to wait, and for the third time that day, he returned to his chambers to bathe. He was annoyed that Polexima had returned alive, but he was eager to hear her account of the Hulkrish threat. He was more intrigued by her rescuer, this Commander General Quegdoth. How could someone so young receive the title of Commander and in what barbarous nation?

"Her Majesty Polexima and the foreigner are here," said an entering acolyte as servant boys used hand fans to dry Dolgeeno.

"Is it true he is very handsome?"

"Exceptionally so, but he is wearing a paint of yellow to conceal his complexion. And his mustache is strange."

"Strange?"

"Yes. It resembles the crimped antennae of a grass. . ."

"Grass what?"

"Roach," whispered the acolyte, hanging his head.

"How invidious!"

Anand and Polexima had been seated for some time in the reception hall. Polexima sighed and looked impatient, but Anand was astonished by the furnishings, which were ancient masterpieces that had taken lifetimes to carve. A newly bald novitiate entered with bowls of sun tea and a platter of dainties.

"Young Pious, do you know when the high priests of the Slope are expected?" Polexima asked.

"Most are already here, Your Majesty. Some are still arriving," said the novitiate. "Pious Kwilgeeno of Dinth has died in a massacre on the Seed Eater border."

"Blessings of Grasshopper upon his soul."

"And may Worm judge him as dutiful to his caste."

As they waited for Dolgeeno, Polexima reached for some tarts filled with creamed aphids in their own syrup.

"Best not to eat that," said Anand.

"And why not?"

"You can't be sure of what they put in it."

"They wouldn't dare poison a queen."

Anand just shrugged as Polexima brought the tart to her mouth, then reconsidered as Dolgeeno's attendants pulled him into the room. As he stood, his voluminous purple garments bloomed outward like an iris to reveal the tourmaline amulet of the holiest office in the land. He bowed to Polexima. Anand stood for Dolgeeno, and then seated himself when the Ultimate took his chair. Dolgeeno glared sideways at Anand, refusing to meet his eyes as the attendants straightened the flow of his garment.

"Truly we are blessed, Queen, to have you grace us again. Thanks to the gods," Dolgeeno said.

"The thanks go to this young man. This is my savior, Commander General Vof Quegdoth."

"My thanks to you, Quegdoth—and to the gods.

Is it your usual custom to sit before a queen and an ultimate holy priest?"

"Yes, Dolgeeno," said Anand, and smiled to see the priest wincing at the familiarity. "How do you know what rank I hold in my own land? Perhaps *you* should be standing before *me*."

Dolgeeno gripped his armchair, his nails digging into the upholstery. "Such a strange name you have, Commander. From what country do you derive your customs?"

"My customs are all my own," said Anand. "I declare myself to be of no specific race or country, but of all people, and I remain suspicious of any nationalist. My race and heritage are insignificant."

"To what station were you born in your country?"

"We are not born to stations. All individuals in my country are allowed to pursue their life's work, as it suits them."

"What rather interesting notions! But the gods have created an order, dear boy. We are all of us born into castes, each with a specific duty. The welfare of the mound comes first, not the desires of an individual. Letting people choose their stations would lead to chaos."

"Respectfully, dear priest, I know that's untrue. The Slopeites have made a tragic mistake in modeling their society after the ants they have parasitized."

"The ants we have *parasitized*? Boy, you know not of what you speak."

"Priest, you know very well that leaf-cutter ants

switch their castes as they need to. A leaf-cutter may spend her youth foraging for leaves or tending the young, but as she grows older and larger, she will be sent to wars as a soldier. When a queen ant dies, a humble worker may swell and start laying eggs."

"Respectfully, you are unwise . . . as a boy your age would be."

"*Respectfully*, priest, you are unaware of life outside these United Queendoms. The Hulkrites, for example, make excellent soldiers of low-caste defectors from places like the Slope."

Dolgeeno squinted and his jowls shook. "You are a *Dranverite!*" he said, rising from his chair. His fat finger pointed at Anand from under a cascade of silk. "You are *that* Dranverite who attempted to lure the Cajorites to your poisonous ideas with jars of watered honey."

"I am proud to be a citizen of my own volition in the Dranverite Collective Nations," said Anand. "And our thick and fragrant clover honey is prized everywhere."

"I will have you arrested!" shouted Dolgeeno. "Where are your clever bodyguards now?"

As Dolgeeno went to the portal to call his guards, Polexima stood. "Dolgeeno . . . you must listen to him," she shouted. "I know everything."

"What are you talking about, woman?"

"*Woman*, you call me," she said and glared at him. "I am Your Majesty." She shook her head in disgust. "Of all men, it is priests who hate women most."

Dolgeeno stopped breathing, then forced himself to inhale. "Why do you stare at me like that?" he asked. Her eyes continued to stab him.

"I know what the source of my magic is, why I and other queens are forced to eat the eggs of roaches."

"How dare you refer to those creatures in my presence . . . at the Divine Mound!"

"I know this, too," she said, ignoring his bluster. "The mushrooms are the source of our fertility. And they are the curse of our laborers, whose lives are a constant struggle to feed their children."

Dolgeeno staggered, bending his head to avoid fainting.

"And I know the humble origins of you and me," Polexima continued, "and of our yellow-hued nobles. Thousands of our kin wait on the borders of the Dustlands. Dolgeeno, our grassland cousins are nearby and riding on roaches . . ."

"That word again!"

"They sit upon *roaches,* Dolgeeno! Our cousins from the grasslands speak our same language with breath fouled by roach eggs."

She stood and locked his eyes. "This is a momentous time, priest. The Slopeites must abandon the leafcutters that ravage these lands, force us into hostile migrations, and keep us in ignorance and isolation."

"You blaspheme, woman. There are places for royals in the Netherworld, places with royal torments! You will desist from this talk and return to your duties at Cajoria!"

"If you wish to save yourself and the people of this Slope, it is *you* who will take commands from *us*. The Hulkrites are preparing for an invasion. It will conclude with our extermination."

"This Dranverite has poisoned your mind, made you fearful with his lies!"

"Don't speak to us of lies, priest," hissed Polexima. "You use lies to justify the murder of infants."

"What?" gasped Dolgeeno.

"The killing of royal females—to control us, limit our number and increase your powers. From now on, anyone who applies the sting of a wasp to an infant will be executed for murder."

She rose and walked to him on her hobbled legs. When she reached his chair, she exploded in rage, her arms a whirl of blows that bashed into the quivering flesh of his face. "Murderer!" she screamed. "Murderer of *my* babies!"

He barely resisted her assault before shielding his face with his arms. She collapsed and brushed at her eyes. Gaining resolve, she struggled to stand at full height.

"You will cooperate with Commander Quegdoth, Dolgeeno. You will do everything he asks and supply him with everything he needs."

Anand saw Dolgeeno was glaring at him sideways, brimming with contempt.

"Just what does he want, Polexima? What is the price we pay this barbarian for his rescue of you?"

"This *barbarian* was a solder in the Dranverite army,

and an officer in the Hulkrish army," said Anand. "I know the Hulkrites' leader, a former Cajorite. The depth of his hatred for the Slope cannot be fathomed. His only goal is the murder of its people. Only a Dranverite is capable of leading an army in tactics that can defeat the Hulkrites."

Dolgeeno collapsed in his chair. "This Quegdoth is barely a man!" he said to the queen.

"He is a most exceptional man and our only hope," said Poleximo.

"He still hasn't told us what he wants! To become king? To annex us to his unholy republic?"

Anand stood, stepped towards Dolgeeno. "I want what you want—to prevent the slaughter of millions of Slopeites. Only one other army has ever repelled Hulkrish forces, an army that is now under my command. The Dneepers wait to join forces with the Slope. Do not make them your enemy."

"How soon do you expect this war?" asked the Ultimate, still looking at Poleximo.

"They may arrive as soon as two moons. We must mobilize now," said Anand.

Dolgeeno sobbed. Poleximo and Anand allowed him to gather himself.

"I know what you are saying about a coming invasion . . . is true," said Dolgeeno through his tears. "The southern mounds have reported that their ants are over-feeding their larvae to grow giants."

The Ultimate Holy finally met Anand's eyes. "What are we to do?"

# CHAPTER 48

## A BOY TO LEAD THEM

The emergency conference in the feasting hall was noisy like a locust swarm, with the buzz settling here, settling there, and then rising up again to wander. The hall quieted when the procession of high priests entered and assumed their seats on the dais surrounding the pitched throne of the Ultimate Holy. The veiled and celibate Nun Queen of Venaris entered on a sedan chair carried by the Infertile Princesses. They took their seats behind the gauze of the nun queen's royal pen.

Anand and Polexima entered the hall with Dolgeeno on his sedan chair. The chair should have been carried by strong, young novitiates, but instead it was supported by brown-faced men, culled from the different working castes of Venaris. When they set down the chair, Anand noticed how nervous the men looked inside the astonishing interior, as if the high ceiling above them might collapse and fall on their heads. He remembered his own first reaction to seeing such splendors and smiled.

Anand and Polexima had assumed the dried grass cowls of a priest of Locust and a priestess of Cricket which had not been seen in centuries. She had shaved her hair and eyebrows and added a pair of crinkled cricket antennae to those of the ant in her headband. Opposite her at the front of the assembly were King Maleps, General Batra, and Sahdrin in his new role as King-Father. Anand looked at the man who had been his king and saw that he had aged far beyond his years in the last few seasons. His false eye stood static in the socket while the other shifted at the sight of the wife he had assumed was dead.

Dolgeeno had the flat tone of defeat in his voice as he addressed the conference sitting on the Golden Throne of Ant Queen whose edges sprouted with carved and jeweled mushrooms. He was without pollen and his skin had taken on an ignoble greenish tint. "This is a day to celebrate," he began, "for our beloved Queen of Cajoria, Polexima, has returned with the hero who saved her. Sadly, she returns with a dire warning. We are aware that all over the Slope the ants are raising giants in their nurseries. These will be vaunted against the ghost ants of Hulkren, whose terrifying masters prepare to murder our people and occupy our mounds. We expect their attack within two moons."

A great murmur went through the crowd.

"We cannot defeat the Hulkrites on our own," continued Dolgeeno. "They have strengthened the Termite Demon and all his legions with uncountable sacrifices of red and green blood."

Dolgeeno looked to Anand, who made the slightest nod of his head. The Ultimate took a great breath and continued. "But fear not! I have descended to the Great Cathedral and spoken with the gods. Mantis has told me our one chance at victory is to accept this man, the savior of Polexima, as our leader during the crisis. All rise to your feet and hail Commander General Vof Quegdoth."

Anand looked imperious as he stood and pulled back his cowl to reveal his head. His face was powdered with a Dranverish red of frightening intensity. The kings, priests, and commanders were slow to rise on their feet. Batra did not stand until Dolgeeno jerked his chin up in a silent command. Once Batra stood, Anand spoke in masterful tones.

"Sit, please. I extend to you the warm greetings of the Dranverite Collective Nations. Some of you will understandably resist the authority of an outsider, but those of you familiar with the Dranverites' forces might attest to our capabilities." Anand turned his gaze on Batra, a gesture that was not lost on the assembly.

"It is our practice to learn the ways of an enemy in order to defeat them. That is why I became an infiltrator in the Hulkrish army. I am aware of their strengths and privy to their weaknesses. In order to conduct this war, you will accept that I am the commander of a new laborers' army, one that will fight in conjunction with your own."

Some gasped. Some laughed. Some muttered obscenities.

"Silence!" shouted Polexima as she pulled herself up. She leaned on a cane of a cricket femur to attain her full height. "If you want to save our lives, you will listen to this man!"

Anand resumed. "Every willing Slopeite, male or female, is welcomed into this defensive effort. As well as a people's army, the Slope will need the help of our neighbors. In order to win their alliance, you will return all mounds and territories you have misappropriated over the last hundred years."

The kings and princes of recently annexed territories stood on their feet and glared.

"Just what is it you want, outlander?" shouted Maleps, rising to his feet. "What price do we pay you for saving our nation?"

The rest of the hall rose to their feet and barraged Anand with questions and accusations. Some walked out. Polexima glared at Dolgeeno until he stood and raised his golden scepter of mantis antennae. "Quiet!" Dolgeeno bellowed. "You will remain in this hall. If you leave, you and all at your mound will be excommunicated!"

Anand, still as stone, waited for silence before continuing. "All of you are right to question what I want in this."

Anand paced a moment, then turned to his audience. "Wars are won by the will, and the will of your people must be inspired. The downtrodden of this land will not fight for the nobles and their cruel ways, but they will fight for themselves and the chance to create a place of their own."

Whispers of outrage rolled through the hall then erupted into shouting. Some were walking out again. Neither Polexima nor Dolgeeno could quiet them. Only Batra could win silence when he stood atop his pew.

"Listen!" he shouted, then turned to Anand in the sudden stillness. "Where are your Dranverites now?"

"In their own country. Where they will stay."

"If they are the invincible force you claim, why not recruit them for this war?"

"The Dranverites will not interfere in the conflicts of nations outside their collective. That remains my duty."

"I will kill myself," Batra thundered, "and so will my soldiers, sooner than allow this barbarian to carry out his agenda under the guise of defeating the Hulkrites!"

"Then take my dagger," said Anand, and removed it from under his cassock. He threw it before Batra and it rattled over the tiles. "Kill yourself now, General, and fulfill your selfish notion. Or join with us to prevent the Hulkrites from murdering your wife, your concubines, and your hundred children."

Batra picked up the dagger and raised it to disembowel himself—Anand was astonished and giving the general credit for his convictions when Dolgeeno rose from his seat.

"Do you defy Mantis?" bellowed Dolgeeno. "Will you go to Worm with a soiled soul and be judged a traitor and coward?"

Batra stiffened as the assembled stared at him. His garments clung to him from the sweat that had burst from his skin.

"If the gods have decreed this man as an authority," Batra mumbled, "then I offer him my cooperation." Batra bowed, then returned the dagger to Anand who immediately beckoned to a group at his right.

Dark-skinned women entered and unrolled a map of both accuracy and artistry in a blend of Dranverish and Britasyte styles. In the map's east was the demarcation of a new land colored in the Dranverites' red.

"The area shaded in red is the new free state. Its name will be revealed at a later time after I discuss the issue with its future inhabitants."

Sahdrin looked at the map and clutched his heart. Maleps rose and shouted. "Perhaps your mapmakers have made a mistake, but it appears you have included Cajoria in your new 'free state.'"

"It will be our capital."

"And where will the Cajorites go?"

"Everyone will be allowed to leave or stay as they like."

"Will you allow this, Queen?" Maleps shouted at Polexima. "Will *you*?" he shouted, looking at Dolgeeno.

"What I will not allow is the annihilation of the Slope by Hulkrites," said the priest.

"And need I remind you," shouted Polexima, "that your military caste is depleted due to someone's idiotic notion that you war on two fronts."

Silence. Maleps turned red through his sweat. The creak of his armor filled the quiet as he marched off. Anand did not wait for Maleps to exit the chamber before he revealed his next steps.

"We have very little time. Over the next ten days, I will make an appeal to the laboring peoples of the mounds to enlist them in our efforts. Kings, you will be informed by runners as to when your people should be assembled." He turned to Dolgeeno. "That is all for now," he said, with a nod of his head.

The Ultimate nodded back, eyes wide, and made what was for him the hastiest retreat possible. The nobles and generals followed, exiting amidst low murmurs. Anand, however, declined to exit the hall on the sedan chair and lingered. Standing with Polexima, he called the dark-skinned people to a corner of the hall. As usual, their heads were bent in submission and their eyes were fixed on the floor.

"Good laborers, I thank you for your service today," Anand said in his old dialect. "Look upon my belly."

Anand lifted his garment to show them his pure skin, as dark as any of theirs. "Now look upon my face and know that I am one of you. Tell all of what you have heard today, what you have seen. Those who fight with me against the Hulkrites will return to a life forever changed. You can become your own masters and need never fear the lash of an overseer again."

The laborers looked at each other, still avoiding Anand's eyes. He could see them make furtive glances at the nobles filtering out of the chamber. Anand was grated by their diffidence and swallowed his contempt—how easy it had been to forget that he had once been one of them. He looked at the chamber's altar and saw the blue idol of Locust with his dark face, nearly hidden in the back, cloaked in a woven grass robe. Anand reached for his new tactic. He walked to the altar, lifted the idol of Locust and shook off its dust before setting it at the front.

"All your lives you have been told you are less than others. You are not," Anand said. "All brown people are descended from their ancestor, Locust the Sky God. Locust grows strong again and wants his descendants to prevail, to be nobles in their own domain. Tell all Venarite laborers who wish to win a place in the new nation that they should assemble tomorrow at the great stadium when Sun begins His descent."

The laborers were all too quiet when Anand walked off. *Perhaps they love their suffering,* he thought to himself, *and they can suffer all the more at the hands of the Hulkrites.* He cursed the Slope as he made his way out, convinced his plans were useless and that everyone would die.

# CHAPTER 49

## THE TYING OF SASHES

Among the first of his commands to the Slopeites, Anand ordered the delivery of two Cajorite outcastes to his camp at Venaris. He then requested the capture and caging of blue-mottled locusts from the local hunters' caste. From the local priests he demanded the delivery of some rather odd potions he assumed were in their secret stores.

Arriving in the weeds of Venaris were the Britasyte clans who complied with Anand's summons to gather as a tribe. Some of the Pleps had trickled back to the Slope on foot, but some had been hunted down in Hulkren while others were still lost in Dneep. The hapless clan was aided in the building of new sand-sleds by the Entreveans and in the breeding of new roaches by the Fallogeths.

The gathering was a joyless one as the Pleps counted the number of murdered or missing. Anand reflected this somber mood as he addressed the wanderers after the evening meal.

"Pleps, you have suffered much and are weary, but I must divide your clan and send you with messages to the Seed Eaters and Carpenter nations. You will carry the generous terms of the Slopeites' surrender so that all who share this region may avoid future wars. You will then give testimony of the cruelty and power of the Hulkrites. You will relate the wishes of the Slope's commanders to unite with their neighbors against the southern threat. And you will offer chests of real gold flakes from the treasury of the Slopeite's Ultimate Holy, gold you must not pinch."

"Pinch, no," Zedral said. "But as the price for delivery we will take a tenth as our share."

"Beloved elder," Anand said with a scolding grin. "The Hulkrites are intent on destroying the Slope and will show no kindness to the Britasyte people. This mission is to protect both our tribes. No pinching, no commissions. Are we understood?"

"You wound me," Zedral said.

"I know you," Anand replied.

"We will carry out this mission," Zedral said, looking smaller. "And deliver all that has been entrusted to us."

"Swear it by Madricanth."

"Who is chieftain here?" said Zedral, looking very much annoyed.

"You are. Now swear by Madricanth and on the eyes of your grandchildren."

"My grandchildren have nothing to do with this!"

Soon after Anand had procured Zedral's best promise, Slopeish hunters arrived at the camp with cages of locusts. While the rest of the tribe slept, Anand sat in a sand-sled with Daveena, where he re-created reins and flying prods as well as the Dranverites' steering gloves. He hesitated, as he was unsure which of the scents he should apply to the gloves' fingers. He was even more uncertain as to the scents' potencies since they were from the stores of Slopeish priests. *Hopefully this is going to work,* Anand thought before he succumbed to sleep in Daveena's arms. However, he just as soon woke from a dream of Pleckoo chopping off his head and leaving it to bleed in her lap.

*What if no one joins me tomorrow?* he asked himself while looking out the window at the half moon. *The Hulkrites will attack at night under a full moon,* he reckoned, *when their ants are at their most powerful and the leaf-cutters are at their weakest.* Unless the Hulkrites were delayed by rain, he guessed he might have as few as forty-two days to ready an army. Dolgeeno had confirmed that the leaf-cutters were gorging their larvae to breed soldier ants even at the northernmost mounds of the Slope which meant that the Hulkrites had begun moving north and were force-breeding their own ants to swarm by the millions.

The following morning, Yormu and Terraclon arrived at the Britasytes' camp atop fleet ants driven by Slopeish escorts. When Anand saw them, they looked both scared and invigorated by their first insect ride.

"Would you mind telling us why we have been summoned?" said Terraclon, affecting a priestly voice. Anand ushered them to his sand-sled where he had laid out Britasyte finery.

"The best friend and the father of the groom must be suitably dressed for a wedding," Anand said.

"Wedding!" Terraclon repeated and slapped his hand over his heart. Yormu got teary and hugged his son. It took much convincing from Anand before Yormu dressed in a tunic of lavender moth felt, then donned a conical headpiece of damselfly chitin. Terraclon rejected Anand's choice and picked his own outfit, a gauzy cobweb caftan and a turban made from the wings of a lace fly. Anand laughed to himself and did not tell his friend that he was wearing a woman's clothes. For himself, Anand greased his hair with a fragrant seed oil before tying it off into the twin tails of a mayfly. After, that he used a fine brush to give his face a thick dusting of pink sugar-powder. He donned the clan's wedding poncho, which was studded with the rarest jewels. Once all three were ready, they left for the center of the camp where the Britasytes gathered before the sand-sled of the Two Spirit.

**D**aveena, her beauty restored, wore a multicolored wig from hair donated by her clanswomen. Only Eturra refused to contribute some of her own rose-dyed locks. Over Daveena's face was a veil that was a cunning miniature of a spider-web. She sat on a baby roach and circled Anand three times, her father baiting the roach, before she dismounted to join the groom. The layers of her forty gossamer gowns began with that of a distant ancestor. The final one was of her mother's embroidery, which depicted the foamy ripples of the Freshwater Lake.

Daveena trembled with clashing emotions as she walked towards her groom before Da-Ma at the altar to Madricanth. The sweet pain that jolted through her was an almost unbearable love for a boy whose fame and heroics increased each day. The fear that made her tremble was that she might lose him to any number of enemies. As she looked at him, she decided in that moment that he must do something for his own survival—even though it would compromise their marriage and her own happiness. *I would do anything to keep my love safe,* she thought, *even if it means sharing him.*

As she considered her plan, one she knew he would resist, she was overcome with a terrible ache that crippled every muscle. Anand saw she was struggling and walked to help her, assuming the weight of her garments held her back. When he looked in her eyes, she knew he could see her inner turmoil.

"Whatever it is, it's all right," he whispered. Looking into his face, she saw certainty and strength. They joined hands and reached the altar.

As the two stared into each other's eyes and Da-Ma sang the wedding prayer, the tribe's presence faded into mist. Anand's hand burned in Daveena's, and when he blinked, tears escaped and slid down the sugar powder. Daveena caught his tears in their tracks and licked them from her fingers. The taste was bitter . . . bitter and then sweet.

After Da-Ma tied their waist sashes together, Anand lifted her veil and kissed her in a way so intimate that the tribe's women swooned. Forced to acknowledge the crowd, he turned to them and spoke. "Wanderers, my bride and I apologize that we have neither the time nor the means to offer you a wedding feast. Know that in the future, in an unexpected place, you will all be treated to a matchless celebration." The crowd applauded and threw shredded chrysanthemums.

The newlyweds went to a new sand-sled, where piles of wedding presents waited to be unwrapped. Pressed to depart, Anand would leave Daveena to open them on her own as she traveled to the Seed Eaters' country. The one gift both took some time to enjoy was a new mattress of a stuffed and polished silk cocoon. Afterwards, with her arms wrapped around him, they lay on their sides as sunlight spread a honeyed warmth over their naked skins. Anand left himself to throb inside her, his hands cupping the softness of her breasts. "I know now that before we met, I was never truly alive," he said. One of Anand's men whistled for him a third time.

"You must go," she said.

"I can't tear myself away."

When he finally rose and left Daveena's side to dress, she remained on the mattress and tried not to cry.

"My sadness is small, my heart is brave," he said in a hoarse whisper, "for I know I return with new tales of roaming." She saw his eyes were watering.

"Bitter tears do not commence a sweet journey," she faintly scolded. He was almost out the door when she called him back. She had to reveal her plan before he left.

"Anand . . ."

"Yes?"

As she reached for her words, each one felt like a heavy rock. "Anand . . . how . . . many . . . wives . . . can a Slopeite take?"

"One. He can turn her out only if she is infertile. Why do you ask?"

She grimaced, spoke through gritted teeth, determined to get her message out.

"The Slopeites will use you to defend themselves, and just as soon destroy you once your usefulness has passed. You will have to do more than raise an army and make an alliance. You will have to mix your blood with theirs and seed women of their highest rank. You must be the father of their princes and princesses."

Anand looked as her as if he was trying to swallow a boulder. "The idea of your coupling with another man is . . . unbearable to me. Don't you feel the same? I want no other woman than you. Not from our tribe, and certainly not from theirs."

"You may not want another woman, but you need one. I know where your heart lies. No marriage with a Slopeite can dissolve our union."

Daveena jumped up and clutched Anand to her. "I won't lose you again," she said, "and that is why you will do this . . . once we have won this war."

His men whistled for the fourth time and one even poked in his head. The young couple tried to pull away, but could not. It was only when she suddenly turned her back to him did he even think to move. She kept her eyes firmly on the wall and waited to hear his steps.

Once he was gone, Daveena allowed herself some muffled crying on the mattress. She buried her face in all the places where his body had left its scent. A short time later, though, she had recovered. Her fear warred with her love and pride but she knew her husband expected her to fulfill her duty. She began her preparations to join the other Pleps. They would travel east to relay her husband's message to the people of the harvester ants.

*I will never fail you, my love, as you have never failed me.*

**A**nand walked with some young Britasyte men to the cages of locusts that had been set in a clearing. He noticed his tribesmen gave him complete deference now. Though it was not in their tradition, they walked behind him, as if he were a king. "Come along now," Anand said, and waited until they were all abreast of each other.

Each cage was small and housed a single locust. Anand examined several, and then selected one that looked younger, its wings glistening. Slipping into the cage, he climbed up the locust's leg and patted its head to still it. Another man helped him fit the mandibles with twin bits and attach the reins to Anand's wrists. Kneeling on the locust's natural saddle, Anand thrust the prod in his mouth, pulled on his gloves, and took hold of the short antennae. The locust bucked. "Open the cage!" he shouted from the side of his mouth, and the others yanked down the gate.

The locust sprang out and up on its powerful legs and buzzed its azure wings. Its chitin disappeared into a sky just as blue. Anand was surprised by the speed of the locust and tightened his grip on the antennae to slow it. He swung west and flew until he reached the stands of red-barked pines in the Carpenters' country.

Veering upwards, he turned east and flew parallel over the Insurmountable Boulders of the Great Jag. Leaf-cutter ants of the westernmost mound of Gagumji were returning with leaf shards from weeds south of the boulders. Their parade disappeared as they entered into the natural tunnel that cut under the Boulders and led to their mound. *The Hulkrites might attack through this tunnel,* Anand thought, and continued his flight, *but not before drawing out and defeating the enemy first.*

Sometime later, the Great Jag came to an abrupt end and yielded to the narrow clearing of the Petiole, the channel used by Palzhanite ants to reach the vegetation bordering the Dustlands. *The Hulkrites attacked Palzhad from here once*, Anand thought, *and they may come this way again*.

Scents of sulfur and decay reached Anand's nose as he next flew over the Tar Marsh. He looked down on the murky bogs that stretched from the Petiole to the Slope's distant border in the east. Leaf-cutters were parading over the natural stone bridge that thrust above the Marsh and led to Culzhwhitta in the southeast. *And surely they might march over this bridge*, Anand thought.

*So many ways to destroy us.*

As he flew past the Slope's border, Anand looked down on the grain-bearing weeds that filled the Seed Eaters' country. Atop their stalks were harvester ants of the grinding caste. When the hungry locust sensed ripe grain, it coasted towards the grinders, who raised their gasters and wagged them. They sprayed an acrid repellent that sent the locust back into flight.

Anand coughed on the spray and veered the insect towards the Slope's capital. The return flight home was full of dives and dips as the locust fought the southbound wind. *The wind always blows south in this season*, he remembered.

Anand was sick with fear as he flew to Venaris to inspire a new army. *Will any recruits be at the stadium? Has anyone passed my message?* Then another thought invaded his mind. *Do these* sedites *even deserve their own country?* he asked himself as his old hatred returned. *Likely, I will have to wage this war with the Dneepers alone.* He saw the stadium from its south side, its stands as dark as night in the shadows.

It was all too quiet as he guided the locust into a spiraling pattern to make his approach. Blinded with sunshine, his eyes ached as they adjusted to the sudden shade and his ears were met with silence. His disappointment was crushing yet familiar—had no one come? As his eyes opened to the shade, he looked up in disbelief to see that the stands were filled. The Venarite laborers had filtered in by castes, taken their usual seats and waited in dutiful silence. It was not all of them, but there were thousands. The first sound they made was a collective gasp as a pink-skinned locust-rider landed in the arena.

Anand caught his breath, and then coaxed the locust to crawl into position behind the amplifying-cones. The crowd watched in confusion as he squeezed his water bladder into his palms. They were gasping again, loudly whispering as he washed away the sugar powder to reveal his brown skin.

"My name is Vof Quegdoth," he shouted, "and I . . . am one . . . of you!"

The laborers jumped to their feet, clapped their hands and filled the heavens with cheering. Anand felt as if he was floating on the waves of their applause and he could not help but chuckle. Through the blur of his watering eyes he saw the Venarites shaking the idols of Locust plucked from their altars. Some waved flags with hastily painted images of the Sky

God. Anand was glad the cheering continued, for he needed the moments to gather himself.

"Sons and daughters of Locust," he began, and the crowd exploded again. "Not to wage this war against the Hulkrites means forfeiting your life. Winning this war means winning a place in the New Country . . . a place where every man and woman will have the rights and dignities of a noble."

As the crowd roared in response, Anand imagined the priests shuddering in their rectories. Laborers who had been reluctant to attend were rushing to the stadium now, eager to hear the message of the Dark-skinned Savior.

A few days later, Anand, his tribesmen and the earliest Venarite recruits rode on ants and roaches to the weeds south of Palzhad to make the first of their camps. Anand sighted the white rock with spider-webbed veins and halted the procession to unearth the articles he had buried so long ago. In secret, he donned his Dranverish armor, so light and yet so difficult to penetrate. It was almost comfortable to wear under his clothing, silent when he moved, and completely imperceptible.

As they had been instructed, the Dneepers were breeding roaches by nursing every hatchling and gorging them with food to force their growth. Anand added to their duties by asking them to capture and cage locusts for an air force. The Slopeish recruits were assigned to the building of leaf shelters and then to the collecting of the locusts' foods. The next wave of recruits was put to clearing weeds and digging pits on the southern perimeter of the Petiole.

At an informal assembly of what was becoming the New Laborers Army, the soldiers segregated, out of habit, into yellow-brown, brown, and dark brown formations. They encircled Anand when he entered a cage to fit a locust with reins and rigs. He had given other sets to the Britasyte craftswomen to reproduce by the hundreds, including the prod for the pilot's mouth.

Before he made his first flying demonstration, Anand donned a fat and mysterious turban, then strapped refilled shells of roach eggs to his thighs. Standing atop the locust's cage, he addressed the Slopeites, Dneepers, and Britasytes in all their different tongues.

"Every willing man and woman among you is as capable of this as I am," he shouted. "You will have to practice, master it on your own, and then teach ten others." The gate was opened, the locust leapt out, and Anand found the patch that coaxed the locust into a level spiral. As it went higher, he ripped open the turban and smashed the shells on his thighs to release streams of red powder. They drizzled onto the crowd to color their faces and hair.

Anand coasted to the ground and shifted pinkies instead of thumbs to the roots of the antennae to land. He realized his mistake too late and the locust responded with a too sudden halt. It threw him over the locust's head, where he dangled in the reins. "That's how you should *not* land," he said. As he swung, he expected a barrage of laughter but looked around to see faces stunned with admiration.

*Even my mistakes are working in my favor,* he thought.

A short time later, the Britasytes distributed new reins and riggings based on Anand's model. Sitting astride a dead locust, Anand demonstrated how to rig a flyer, then gave instruction in the essential steering, landing, and docking techniques. The Slopeites did not ask direct questions, but observed in silence and questioned each other in whispers. The Britasytes were impatient to fly, and before Anand approved, they were rigging the locusts in their own fashion and taking the first erratic flights.

Ignoring Anand's command not to "fly too far south," several students were dumped in the Dust-lands and it took them days to walk back. The end result was a loss of a number of insects and their rig-gings. He commanded the disobedient to capture new locusts and was enraged that they may have been sighted or captured by Hulkrites. "Because you are Britasytes does not mean you are above our regu-lations," he scolded.

The most competent of the new pilots were Dneepers, who approached the new discipline with fearlessness and determination. Confined by veg-etation all their lives, flying gave the Grass men an unbounded exhilaration. As Anand trained them, he realized they already had a hierarchy in place with established officers. *These are my natural captains,* he thought, *and I will assign each of them to his own company. And after that, I'll appoint men and women from the Slopeish servants caste who can interpret for the laborers and the Dneepish captains whose language is so close to the nobles' own.*

While the pilots perfected their flying, Anand scheduled appearances at the stadiums of key mounds and sent messengers to announce the day and time of his arrival. He knew that to make the best impression he needed the right costume. A smile came to his lips when he realized the garment he needed had likely been sewn already. He flew to Cajoria but not before making a quick reconnaissance over Hulkren's northernmost mound.

From above, the deep blue of the Great Brackish Lake was startling. Its waters seemed to stretch forever in the east. To the south of its shores, Jatal-dozh was all too quiet. Anand could not smell the carnal odor of ghost ants nor sight any Hulkrish warriors or slaves. Had all at the northernmost outpost been recalled to the Hulkrites' center for redeployment? Was Jatal-dozh truly abandoned or were the Hulkrites in the tunnels brewing some new offense?

Were the Hulkrites coming at all?

# CHAPTER 50

## HIDDEN FEELINGS

It was nearing sunset when Anand reached Cajoria and landed his locust outside the midden. He called to Yormu at the carrion piles and to Terraclon who ran from the chamber pots to wash his hands. The rest of the middenites halted in their tasks to gape at the stranger sitting on a locust. Anand grinned to be regarded with religious awe in the place where he had suffered as a half-caste. Terraclon approached and watched Anand pat his flyer's head with the flat of his hand.

"Why do you smack it, Anand?"

"To keep it still. Come up, Ter. Come up, Father."

Out of habit, the two looked to Keel for permission. Recognizing Anand as the infamous Dranverite, Keel turned his back in shame and pretended to be busy. Anand smiled to see Keel no longer carried his whip.

Yormu sobbed with pride as he climbed up the locust's leg and hugged his son. He descended to let Terraclon climb up and Anand looked at his friend's face to see his beard had grown thick and made him handsome.

"Have you ever seen a mirror?" Anand asked.

"Not a real one."

"You'd like what you see, Ter. Do you still have the bolt of blue cloth I gave you, the mottled one?"

"Well, yes, Anand. In a manner."

"How long will it take you to make me a royal-looking garment of it?"

Terraclon chuckled. "I must confess I have already done so."

Anand let loose with a long, loud laugh. The middenites turned and stared at him as laughter was so rare to their ears.

"Go and get it, please."

"I can't, Anand. If someone sees I've sewn something in imitation of the royals, I could be . . ."

"Those days are over. The new way has begun and everyone dresses as it pleases them. Hurry, Ter. I haven't much time. Locusts don't fly once night falls."

When Terraclon returned with a folded garment, he looked sad.

"Anand, I must tell you something," he said, dropping his head.

"No need to, Ter. I have always known. It is not stigmatized in Dranveria. It is even celebrated. You are like many of the priests on this Slope who practice it in secret, like the priests of many faiths. Our own revered Da-Ma, the Two Spirit is . . ."

"It's not that, Anand, I . . ."

"I know, Ter. I have feelings for you as well. I have always felt close to you, like a brother of course, but . . ."

"That is not it, Anand. Don't flatter yourself!"

Terraclon took a great breath and exhaled it noisily. "I am jealous of you, Anand, so jealous it prevents me from wishing you well."

"What are you jealous of, brother?"

Terraclon looked down at the sand. When he looked back up, Anand was surprised by the fierce burning in his friend's eyes as he choked out his words.

"You have escaped! Seen other places, had adventures! And now you are flying on locusts and creating an army! That was you at Venaris who addressed the nobles and military, wasn't it?"

"Yes, Ter. What do the people say about me?"

"The most incredible things! Some say you are the avatar of some Britasyte roach demon. Some believe you are the Son of Locust, the long awaited Dark-skinned Savior who will lead us to Bee-Jor."

*Let them think that,* Anand thought as Terraclon's resentment seemed to deepen.

"Have you been lying to me?"

"What?" said Anand, snapped from his reverie.

"I thought I knew you! Have you always been some god in disguise?"

"Get back up here."

Terraclon climbed up and Anand put his free arm around his shoulder. "Ter, I can easily find someone to sew me a costume. The real reason I came here today is because I miss my father and I miss *you*. You know I am no god, but I have found a way out of this terrible place. And you are coming with me, into battle, I hope, and later into the new way. If you like, you will live with us one day—for you are my family. And I love my family."

Terraclon blinked in silence.

"That's not all, Ter. Though I cannot tell you how or why, you will wield great powers in the new country in a new role."

Terraclon looked stoned with emotions. "I . . . I love my family, too," he said, and tucked the garment into Anand's backsack.

"The easy time is still a ways off, Ter. But some day we shall sit and do nothing but feast for days. And you will have a different garment for every day of the year." Anand looked suddenly stern. "I hope you and Dad will fight with us. I'll send my pilots here soon. If you want to join us, you'll fly back to our camp with them. Jump down, now. I really must go."

As soon as his friend hit the ground, Anand prodded the locust and it leapt into a darkening sky.

The cold wind that blew through Anand on the

return flight stirred his apprehensions. Behind all his bluster, he had no complete strategies for defeating the Hulkrites. He had no idea how large his army would grow or how quickly they could train. *I'm a young and foolish fraud*, he thought. And with Daveena gone once more, he suffered the weight of keeping in these secret feelings.

As the light disappeared, the locust suddenly dropped from the air and into the weeds. As it grew darker, the locust grudgingly took short and low leaps until it neared Palzhad. Just as Anand neared camp, he prodded it one more time and the locust smashed blindly into a tree and was stunned and fell. Anand grabbed at the tree's bark, swinging himself inside a crevice. When his heart stopped thumping, he scaled his way down. *If only the locusts would fly in the dark, I could defeat the Hulkrites from the air*, he thought.

When he arrived at the camp's outskirts, he saw the supplies he had demanded from the priests had arrived and were arranged on the edges of the first pit. For now, he would implement the parts of his strategy he did know, but his mind kept going back to the flying of locusts at night. What did they fear most that would send them into a dark sky?

And then Anand remembered his time spent in the lair of a spider.

# CHAPTER 51

## STRATEGY

"I need the bravest among you," Anand said in the midst of the Slopeites' camp as they finished their evening meal. "Who will risk his life for the New Country to bring me a living lair spider?"

A few men from the servants' caste filtered through the crowd. Their elder, a one-armed man named Benjul, crawled on his knees and used his antennae to nuzzle the hem of Anand's garment.

"No need for that," said Anand, trying not to look disgusted. "Stand proud, soldier."

"Savior, we have accompanied the nobles on lair spider hunts," said Benjul. "I was used as the bait."

"You were used as *bait*?" Anand shuddered at the

idea. "And please, do not call me 'savior.' I am your commander."

"Yes, Commander. Forgive me."

"Nothing to forgive. What do you know about lair spiders?"

"I know where to find them, can identify their lairs. I was made to run over the spiders' doors. I would risk it again for the New Country."

"And the New Country thanks you for it. But none of us will ever be used as bait again in the nobles' pastimes," said Anand. "You will do this, in as safe a way as possible, and only if you want to."

"Gladly, yes."

"Excellent. Please, bring us a lair spider of any size. You may break its legs, but I need it alive."

The following morning, Anand gathered the Britasyte men in the excavated fire pit and warned them of the dangers of the task they were undertaking. "You will be using the most destructive force on the Sand to make the most dangerous substance. It looks and tastes like aphid candy, but I command you not to eat it, not even to *touch* it," he said.

As usual, the wind blew south, away from the Slope and towards Hulkren. The Britasytes had arranged layers of straw, kindling, and wood. Dispersed through the fuel were barrels that contained a fortune in silver pyrite crystals, some of it recently mined, some plucked from the royals' garments, but most demanded from the priests' own hoards. Anand led the Britasytes in a song while they rocked an enormous bow that twisted a twig in a divot.

Smoke filled the pit and wafted up to dance in spirits that both faded and multiplied. When the flames emerged and climbed through the twigs, Anand's heart leapt in excitement. He had made fire! "Now!" he shouted.

The Britasytes scrambled up the ladders. Anand was last, and when he crawled out of the fumes and over the pit, he saw Slopeites and Grass Men on their knees in worship. He joined them to watch the spectacle of flames flashing and curling from deep in the pit. The barrels of pyrite plunged deep in the fire with a noisy crash. Their burning sent up a bittersweet stench that sickened those whose noses caught it on a rogue draught.

The following day, Anand and the Britasytes descended into the pit wearing gloves and tight clothing while breathing through filtration masks to gather the pockets of white crystals. These were shoveled into barrels that contained a blend of honey and insect fat. After the barrels were tightly sealed, they were left in the pit, covered with sand, and guarded.

"Neither insects nor humans are allowed near this place," Anand commanded his men as the Britasytes arranged rocks stained with roach-scent around the refilled pit's perimeter. "Until the day these barrels are hauled into Hulkren, they must remain buried. Guard them with your lives . . . or surely we will all lose ours."

Anand's success at creating arsenic in the pit raised his spirits, but he was crushed anew with worries and indecision, sure that he needed more time than anything. One good piece of news was that Benjul's men returned late in the afternoon with a small and crippled lair spider that they carried on a sedan chair as if it were a royal personage. The sight made Anand laugh, and when his belly ached, he realized how long it had been since he had laughed.

Anand could barely wait for night to conduct his experiment. He set Britasyte women to soaking up the spider's scent. As he waited for darkness, Anand inspected the second and larger fire pit, the fuel of which would not be ignited until the night of the invasion.

While the Britasytes layered the kindling, Slopeites beyond fighting age were engaged in the fashioning of one hundred and thirty separate components of an enormous effigy of wood. Its twigs were wrapped with human hair that was soaked in stinking grease. The figure would tower as tall as a tree but would be light enough for a thousand men to raise from the ground with ropes. The caste of basket makers who worked at it guessed at the final image, but until the night it was raised, none but Anand would know its shape.

Basket makers from different mounds had bickered with each other and argued over how to secure the separate components. When they could not agree on knots, lashings, or materials, Anand placed one man, Tafro the Fuzzy-Eared, in charge. He convinced

Anand he was the man for the task when he demonstrated his ideas in a small model. Anand put his faith in Tafro, and then turned his concerns to another direction: his hopes for flight at night.

Right before sunset, Anand flew a locust in lazy circles before landing it in a clearing just outside the cages. He waited for the moment the insect would grow confused by darkness and crawl under a plant and cling to a leaf. When it refused to fly, Anand changed his gloves and pressed lair spider-scent to the highest segments of the locust's antennae.

The locust bucked. It pivoted, jerked, and fluttered its wings in some defensive movement. It jumped but did not fly. Anand tried different segments in different combinations and ran the scent through the sensors of its head. The locust's mandibles pulsed and beat its mouth-slime into brown foam. It kicked up its back legs and pushed its own face into the sand . . . but it would not take flight.

Disappointed, Anand walked back to the cages. He tried the spider-scent on several other locusts with the same results. Some would not even leave their cages but smashed themselves against the bars, tearing off their antennae. *Very well. Blue-mottled flyers will not take wing at night. How stupid of me,* he thought. *If the Dranverites were unable to achieve this, how could I?*

That evening as he slept in his hammock, Anand dreamt of Hulkrites raping Daveena. He was screaming in his sleep when two men grabbed him by his shoulders and shook him awake.

"Who are you!?" he screamed, searching for his dagger.

"Your family," said Terraclon. Anand could make out his friend's face and then his father's. "We came this afternoon on the locust you sent. We left our stomachs somewhere over Abavoon."

Anand wiped sweat off his face when he heard screaming in the field of leaf tents housing the recruits. They ran outside.

"What happened?" Anand shouted to the gathering men.

"An orange-winged demon," said a shuddering recruit whose beliefs prevented him from saying the true name.

"Who did it take?"

"Benjul, the one-armed."

Anand looked to the sky. Above him and heading for the trees was a night wasp, her wings a fiery blur in the distance. She had knocked over a tent in silence, clutched and then paralyzed the hero who had brought Anand a lair spider. He remembered the night when a wasp had flown him to her nest, how he was sick with fear. *Poor Benjul must be drowning in fright,* he thought.

"Let us pray for Benjul," Anand said to those who gathered round, "a man who sacrificed his life to build the New Country." As friends and kin of Benjul gathered, Anand hung his head. As an idols keeper mumbled the prayer for the working dead, Anand looked up at the new moon and grew queasy. *I have less than twenty-eight days!* he thought as he looked into the trees, searching for the wasp nest. Suddenly, a notion dropped into his head like a seed to the mud. Its roots sprung immediately and plunged downwards as its sprout reached up for light.

When Anand returned to his hammock, it was with an idea that would rob him of sleep that night. He questioned certain aspects of his plan, wondering whether it was brilliant or insane. By dawn, though, he decided he had no other choice. His strategy for the war was set.

The following morning, Anand learned Tafro had failed to show up at the effigy site. He had spent the night celebrating his new position with a fermentation party and was passed out with his kin. When Anand replaced Tafro with Bilka the Baggy-Eyed, the two men fought when Tafro arrived to resume his position. Their respective kin were drawn into the conflict when Tafro and his cousins undid all the lashings, igniting a full-on brawl. When Tafro and his men heard the Son of Locust was returning to oust them, they fled towards the Dustlands, vowing to take up with the Hulkrites.

Anand ordered the Dneepers to hunt down Tafro and his kin and confine them to cages—he could not take the chance that they would reach the Hulkrites and divulge any of his plans. *The best thing to do now is gather my pilots for their mission,* he thought. He looked very tired and not at all like the son of a god when the summoned locust flyers gathered around.

"Brave pilots, I must ask you to be braver still. I need a thousand volunteers. You may lose your lives in this endeavor before the Hulkrites even arrive."

Nearly every pilot was willing. A reserve remained to train replacement pilots, but most followed Anand to a new location. Men of the woodworking castes were drafted to bring their tools and follow the pilots. Terraclon caught up with Anand as he marched at the head of the procession.

"You did not say good-bye after breakfast, Anand. Where are you taking these people?"

"To some rather treacherous weeds past the border and verging on the Dustlands. They will train there."

"How long will you be gone?"

"Just a few days . . . I hope. You and Father must train with your divisions while I'm gone. Don't expect special treatment. Tell my father he is always in my heart . . . as you are, Ter."

Aware that others were listening, Anand could not speak freely. But what he passed to Terraclon in a brief gaze suggested they might never see each other again.

Anand grew nervous as he led his pilots through burgeoning camps that had popped up like mushrooms after a storm. All these men were looking at him, pulling away to bow in reverence. On the outsides of their leaf tents, many had scratched crude pictures of God Locust with His Son riding upon His back. As Anand looked in hundreds of their faces, he was overwhelmed with the risks of his endeavor.

When they reached the weeds south of the Petiole's mouth, Anand fell back to address his builders.

"Woodworkers, on the eve of the invasion, I will command our troops from this spot," said Anand. "You will build the first of forty observation towers here, tall enough for a view of the Dustlands, twice as tall as Palzhad. It must be sturdy enough to support a chain of messengers spaced along its ladders. They will be the first to relay my commands in a link that will stretch all along the Dustlands' border—along the shores of the Tar Marsh in the east and along the rim of the Insurmountable Boulders of the Great Jag in the west."

The woodworkers began the collecting and binding of twigs for a foundation. Anand left them to their tasks and led his pilots to the shadowy weeds that stretched to the shade of distant trees. When he told the pilots what he had in mind, their faces filled with horror. He knew most of them had the urge to refuse his orders, but none of them did.

*They trust me,* he thought. *If only I could have that much faith in myself.*

**W**hile Anand was away, King Maleps and other nobles in the guise of pleasure hunters crawled on their ants up a ledge to spy on the camps of the New Laborers Army. They looked down expecting to see squadrons of buffoons with inadequate weapons playing at soldier. They were horrified to see thousands of men with frightening weapons being drilled in an exotic shielding technique. Maleps and his twin brother, Prince Kep, sniffed the air as if it stank.

"Something must be done about this," said Kep, who had lost his perpetual grin.

"Something very final," said Maleps.

# CHAPTER 52

# THE TURQUOISE INFIDEL

Seven days later, Anand returned to camp. His pilots remained behind. He heard the spreading rumor that the pilots in the weeds were being trained by the god Locust himself on insects that came from the Great Beyond. The other rumor was that the men were dead, that they had sacrificed themselves as blood meals to Locust to make him strong.

Anand returned to the central camp to find an abundance of newly trained pilots. This allowed the passing of messages to distant mounds and border nations within a day. As expected, Pleps in both the east and west reported that proposals of an alliance with the Slope were refused. The Seed Eaters acknowledged that the warnings of an enemy in the south were true, for deep in their own nests, the harvester ants were nurturing giants. The Carpenters confirmed the threat after sighting the vast armies of the Hulkrish Empire from atop their tallest pine. Still, both nations sent the message they might join the Hulkrites in destroying the Slope.

Anand was expecting this news but was surprised by how disappointed it left him. Knowing he needed more men, he commenced a recruitment tour, which was as much about demoralizing the nobles as it was about adding to his army. The sight of pilots on locusts was becoming common on the Slope. They brazenly informed the nobles in the most ill-spoken dialect as to when they were to assemble their subjects to hear the appeal of the person the nobles spoke of as "the Dranverish interloper."

After a series of successful speeches at other mounds, Cajoria was chosen as Anand's final stop. His garment was a deep and brilliant turquoise from an unobtainable Dranverish dye, but even the lowest castes, in defiance of the law, went to hear him in flimsy garments rinsed in the weak dye of sky-berries. Anand saw that more than a few nobles disguised themselves in the clothing of their servants to glimpse the man who had come to save—then split—their nation. Young women screamed and fainted at the sight of his beauty. Young men adopted the hairstyle that concealed Anand's ears. Many wore the red, brown and yellow stripes he painted on his face. Nearly all seemed moved or disturbed by his message when he spoke.

"Cajorites, I ask for your sacrifice," Anand shouted from atop his locust through an amplifying-cone. "All men and women who are willing and able must take up a sword and don armor. They must be ready to lose their lives in order to save those of their families. Once we vanquish the Hulkrish menace, those who wish to reside in the New Country may do so, a nation where all men and women are of one caste, a nation devoted to prosperity for all, where honey will be plentiful and free." A great roar went up in the stadium, and Anand flew his locust about, riding on the current of their cheers.

Most of the nobles, cowering with their families in their dwellings, heard the cheering and felt it vibrate through their walls. The weather was growing cooler and they trembled as they pulled comforters over their fleshy bodies. Some worried that when the assembly ended, the workers would swarm through their homes, plunder their treasures, and stuff their women with polluting seeds.

The nobles and military families were compelled by the priests to cooperate with Quegdoth, but among themselves, they whispered of the time when the gods would restore the Holy Order. The roach and locust-riding Grass men, the Slopeish caste defiers, and especially the turquoise infidel, would all be swept away, like so much dust, when their function was fulfilled.

Conflicting rumors about Anand spread among

the nobles as quickly as they did among the workers. It was said that Quegdoth was not a Dranverite at all, but a noble like themselves. How else was he so capable? Some said he had been a priest at Venaris who was seduced and empowered by the roach demon, Madricanth. Others believed Quegdoth was still a loyal Hulkrite and, at the moment the ghost ants were at the border, he would turn the nation over to his superiors: termite worshippers who were mad on turpentine.

To the horror of their mothers, adolescent girls of noble lineage were fascinated by the Dranverite and had hopes of becoming his concubine. Some had set little Quegdoth dolls, wrapped in pieces of rare blue cloth, on the altars of their bedrooms. To the horror of their noble fathers, adolescent boys attempted to capture locusts and fly them. Some imitated the Dranverish accent Anand used when he addressed the assemblies. These same boys were rejecting their meals to grow thin. They walked with Quegdoth's swagger in capes that fluttered behind them and grew long and droopy mustaches that resembled roach antennae.

When some noble families gathered at meals, they might find an empty seat cushion. Its usual occupant, a son near fighting age, left the dreadful message that he had "gone to the southern border to join the forces of Vof Quegdoth, Righteous Emissary of Dranveria, in his glorious campaign against the Hulkrish invasion."

In every crystal palace on every mound, in every black sand barracks and rose quartz rectory, nobles, priests, and soldiers whispered the same thing: "Something must be done."

They were assured in quieter whispers that something was.

On the borders of Palzhad, the woodworkers completed Anand's observation tower. It was the tallest man-made structure on the Slope and at night, on its north side, its egg-illuminated twigs inspired even greater numbers to leave their mounds and join the Dranverite's forces. Once it was finished, the woodworkers started building the forty shorter ordinal structures, one for each division of the army, which stretched in a vast chain along the southern border. The peaks of these structures would be illuminated on the eve of the battle and serve as reference points in the positioning of troops.

Men, and more than a few women, were fitted with crude but effective armor that was stuffed with a cladding of spent mulch from the mushroom chambers. Slopeites, who once would have been executed for touching a weapon, were granted their own swords. Everyone of every caste carried a blowgun and practiced shooting darts, caches of which were being produced day and night.

Anand would wait until the night of the battle before ordering the darts to be dipped in a paralyzing concoction he had mixed and remixed in secret. Some guessed it was the Living Death, but it was not. Anand guessed at the formula and knew it involved a combination of spider and centipede venoms but what he came up with left a shorter-term paralysis. He convinced himself this was not a bad thing, as he feared the concoction might fall into the hands of the Slopeish priesthood and, Madricanth forbid, be used against himself.

Wives and daughters of the new army prepared the rest of the potions Anand had demanded from the priests. Included were hundreds of barrels of leaf-cutter kin-scent, which was mixed with human blood. In the clearings of the weeds, this was dried, powdered, and poured into casings of resealed eggshells. Later, extracts of herbs, seeds, and insects were mixed into other concoctions. Britasytes and Grass Men had been ordered to gather as much of their own insects' secretions as possible. No one but Anand knew what any of it was for but the supplies he had demanded of the Slope's authorities were received promptly and without protest. They did not question him but accepted his request to address the Slope's rulers on day twenty-one of the lunar cycle at Venaris at midday. The authorities' complete and sudden cooperation roused his suspicions. What were they planning?

Anand doubled the number of his personal guard and kept them posted around him at all times. He knew as the moon grew larger that the Slope's soldiering caste was on high alert, ready to gather at the top of their mounds and wait for the emergence of giant soldier ants to ride into battle when the Hulkrites were detected. General Batra had sent a message to Anand letting him know they were cooperating with his Laborer's Army in one way only—"Make sure your lot are out of our way when the Slopeish Army rushes to face the Termite worshippers."

Seven days before the full moon, Anand hastened his daily inspecting rounds at the divisions of the Laborers Army in order to leave for Venaris by noon. He dressed in his Dranverish armor before getting into deep red robes that Terraclon had tailored and dyed with juice from the hymen berry. Fifty flyers would accompany Anand and act as his guard, men whose darts were dipped in the same red dye. Their color suggested they were coated in the Living Death. They were not. Anand had only one dart left that contained that potion, a dart he kept in his holster. As he flew to Venaris, he could already hear in his head the commanders' noisy objections to his proposal.

Anand steered his squadron over Venaris and saw the usual parades of leaf-cutter ants climbing up or crawling down. At the foot of the mound was a train of garlanded-and-bangled carrier ants that he and his men would ride to the top on the main thoroughfare. Crowds of workers had assembled to wave blue flags. Anand landed with his men in an adjacent clearing near a clover patch, some distance from the training fields. It was a good place where his men could tether their locusts and later pass the night in leaf tents if needed.

As soon as Anand set down, an arrow struck his chest plate and jammed in the cladding. His men and locusts were under a sudden barrage of arrows. Deep in the weeds, assassins in green camouflage were shooting from the leafy shadows, and all Anand could do at that moment was watch his men die.

# CHAPTER 53

# THE WASHING OF HANDS

The head of Anand's locust had been filled with arrows and it could not fly. Anand leapt to another one, whose dead rider hung tangled in the reins. He got this locust into flight and in a spiral above the arrows' range. He reached for his blowgun and its loaded magazine and searched for his would-be assassins. He saw no one, though—they had already retreated to tunnels in the sand.

"To the top of the mound," he shouted to those who could follow him. The survivors of the attack flew to the top of Venaris and landed on a platform just under its rain shield. Next to them on a sun-worshipping deck was a crowd of Slopeish officers who were all too silent on seeing the Dranverite.

Anand searched their eyes in the awkward silence before they returned to a conversation that surely had been about him. He looked unaffected, but rage pumped through every part of his body.

Next to the officers was a confused crowd of greeters with sweets and gifts. They were surprised to see the Savior had skipped his welcoming parade. Among them was Polexima, who was jubilant to see Anand, and went to hug him. Her smile vanished when she saw his furrowed brow. His men had their blowguns raised. They pushed Polexima back, and encircled Anand in the fashion of gottallamos.

"Forgive them, Polexima. These are dangerous times. The commanders must gather now," he said, throwing open his cape. Polexima gasped when she saw the arrow extending from his chest plate.

"No apology needed," she replied. "My son and I have prepared what you requested."

Anand's men used their maces to break the walls of the feasting hall and bring their locusts inside. This way they could escape in flight in an instant if needed. Anand sent a passing priest running with orders for Dolgeeno to come from his chambers, sit on his throne and call the assembly to order. When Dolgeeno dragged himself in, Anand could see the Ultimate Holy had lost much weight. He slumped as he sat, idly scratching the fleshy folds under his chin that had become difficult to shave. Polexima and her son, Pious Nuvao, quietly appeared in the hall and stood by a service portal.

The hastily assembled commander generals failed to hide their contempt for the Dranverite and their disappointment that he was still alive. Anand paced before them in his piercing red cape, surrounded by his stone-faced guards. The wings of the locusts would suddenly flutter while spittle dripped from their mouths. The guards' conspicuous darts protruded from the barrels of their blowguns.

Anand raised his free hand to quiet the hall, using the other to keep his cape tight at the neck. A great wooden gong was banged but some men kept their backs turned and continued to murmur. Anand looked to Dolgeeno, who called for silence, but the room would not come to order.

"Commanders!" shouted Anand with a sharp blast. With that word, he threw open his cape to reveal the arrow lodged in his chest plate. The chamber was shocked into silence and the commanders turned to him and took their seats. Anand turned to Dolgeeno, who colored and blinked.

"Commanders, I am so sorry to yank you from your feasts and your women," Anand shouted, then paused to obscenely stroke the arrow in his chest plate. "You have not shown me respect today, but it is with all due respect for your rank that I propose a new type of warfare. My ideas will sound foolish at first, but they will best serve your soldiers."

Anand looked into the eyes of the commanders, who sat with folded arms, squinting at him. "My suggestion is that you give up your ants as mounts. Do not ride them into battle, but allow them to face the ghost ants on their own, as the Hulkrites do with their ants, as our first defense."

The hall filled with derisive laughter that swelled and crashed like a wave. Batra stood, his chin jutting. "Are you making a joke, Quegdoth? We have no time to indulge your whimsies."

"I am most serious," Anand shouted. "This war must be fought on foot behind a defense of locked shields. If every soldier wears an ant-repelling potion, Hulkrites and ghost ants can be slowed or even stopped from penetrating the Slope."

"We will destroy the Hulkrites before they even reach our borders," Batra shouted.

"A soldier of the military caste would no sooner give up his mount than he would give up his sword," shouted Commander Dushan of the Jukatha mound.

"Just what is this so-called repelling potion? How could it possibly be effective?" asked Commander Bevakoop of Mound Abavoon.

"It is entirely effective," said Anand, "for it is a concentrate of roach-scent, the same substance that allows the Britasytes to travel these lands without molestation by any kind of insect."

Angry muttering spread like a stink through the hall.

"We must convene among ourselves before giving our answer," said Batra.

"I will wait," Anand said.

The commanders discussed the matter in several

circles that re-formed into two circles and then into one large one. Anand paced as Dolgeeno shook his head. "Quegdoth, your demands are ones that soldiers will never obey," said Dolgeeno, "even if I tell them the gods demand it."

"But they will listen when you tell them the gods want me dead."

Dolgeeno took shallow breaths and hung his head as Batra broke from the circle to make the pronouncement. He could not hide his hatred for Anand and shouted through gritted teeth.

"Sir, we are united in our response. We have agreed it is possible your New Laborers Army might make some contribution to the Slope's defense. But we must insist on this point: we will fight atop our ants with our own weapons and in our own way. It is inconceivable that we should allow ourselves to fight as foot soldiers wearing a potion derived of the . . . of the . . ."

"Roach," said Anand for him, as if he were biting into a savory slug-roast. A silence followed as he paced again.

"Commanders, you would be fools to believe everything I tell you," Anand finally said. "I conceal some of my intentions as well as my strategies for winning this war. But I swear upon the lives of my loved ones that what I tell you now is true: if you choose to fight the Hulkrites in your usual way, you doom yourselves and endanger your people."

Anand's voice was full and chilling as he stared at

Batra yet addressed them all. "I cannot exaggerate the numbers of the ghost ants—more than leaves on your trees, more than stars in the sky. The Hulkrites are not strategists, but base their efforts on overwhelming force. The first wave of ghost ants will come unmounted. They will destroy you and your leaf-cutters before you ever see the Hulkrites at their rear."

"Slopeites and leaf-cutters are invincible against any enemy," said Batra.

"You lost your most recent wars," Anand countered.

"We retreated prematurely—to follow your commands, Quegdoth." Batra turned to Dolgeeno. "Ultimate Holy, what are the omens for the coming war?"

Dolgeeno had not been paying complete attention and was focused on scratching his flaking ankles. "What? Oh, why, they are good, Commander Batra. Victory is predicted."

"When have your oracles ever predicted defeat?" Anand asked.

"You blaspheme, Quegdoth," said Batra. "If the gods have said they are with us, then we put our faith in them."

"The gods are with whomever has the greater force," said Anand, quoting from Dranverite wisdom.

"We will destroy every ghost ant that nears our border and then slaughter every Hulkrite who waits like a coward in their rear," shouted Batra, brimming with rage. "We do not question the word of our gods and don't allow foreigners to do so either."

"What you do not question are the words of your priests," said Anand.

Dolgeeno's eyes shifted left and right in their pockets of wrinkled fat. Anand paced again. This last silence was his longest yet and with each passing moment, it incensed Batra, whose hands gripped the pew to halt their trembling.

"Very well, commanders," Anand said and then clapped his hands twice. A servant entered from the portal with a wash basin that he handed to Polexima. She hobbled with it to Anand, supported by her son, as over one hundred witnesses, from every working caste of Venaris, squeezed through the service portal and spread throughout the hall.

The commanders turned to each other, then glared at Anand, wondering what he had contrived. When the witnesses were settled throughout, Anand made a show of dunking his hands in the bulging dome of water in the basin. Polexima handed him a rag. Pious Nuvao sat on the floor and recorded what had been said and done in writing, then dipped the corner of his document in the basin's water to stain it.

"Commander Generals of the United Queendoms of the Great and Holy Slope, I wash my hands of your decision," shouted Anand. "You choose your own way in this war. The New Laborers Army will follow mine."

Anand plucked the arrow from his armor and threw it before Batra.

# CHAPTER 54

## PLECKOO'S PRAYER

Pleckoo's first step toward conquering the Slope took him to mysterious Foondatha, an isolated and rocky country south of Dneep. Foondathans were a farming people whose religion required them to live without insects, but they had legendary weapons made of local obsidian that were handsome and exact. They had enormous crossbows set on carts with razor-sharp missiles that could kill any insect and send it flying before it landed as a skidding corpse. Their highest holiday celebrated a powerful army that had maintained peace for hundreds of years.

After centuries without conflict, the Foondathan army had dwindled to a token force that performed re-creations of ancient battles as a kind of entertainment at festivals. The people enjoyed security behind what they believed were towering and impenetrable walls topped with thick, black clusters of razor-sharp barbs that no living being could cross.

But the Foondathans has never known of ghost ants.

Foondatha was asleep when hundreds of thousands of nocturnal ants made a living hill of themselves and then became a bridge of punctured corpses the rest of their sisters could crawl over to raid the farms and villages. By the time the Hulkrites arrived to steal their weapons, most Foondathans were being digested by ghost ants.

Pleckoo loved unsheathing and staring at the black glass sword he had found on a wall in the palace of the Foondathan king. It was shiny enough to see the pores of his cheeks reflected in it. The blade was so sharp that its translucent edge seemed to disappear in air. He and his captains were thrilled to find armories filled with endless numbers of different-sized arrows that looked as if they were ritually cleaned each moon as well as skillfully made bows that were freshly strung.

As the Hulkrites loaded their sand-sleds with shiny, black weapons, a messenger reached Pleckoo with a report from the border on the Slope. Pleckoo's scouts, disguised in the husks of dead leaf-cutter ants, sent the message that Grass men of Dneep and their roaches were stretched along the Slope's southern borders, sitting as a living repellent to a ghost ant invasion. The scouts also reported the sight of rising observation towers and surmised that a people's army had been mustered and was camping at the edge of the Dustlands.

The Second Prophet worried little about this on his return to the capital. During the Living Death, he'd had plenty of time to ponder his strategy. His greatest worry was not that he would lose the war, but that he would be unable to hear the shrieks and squeals of the Slopeites as they were lifted to the mouths of hungry ghost ants. *It's only a matter of days,* he thought to himself, *and on the last day I will have all my forces gathered under a fat and golden moon.*

As the eve of war approached, chaos reigned in the camps of the New Laborers Army. The Dneepish captains were overwhelmed with the dull-witted, hunger-weakened recruits who poured in, each one anxious to claim a stake in the future nation. Every recruit was needed but so many had yet to be trained in the shield-locking technique. Anand knew it was effective, but without everyone working together, it could be disastrous. He pushed his captains to reinforce the notion that a break in the shield front must be immediately filled. Taller men who had proven their aim were to stand behind the shield-bearers to shoot arrows and hurl spears with tips dipped in poisons. When Anand tested the poisons on leaf-cutter ants, he panicked to learn that its potency varied from batch to batch. It stunned some ants, killed others, and left many un-affected. That was frustrating enough, but then he learned some of these batches had already been sent out and would have to be recalled.

And that seemed the least of his problems.

The last recruits to pour in from the northern mounds were the most difficult to train. They could not always understand the chain of instructions translated from Dneepish to the Noble Tongue and then to a confounding southern workers' dialect. Having no experience of warfare, these men were stymied by the idea of standing behind locked shields while aiming darts through a slit. Warfare, as they had heard of it, was conducted on the backs of ants with swords and bows and arrows.

Two days before the invasion, many laborers deserted, convinced there were enough soldiers to fight the war. Others were failing to show up for drills and spent the time gathering honey grass to ferment overnight and drink in the mornings. The army's usual adulation for Anand was slipping away and sometimes when he walked through camp the men failed to stand for him. With his heart racing and his chest tightening, he sent for Terraclon to ask what he knew.

"The men are jealous that the noble and military castes are preceding the laborers into battle in order to reap the first glories," Terraclon said.

"What?" Anand said, but in his mind he was thinking, *What idiots!*

"Yes. Lots of them expected to bear pretty weapons with carved handles instead of these makeshift blades. They are also complaining that they don't have engraved armor. Some are talking about leaving their divisions the night of the invasion to jump on ants and ride them into battle with the upper castes."

Anand's head fell into his hands as he staggered. "I have told them . . . no ants! That would be killing themselves!"

Terraclon could only shrug. "Others are convinced we won't need to fight at all. They expect that on the eve of battle you will call out to your father, the Sky God, who will march ahead of us as a towering giant. He will crush the ghost ants and Hulkrites under his feet, then uproot a bortshu tree to sweep their corpses into the Tar Marsh."

Anand's lips were suddenly thin. His eyes were wide and unblinking.

"You're frightened," Terraclon said.

"I am not!"

"If you aren't frightened, then you're a dimwit, Anand. You're pitting a bunch of Slopeish laborers against the most vicious force on the Sand."

Anand felt a sudden, crushing exhaustion. He blacked out and when he came to, he was slumped on the ground before Terraclon and knowing he did not look at all like a commander general.

"Terraclon," he said quietly. "I have no idea what to do now."

"Be an overseer! Threaten the lash and withdraw rations."

"That is not right. That is the old Slopeish way."

"Then go and figure out a new way. Do it fast because you might be aware that we have some rather unfriendly strangers arriving shortly and they aren't bringing sweets on crystal platters. Go!"

"I can't. I still have so much to inspect, so many final preparations, so many . . ."

"*Go! Somewhere.* You are useless until you find yourself. Put your captains in charge. It is still morning."

"Perhaps you're right," Anand said. He knew of one place he must go immediately. Before departing, he assembled the soldiers of his central division and gave the following speech mounted on a locust, knowing his words would be passed to the other divisions through the relay system.

"Soldiers, your gods will not protect you in the coming battle. We must rely on ourselves, on our skills and on each other in order to save us from the Hulkrish killers. Because we must have victory, we will not ride to our slaughter on the backs of leafcutters. Mighty laborers, the task of winning this war falls to those who will fight on their feet. Until you are ordered to advance and shoot, you will lock your shields and wait. Victory will be ours because you will stand firm for the New Country!"

The soldiers cheered. A breeze filled Anand's turquoise cape, the color of which intensified his brown skin. "Truly he is the Son of Locust," he heard the men whisper.

"Commander, what will we call the New Country?" one soldier asked.

"Let us win the war first," Anand said.

Anand was relieved to fly off and hide his face from his fledgling, ill-equipped army. *They have no idea how hopeless this cause is,* he thought. *In two days, all these men will be dead and the Slope will be crushed forever.*

*And I will be the one who led them to their ruin.*

It would not be hard to find Daveena and the glittering caravan of the Pleps in the grain-rich weeds outside the capital mound of Worxict in the Seed Eater nation.

**D**aveena was napping in bed, mildly nauseated, when she heard a loud buzz and then a thud outside her sled. She rose to look through her window and saw the massive head of a locust dripping brown spittle. She came closer and saw her reflection in its great blue eye and then the boots of her husband above it. He peered down at her with a face so sad it looked as if it were melting. She was most unhappy to see him and tried not to scowl. They stared at each other in silence as he slapped the locust's head.

"You aren't supposed to be here," she finally said.

"Why not?"

"Because the ghost ants approach your border. The Seed Eaters are having an emergency conference in their southwest."

"Will they battle the Hulkrites?"

"It is uncertain. Some Seed Eaters have hopes that the Hulkrites will end the Slopeish problem forever."

She saw Anand's eyes shifting frantically as he bit his lip.

"You're frightened," she said.

"So people keep telling me."

"We both know you've come to tell me something. Out with it."

She climbed through the window and scaled up the locust's spikes to reach Anand's saddle. When she was close to him, he saw that her belly was full and her breasts were larger and heaving. He stopped breathing.

"You are . . ."

"Pregnant. Yes. From their kicks I can tell they will be good dancers."

"Twins?" They were silent for a moment. Anand looked away from her to wipe at sudden tears. "Daveena, if I fight this war, I may never see these children."

"Then I will tell them that their father was the bravest hero, that he did what he could to spare them from Hulkrish cruelty." She hugged him and rubbed his back. "To live in fear is not to live," she said.

"Feel the fear and wander anyway," he said, completing the tribal adage. He gave out with a great sigh and fell limp into her arms.

"I just had to see you," he said. "Just in case . . ."

"Shhh!" she said, forbidding him to speak the words.

"But this could go badly," he whispered. "If the

Hulkrites win, you must not come and look for me. The clans must make it to Dranveria. If you do, paint this symbol in red on the sleds. They will know you have come to join them and live by their principles."

Anand peeled off a glove and drew the Dranverite's five-sided symbol of peace into the velvet of the locust's skull sensors. Afterwards, Daveena took his fingers and pressed them to her mouth. Anand kissed her tenderly, pulled her tight and let his tears run down her cheeks. Within the warmth of her embrace, he allowed himself to sob without control. She held him until he was still.

"Can this be our secret?" he said.

"Of course. Should you be going?"

He looked to the sun, blazing in the southern sky. "If I hurry, I'll just have enough time to see what the Hulkrites have gotten up to."

He kissed her mouth, her belly and then flew off.

**A**nand saw the first of the unmounted ghost ants at the northeast shore of the Brackish Lake, where they drank water, passing drops with their mandibles to the masses behind them. He assumed he would see the first divisions of the mounted army at Jatal-dozh, where they would replenish their supplies.

He was wrong. He spotted a few men in dust-camouflage scaling up the mound or coming down, but all were on foot and entering the mound through side portals.

*Are they hiding something?* Anand asked himself, and felt a rush of water in his bowels. Fear was still having its day. The rain shield of the mound had been lowered to keep ants out. *Or to keep something in,* he realized. *But what?*

"Expect the unexpected," he said to himself. "I am not without my own surprises." He steered the locust farther south, determined to see their numbers. At first he thought he was seeing another lake, a crystal and shimmering body of water. He soon realized, though, the phenomenon unrolling before him was hundreds of thousands of unmounted ghost ants. Deep in their center, he finally sighted thousands of Hulkrish tents in a camp.

*So they'll attack us through the Tar Marsh Bridge to take Culzhwhitta first,* he thought. A moment later, his heart sank when he saw the Hulkrish relay system set in place: spaced at intervals and linked by ropes were portable towers on sand-sleds. The men in the towers would pass their leader's orders from a central command across vast distances. There was no need for this unless there was a second camp of Hulkrites. He looked west.

Anand flew over a sea of dormant ants and, sometime later, his suspicions were confirmed. He saw thousands of Hulkrish tents pitched directly south of the Petiole. While the Hulkrites in the east attacked Culzhwhitta, these soldiers would march to Palzhad. But the relay towers continued to stretch west. He had to assume this third camp would attack through the

natural tunnel of the Great Jag to overcome Gagumji.
If they went unimpeded, eventually, all three divisions would coalesce to march on Venaris.

*Wise of Pleckoo to use the trident strategy against such
a lengthy border. His scouts have seen that we are stretched
all along our southern reaches,* Anand thought as he recalled a similar triumph in the Dranverites' past. He
knew that in the coming battle, the Hulkrites would
launch their assault at different times and places. If
the Slope's forces shifted to face one army, the second
or third army would smash through at the vulnerable
spot.

Anand felt sure that the Hulkrites could not know
he had espied their strategy by flying overhead on
a locust. But he felt anything but confident as he
viewed what looked like an infinitude of the deadliest
ants and a human force that had grown since Tahn's
demise.

A gust of wind came up, jerked the locust, and
sent it into a plummeting spiral. Anand fell off the
saddle but held tight to the reins as the locust spun
and flared its wings. It righted itself, veered over the
ghost ants, then swooped back up to the sky. Anand
pulled himself against the gusts, regained his seat and
took hold of the antennae.

It was time to return to camp, time to take command. As he flew north, Sun died in a lake of blood as
Mother Sand shred Him with Her fangs. Moon arose,
nearly full, Her face a tilting mask of pity.

The ghost ants reflected Sun's blood as they roused to the spreading darkness. With their translucent bodies, they looked like a flood of crimson phantoms as they flowed in a mass toward the Slope. *I must use a wedge formation,* Anand decided, *and drive this enemy east and west.*

The locust stalled after sunset and halted on Palzhad's eastern edge. Anand stripped the reins from the locust, released it, and walked back to his sandsled through the camp's many divisions. He was not assured to see his followers scrambling to finish their tasks. The tops of the ordinal towers were coated with sap but only a few were glowing with lightningfly eggs. At his sled, he rejected a meal at a platter and instead chewed on some gnat pickles Terraclon had left him before leaving to join his division. Anand listened to reports and received assurances that all projects were *nearing* completion. Voice-runners in a chain practiced their relay system and passed news from the distant divisions. Each captain assured Commander Quegdoth that their men were *almost* ready and their weapons were *being* sharpened.

"I have some final preparations in the border weeds," said Anand to the captains of the central divisions. "I'll return by early morning."

Anand raced on a speed roach down the Petiole to the distant weeds. He was heartened when he saw the vague lights of his pilots' camp—these men were still alive.

The following day, a full but ghost-like moon was floating low in the afternoon sky. The sight was pleasing to Pleckoo when he left sleep and his darkened tent to ride north. Soon the leaf-cutter soldier ants would be catching the war-scent of the ghost invaders. And soon the leaf-cutters would be pouring up from the bowels of their mounds to hurtle south with Slopeites strapped to their backs. *How delightful,* Pleckoo thought.

Pleckoo's official counters submitted wildly different estimates as to the number of ghost ants that had been pulled into their three-pronged campaign and some added extra strings to their counting knots. At first this was aggravating, but when Pleckoo and Captain Aggle reached Jatal-dozh, they rode to the mound's top and looked out on their central forces: a lake of fighters without end. Pleckoo laughed and Aggle stared sideways.

"Why do you laugh, Prophet? We are almost at war."

"I am filled with Hulkro's joy, Captain Aggle."

Before the sun had set, the men watched as the hungriest of the ghosts were up and pacing, having caught the leaf-cutter's rich and fungal odor on the south wind. These ghosts crawled over the dormant ants, rousing them. The ghosts that caught the first sprays of the leaf-cutters' *alarm-scent* were up and lifting their gasters to spray war-scent. Pleckoo breathed in the dank odor he had grown to love, and spread out the locks of his hair to catch its heavy perfume.

"Aggle, tell our men here at Jatal-dozh it will soon be time to release their captives."

"Yes, Prophet."

Pleckoo and his captain journeyed for some time to rejoin the end of the central formation. Pleckoo switched to his final mount, the largest and tallest ghost ant of all which required its drivers to pat its massive skull with both hands to keep it from racing ahead to the Slope. Archers joined Pleckoo on the ant's head, while others took side-saddles on the thorax and abdomen to defend the Second Prophet in the unlikely event of a human attack. Surrounded by a circle of captains/advisers on mounts, he shouted to the first of his message relayers in the chain woven through his distant forces.

"Good Hulkrites, we must not rely on our numbers. We cannot be overconfident. All of us must fight this battle as if it were our greatest challenge. The aroma of an enemy's blood is more pleasing to the Termite when it is mixed with the blood of our own fallen soldiers, and indeed, some of you will be martyrs by tomorrow. But Hulkro wants you all alive—alive to slaughter every Slopeish infidel whose existence is an abomination. Mighty Hulkro, we dedicate this battle to Thee."

*By morning, I'll be eating my breakfast in the stately chambers of Palzhad,* Pleckoo thought. *Sometime after that, we will reach and subdue Venaris, and from there take control of all the Slopeish mounds. A short time later and I will reach Cajoria! How clearly I can see it: the moment when the banners of Hulkro are stretched over the palaces of the royals!*

Pleckoo looked to the sky and prayed aloud. "Benevolent Wood Eater, I dedicate the destruction of this pit of idolatry to Thy name. I will arrive in Cajoria without my mask so all who knew me as Pleckoo the Noseless will tremble before me as Thy favorite son and Thy holy executioner. So say I!"

"Then so says Hulkro!" his men roared.

# CHAPTER 55

## WAR

All along the southern frontier, tens of thousands of soldier ants erupted from the leaf-cutters' mounds. The ghost ants' scent had not reached Cajoria, or the other northern colonies, but the priests were down in the deepest chambers inciting the ants to join the war by splashing *alarm-scent* from censures.

On top of Cajoria, King Maleps and his princely brothers-in-law were awaiting their mounts in front of Commander Batra and his captains. The giant soldier ants that emerged had long antennae, bright, new chitin, and mandibles that were sharp and fresh. Their long, strong legs would allow them to speed to the southern frontier by mid-evening as the last to enter the battle. The giants were already fitted with reins, and as they poked their heads up, the nobles grabbed at their ropes, leapt onto their heads and then slid back to a saddle. Commanders and captains were next and were followed by subordinate soldiers. When all were racing south, smaller unsaddled ants emerged to chase their sisters down through the Petiole to the battle in the Dustlands.

**F**ar in the south, the Slope's mounted forces converged in a single column, racing towards the Petiole. Anand heard their noisy clamor as he smeared his face with stripes of yellow, brown, and red. He dressed in his turquoise robes, and then crossed the clearing where the effigy makers applied the last lightning-fly eggs to the monstrous structure of conjoined twigs. In the pit south of this clearing, the Britasytes waited to make fire. They were silent when Anand arrived for an unannounced visit. He bowed to them and they bowed back, absorbing the somber look on his face.

In a niche between the effigy's massive feet was an idol of the roach deity. Anand lay on his stomach with his face to the ground and pointed his palms up. His prayer to Madricanth was mouthed in silence.

With a final nod to the Britasytes, Anand rode a roach to his observation tower and began the long climb up the central ladder. The tower had two other ladders, one curving east and one curving west. Along the rungs were voice relayers stationed within shouting distance of each other. The two chains extended in back of the lines to the farthest divisions on the frontier. The relayers on the ground were prepared to run with their messages should their sequence be broken.

*Let us pray it doesn't come to that.*

Anand was but a few rungs up when the last of the ants, the Cajorian contingency, bottlenecked near the tower. As Commander Batra's ant slowed, he noticed Anand climbing in his blue robes. The two stared at each other when Batra scowled, as if Anand were nothing but an irritating child.

Anand simply went back to climbing.

When he reached the top, he looked down at the swath his soldiers left free to allow the Slopeish ant riders to funnel down the Petiole. Their random parade had thickened into a great and irregular blur that was subject to the ants' own speed and instincts. The moon was floating at mid-sky when the column thinned into stragglers and unmounted ants too old or small to keep up. Anand shuddered with grief as he watched the distant head of the column fade in the blackening horizon. Despite his contempt for the royal armies, he grieved because he knew their fate.

"Fill in the gap," Anand shouted down the ladder, as his first command. The twentieth and twenty-first foot divisions marched towards each other, then slightly south, spreading out to defend the route the Hulkrites had taken on their raid of Palzhad. The defenders in the eastern and western divisions extended in a vaguely diagonal line, whose distant ends were farther inland, creating a vast wedge formation.

The soldiers were concentrated in staggered clusters before the bridge in the east, the tunnel in the west, and the Petiole at the center.

The Grass Men were mounted on their roaches and behind the lines of foot soldiers in a second parallel line. The roaches were bound to each other by ropes to keep them in formation. Their antennae were whipping like barley stalks in a tempest. They had picked up the scent of ghost ants as well as the war-scent of leaf-cutters. Some Grass men had to wrap their mounts' antennae in order to keep them docked.

"Distribute the Blue and Green" was Anand's second command. It was quickly repeated and reached the Slope's furthest extremities in less than a thousand breaths. Moments later, the much-discussed and mysterious potions were passed through the divisions to be explained and applied.

Terraclon's division in the east was positioned in front of the dry shores of the Tar Marsh, near the divisions defending the stone bridge. "Spread the Blue on your armor, your shield, your skin," shouted Caleery, Dneepish captain of the 38th division whose yellow skin set off his violet eyes. His interpreter shouted in kind as a barrel of the Blue was rolled Terraclon's way. The Blue had a familiar stink, something he had smelled on Anand several times. *Roach oil!* he thought to himself, not daring to repeat it aloud.

*Just what were you thinking, Roach Boy?*

In the west, Yormu and his division were positioned along the boulders of the Great Jag to defend the tunnel that led to Mound Gagumji. They were already smeared with the Blue and were following the example of their captain, who dipped his dart tips in the narrow-necked jars of the Green.

"Do not pierce yourself or your fellow soldiers with this potion," shouted the captain's interpreter, a tubby palace servant whose voice trembled in fear. "You are dipping your darts in a concoction of venoms that will stun both ghost ants and Hulkrish warriors. When a Hulkrite is stunned and you are close enough, gut him or chop through his neck."

As Yormu and his division dipped their darts, they heard a distant shouting from the next division, something they didn't understand. Just visible on the horizon was a strange sight lurching closer, something that made even less sense. To their eyes, great clusters of weeds were moving toward the boulders: tall and thick plants that looked to be walking on their roots.

South of the border weeds, Batra and his fellow commanders, as well as kings, princes and Slopeish soldiers, were singing war prayers as they left the Petiole and sped into the Dustlands. Their chest plates were emblazoned with the image of Mantis in an ink of lightning-fly eggs, an image they knew would pierce the Hulkrites with fear.

The Slope's commanders were employing their usual field strategy for an offensive: they let the ants race towards the enemy in a single column that would puncture the Hulkrites' first defense of unmounted ants. The Slopeites would then cluster to fight from the center out, while the leaf-cutters used their mandibles of fabled sharpness to eviscerate the ghosts. As soon as the Slopeites sighted the first lines of mounted ants, they would ready bows and arrows for the human targets in their rear.

The problem was, all they saw were endless, shifting walls of ghost ants and not a single warrior for Hulkro.

Batra panicked when his ant was overcome with ghost-scent. All the leaf-cutters raced beyond control into a widening sea of enemy ants, which surged towards them in a deluge. The crash of chitin and the screams of men drowned Batra's call for retreat. The sea of ghosts and river of leaf-cutters crawled and collided over each other to bulge into a stupendous, living hill of biting, slashing, and bleeding.

The deathly hill grew higher as the entanglement thickened. Soon it was as tall and wide as the mound of Palzhad. Inside its center, the Slopeites were suffocating or succumbing to attacks from ghosts. The humans who managed to dismount and run were tumbling over ants to the sand.

They landed only to face more hungry ghosts.

King Maleps and his Cajorian brothers-in-law were in the rear of the column and the last to reach the great death pile. Maleps jumped off his ant and turned to run north through a forest of glassy ghost legs. It was only a brief moment before an enemy ant caught him. Sharp pincers reached down to pierce and lift him, quite alive, to be swallowed. The ant reared up on her abdomen so her meal could slide down.

Maleps squirmed and spun inside the ant. He was able to see through her as his lungs sucked in the scalding fluids. As he prayed to Grasshopper for mercy, he glimpsed other ghost ants swallowing fellow Slopeites. In the moment before he drowned, Maleps's thoughts turned to Hulkro. "I offer myself to you, Termite. Surely you are the greatest god. Forgive my negligence at your altars," he mumbled into the liquid. He thought he had died and was ascending to the next world as he felt himself gushing in a rush of fluid only to realize he had been spilled on the sand. Far from being relieved, he panicked as he drowned inside the dome of a drop. His vision swam in blackness once again when suddenly the bubble's surface tension was broken. He was coughing, struggling to breathe, when he was jerked up to look into the mirror image of his brother's face. In Prince Kep's hand was the sword he had used on the ghost and to release his brother.

"Maleps!" Kep said, wiping the liquid off his brother's face. "This battle is lost, but we're alive."

"We've got to fight," Maleps said.

"Don't be stupid. We'll hide under this ant," said Kep, "and let its scent disguise us until it's clear."

Maleps looked in astonishment at the boiling mass of ants and humans as the living hill rebuilt itself with insects and their riders. "Get under here!" Kep shouted and Maleps squeezed under the corpse of the ant that had swallowed him. Just as they had done as children on cold nights, the brothers clasped each other and waited for morning.

*You have saved me, Hulkro,* Maleps thought—and then thought better of it.

**B**atra clung tight to his ant while it struggled to the top of the living hill. He was determined to find a human enemy, a captain or lieutenant or just a warrior to engage, but the only men were panicked Slopeites.

"Cowards!" Batra screamed at far-distant foes when his mount was grabbed by its mandibles. It was shaken until its head snapped off. As his ant's corpse fell down the hillside, Batra tried to dismount but he was tangled in its reins and landed under his ant. His chest armor was pierced by the ant's saddle thorn, puncturing his lung.

*The Dranverite was right,* he thought as he coughed up blood, then felt his ears poked by something sharp. Crystal mandibles sliced into his head while another ghost picked him up by his legs. Stretched between two ants, Batra was torn into halves and swallowed.

The tail of unmounted leaf-cutters entered into the conflict. Ten leaf-cutters banded together might subdue a single ghost, but every unmounted straggler was overwhelmed and destroyed. The smallest of them resembled human children, happily running to mothers. But rather than swinging them high in a joyous show of love, the ghosts tossed the leaf-cutters in the air only to catch them in their maws and swallow them whole.

Once finished with the last of the leaf-cutters, the ghost ants continued northwards with their meals on display in their abdomens.

Just as the death pile had stopped growing, Anand received messages from the distant east.

"Unmounted black ants approaching," said the relayer. The message was repeated sixteen more times, and Anand knew that black ants threatened the forces guarding Culzhwhitta. *Black ants? Bitter ants!* Anand realized. *So that's what they were breeding inside Jataldozh!*

"All divisions! Do not attack the black ants! If injured, they will explode!" he shouted. "Deflect them, but do not attack! Leave them to the ghost ants!"

Terraclon's far-flung division did not receive Anand's command in time. Fleeing the ghosts who chased them from behind, the black ants rushed north and into the front lines and the Laborers' captains ordered an attack. Marksmen hurled their javelins into the bitters' heads, which punctured with a hiss, then flashed with blue light as they exploded in deafening blasts. Their flying parts tore into other bitters and set off a chain reaction. The laborers' shields blew from their arms or smashed into their heads and chests. Sharp thorns and dagger-like hairs from the bitters' flying chitin pierced their exposed skin. Some men had their heads and limbs torn off.

"Shields over head!" shouted Captain Caleery. Terraclon scrambled through bloody corpses to find his shield and raise it. The standing soldiers deflected the falling debris but some were blinded by the ants' toxic blood. Blisters raced and bubbled over faces, legs, and arms. Whole companies ran north to cower in the Tar Marsh. Some swam the wrong way and stuck in islets of floating tar. Others drowned in the bubbling water.

Terraclon looked around and saw that a third of his division was dead or had deserted. The wounded were pulled to the rear in back of the roach line. Trembling reinforcements stepped in to lock shields.

**E**stimates of casualties reached Anand from the east. As he resisted every urge to panic, a message was coming up the ladder from the west.

"Clusters of walking plants approaching the first through fifteenth divisions," said the relayer.

*Walking plants?* thought Anand, and searched his mind for any clue. *What would the Hulkrites send against troops whose backs were against a boulder?*

"Prepare for an attack!" Anand shouted and instantly felt foolish.

*But what is attacking?* he asked himself.

**Y**ormu and his comrades watched as the weed clusters pushed closer in. The division's captain realized the weeds were camouflaging great boxes on runners. They were lugged by teams of low and squat longhorn beetles. Yormu knew something alive was inside them, something other than ants that would not be repelled by roach scent.

"Look out, men!" the captain shouted, as the boxes suddenly tilted up and their lids fell open. Thousands of shooting creatures, too fast to be seen, leapt from the boxes to attack the army.

"Fleas!" came the shouts as leaping blood-suckers landed on the foot soldiers. Yormu spun and hacked at the monsters clamping on his comrades. Around him were men whose screams faded as they were drained to husks. The largest fleas leapt off with their victims to drink their blood unmolested.

**P**leckoo's scouts in the east and west filtered back to pass their messages. For some time the Hulkrites' commander had cherished looking at the death pile of the

Slopeish nobles, but when he had news of a devastated people's army, he nearly fell off his mount in laughter. He looked up at the conspicuous observation tower, knowing this was the seat of his enemy's command.

"Let our central forces dismount," Pleckoo said, "and march up this Petiole. We will chop down this tower, so offensive to the True God, and capture the sinner that leads these infidels."

In his tower, Anand heard a single-word message from the west: *fleas*. His heart thumped in his chest as reports of western casualties poured in. He gripped the rail of his platform as he listened to the mounting numbers. *This will never work! I am just a stupid boy,* he thought as he struggled for outward composure. He steadied himself only to hear reports of Hulkrites on foot and marching out of the legs of their ants to his tower. Their front lines were lugging sleds with panels that concealed their contents.

"Yes, come closer to me. It is nearly time," Anand whispered as rage replaced his grief. He picked up and waved a large and luminous flag.

At the fire pit, the Britasytes waved a flag of their own as acknowledgement of Anand's order. They set to making a blaze in their pit and soon had sparks and smoke. The grease-soaked kindling caught quickly and soon a great and hungry fire was roaring for fuel.

"Hoist!" Zedral shouted to the rope carriers in the clearing behind the pit. A thousand Slopeites picked up the web of ropes connected to the effigy. They marched and tugged up the effigy whose feet were rooted in the pit filling with flames.

**H**ulkrites stared at a rising figure with hundreds of thousands of lightning-fly eggs pasted to its frame. As it rose, it grew taller than any bortshu tree. Its illumination outlined the figure of a great, fat roach with a human head: Madricanth waving swords! The idol's long and sweeping antennae bent with the wind. The Hulkrites were slashed with fright and halted their advance.

Pleckoo attempted to stuff his fear back inside him. It would not stay put. *Anand!* he thought to himself as he quivered. *The Roach Boy leads the Slopeites and flaunts his demon idol!*

"What . . . what is that, Prophet?" Aggle asked, unable to tear his eyes away.

"Do not be afraid, men. It is only the bluff of an idolater," Pleckoo shouted to his messengers. The shake in the commander's voice revealed his own fear and it passed east and west in his relayers' voices. The Hulkrites advancing up the Petiole remounted their ghosts and waited for a call to retreat. Those who had hauled the sleds abandoned them.

The fire in the pit caught the legs of the Madricanth, where it raced up its oily straws. Hulkrites staring at the effigy saw it was suddenly illuminated from below with an orange light. In moments, the Madricanth was blazing. It seemed to breathe as it staggered in the wind like a drunkard. The terrible stench of burning hair and roach oil blew south over the masses of ghost ants.

The fire's roach-infused vapors spread through the ghosts and plunged them into turmoil. They smashed into each other before retreating south, resistant to human prodding. The Hulkrites on foot who wove among them were revealed and open to attack. Showers of arrows from the laborers poured down on these Hulkrites and pierced their armor.

Zedral looked to Anand who waved his flag again. "Tilt!" Zedral shouted, and the men strained to angle the Madricanth downwards. "Drop!" Zedral commanded and the men released their ropes and ran back to the pit.

The effigy fell on the southbound wind and crashed. Its flames exploded into jumping, whirling embers. Hundreds of ants and Hulkrites were immolated in an instant, reduced to burnt flesh and smoking bones. The faces and hands of Hulkrites who caught the embers were covered in ulcerous wounds. Those whose eyes met with fire were robbed of sight.

What was this torture the Roach God had visited

on the Holy Warriors of the Termite? The Hulkrites' screams ignited a deeper panic, which spread to Pleckoo and his captains. Some Hulkrites shouted out that this was "fire," the most feared element on all the Sand. The panic spread as quick as a thought to the distant divisions of the Hulkrish army.

"Hulkro tests the faithful!" Pleckoo shouted into the deepening chaos. He was sure he was sweating blood as his ant was jostled in the crushing waves. "Take control of the ants!" he bellowed.

But the ants were beyond control. Thousands of them had their antennae burned off and they spun and sputtered in a daze with opened mandibles, piercing and killing their kin. Some ants plowed their heads into sand to leave their hind legs up and twitching behind them.

Anand watched as ghost ants nearing his tower retreated south to expose Hulkrish foot soldiers that had been hiding under them. Emboldened laborers broke their lines to run out and shoot these Hulkrites with darts. They fell and twitched in agony as their tongues wagged in foaming mouths. When the laborers saw this, they ran out with swords to slay the fallen. They hacked at their armor and through to their stomachs, then stomped on their chests until intestines issued.

The captains ordered these men back into line. They laughed as they returned, their boots dripping with blood they had danced in. Anand saw that the battle had stopped, but he was not comforted. He knew the Hulkrites would regroup at a center in the distance, while their divisions in the east and west were activated.

"Prepare for an onslaught!" was the message he shouted.

When the burning roach scent had blown away, the fleeing ghosts settled in their swarm. Pleckoo wiped the sweat from his face, looked to the moon still high in the sky, and communed with his god. *You will have your cousin's corpse tonight,* said a godly voice inside him, *and will sacrifice it to Me on the Slope.*

The Second Prophet returned from his trance and was assured by his counters that he retained nearly half of his forces at the center. He was fully intact in the east and west. Fear gave way to utter confidence. Pleckoo ordered his warriors to smash new eggs with concentrates of war-scent, which incited the ants to release their own.

"Lord Termite has said we will have the Slope and we will have it tonight," he said to his messengers. "Let the true war begin."

# CHAPTER 56

## THE TRUE WAR

**A**nand looked out at the Dustlands. They were empty of life as the moon shed its cold light. The distant sand looked like the skin of a corpse. The crickets, which had long abandoned the nearby weeds, had left a terrible silence. A message made its way on his left, its quick repetition a long and slow reverberation in the quiet. Anand already knew what the message was.

"Ghost ants nearing Culzhwhitta."

A moment later, the same message came from his right: an attack in the west at Gagumji. Anand felt outside of himself as he gave his commands, like a specter pitying a suffering stranger. His twentieth and twenty-first divisions remained before him to guard the Petiole, staggering their formations before its entry.

"Push!" was the command he gave his eastern and western lines, and they marched from the middle like two great arms breaking from prayer. The Grass men and their roaches followed behind the foot soldiers in a second, unbroken line, all of them rolling the ghosts to the extremes of the Slope's borders, east and west.

Terraclon was giddy as he marched forward with his division, watching the ghost ants rushing backwards in chaotic and glittering waves. Some tumbled and landed on their backs to squirm and wave their legs at the moon. When the laborers marched past these ants they punctured their brains with javelin thrusts through the eyes.

*This is all so easy!* Terraclon thought when suddenly the roach behind him was excited by an irresistible lure. It dragged forward the other roaches and they burst through the foot soldiers to race ahead of them, tripping them with their tethers. They entered into the ghost ant sea to create sudden clearings. The roach riders attempted but failed to guide their insects back.

Farther distant, through the slit in his shield, Terraclon saw an undercurrent of Hulkrites on foot seeping through their ants' legs and into the clearing. The warriors hauled sleds smeared with the rancid odor of fly larvae, something the roaches could not resist.

The roach riders gave up on halting their insects and slipped under their head scales as they rushed to meet the Hulkrites.

When the roaches got close, sides dropped on the sleds to reveal crossbows and shoulder-wide arrowheads of fabled Foondathan obsidian poised in their quivers. The arrows flew with a force that picked up the roaches and sent them crashing into the laborers. Terraclon dove for the ground just as the roach that had been behind him came flying over, crushing to death the reserves of men at his back.

Yormu and his division were herding ghosts west when they faced a similar assault. His arm was already scraped and bloody after a frenzied roach scuttled past him and to the Hulkrites' arrows. The crossbow misfired and its arrow flew at the laborers. It was of such width and sharpness that it sliced through the shields and cut two of Yormu's neighbors neatly in half before slicing through two more men in the reserves behind them.

"Forward!" commanded Yormu's captain. "Re-form lines! Blow darts!"

The marksmen behind Yormu stepped over the corpses to replace the dead, locked their shields, and switched to blowguns. As the line pushed forward and Hulkrites fell to the darts, the shield bearers trampled over them, stopping briefly to slice with their swords through their enemies' necks.

The line reached the Slope's sanctified borders. The men broke formation to climb over the piles of ant pellets and enter into "the place where priestly magic ends." This frightened Yormu more than any horror he had witnessed that night. He worried that the potion on his shield was suddenly worthless and that the ghosts could now advance. When the captain called for re-formation of the shield wall, Yormu obeyed but prayed to Mite to protect him.

South of the border, Yormu watched as Hulkrish and Slopeish men fell by the hundreds. The ranks of the roaches rapidly thinned as they were turned into arrow-pierced missiles that picked them up and splattered them against the boulders of the Jag. Soon their corpses would exude a death stink that was an invitation to the ants to invade. Dizzy with exhaustion and on wobbling legs, Yormu endured with his division and pushed the Hulkrites and their ants toward Red Pine Country.

In the tower, Anand knew death and devastation ruled in the extremes of the frontier. Was Terraclon alive? Was Yormu? Messages came from the Slopeish civilians of every mound: Which way went the war? Should they flee north and take their chances in the Buffer Zone of the Dranverites?

"No victory yet," Anand said as he searched the darkened distance for an invasion at the center. Far from his eyes and ears, his men were dying by the

PROPHETS OF THE GHOST ANTS 553

thousands. Were enough of them alive to fulfill his plan?

**N**ews that every last noble and soldier had been slaughtered at the outset reached Cajoria. Trellana was supervising the packing of her chests when Poleximа appeared at her portal, as pale as a lily.

"Trellana. Your husband and all your brothers . . . they're . . ."

"What . . . injured? Missing?"

"Dead. They have all been destroyed." Poleximа was woozy, too weak to reach the bed, and sat on the floor.

"You're a horrible woman to play such a cruel game," Trellana screamed. "No one has died but those horrid Hulkrites!" Trellana fell to the floor and clutched her face. "Oh, Mommy!" she screamed, and crawled toward her mother, falling into her arms to sob.

**I**n the east, the Hulkrites were leaking through their ants' legs in unstoppable numbers on foot. As Terraclon toiled eastward, he grew dizzy from sharply exhaling through his blowgun. It was a struggle for the laborers to march in lockstep, but the men pushed until they were halted by a barrage of arrows so numerous and powerful it sent them tripping backwards. They scrambled to re-form; there was no choice, as they had no replacements for their front line.

Terraclon stumbled over a corpse. As he recovered, his shield was filled with arrows. The enemies' arrowheads were of such sharpness that they burst through the shields to pierce the man behind it. Terraclon looked at the glistening weapon that had grazed his stomach. What strange black stuff was this weapon made from?

"Push forward," he said to himself and rose to relock his shield. But there was nothing to lock it against—he stood alone. His neighbors were dead or scattered. The arrows continued to fly. The other survivors crouched behind shields shredded by arrows. These men waited for orders, but none could come from Captain Caleery, for a Hulkrish arrowhead had pierced his lung. The captain lay on his back and mouthed a prayer through the blood spilling up his mouth.

The Hulkrites gushed out of their ants' legs in thicker streams with great plows, pushing away shields and corpses of men and roaches to clear a path for their ghosts. The plows left a scent of trunk-trail mixed with food-alert. The ghosts' antennae found the scents and took tentative steps towards the Slope. The trickle would turn to a stream and then to a deadly deluge.

Terraclon was paralyzed. What to do? If he ran, his back would be filled with arrows. If he sat, his shield would be torn to pieces and leave him vulnerable. He was praying when the shield was picked up by a barrage of arrows and blown over his head. He scrambled to a corpse to use as his shield. It soon filled with arrows and was hacked to pieces, but at least he was still alive—this was little comfort when he turned to his left and saw a small ant with a giant head. It was a brown stinger ant, and it jerked up and ran when it caught the roach oil on his skin.

Terraclon gawked at Hulkrites and ghost ants, which were suddenly overwhelmed by thousands of the harvesters' stinger ants gushing from the east like a mudslide. *So this is what Anand wanted,* he realized, *to herd the ghost ants to Seed Eater country and draw them into the war!* Low and agile, the stingers swarmed through the ghosts and overwhelmed the Hulkrish infantry. When the stingers attacked, they grabbed a Hulkrite by the neck with their pincers, and then bent their gasters to pierce him through his stomach or buttocks. The injection turned the victim's blood into a paste that would not flow. Bodies of the stung Hulkrites went rigid as wood and their eyes popped from their sockets and burst.

The ghosts attacked the brown stingers, which evaded the larger ants by crawling onto them, ten or twenty at a time. The stingers bit into the ghosts' chitin to anchor themselves, then plunged their gasters to puncture and pump the ghosts with the fatal coagulant.

Terraclon and his fellow survivors stood firm as a wave of brown stingers scurried near, sniffed roach scent, then raced away to attack the ghosts. As Hulkrites fell to the brown ants, Terraclon saw their chance. "Run!" he shouted, and the defenders retreated north.

As the Hulkrites struggled to combat the stingers, the Seed Eaters released their next wave of ants. These were giant brown soldiers with formidable pincers, but their real weapon was a noxious spray from enormous gasters, which they held upright and shook. The spray carried on the south wind. Ghost ants whose ventricles absorbed it vibrated in place, then suddenly stilled. All through their ranks, Hulkrish men were dizzied and fell to the sand in coughing fits.

The Seed Eaters' human army appeared last. They rode magnificent brown strider ants, made even taller with the addition of stilts to their legs. Atop the ants, bowmen aimed down and picked off the Hulkrites stumbling in retreat to complete a rout.

In the west, human blood blinded Yormu as arrows of every size flew at the line. He did not have a free hand to wipe at his face and he dropped his blowgun. As he stumbled forward, he realized his shield was no longer locked with the others. The blood that blinded him came from the headless necks of the soldiers on his right and left. Their corpses slumped to the ground to drain.

Yormu knelt to pray when the Hulkrites advancing ahead of their ants fell to an abrupt onslaught of tridents hurled from the west. When Yormu cleared the blood from his eyes, he saw thousands of new attackers surging on his right.

The Carpenter nation had entered the war.

High on their massive wood beetles, Carpenter squadrons were lurching into battle to hurl their tridents, shoot their arrows, and wield their stone hammers. Hulkrites ran to mount their ghosts and retreat but the ants would not obey as they were drawn to the beetles' scent. The beetles kept their low, almost invisible heads to the ground. The ghost ants bit into the beetles' backs but the effort was futile as the chitin was hard and greasy and their heavy paddle-like legs rooted in the ground and prevented them from being flipped over. The men atop the beetles protected themselves with thick shields that deflected even the largest and sharpest arrows as well as the mandibles of the ghost ants.

Smaller ghosts crawled onto the beetles to attack their riders but these ants met with stone maces that shattered their mandibles or smashed through their skulls. The larger ghost ants were targeted with tethered tridents that had reversed thorns, and when they were yanked out, the wounds they left gushed with green blood. Hulkrish soldiers met with the same fate as their chests were pierced by tridents that were yanked back to rip out their hearts and lungs and rib cages.

The laborers were cheering the Carpenters when suddenly their tridents and arrows flew at them, too.

"Retreat!" came the call across the west. Yormu and the laborers had no choice but to run from the Carpenters and let them fight the war.

Pleckoo was giddy with ecstasy, until he received reports that his western and eastern divisions were retreating to the center. Both had suffered tremendous casualties at the hands of the Slopeites' neighbors. The Second Prophet's joy flipped to fury and he felt heat pounding in his face. "That roach-eating brat—he planned this! For the first time I am proud to have him as my cousin," he muttered to himself. "After I subdue the Slope, I will destroy their neighbors."

When his rage subsided, Pleckoo was heartened to learn that Anand's triumphs had come at a terrible cost. Survivors of his army were fewer and far distant. Without ants to ride, they could not regroup with the central divisions protecting the Petiole. Pleckoo smirked to remember that Tahn had defeated larger nations with fewer ants and warriors.

Pleckoo looked to the moon and saw it had floated low to the western sky. Night was leaving. Pleckoo's force would still be overwhelming but they would have just enough darkness to combine and attack and avoid a daylight battle. His confidence grew as confirmation of his numbers trickled in. They were facing just a puny army south of Palzhad, a force with no ants and very few roaches.

"We will march up the Petiole and destroy what remains of these pests. Palzhad will be ours before dawn," he shouted to his messengers. "Advance!"

The captains saw their Prophet was smiling. Soon his glee had infected them and banished any doubts. A short time later, Pleckoo was thrilled when the tail of his column came close enough to see Palzhad, so famed for its decaying beauty. Though its crystal palaces were caked with ancient grime, it glittered prettily in the moonlight. *Soon the extermination begins,* thought the Second Prophet.

**A**nand also checked the moon's position, then looked down at the ragged divisions bravely waiting to meet an unbeatable force. The laborers could already hear the rumblings of the Hulkrish army as they descended from their ants to advance on foot. The laborers knew the unthinkable had happened, that Hulkrites were pouring up the Petiole and little stood in the way of their taking Palzhad. When the Hulkrites became visible, Anand saw they were still as numerous as the stars above.

The Hulkrites' foot soldiers approached in a spearhead formation. Their outer-line pushed the baited bow-sleds that drew out the last of the laborers' roaches and soon destroyed them. The laborers' darts would be depleted after taking on this front line alone.

Anand spoke without emotion to his relayers. "Divisions twenty and twenty-one are ordered into an immediate retreat north," he said. "All will do what they must to save their own lives."

As the message shot down the ladders, Anand picked up his luminescent flag again. This time he looked into the bortshu tree on his left as if appealing to his god. He waved the flag three times as the laborers ran north then dropped his head.

The relayers stared at Anand, who was all too still. Was he praying? As the Hulkrites marched closer, they chanted all of Termite's names in a round. Anand left his trance and turned to look at the relayers.

"Good laborers," he said to with a tremble in his voice they heard as cowardice. "You have been brave soldiers in this war. For your own safety, all of you on these ladders are to climb down and retreat into the weeds."

The ladder messengers passed these words among themselves. The two at the top were preparing to descend when they heard a faint and melodic buzzing. They looked up to see bright orange wings and enormous eyes of shining black that reflected twin moons.

A night wasp.

The relayers dove for the floor and muttered their prayers as they clutched the platform's splinters. They peeked up to see Anand had not dived to the floor with them but stood with opened arms to the wasp, welcoming his own destruction.

When the buzzing grew faint, the boys stood and caught a glimpse of Anand's cape as it flapped from under the flying predator. Once the boys had recovered, they descended to pass this message: the Dark-skinned Savior has given up and surrendered his life to a night wasp.

All across the Slope, fleeing relayers passed the message that the war was lost and the Hulkrites marched on Palzhad. The ghost ants would soon be ravaging the country and no human or ant would be spared. Ants inside the border mounds had realized the war was lost and sprayed *abandon-scent* as they gathered eggs and larvae and pushed their ant queens out of their chambers and down to a pointless refuge.

Evacuation of the humans followed. Hundreds of thousands fled north to risk lair spiders and tree cannibals and throw themselves on the mercy of the Dranverites. The royals set out on sand-sleds, bringing as much of their treasure as possible. Since team ants had been lost in the war, low-caste Slopeites were granted the privilege of hauling the surviving nobles to the north.

Polexima fought with Trellana when the latter picked up a whip to lash at the humans lugging their over-packed sled. It was weighed down with chests of gowns and jewelry with which she simply couldn't part.

**T**he Hulkrites had not found Anand atop his platform. Captives swore that Vof Quegdoth was last seen in the clutches of a night wasp. When Pleckoo heard the report, he rejected it. *I know he's alive. I will hunt him in the country north of here. Anand will bear the shame of revealing my next conquest to me, this place called Dranveria!*

Pleckoo and his captains were reaching the southern weeds of Palzhad when the entire procession halted. Suddenly the ghost ants clustered tightly. Their gasters were up and shaking with *warning-scent* as their antennae rose in unison above them. Pleckoo assumed his ants had encountered a last reserve of roaches and ordered their destruction.

In the stillness, the Hulkrites heard a strange, almost musical buzzing from over their heads. From the front of the procession came screams of terror.

The Second Prophet and his captains felt a light powder filter onto their hands, and when they looked to the sky, their faces were dusted with it. More and more of it was falling now. Pleckoo wiped the powder from his mask and saw that it was reddish, like powdered blood.

The ghost ants' antennae lashed and snapped. They were maddened by the falling powder. Trapped by their own numbers, they scraped against each other and tangled their legs. Their heads jerked in circles as their mandibles widened and stilled. They scattered from the column or knotted in masses.

As Pleckoo's giant ant jerked and spun, he heard a symphony of buzzing. The sky filled with a spreading blur of flame-colored wings. Those who had survived the fire of the Madricanth effigy were afraid that a second one had been unleashed. What they saw now was far more frightening.

"Night wasps!" screamed the men.

All along the chain of the procession, the warriors spread flat on their ants or slid under them. Pleckoo and his captains stayed seated and stared at the threat. "Hulkro tests the faithful!" he shouted as the wasp swarm lowered and circled his officers.

*Night wasps do not fly in formation!* Pleckoo thought. The captains clutched at their chests as a sudden storm of darts rained down and pierced their armor. How? From whom? As the wasps whirled lower, Pleckoo's mouth opened in shock. Every vein in his body pulsed with dread.

Men were riding the wasps.

The Hulkrites were horrified into silence followed by whimpering and screams. Mostly, though, they were all too stunned to act. Pleckoo's campaign disintegrated before his eyes bulging through the holes of his mask.

One of the wasp riders circled Pleckoo. Behind the pilot was a stripe-faced man in blue mottled robes and a cape that fluttered behind him. When Pleckoo caught the man's eyes, he saw it was Anand, grinning as he aimed a dart that grazed Pleckoo's shoulder. The Hulkrish captains abandoned their ants. Some clenched their teeth to stop their chattering. Others wet or fouled themselves as they were bandied between the ghosts' legs.

Pleckoo sniffed the red powder on his arms as the howls of his men filled the night. The red powder stank of leaf-cutter kin-scent. "That roach-shit!" he shouted. "Anand has bombed us with the scent of our ants' enemy!"

The Second Prophet looked out at his sea of ravening ghost ants, which identified the Hulkrites as leaf-cutter ants. Within moments, thousands of warriors were attacked by their own insects and torn to pieces or swallowed whole.

"Remove your armor and your garments!" Pleckoo shouted to his captains. "Wipe that powder off you!"

But it was too late. The antennae of Pleckoo's own ant had sensed enemies were on her back. Just as he was stripping, the ant rose up and tried to shake him and his bowmen off. Pleckoo used his tunic to wipe at his skin when he saw the wasps returning.

"Arrows!" he shouted to the archers. "Aim for the wasp riders!" At this point, Pleckoo could only hope that he still had men around to hear his commands. Most of the bowmen had left their saddles. They climbed down the hooks of the ants' legs and fumbled to draw their bowstrings.

**A**nand looked down as arrows flew, most without aim from the jumble of ghost ants, most of which were attacking each other. Pleckoo's arrow pierced the wing of Anand's wasp, then shattered his armor to puncture his shoulder. As a fierce pain throbbed through his arm, Anand wondered what had cut through Dranverish armor. His wasp weakened on its wounded side and soon its wing went still. It tumbled into the ants, which scattered from its scent.

Anand rolled to the ground and found himself near his cousin's mount, where a cluster of Hulkrites ran towards him with swords. Anand drew his own and in a singular swing of his arm, severed the head of one attacker and then sliced off the arm of a second. A third attacker ran from Anand into the legs of the largest ghost ant. Anand looked up at the giant's head where he saw Pleckoo on top of it taking aim with a bow. Anand deflected the arrow with his sword, then stared at his cousin, their eyes locking.

Time slowed as Anand had a strange and sudden remembrance of Pleckoo, when he had been the most hopeful and handsome boy in the midden. For a moment, Anand was crushed with pity for Pleckoo and identified with the hatred that had driven his attack. *No time for this now,* Anand thought, as Pleckoo reloaded his bow. The night wasps lowered and encircled Anand, forcing Pleckoo's ant to flee.

"Commander!" shouted a pilot to Anand, extending his hand. Pleckoo released his arrow from atop his racing ant. The arrow missed as Anand was yanked up and onto a wasp. He clung to the waist of the pilot who steered them away from a barrage of Hulkrish missiles.

Anand plucked out the arrow from his shoulder and turned to look behind him. The giant ghost was racing south, but Pleckoo was not on it. *Was he on any of the ants speeding south?* Anand wondered, as the wasp rejoined the swarm.

"Formation up," Anand shouted. The wasps spiraled out of reach of the deadly arrows. "Head north, then turn south to assume the repelling formation!"

Every last Hulkrite had given up the attack and most of their ghost ants were dead or occupied with killing each other. Thousands more, who had escaped the powder, were running north. The night wasps swept over them, then turned and gathered in a chevron above the ghosts' column.

Anand led the wasps into a low flight over the ants, driving them east, then south. Wasp-scent forced the ghosts into the poisonous waters and sticky lumps of the Tar Marsh. Other ants scattered up and over the jagged boulders in the west before re-forming into broken columns bolting south.

The moon had grown orange and faint, just avoiding the fangs of Mother Sand. Anand knew his battle was incomplete if he did not vanquish Pleckoo and the surviving officers that might rise up and take his place. "Formation south," Anand commanded. The squadron soared over the ghosts retreating to the Dustlands.

Laborers hiding in the weeds emerged as the few surviving Hulkrites fled back to the south on their ghosts. Using the last of their darts and arrows, the laborers picked off straggling riders and cheered as they ran out to stab and stomp on them.

Above in the sky, Anand did not cheer. A grievous melancholy blew through him like cold wind in a cave. Spread below him like the bulky fibers of some rough cloth were dead insects and human corpses. None of these dead would see the New Country or the Promised World. Anand sighted a cluster of a hundred naked riders speeding on the giant ghost ants of Hulkrish officers. He sensed the Second Prophet was among them.

*We end this now, cousin.*

**P**leckoo's latest frustration was that the ants on which he and his surviving soldiers had fled were uncontrollable and frighteningly swift. They had been driven too far east, to the shores of the Great Brackish Lake. The last of the Hulkrish officers would have to detour alongside the water before going south again. He looked up in complete exasperation to see the night wasps gliding above them, herding them farther south. *Why don't they just kill me now?* Pleckoo thought when he saw ahead of him a second cluster of ghosts and their riders. Pleckoo reached the tail of their parade and saw Captain Aggle. "Aggle!" Pleckoo shouted and his captain slowed his ant, his eyes wide and blinking to see the Second Prophet was still alive. "I have one last command for you, Captain," Pleckoo shouted. "Do you still have faith?"

**A**bove them, the wasp pilots readied their blowguns. The last of the Hulkrites had veered left to Jatal-dozh, and were racing to its opening. Anand reached for one last dart dipped in something more awful than yellow jacket venom. As he pondered the dart's intended target, his mind turned again to memories that sundered his already tender soul.

# CHAPTER 57

## TESTS OF THE FAITHFUL

**Y**ears before, following the death of the caste's old idols keeper, Pleckoo had been summoned by the demi-priests to a clearing in the weeds. They had set up a grass shield between themselves and an untouchable with lighter skin to ask him questions as they tossed an oracle bone. They had selected one other middenite, Glurmu the Floppy-Eared, and performed the same ritual in search of a new sub-shaman to preside over the outcastes' altar.

Pleckoo won the position. He would get to wear a yellow sash and have parity with the foreman. It had been a time of famine, a time of even less joy, but Pleckoo was ecstatic over his recent elevation. "All my life I have felt as if I belonged somewhere else," he said to Anand on his final day of washing chamber pots. He bragged that he was leaving on a journey for the Holy Mound, where he would train for his new responsibilities. Once there, he met the outcaste acolytes of other mounds and one of them stole what little stash of food he had.

Venaris had fewer mushrooms for its laborers than Cajoria, and all but its priests and nobles were starving. One night when Pleckoo could bear his hunger no more, he stole a rotting mushroom from a pile being returned to the ants. The sheriff who caught him was supposed to cut off his hand, but he found him too good-looking and decided on his nose.

Pleckoo did not return to Cajoria with a yellow sash, but with a blood-soaked rag tied around his face. Gone forever with his nose was his smile. He seldom spoke to anyone unless it was to demand they get out of his way.

Anand asked Corra if he could take some of their food to the shanty on the midden's outskirts for pitiable bachelors where Pleckoo had withdrawn. When he saw Anand approach with a leaf-bag bulging with mushrooms and sweets, Pleckoo burst into sobbing. When Anand set the bag down and went to comfort him, Pleckoo picked up the bag, hurled it away, then kicked Anand to the sand and beat him until he was bruised and bloody.

**A**s Anand flew closer to Pleckoo, the next memory of him was so vivid it was like a dream from which he had not awakened. Anand remembered the day when Pleckoo, sometime after receiving his fourteenth age chit, turned on his father when he attempted another public beating of him for hoarding his mushrooms. In front of all standing in the rations line, Pleckoo broke from his father's grip, pivoted, and backed away as his face filled with rage. He crouched, then charged his father, knocked him down, then knelt on his chest as he struggled for breath. "You are not my father!" Pleckoo shouted. His fists made a bloody pulp of the dark face of a man who bore him no resemblance, a man who had groped him at night on his mattress. As Pleckoo's mother pleaded for her son to end the beating, others whispered of the time she had returned from the weeds, wailing and in torn rags and insisting she had not been raped by drunken, yellow-skinned sheriffs.

**A**nand's mind jumped to the moment when Pleckoo had argued with Keel before the Fission Trek. "I told you, I will not go," Pleckoo had shouted in utter defiance. He had puffed out his chest and declared, "I will go to Bee-Jor!" Pleckoo had not wilted under the laughter of the others but sneered at their ignorance. That day, Anand wanted to ask Pleckoo if they could run away together. The two of them would have ended up in Hulkren, where freed from the Slope's conventions, Pleckoo would have forgiven his cousin's darker skin. Anand knew that deep in the Dustlands they would have bonded for eternity in their hatred for the Slope. *I would be fighting with him,* Anand thought. *Tahn would be alive and ruling over the Slope and I would be a husband to Hulkrish women.*

The shock of Anand's realization jolted him back to his mission. The last Hulkrites and their ghosts had raced to the top of Jatal-dozh and were circling the opening under its raised rain shield. Above them, Anand led his wasp riders in a counter spiral. He looked for Pleckoo among the Hulkrites, then saw his masked figure atop his massive ant, attempting to control her.

The Hulkrites were losing the struggle to steer their ghosts, which strained to attack the bitter guard-ants who clustered under the dome of the mound's opening, their giant heads locked together. One ghost could not be held back and her mandibles stabbed the head of a bitter guard-ant—she exploded and set off her fellow guards. Their bodies fell away as the last of the bitter ants poured up from the mound and rushed to the ghosts who nabbed them with their mandibles to raise and swallow but instead were destroyed by an explosion that ripped through their heads.

*Why was he so stupid to lead his men to this death trap?* Anand asked himself as he sighted Pleckoo, directing with one arm and shouting commands through his mask. Anand signaled the wasps to land and crawl to the opening. Under the rain shield, Pleckoo had dismounted and was herding his men on foot to the opening's edges. They were not taking the spiraling stairs for humans, but throwing themselves off the opening's rim. Blue lights flashed as bitter ants attacked and exploded, their smaller sisters arriving to carve up and cart off the Hulkrites' corpses. *They're killing themselves!* Anand realized.

"Stop! Don't do it, Pleckoo!" he shouted at his cousin as he prepared to take the last plunge. Pleckoo halted before the rim, looked at Anand, then stepped forward. Anand raised his blowgun, inhaled and blew.

The dart pierced Pleckoo's neck. He raised his arm to pluck it out but it spasmed before he slumped and fell to stillness with his head hanging over the opening's edge.

Anand dismounted from the wasp, ran to his cousin. He pulled the dart from his neck, raised his head up and laid out the folded limbs of his body. "I cannot let you die, Pleckoo. You have fallen, as far as any man can fall, but I love you, cousin. I always have."

Anand bent down his ear to hear if Pleckoo was breathing. When he pulled away, he looked harder at the masked face below him, suddenly unsure. Anand's heartbeat boomed inside him as his breathing grew shallow. He reached for his dagger and cut the mask's ribbon. Under the mask was a face with a missing nose. Anand pushed back hair to reveal two unclipped ears.

"Aggle," said Anand, and it felt as if he had lost the war.

**P**leckoo was naked, crawling over rough sand grains and through water-smoothed pebbles towards the rough, black waves on the edge of the Brackish Lake. As a harsh wind blew, he felt the weight of the world on his back, crushing him to something less than the stinking pond scum before him. *At last, this cruel joke of life will be over,* he thought as he reached the mud ringing the water. He tried to rise and walk over the deepening slime but fell on his face with a painful splat. Mud and algae clogged the cavity that had been his nose and he rolled over, choking and coughing. He looked into a sky emptying of stars and fought the urge to sob but his body shook with a venomous grief and he fainted into a tarry darkness. He came to in a fog of pinpricks and determined to slither to the choppy water. He paddled to pull himself in and drink the water's poisons when a sharp wave picked him up and threw him on shore. He banged his head on a pebble and watched the world spin around him and dissolve.

Sudden sunlight hurt his eyes as he looked up with a start. The Brackish Lake was gone and in its place were two altars set side by side. One altar was ornate and sparkling, set in a thicket of fragrant flowers. A quartz platform was covered with statues of the Slope's hundred idols coming to life and beckoning with multiple arms and kind faces. Grasshopper poured an endless stream of jewels from his six arms, honey oozed from Bee's golden cups and Mantis offered swords of gold with jewel-encrusted grips.

The other altar was a plain and empty platform with a single block of wood. Its only features were a termite track and the vague scent of turpentine.

"Choose," said a female voice behind Pleckoo, a voice of seductive warmth.

Pleckoo looked to the two altars and then to a mountainous rise behind them. "You must choose now," said the voice, and he felt warm, invisible hands pulling him towards the Slopeish idols. Mite was rising up from the platform, fat and jolly, seated atop a multiplying feast for thousands.

Pleckoo looked at the gray, dead wood of the other altar.

"I choose Hulkro," he said.

The Slopeish altar succumbed to a fast-growing mold and melted into slime. Hulkro manifested as the Great Blind Drone, crawling out of the wood block and shaking wood dust off His wings.

"Hulkro tests the faithful," he said. "And you, Pleckoo, my Living Messenger, have passed the greatest test of all." Pleckoo watched as Hulkro flew up and disappeared into the brightening blue of the morning sky. Lowering his eyes, Pleckoo looked out on the lake's water dancing with pink-and-orange sparkles.

The sun was rising, proud and gaudy, and splashing its gold on clouds growing thick and muscular.

Pleckoo slipped and slid through the mud before his feet found dry sand. Something sharp was tapping at his ankle and he realized, he was still wearing his sword belt. He unsheathed his weapon which reflected the orange sky, then looked to the heavens for guidance. *Go south*, said the voice in his head when a riderless ghost ant raced up from behind and probed his shoulders. "Eat me," he said, closing his eyes as he turned and let her antennate him. She smelled/felt the scent of a ghost sister under his filthy skin. Pleckoo opened his eyes, stepped forward, pulled himself onto her mandible and climbed atop her head. He had no gloves to guide her. "Take me where you wish," he said, as she crawled off, her antennae waving in search of prey or a sister's trunk-trail.

**A**s the pilots hiked with Anand to the Slope, they grew giddy as they wove through the corpses, collected Hulkrish weapons, and relived their triumphs. The Grass men among them talked of sending for their families. The Slopeites talked of their new dwellings in the old chambers of the military caste. Some laughed as they imagined the widows and children of the noble soldiers leaving with bundles for the shanties of the rings. Anand frowned at his men in disapproval.

"Men, save your laughter. The families of the military caste will be compensated for their losses. In the meantime, I must remind you this war is not ended until we have exterminated every ghost ant and freed every slave in Hulkren. Only then can we build the New Country."

A silence passed.

"Commander, do you know yet?" a Slopeite asked.

"Know what?"

"The name of our new nation."

Anand rubbed his chin. "We must invite the men and women enslaved at the Hulkrish beehives to be honored guests at our mounds. We will need their know-how if we are to have free and plentiful honey in the Free State of Bee-Jor."

# CHAPTER 58

## BEE-JOR

Waiting for Anand at Palzhad were hundreds of messengers and a thousand requests. Among those waiting were Terraclon and Yormu. They were bandaged but smiling as they waited their turn in what seemed an endless queue.

Slopeites who had fled north were slowly returning. Some reported contact with Dranverish sentries on red ants that did not administer the Living Death, but allowed for refuge until the conflict subsided. Anand learned the Seed Eaters had sustained their border agreements with Bee-Jor but the Carpenters had absorbed the mound of Gagumji, were planting pine seeds, and were poised for more conquests of the divided Slope's crippled west. The Britasytes learned that the Carpenter Nation was furious with Vof Quegdoth for forcing them into war.

*I suppose they have a point,* Anand thought wearily. *But they would have dealt with the Hulkrites eventually.*

Among the last in the queue was Pious Nuvao, Polexima's son, who approached Anand with gravity. "I risked my life to escape and relay that a reserve of Slopeish nobles and military elite lie in wait for you at Venaris," said Nuvao. "They intend to torture you to death, dress you in your mottled robes, then parade your corpse on a cross through the rings of every Slopeish mound."

Anand donned common rags before informing his soldiers they would not be marching past Venaris but to it, where they would fight a different enemy. The Laborer's Army was diminished but they had Hulkrish weapons and roach-scent to repel any mounted attackers. Laborers who had been too cowardly to fight in the Hulkrish war were offered the chance to join and attack the Holy Mound.

When the nobles' scouts related that Anand was returning with an emboldened army that outnumbered their own, surviving princes and nobles fled into the night. They dispersed to all the western mounds that Anand designated as the Old Country, to what the BeeJorites called The No Longer Great Nor Holy Slope. At Venaris, the Laborer's Army was unopposed.

As the Army marched out of Venaris, women and children in the rings dropped their tasks to cheer the soldiers who had saved them from the Termite demons. They cheered even louder when these same men marched down the mound with the priests before them, their arms and ankles bound in cuffing grass. The clerics were forced to wear their most beautiful robes and their gaudiest miters, the ones saved for the feast day of Mantis.

His Ultimate Holy Pious Dolgeeno had been cuffed as well as leashed around his neck. He was set high on the platform of a sand-sled. Anand sat with him, surrounded by his guards. Terraclon was given the leash to hold.

"Why this, after I complied with your every wish?" asked Dolgeeno.

"I am sorry you find it humiliating," Anand said.

"You said we would have two separate nations."

"We will, but you've been down in your cathedral, plotting my assassination. It appears I shall have to contend with some secret reserve of royals and military who will attempt to reclaim our portion."

"And what will you do with me?"

"You will live. You are the Ultimate Holy Priest of the Slope as well as of Bee-Jor and as long as you are, you will carry out your duties. Of course, you will do so from Cajoria, as my guest."

"You mean as your hostage."

"However you choose to think of it. It does not matter to me." He nodded towards Terraclon. "I should like to introduce you to someone, this young man who holds your leash."

Dolgeeno's eyes squinted in contempt. He barely looked at Terraclon.

"His skin is dark."

"So is mine. Again—it matters not. His name is Terraclon and he is your novitiate. The priesthood is now open to all who aspire to it. Terraclon will succeed you as the Ultimate Holy of both our nations. He will return Madricanth to your pantheon as well as revive the cults of Locust and Cricket."

Terraclon had not anticipated that. His knees went weak and he lowered his head to keep from blacking out. "Me? The Ultimate Holy? *Why?*"

"Brother, you have played an invaluable role in my life. Without your love for me, I would have despised all Slopeites, hated them to the point that I might have let the Hulkrites tear them into bloody scraps."

Terraclon, overcome, felt as if dust was in his throat as he tried to speak.

"Besides . . . you've always had a taste for pageantry," said Anand, "and Bee-Jor will have pageants."

Anand took Dolgeeno's fabled tourmaline and set it around Terraclon's neck. "Ter, as Dolgeeno schools you in his knowledge, I will school the both of you in the principles of something called *The Loose Doctrine of Dranveria*. Together, we will build a nation based on inclusion and equality for all."

Terraclon was still trying to recover. "And with much better clothing, I hope."

"Just wait until you see Dranverish fashion,"

Anand said through a grin. "I think you'd look good in red."

Some days later, the Dneepers were assigned one last mission to finalize the war. They were not to return to the Grasslands until they had stopped at every mound in Hulkren with the exhumed barrels of the potion known as the Yellow. Anand flew on a locust to meet with their caravan headed to the northern mound of Fadtha-dozh, still active with ghost ants. He handed a map of Hulkren to Medinwoe to identify its 107 mounds but warned that there might be new ones with wild ants.

"After liberating and warning the slaves, open a barrel of the Yellow and set it at the base of each mound. When your roaches have left, the ghost ants will appear. They will find the Yellow irresistible and take their fill. The potion is sweet, slow-acting and utterly fatal. The ghosts will pass it to each other's crops until it reaches their queens. Once an ant has been contaminated with the Yellow, it is no longer edible to humans." Anand thought a moment, then added, "But spare Jatal-dozh," he said. "Or rather, Mound Jalal as it was known."

"Not Jalal?" asked Medinwoe. "It may still be full of bitter ants."

"Yes," said Anand. "Which may be of some use to us."

Before saying good-bye to the Grass Men, Anand

extended his gratitude with words moistened by happy tears. The Grass Men had been obedient and brave, having followed him without question to capture a night wasp and steal its scent in order to infiltrate their nest and tame them. He knew the Grass Men would be meticulous in their final assignments. Medinwoe promised to bring Polexima's children to Bee-Jor on his return and Anand promised Medinwoe he would prepare the Promised Clearing for its new occupants. There, they would return to learn practices called farming and insect husbandry.

Daveena was much on Anand's mind as he completed his last task for the day, knowing that when he returned to Cajoria he would share a mattress with her for the first time in weeks. He flew east and searched for the Entrevean caravan he had sent to Halk-Oktish to invite the Bulkokans and their hives to Bee-Jor. From above, he saw what looked like his and Daveena's own sand-sled. His heart leapt in excitement, then flipped into injury. What was she doing with them? When the caravan halted to freshen the roaches' lures, Anand surprised Daveena by landing his locust next to the sled.

"Good travels, beloved wanderer."

"What are *you* doing here?" she asked him, coming to the window. She was trying to look angry but her eyes danced as she fought back a smile. He was reminded of the first time he saw her.

"I was going to ask you the same," he said, noticing her face and body were thicker with pregnancy.

"You assigned the Entreveans to a mission," she said.

"You are a Plep. And you are supposed to be waiting for me in Cajoria."

"If I'm married to you, I'm an Entrevean. And our clan has been given an important mission. I don't want Bee-Jorites or Britasytes thinking I have special privileges as your *first* wife."

Anand suddenly understood and was pierced with sadness.

"You don't want to be there for the ceremony," he said.

"No."

"But it was your idea."

"It was."

"Daveena, you know I will always hate her."

"Yes."

"Fly back with me. Someone else can look after our sled."

"No, Anand."

She turned from him to hide her distress before she met his eyes. "Because I love you, and thousands need you, you must go through with this. But now that the time is near, I find the idea of the two of you . . . it feels like a flea piercing my heart."

"I'm sorry," he said, and he truly was. The two were silent, then looked away from each other.

"Promise me something," she said, lifting her eyes to his.

"Anything."

"When that . . . time . . . comes, you will close your eyes and think only of me."

"I promise. I only ever think of you."

"I don't believe that," she said with the mildest of snorts. "Our first time was not *your* first time."

Anand was silent, looked away. Daveena crawled up the locust's leg and into her husband's arms. He cradled and kissed her and rubbed her swelling belly in the crisp autumn air. He looked to the sky and the tatters of gray clouds blowing in. He knew from the sun's position that he must leave now in order to make it to the Slope on time and partake in the first official function of the Free State of Bee-Jor. When Anand was back in the air, he did not feel whole. He had left half of himself with Daveena, the half of him that had been happy.

As Anand flew over Bee-Jor, he saw that everywhere, it was calmer. The corpses of the ghost ants had provided the people with a bounty of food that would last for many moons, long enough to learn the Dranverish methods for food production. The scuffles over housing were ongoing but for the moment, the neighboring Seed Eaters posed no threat.

Regardless of the peace, Anand knew his real work had just begun. Defeating the Hulkrites was far easier than the building of a new nation. Slopeish merchants and craftsmen, who had burrowed in their dwellings to protect their hoards, had to be urged out of hiding to renew the flow of commerce. Anand would have to contact the Dranverites and invite their ambassadors to bring inseminated red hunter queens before the leaf-cutter ants could be phased out, a process sure to invite resistance.

When Anand landed atop Cajoria, he saw women in widow's whites scowling at him as they strolled over what had been the royal decks for Sun and Moon worship. Many widows of the military castes had killed themselves and their children rather than allow the dark-skinned victors to live near their chambers. A few widows had attacked the new class of soldiers with knives or attempted to poison them. Some soldiers wanted to kill these women on the spot, but Anand ordered their imprisonment instead. He sighed, knowing that one of many things he would have to explain and institute was a justice system.

As he stared back at the scowling women, Anand suspected they fidgeted with daggers under their robes. *I can never be alone again,* he thought, *and must always be on alert.* And as if he had commanded them with his thoughts, loyal soldiers surrounded him. Each considered it an honor to act as the living shield that absorbed an assassin's weapon.

**P**olexima had assumed her new role as Bee-Jor's Priestess of Cricket. She was conducting funeral rites for the thousands of Cajorian dead when a messenger arrived at the altered cathedral. Vof Quegdoth sent warm greetings and requested she prepare her daughter for the nuptials. Priestess Polexima would officiate at the ritual with the holy person of Anand's roach tribe. She hobbled in her robe of polished straw towards Sahdrin's darkened chambers where Trellana had gone to live with her decrepit father so that they could drink fermentation from morning to night.

Polexima's nose was smacked with the stink of overflowing chamber pots as she entered her daughter's bedchamber to find her slouched and staring at the wall as a servant filed her nails.

"Good gods, it stinks in here, Trellana!"

"The servants aren't emptying the pots."

"And they won't be. Quegdoth's first edict was that all citizens of Bee-Jor are responsible for removing their own waste."

"I've been busy."

"Oh, I'm quite certain you have been. He is coming. His holy person and his family are descending to the cathedral."

"I will kill myself rather than go through with this," Trellana said. She threw herself on the bed and pulled fetid blankets over her face.

"But you agreed to it."

"I was drunk."

"When are you not drunk?"

"I want to go west and live with Cousin Prettana in the Kobacynth Mound."

"Mound Kobacynth is under attack from the Carpenters. The entire west will soon be under siege. Is that where you want to take your children?"

"They can stay with you."

"They are *your* children."

"But, Mother—he's a Dranverite! Supposedly he's as dark as night under his powder."

"He is your moral, mental, and physical superior. Marry him, Trellana. He has promised that you can live in the palace, with all your usual comforts."

Trellana sucked from a bowl of spirits until she coughed on them. "Why me? Why must I always suffer?"

"You don't know a thing about suffering. This marriage is not about your happiness. If you care about anyone other than yourself, you will fulfill your duty."

"My duty is to myself."

"Fine. Pack a trunk. Leave. I'm sure you can scrounge up a hovel on the flats. "

Trellana fumed in silence, then reached for a second bowl and slurped it up. "Bring more from the best casket," she shouted, flinging the bowl at her servant. "I'm wedding the Son of Locust!"

**A** short time later, Trellana was in a dark haze, wearing her finest gown, sitting atop an insect being lured to the cathedral. *What am I riding on?* she wondered as she considered the strange gait of the creature that sent the ants scattering. Before she realized it was something other than an ant, she was helped down and pulled through the portal's flap to some very strange sounds when it occurred to her she might have been riding on a *roach*. The Dranverite had invited clans of roach people, as well as foot soldiers of the lowest castes who sported swords and blowguns in a holy place. The Britasytes had brought instruments and were making a frantic music they danced to. *Dancing roach people in the cathedral!* "Desecration!" she shouted, but her outcry was drowned in the din.

No Slopeish priest was at the altar, but her own mother—a woman!—was there with a dark-skinned person of indeterminate sex. Someone had replaced the idol of Mantis with an idol of Madricanth and his/her consorts were Locust the Sky God and Cricket, the goddess worshipped by the fatuous Palzhanites.

"Blasphemy!" Trellana screamed through her veil as the cathedral quieted. Her cries were ignored as Cricket novices stood at her side to hold her up. The dark roach priest (or priestess?) conducted half the ceremony in an ugly language sung to garish melodies. Polexima conducted the second half in a bizarre ritual that involved the rubbing of insect wings against femurs as Cricket's different names were invoked: Night Musician, Defender of Peace, Wisdom Queen. Trellana heard her mother spouting nothing about the joyful union of a man and woman, but there was gibberish about the uniting of peoples, the equality of races, a new era of love and tolerance.

At one point, the Priestess of Cricket and the Two Spirit took the sash of Trellana's garment and tied it to that of the Dranverite. She barely realized he had been standing beside her. His face and hands were powdered with yellow pyrite, which made him gorgeous, even divine, in appearance. When Trellana's veil was pulled away and she could see him more clearly, she found herself both enchanted and repulsed. He thrust a honey-sweetened egg wafer in her mouth, then ate the one that had been smashed into her own limp fingers. She passed out again.

Trellana awoke in her own chambers sometime later. They smelled sweet and she realized servants had exchanged the chamber pots and rubbed the floors with a fragrant flower essence. Vof Quegdoth was across from her, in a simple tunic, sitting and looking out the window. *How handsome he is,* she thought, no longer certain of who he was. He wasn't puffy like a Slopeish royal but was lean and sinewy. Under his taut skin were rippling muscles that she didn't know humans possessed—Maleps didn't look like that out of his clothes. She wondered why the Dranverite looked so sad.

**A**nand cast a forlorn gaze out the window, saddened because his father would not attend the evening's wedding feast. Yormu had motioned with his hands that he could not stay inside a crystal palace, much less live in one. He shook when he looked up at their distant ceilings, seemed frightened by the opulence. He kissed his son's cheek before he left to sleep in his hovel at the midden.

Anand watched as his father's hunched figure disappeared in the crowds of the wedding celebrations.

As Anand had ordered, great spaces on all levels had been cleared for everyone to gather. The clearings were crowded with celebrants who paraded idols of old and new gods on palanquins. Some worshipped the Lord of Fire and Nephew of Bee, while others chanted to Quegdoth the Godling and Master of Night Wasps. The new deities were all fashioned to look like Anand and were dressed with facsimiles of his mottled blue robes. He laughed to himself, none too quietly.

"What's so funny?" asked Terraclon, who had entered without announcing himself. Anand looked at his friend, standing tall and imperious in yellow robes. His arms flared out to display brocaded silk so abundant its folds gathered in puddles around his feet.

"Terraclon, they think I'm a god."

"You will have me to remind you that you are not," said Terraclon, who had taken on something of Dolgeeno's accent.

"And you, shit worker, will have me to remind you of your own humble origins," said Anand as he affected the royal accent in kind.

"I'm as royal as any of them," said Terraclon, returning to the harsh accent of his old caste. The two friends grinned at each other, then turned to look out the window. Anand smiled to see the Britasytes being tolerated by the crowds as they paraded their idol of Madricanth up to the highest level. They set it on the place where Maleps and Trellana had once sat on thrones to enjoy torture spectacles. Anand turned from the window to see Trellana awake and squinting at him in drunken anger.

"Will you excuse us, Ter?" Anand said.

"Excuse you?" Ter asked, cocking an eyebrow.

"It's a polite way of telling you to go."

Terraclon rolled his eyes and made a mock bow before floating off in a cloud of silk. Anand turned to Trellana.

"Good evening, Trellana."

"There is nothing good about it."

"I regret having wedded you as well, but it serves our purposes."

"What purposes? Why not just send me to die in the west?"

"This was not my idea, it was my wife's. She realizes, as you should, that transitions are best when they are gradual. Many of your subjects still accept you as their queen. Most accept me as the new ruler. They have even elevated me to divine status, something I will have to decline. Silly, isn't it, this idea of me being the Son of Locust? Why, it's almost as silly as when they thought you were a sorceress descended from Ant Queen."

"It is not silly at all. I was born to rule . . . it is the duty of my caste."

"Castes have come to an end. This is Bee-Jor now and no race will ever dominate another. Not here."

Anand saw her face grow long and sensed her grief.

"I will never love you," he said, "and you will never love me. But perhaps we will both love our children."

He breathed deeply with regret as he looked away, then back at Trellana. Her breath was acrid from thornroot liquor, but he knew what he must do.

"Your mother has told me you are not in a time of bleeding. It is with all gentleness that we must fulfill our duties as sovereigns. We should remove some of our clothing and . . ."

"Yes, I know how it goes from there," she said. She started to pull up her garment, then stopped and glared at him. "You murdered my husband," she shouted. "You murdered our kings and princes and our military caste."

"The Hulkrites killed them. Or most of them anyway. I told them how to save themselves. They ignored me."

"Yes, of course, the infamous washing of hands. You know your arguments were purposely weak."

"They decided on their own strategy," said Anand. "Would your husband have fought on foot and smeared his body with roach secretions? Would you?" Anand nodded toward the lower part of her body. "Please, Trellana. Let's be quick about this. I apologize for this . . . intimacy . . . we shall have to engage in from time to time."

She lifted her garments and sighed. After Anand dropped his tunic, he turned to see her pinching her nose with her fingers. His face was dusted with gold, but he knew the hue of his buttocks was something else entirely.

"Is that the normal color of a Dranverite?" she asked.

"We are all different colors," he said.

"You repulse me," she spat out.

"I am not so fond of you."

"Come on," she said. "Let's see if it's true."

"If what's true?"

"That dark skinned people are savages who keep their women in ecstasy."

"Our goal is not ecstasy," Anand said as he climbed atop her. "It is to make children."

Anand could not look at her and closed his eyes as he needed someone else to think about if this was going to succeed. He tried to think of Daveena, but that seemed obscene. He turned to memories of his afternoons with Jidla, which was more helpful. He was yanked from his trance when he heard Trellana gasping with pleasure and saw her eyes were open. She grabbed him by his head and yanked him to a kiss.

"No! No kissing!" he said, wiping his mouth. She laughed as he closed his eyes, exerted himself. It was over quickly.

"Thank you," he said as he rushed to his clothing, never more anxious to leave a room. Trellana sat up looking smugly satisfied, but a moment later her nose was in the air and she scowled.

"Was that the best you could do?" she taunted. "I felt nothing. Perhaps you're saving yourself for that little butterfly that was here. What's his name—Terraclon? Just wait until I tell the world—the Destroyer of the Hulkrites, the Tamer of the Night

Wasps is one of *those*. Would you mind dressing my hair before you leave?"

Anand froze and pinned her with his eyes. All his old hatred was burning again, threatening to become a wildfire.

"It occurs to me that you are a victim, too," he said, "of this ridiculous system where people are born to their stations in life. You've little idea of how ignorant and incurious and mean-spirited you are."

"You'll find out just how mean-spirited I can be," she said, sitting up and grabbing a hand mirror to grin at her image. He was quiet a moment as he tied his garment. But then he smiled.

"What are you simpering about?" she asked.

"You know—this was not the first time we've touched," he said.

"What are you talking about?"

"The first time I touched you, by accident, was in a rolling cage in Dranveria."

Trellana jerked up, backed away on her mattress. She held her breath as Anand picked up a string and tied his hair back. He turned in profile to reveal his ear with its missing lobe.

"Yes, little darling," he said, dropping all pretenses of a Dranverish accent. "You tried to have me executed, torn into little pieces, merely because I brushed your arm."

He smiled, even more broadly now, as he sat on the mattress and waited for the moment of realization. Her eyes grew wide as her face blanched and her body shook. She screamed as she ran from the room and hurled herself into a scent tub. Anand watched as her servants stared at her as she thrashed and shrieked in the dome of water.

Anand was clenching his teeth to keep from laughing when a guard squeezed through the portal with a shining red tube.

*A Dranverish message scroll!*

"Where did you get this?" he demanded of the guard.

"Someone on a locust, an impressive young man named Dwan, gave it to me. He said it was from the People's Agent of Dranveria and that it was very important you get it."

"Where is he? Tell him I'll be right with him!"

"He did not wait. He flew right away."

Anand was crushed with disappointment. To see Dwan on this day would have been like a rich sweet at the end of a feast. Now the day was ending in confusion.

"Thank you," Anand said, taking the scroll. He saw the insignia of the People's Agent. The letter was addressed to Lick-My-Testicles.

"Uh-oh," he said as his mouth went dry. His stomach rumbled with dread as he uncapped the tube and read:

*Anand,*
    *We must reconsider membership of your new nation of Bee-Jor within our collective for an indefinite*

*time. If what we have heard about your war with the
Hulkrites is true, we must express our utter dismay
at the means by which you achieved victory. We are
most distressed by your careless use of fire in warfare,
especially as it appears you used it to promote your
personal religious beliefs. We also question the name
you have given your new nation, which is likely to
attract a migration of displaced people you cannot
possibly absorb. We are reinforcing our own Buffer
Zone at this moment in anticipation of . . .*

Anand could not read the rest of the letter. All
his joy was gone and in its place was the same anguish he had known all his life. "Is there anyone on
the Sand who understands me or appreciates what I
have done?" he asked of no one at all. A moment later,
he chided himself, for it was not the Britasyte way
to ever take pity on one's own self. No matter how
long and difficult the next journey, he must prepare
for it . . . then take the first step.

# ABOUT THE AUTHOR

**CLARK T. CARLTON** is a journalist, screen and television writer, and an award-winning playwright and novelist. He was born in the South, grew up in the East, went to school in the North, and lives with his family in the West. As a child he spent hours observing ants and their wars and pondered their similarity to human societies.

Discover great authors, exclusive offers, and more at hc.com.